MEMORY
RESTORED

Book Two of the Memory Lane Trilogy

MEMORY
RESTORED

AMANDA DIAZ

Clovercroft Publishing

Memory Restored
©2023 Amanda Diaz

Published by Clovercroft Publishing, Franklin, Tennessee

Cover image by Sarah Scott

Edited by Tiarra Tompkins and Ann Tatlock

Developmental Edit: Tiarra Tompkins-The Legacy Architect

Cover and Interior Design by Suzanne Lawing

ISBN: 978-1-954437-9-37

Printed in the United States of America

For my niece, Sarah:
May you always be proud of yourself and know
that you came out stronger on the other side.

For my nephew, Aden:
May you always love reading and let it
take you to far-away places.

Chapter 1

You aren't supposed to smile at a funeral. Don't get me wrong; I was sad that Kate's Mom was dead. Kate was one of my best friends and I mourned with her at such a huge loss. Yet, I was ultimately still in blissful shock that my younger sister, Leslie, was alive and sitting next to me. I looked down at her and thought about how lucky I was to have my sister returned to me, one who loved me and still remembered me. Just a short while ago, we thought she was dead. We spent the past four years grieving, thanks to Memory Lane and their lies.

As if sensing my train of thoughts, Leslie squeezed my hand. The service continued as the preacher read aloud from the Bible. Mom sniffled next to me and reached into her purse for a tissue.

"Who can separate us from the love of Christ?" the preacher asked of the crowd. "In John 14, the Bible tells us that…"

Unable to focus on the service, I stole a glance at Kate who was sitting several rows in front of us, next to her Dad, Gideon. My smile faded when I thought about what a terrible person he had become after creating Memory Lane. I felt awful for Kate, knowing that her Mom was dead and all she had left was her Dad.

The church was filled with people from all over the state. Danielle Wesley was a high-profile case, considering the police had ruled her death a homicide. She also happened to be the wife of the CEO, CFO, and COO of Memory Lane. In short, everyone's interest was piqued. The Wesleys were extremely rich. Both Gideon and Danielle had personal security teams and bodyguards that went everywhere with them. How someone got close enough to murder Danielle was beyond me. My only thought was that it must be someone on the inside. Either on their security team or Gideon himself.

With everything going on, I hadn't had a chance to talk to Kate just yet about what she knew regarding her Mom's death. She and her Dad had been overwhelmed with making funeral arrangements for her Mom the past week.

The only reason I was able to be here at all was because Danielle Wesley was dead. Gideon poured all of his money, time, and investigation team's power into finding her killer. Thanks to a clever disguise with some heavy makeup and a wig, no one was able to tell that I was here at the funeral. We made sure to disguise Leslie too so that no one from Memory Lane suspected anything was amiss. As additional protection, we had Jenson lay a digital trail of myself and Thomas traveling to various motels and hotels across the country. The guards were likely chasing us through Georgia as I sat here at Danielle Wesley's funeral.

As the preacher droned on, my eyes were drawn to the picture of Kate's Mom by the casket. It was surrounded by bouquets of orange flowers—her favorite color. Danielle was at the beach in her picture, and she was laughing at something. Her eyes sparkled. My heart ached for Kate. I knew what it was like to lose someone close to you and have the world crash down around you. You can never prepare for it and the ache remains daily. For four years I had grieved Leslie's death only to discover that she was alive the entire time. Joy and anger replaced my grief. Despite my feelings, my world had been set right. I knew the same wouldn't happen for Kate.

Lining the walls inside the church were policemen and Memory Lane guards. No doubt, with a murderer on the loose, they were there to protect Gideon and Kate. I slowly surveyed the room, trying not to hold eye contact with anyone for too long. I was still uneasy around the Memory Lane guards. Understandable, considering I spent several weeks running for my life while they pursued me and Thomas.

My new burner phone buzzed, and Mom shot me a warning glance to keep it quiet. I suppressed the urge to roll my eyes and slid the phone from my pocket. I snuck a quick glance to see that Thomas and Jenson had both texted me in a group chat. Thinking about the journey that led us to finding Leslie made me so thankful for my cousin Thomas and all that we went through at Memory Lane. Despite being found by the guards over and over, he made sure that I was taken care of and didn't die. Jenson was another person I was thankful to have on my side at the moment. Kate's ex-boyfriend was "The Man With the Plan" when it came to our breaking into Memory Lane (for the second time) to find the truth about Leslie's presumed death.

> **JENSON**: what time r we meeting later?
> **THOMAS**: i think 8 tonight should work. ok hannah?

With Mom's piercing gaze bearing down on me, I sent a reply and then quickly put the phone back in my pocket.

> **ME**: that's fine where at?

Leslie shot me a questioning look and I promised to explain later. Someone stood from the front pew and walked up to the podium at the front of the church. He unfolded a piece of paper and stepped closer to the microphone the preacher had been using a moment ago.

"Danielle was the best sister a guy could ask for. She took care of me when we were younger and always made sure that I was happy. The world lost a special person when Danielle" —his voice caught, and he wiped a stray tear from his cheek— "passed away suddenly. We are all a little better off for having known her."

As if I didn't already feel like I was bombarded by new information moment by moment, I got hit with another one. I didn't know that Danielle Wesley had a brother! All the times I was at Kate's house when we were younger, she never mentioned an uncle. I supposed Danielle and her brother weren't close. Curiosity stirred and I wondered what could have happened to pull them apart.

Her brother continued his eulogy. "Danielle loved her daughter, Kate, and her husband, Gideon. She always put family first and made sure that they knew they were loved."

It felt like he was talking about someone completely different. I wasn't sure how much of his eulogy was true. Kate had told me on many occasions about how her parents treated her over the past few years. Danielle's brother was acting like she was a saint, but Kate told a different story. Her Mom was always caught up with work at Memory Lane and ignored Kate most of the time. So did her Dad. I felt sorry for her. I'm sure that was true for most families though. My family isn't perfect, either. Far from it, actually.

Dad was still being held at Memory Lane and we had no way of contacting him. I asked Mom several times how we could get him out, but she told me that she didn't want me and Leslie near Memory Lane and that she didn't want me asking about it again. That led to me, Thomas, and Jenson coming up with a plan on our own. We were going over the logistics tonight.

Danielle's brother finished his eulogy, shaking me out of my reverie as he stepped down from the podium. The preacher spoke again. "Let us pray. Heavenly Father, we are gathered here today to honor the life of Danielle Wesley. She was loved by many, and we are comforted knowing she is home in heaven with you now. Even though we may not understand why she was taken so soon, we believe your plan is perfect and that we will one day get to see her again. In Jesus' name we pray, Amen."

I opened my eyes and looked over at Kate and her Dad. He had his arm around her as she sobbed into his shoulder.

The preacher spoke again. "The family would like to welcome you forward to pay your respects."

I watched as, row by row, most of the people stood up and formed a line to go and talk to the Wesleys after pausing by the casket. They had opted for a closed casket, and part of me wondered about the significance of saying goodbye to a box. I didn't understand, but to each their own. I planned to go talk to Kate to make sure she knew that I was there to support her during this difficult time. Mom, Leslie, and I moved to the end of our pew to join the line to talk with the Wesleys and pay our respects.

Leslie followed behind me as we got in line. There were tons of people ahead of us due to the publicity surrounding Danielle's death and who she was related to.

"That poor woman. Her husband probably killed her. It's always the husband," whispered a woman behind us in line.

The woman she was with whispered back, "I feel bad for the daughter. It's just a tragedy to continue living without a mother."

Leslie and I exchanged a look and I winked at her to let her know to play along.

"How do you know the daughter didn't kill her mother for attention? That's just as plausible," I said to the two women.

"That's horrible! Why would you suggest that?!" asked one of the women.

"I bet Kate killed her Mom for the money she'll inherit. That's what I would do if I was rich," added Leslie with a smile.

One of the women clasped her hand to her chest and gasped in shock. "Where is your mother?"

"She's dead. We killed her," Leslie and I said at the same time as the line moved forward.

Both women looked disgusted. "That's not funny. How dare you even suggest that, at a funeral, no less. So crass!"

"Almost as bad as speculating that Kate's Dad killed her Mom when you don't even know them," I retorted, coldly.

"Girls, be quiet. It's almost our turn," Mom interrupted.

With one last dirty look at the two women, I turned and faced forward with Leslie. The black casket was about twelve feet in front of us with a line of people just past it, hugging Kate and her Dad off to the side. As we approached the casket, the familiar feeling of losing Leslie gripped me, and I grabbed her hand, silently reminding myself that she was here, alive with me.

Mom placed her hand on the casket, and was silent for a moment, as if in prayer. Anxiously, I waited for her to move away from the casket and toward the Wesleys, mimicking her motion and moment of silence because I didn't know what else to do. After a moment, Leslie nudged me, and we walked over to join Mom.

Kate looked a mess with red, swollen eyes and immediately I grabbed her shoulders to hug her. "If you need anything, I'm here," I told her, quietly. She nodded her head. I pulled away and shook Mr. Wesley's hand next.

"I am so sorry for your loss," I told him sincerely. He smiled at me and wiped away some stray tears.

"Thank you." Mr. Wesley's eyes darted from me to Leslie. His brows knitted together in confusion as if trying to place who we were. I breathed a sigh of relief that our disguises worked.

Before turning away, I looked back over at Kate. "I'll call you later."

As we left the Wesleys, Mom ushered me and Leslie out of the church and into the parking lot. "What a nice memorial service," Mom said, absent-mindedly.

"I still want to know who killed her," I responded.

"Hannah! That's not something you should be talking about."

"Well, I want to know. It could be Gideon. Kate could be in danger. Excuse me for caring about my friend."

"There's no evidence that Gideon killed his wife. Leave it alone," Mom warned.

The three of us walked toward the car and I climbed in the passenger-side door while Leslie climbed into the back seat. As Mom backed slowly out of the parking space, careful of people loitering in the parking lot after the service, I absentmindedly turned on the radio.

"Have you talked to Dad?" asked Leslie.

"Are you asking me or Mom?"

"Either of you."

"I haven't heard from your father. With everything going on in Memory Lane, I'm sure he is being monitored and can't call us."

Leslie leaned forward and put her arms around my headrest to get a better view of Mom in the front seat. "And you're okay with that? He might be in danger."

There was a beat of silence as the radio played on.

"Have you tried calling him?" asked Leslie.

Mom huffed. "You mean calling Memory Lane and asking them to put Robert on the phone for a second? Somehow, I don't think that will work."

"There has to be something we can do!" Leslie sounded exasperated.

"I know you're worried, Les. I am too. But I have to make sure it's safe for our family to be anywhere near or involved with Memory Lane. We have already had more than our fair share of tragedy and loss. I just got you back. You know it is my job to keep you and Hannah safe."

Without a beat, I rolled my eyes. "I appreciate the sentiment, Mom, I really do, but I'm eighteen now. I love you, but there isn't anything you can do to stop me from helping Dad."

"Are you planning another break-in? Have you learned nothing from last time?! I can't believe you're even considering—"

"Don't tell me what to consider! He's my Dad!" I yelled back.

"Stop!" Leslie yelled from behind me. "I hate when you guys fight."

"We aren't fighting!" Mom and I yelled at the same time.

Leslie leaned back in her seat and crossed her arms. "Sounded like fighting to me."

Mom sighed. "Everyone, just calm down. We can talk about this when we get home in a little bit. Like rational adults. Okay?"

Nodding, I agreed silently and turned the radio up to fill the awkward silence. A few minutes crept by, and I finally couldn't stand it anymore.

"Are we going to bake Kate a casserole? Isn't that what you are supposed to do when someone dies?" I asked.

"Not unless you want to," Mom responded.

Despite my need to fill the silence, I actually hated all the casseroles we got from people when Leslie died four years ago. Appeared to be dead. Whatever. My brain hurt from going in circles regarding what really happened to Leslie. Despite it feeling almost as if she had never left, I wasn't used to saying it yet.

My thoughts turned to Kate's grief. "I think Kate would appreciate cake more than a casserole." I turned around and asked Leslie. "Wanna help me bake her a chocolate cake?"

"Sure. We should add sprinkles too."

"Good call. Nothing says I'm sorry your Mom died like some sugar-coated candy on a cake."

"Hannah! That's terrible."

"Well, it's sorta true," I replied. "Giving people food when someone dies is weird. Admit it."

"It's so the family doesn't have to worry about meals while dealing with the aftermath of losing a loved one," Mom explained.

"I know the reason; I just think dessert will be more appreciated."

"Very much so," Mom agreed.

We pulled up to our house and Leslie and I got out of the car and headed to the kitchen. I discarded my wig on the counter and watched as Leslie did the same.

Opening the pantry and the spice cabinet, I began to survey our available ingredients. "Let's see if we have the ingredients to make a chocolate cake. If not, we can go to the store."

The shelves held flour, cocoa, and baking powder among the other items in the pantry and I made a mental checklist of things that were still necessary to make the cake.

"Check for eggs in the fridge, Leslie."

Scanning the shelves, I continued to look for the rest of the items. "Crap. We don't have any sugar."

"Double crap. We need eggs too."

"Mom!" I called out from the kitchen. *Where did she go?* "When are we due for our allotment of eggs and sugar?"

Mom entered the kitchen from the direction of her bedroom. "What was that, honey? I couldn't hear you."

"When do we get more eggs and sugar?"

"Not for another four days, I think. I keep forgetting to change the amount of people living in the house since Leslie…" she said, her voice trailing off.

"Can't we make the cake without eggs?" asked Leslie.

"Not if we want it to be edible." I chuckled. "Well, we can wait a few days to bake the cake, I suppose. Or buy Kate a chocolate cake. Although, I really wanted to make her one to show her that we care. Plus, the store-bought cakes are gross. I swear they count out each sugar granule to make sure there is enough for rations."

"At least you've had cake," said Leslie.

My heart sank for a minute and the elephant in the room was back. I was still trying to pretend that everything was normal again. Of course Memory Lane wasn't feeding the kids in the program cakes, cookies, and their favorite sweets. They were experimenting on children in disgusting ways. Within seconds, I got angry at Memory Lane all over again. We still had no idea what Leslie went through. She had yet to share with us what happened and I didn't want to pressure her into talking. She would tell me when she was ready.

A strange noise came from the other room, interrupting my thoughts. It sounded like a phone was ringing but it wasn't a ringtone I recognized.

"Is that your phone?" I asked Mom.

"No," she replied.

Mom and I both turned to look at Leslie, assuming she had to be the culprit of this ringing phone. She rolled her eyes. "I don't even have a phone!"

"Well…then whose is it?" I asked.

"Don't just stand there. Go answer it," prompted Leslie.

The three of us walked toward the noise that had now stopped. Our discussion about the mystery phone took longer than the effort to find it.

"Well, how are we supposed to figure out where—"

A three-note trill went off soon after the phone stopped ringing. It was probably a text message. The phone kept trilling as text messages came in. One right after another. We followed the sound to my parents' bedroom. It was coming from the nightstand next to Dad's side of the bed. *That's weird. Why would my Dad have a phone in the drawer that Mom didn't know about?*

Approaching the nightstand, Mom opened the drawer and dug under some old papers and various other things to find a phone she had never seen before. Her face went ghostly white as she read the messages as they scrolled across the screen.

"Mom? What's wrong? Who is it?" asked Leslie.

Silence. Mom stared at both of us.

"Mom?" I urged.

"It's your Dad. He's in trouble."

Chapter 2

Silence stretched on for what felt like forever.

"Mom! How do you know it's Dad?" I asked, confused.

I was met with heavy silence. Mom just stared at the phone in her hands.

"Mom?" asked Leslie.

Mom's hands began to shake. This must be serious. I had to try to get Leslie out of the room. Maybe then Mom would tell me what was going on.

I faked a smile at my sister. "Hey, Les. Can you go get me a snack?"

"What? Why? I need to know what's going on too."

"I know, and we'll tell you later. Promise."

Leslie crossed her arms, unimpressed. "I'm not the same eight-year-old who "died" anymore. I deserve to know what's going on with Dad."

She wasn't wrong. I conceded. "Spill, Mom. What's wrong?"

She handed over the phone to me so Leslie and I could read the messages.

UNKNOWN: It's Robert. Linda?

UNKNOWN: HELLO????

UNKNOWN: I have no way of knowing if you are getting this message but Memory Lane has decided they are done with me and want Hannah or Leslie. Why would they want Leslie? That makes no sense. Hello? Linda? Please answer.

UNKNOWN: They are watching

UNKNOWN: I think they are going to kill me

"What? They want to kill Dad! I thought he was an asset because of his memory retainment?"

"We can't let him die, Mom!" Leslie pleaded.

"No one is dying!" Mom yelled. "Just give me a minute to think." She paced the room back and forth. I could see the wheels spinning a thousand miles an hour as she tried to puzzle out what came next.

A minute went by in silence that seemed to stretch on forever.

Leslie broke the silence first. "Are you gonna reply?" She handed Mom the phone back as if silently demanding a response.

Mom put the phone down on her bed and rubbed her temples like she had a headache. "What would I say?"

"Ask him why he thinks they want to kill him," I suggested.

"We don't even know if this is your Dad. It could be someone pretending to be him in order to scare us or get information."

"That's a good point. I didn't even think about that."

"Where did this phone come from, anyway?" asked Leslie, picking the phone back up off the bed to examine it.

"No idea. It has to be your Dad's because it isn't any of ours. Maybe he kept it for emergencies."

Immediately I thought about every mystery book I had ever read. "Ask him something only Dad would know."

"There could be a guard forcing him to give information. We couldn't be sure he was giving the answers willingly," Mom countered.

"But how could they know the number for this phone or that this phone was even here? You didn't even know this phone existed until five minutes ago."

"What if they stole the number from his memory using The Mnemonic?" asked Leslie. Mom and I both looked at Leslie at the same time.

"That's a far-fetched possibility, Les." *Not that I was trying to point out the obvious, but this isn't a science fiction movie!*

"I'm just brainstorming too."

Mom sighed. She looked as though she had aged ten years in just a few moments. I could see the worry lining her eyes, and the down-turned corners of her mouth were too deep to hide. "I'm going to ask him why he thinks Memory Lane will kill him," she finally said.

With the idea on the table now, it seemed frightening. "Are you sure, Mom?" I asked.

"Yeah."

She typed out her question on the phone and waited for a response. What felt like an eternity passed and then the phone trilled twice.

Taking a deep breath, Mom opened the text messages. As her eyes darted back and forth over the phone's screen, I could see the color drain from her face. She sucked in a breath as if she had unknowingly stopped breathing and then tears began to fall. Trembling, she dropped the phone and covered her face with her hands.

"What did he say, Mom?" I asked, panic creeping into my voice. Reaching over, I picked up the phone and read the brief messages sent back.

As I read the messages, I stood there in shock. How could we have just gotten Leslie back, and now we were being rocketed back into Memory Lane and their chaos?

As if she knew I was talking about her, Leslie leaned over to read the messages glaring up from the screen.

UNKNOWN: I have three days to hand over Hannah
UNKNOWN: If I don't, they will make my death look like a suicide

She shook her head in disbelief.

"Well, we aren't going to let them do that, Mom." I stated.

Leslie nodded along with me, and we sat down on the bed on either side of her. I put my hand on her one shoulder in comfort and Leslie leaned her head on the other. "It will be okay. We have these messages as proof if they try something."

Leslie chimed in with her own comfort too. "Yeah, the three of us are in this together. No one has to stand up against Memory Lane alone."

The second hand on the clock ticked by loudly as Leslie and I waited for Mom to respond. My impatience got the best of me.

"I hate to bring this up Mom, but do you think we should tell Dad about Les?"

My question seemed to bring Mom back to the moment and she wiped away the tears on her cheeks. "I'm afraid Memory Lane will come after her sooner if we confirm that she is alive and with her family. Even if it is your Dad who is telling us all this, we know they are monitoring it. For all they know, Leslie is a runaway."

"Yeah," Leslie said, "but Randall saw me running with Hannah and Jenson. He watched me get into their car. I'm pretty sure he knows I had help to escape. It's only a matter of time before Memory Lane catches on."

"Besides, don't you think Dad deserves to know that his daughter is actually alive and well?" I asked. "It might give him some hope to hold onto."

"It's too risky. I can't lose Leslie again. I just can't." Mom's voice cracked and she started crying again, hard this time. Leslie and I hugged her tight. *It was time for action. I had already began planning, maybe I needed to bring Mom in on my own hope.*

"Well, I think we need a plan to get Dad out of Memory Lane."

Mom's head snapped up. "I already told you that I am not allowing you or Leslie near that place, Hannah. I mean it."

"What if we had other people do it for us?"

"What? Who?" asked Mom, clearly confused.

"I think Jenson and Thomas might be willing to help us out. Besides, we were all meeting tonight anyway to talk about getting back into Memory Lane in the first place—" *I definitely said too much there!*

"So, you went behind my back and disobeyed me anyway?!?" Mom yelled.

I guess she was done being sad and had moved onto mad.

"I wasn't going to let Leslie go. She's still a little kid. I'm not dumb."

"Hey! I resent that!" Leslie had been gone for four years and it was so tough remembering how much older she was now. Even worse was admitting how much she was forced to grow up under the torture she endured while she was imprisoned at Memory Lane.

My mind may have been wandering, but Mom was still angry. She stared at me with a look that only mothers have. One that said, "I cannot believe you right now." At least she wasn't yelling anymore.

"Look, I think you'll want to hear this plan. It could help get Dad out of Memory Lane and it might even help us figure out the reason Leslie was taken in the first place."

"How?" Mom asked. Her look told me that I better be ready to make a darn convincing case.

When trying to get your Mom on board with a life-endangering plan, you must make sure you present your ideas clearly. I paused for a minute to gather my thoughts so I could tell the whole story of how Kate, Jenson, and I had gotten into Memory Lane in the first place. The break-in that resulted in us finding Leslie by accident.

"Well, Kate went in to relive a memory of hers about the day that Leslie 'drowned'"—I put air quotes up—"at the waterpark. Since she was working with her Dad, she had some information about how a guy in a suit was hanging around the waterpark that day and she believed he was a Memory Lane guard who was possibly responsible for faking Leslie's drowning."

"Okay ... and?"

"Well, Jenson had the idea to plant a device on a computer in the memory storage room so we could view Kate's memory ourselves after the fact."

"Hold on. Jenson is Kate's ex-boyfriend who served time in prison for hacking, correct?" Mom asked for clarification.

"Yeah, he knows what he's doing. Trust me."

Mom shot me a disapproving look but I pretended to miss the look as I continued with the story.

"Anyway, I was responsible for planting the small device after Jenson started a small fire to set off the alarms. We assumed all doors would unlock to allow me access to the memory storage room in the event of a fire. It let me into the building, but not into the storage room," I explained, disappointed in myself again.

Mom interrupted to ask a question. "So, you haven't seen Kate's memory of that day at the waterpark yet?"

"Unfortunately, no. That's why we want to go back and plant his device to retrieve the memory. Maybe it can help us piece together the mystery of why they faked Leslie's death. It was my idea to try and get Dad out too."

"But Dad is at Memory Lane here in Mississippi and Kate's memory is at Memory Lane in Kansas. How does that work?"

"Jenson is pretty sure that there is a database where memories are stored connecting all Memory Lanes."

"Pretty sure? You want to go barging into Memory Lane again on a hunch from an ex-hacker? I didn't raise you this way, Hannah. You've lost all common sense," Mom gasped. "Besides, how do you plan to get Robert away from the guards? He's been under arrest for a while now. They are watching him."

"I know, Mom." I rolled my eyes. "But we have to try."

"What if we drugged the guards to get Dad away from them?" Leslie suggested.

"What?! How'd you come up with that idea?" I asked.

"Well, Thomas was drugged recently and he made it out okay, so I thought it could work. It's also a little less violent and messy if there aren't dead bodies to deal with."

"Who are you and what have you done with my precious daughter?" Mom asked, clearly disturbed. "You are also a minor and I forbid you to have a part in this. Is that clear?"

At the moment, I had to agree.

Leslie started to speak. "But I—"

Mom cut her off before she could finish her sentence and spoke sternly, wagging her finger in Leslie's face. She clearly was not messing around. "No. I mean it, Leslie."

"Where would we even get something to drug the guards?" I asked, mulling over Leslie's idea more.

"We are not drugging the guards!" Mom yelled.

I scoffed. "You would rather us shoot them?"

"Shoot them! I would rather you not go back to Memory Lane at all, but I have this sinking feeling that you are going to find a way in like last time no matter what I say."

I smirked. She was finally starting to realize that I was going back to Memory Lane, regardless of her attempts to dissuade me.

Leslie looked defeated and upset as she hung her head in disappointment. "I guess I'm just chopped liver. Good to know that while I was gone our 'happy little family' just continued without me." She got up to leave our parents' bedroom.

"Leslie, wait! It's not like that!" I called after her. Dejected footsteps echoed through the hallway ending in a dramatically slammed door.

"Great. Now Leslie is mad."

"I don't know how we should do this, Hannah. I really don't. I want all of you safe. Is that too much to ask?"

"No, it's not. We also can't just sit around and do nothing. I won't."

Mom huffed. She knew I was stubborn; she knew where I got it from.

"Look, Jenson and Thomas are supposed to meet with me later. Let's change the meeting to here so you can listen and brainstorm with us until you are comfortable with the plan. Sound good?" I asked, throwing Mom a white flag.

She looked almost as dejected as Leslie did before she stormed out of the room. "It's better than the alternative." With nothing to do but wait for the meet-up, Mom stood up from her bed and walked out of the room in search of Leslie.

I took out my phone and sent a VidChat to both Jenson and Thomas to let them know that we were going to meet here at my house now. I pocketed my phone and went to find Mom and Leslie elsewhere in the house. It didn't take long to find them; I just followed the sounds of their arguing to the kitchen.

"You can't make me!" Leslie screamed.

Wow. I did not miss that yelling.

"As your mother, I can make you do whatever I want."

"I was only trying to help. I hate being left out. I think you and Hannah forget that while you were getting over my death for four years, I was out there dealing with Memory Lane guards the whole time. You can't underestimate me anymore. I'm an asset."

The way Leslie explained herself to Mom again reminded me that she was no longer an eight-year-old kid. She had grown up and learned how to survive and deal with things on her own. I hated that she had her childhood stolen from her. I wish she could have stayed innocent forever, but I knew that wasn't possible. I also hoped she knew that there was no way I was done "getting over" her death. Not ever.

"I think Leslie's right, Mom. She could help us get Dad out. She knows more about the layout and what makes Memory Lane guards susceptible to drugging."

"I also spent years making them believe I had memory loss so they wouldn't know I had memory retainment."

"Wait, you knew that's what they were after?" I asked, shocked that she even knew what memory retainment was.

"It was sort of obvious when they were testing us. Plus, all the kids would talk at night when the guards went to bed. Almost every kid I met the last four years has memory retainment. Of course, we didn't know it was called that until later. We just called ourselves the memory keepers. It's a dumb name, I know, but we were just kids."

"How did they find out all of you had memory retainment? Were they targeting kids?" Mom asked.

"I'm not sure. The day you both thought I died, I woke up with Memory Lane guards all around me and I was freaking out, asking where I was, where you all were."

It felt surreal to listen to Leslie talk about her time away from us so unaffected. Her voice had less tone than if we had asked her about the weather or what she did at school.

Mom gently grabbed Leslie's arm to get her to continue. "What else do you remember about the day you disappeared?"

"Not much. I don't really want to talk about it right now."

"Nothing else?" Mom prodded.

Leslie winced. I could tell she didn't want to talk about it anymore. She would tell us details in her own time. I stepped in to give Leslie a way out of talking to Mom right now. "It's fine. Just help us figure out a way to incapacitate the guards."

"Like I said earlier, I think drugging them would work. It's quieter than guns or other weapons."

"What kind of drugs?" I asked.

"Roofies."

"Pfffttt," I scoffed. "That sounds so cliche."

"Well, it works. It doesn't kill them, but it will knock them out and hopefully they won't remember anything afterwards."

Despite how confident Leslie was, I was still skeptical. "How are you planning on giving it to them?"

"Just like men used to do to girls in the ancient times. Put it in their drinks." Leslie smirked. She sounded pleased with the thought of them getting a taste of their own medicine.

I wondered if the kids in the "program" were ever roofied. My stomach sank at the thought of that happening to eight-year-old Leslie.

"How are we going to even get close enough to put something in their drink? This plan has a lot of holes in it, Les."

Leslie shrugged. "I'm just telling you what my idea is to knock them out. The rest is up to you guys."

Mom chimed in. "Hang on. There are some other logistics to work out. Like the fact that we don't know where to even get our hands on that kind of drug and we have no idea which area your Dad is being held captive in. There are too many things that could go wrong."

"Giving up already?" I asked, annoyed with Mom changing her mind every five seconds.

"I didn't say that." She shook her head. "I just think we need some more information. Maybe a layout of the building."

"Well, Thomas and I have actually been inside. We were also in a holding cell at Memory Lane. I know where some stuff is."

"I know that, but I still think we need to know how to get access to where your Dad is. I doubt he is just in a holding cell. Don't you think they have a more permanent place for people they have arrested?"

It was still strange to me that Memory Lane also functioned as a police station at times. The jails became overrun in the last three years so Memory Lane offered to help out. They had the means and the guards necessary to make it happen. Of course, this was only for offenses against Memory Lane or small misdemeanors. The real police took care of murderers, rapists, and the like. I was worried that one day Memory Lane would take over all policing and then we would really be up a creek. There would eventually be no one else to call if Memory Lane was at fault for something. They would truly be the only people in charge of everything.

Leslie broke me out of my thoughts. "Earth to Hannah."

"Sorry. Just thinking. Yeah, Mom, I'm sure they have Dad somewhere else. Maybe Jenson and Thomas have some more info."

Mom nodded. We silently agreed to table this conversation until later when Jenson and Thomas arrived.

"In the meantime, can we get some food? I'm hungry," said Leslie.

"Sure thing. Let's go see what the Instafood panel can drum up." With plans in the works and help on the way, the three of us walked toward the kitchen in search of something to eat.

Chapter 3

My phone trilled. Glancing down, I could see that Jenson had sent me a VidChat. I opened it just as a VidChat came in at the same time from Thomas. They were both on their way to my house to discuss the plan. How do I tell them both that Mom was now involved? I began to wonder how that would go over.

"Thomas and Jenson are headed over," I chimed.

Mom got up and threw her empty plate away. "Good."

She still looked uneasy about sitting down with a handful of kids to discuss a breaking-and-entering plan that included drugging guards. There was nothing I could do about that now. The best we could do is create the most foolproof plan possible.

"Are you going to ask Dad anything else or just wait until we break him out?" I asked.

A flash of parental frustration passed over Mom's face as she turned to confront my ambitious statement. "I'm glad you are so confident that we'll get him out. That's assuming there are no other surprises."

It only took a second for me to run through my last two break-ins at Memory Lane. She was right about surprises and how things went south quickly.

"We'll over prepare. Besides, now we have an adult helping us." I winked at Mom, hoping to lighten the mood. "That has to be worth something."

It seemed to be worth a hearty roll of her eyes as she threw a damp towel at me and directed my eyes to the crumbs that covered the table where I was sitting. Jeez, I was always such a messy eater.

"What are you planning to do with Leslie"—I pointed at her across the table from me—"while we are on this so-called mission?"

"I guess she can stay with your Aunt Nicole. I can call and ask her."

"Hey! I'm right here! Don't I get a say?" Leslie asked. She couldn't conceal the hurt on her face as she looked at both Mom and me. How do you explain to someone that you just can't bear to lose them again?

In the case of Mom, it took her no time at all to lay down the law, gently. "We already established that you aren't coming, sweetheart."

"I can help! I was at Memory Lane all the time over the last four years."

"Wait, you remained at the same facility full time?" I asked, shocked.

"Pretty much all the time during the day. We were in an area marked for authorized personnel only."

What if there were more kids there who were still being experimented on? I made a mental note to ask Leslie later about where they kept the kids at night. Didn't need to give Mom another reason to be worried.

"Was the area you were in with the other kids near the memory rooms?"

"No. It's on the other side of the building, where the memory storage unit is." Leslie said matter-of-factly.

This was brilliant! I couldn't believe that Leslie was the answer that we needed all along to put Jenson's device on the computer and download all the memories. Even though Leslie was at a different Memory Lane than the one Dad was being held in, this was still very useful information.

Leslie interrupted my thoughts. "I bet Dad is in the same area where they tested us."

"You're probably right." I began to wonder how similar the layout was for each Memory Lane. I knew Kate said they followed the same basic layout but there were subtle differences for each one.

"I still don't think it's a good idea for you to be anywhere near Memory Lane. You escaped their 'program.' There's no way the guards aren't looking for you," said Mom, still working to discourage Leslie from participating.

Leslie started to argue again. "But—"

"I'm actually surprised they aren't looking for you right now." Mom's brow was furrowed and she had a worried look on her face.

"With the murder of Kate's Mom, finding the killer is high priority right now. Unfortunately, give it a few more days, and me and Les are both toast. Even more reason we need to get Dad from Memory Lane and get out of here. The good thing is that Memory Lane thinks me and Thomas are in Georgia at the moment, thanks to Jenson and his digital tricks. That should keep them busy for a little while, but it's not a permanent solution."

"Are you still talking about those fake IDs for all of us?" asked Mom.

"Yeah. I think that's our best bet."

"What fake IDs?" asked Leslie. "No one ever tells me anything."

I smiled at her. That pouty face still reminded me of her begging me to take her with me when I would hang out with Kate. It was still just so hard to believe that she had been gone for four years. "To be fair, you haven't been back that long. It was Thomas's idea. He says he can make legit-looking IDs for me, you, Mom, and Dad so we can all leave the country and escape Memory Lane. For good."

Leslie looked contemplative for a moment. "We're just going to run away?"

"Well, otherwise they will be after us forever."

The doorbell rang. *Well, I guess it is time to get this plan mapped and executed.*

"I'll get it." I left the kitchen and made my way to the front door. As I let Thomas in, he hugged me.

"How are you?" he asked. We had all been through a lot the past few weeks with more yet to come.

"I'm fine," I said, brushing off his question. "Leslie and Mom are in the kitchen." I nodded in that direction. "Jenson should be here in a few minutes."

"Where is he staying, anyway?" asked Thomas.

"I think he got a motel for now. To be honest, I didn't ask."

Thomas made his way over to the kitchen just as Jenson arrived and started knocking on the door. Opening the door suddenly, I could see Jenson's hand was still midair. He looked a little put off at being interrupted mid-knock. "What? Are you psychic now?" he asked.

"Yes, next you will ask to come in…" I laughed a little at my joke and saw Jenson smile. "Thomas just got here so I was already standing at the door. Ready to get down to business?"

Jenson followed me into the kitchen and greeted Thomas with a nod. He smiled and shook Mom's hand. "I'm Jenson. Nice to meet you."

"Nice to meet you too," Mom responded. "So, let's get down to business. What's your plan for getting back into Memory Lane?"

"Straight to the point, like Hannah. I like it." Jenson laughed. "I want to plant a device on the computer in the memory storage room, but it's locked, and you need a key card to enter."

"Last time we thought starting a fire and setting off the alarms would open all doors, seeing as it's an emergency and all, but that plan failed. It only opened exterior doors," I said, filling in Mom with more details.

She nodded along. "Right."

"This time, we need to get a key card from a guard and use it to enter the room," Jenson continued.

"Sounds like a better plan, but how does this help us get Robert out?" Mom asked.

Jenson shrugged. "I'm not sure of that part yet. It's why we were meeting up tonight. We had only talked about getting my device on the computer to download memories."

"Why are you trying to download memories anyway? That seems just as invasive as Memory Lane to me," said Thomas almost accusingly.

Before Jenson could speak up, I defended the plan and Jenson. "We want to see what Kate viewed the night she went into a memory room at Memory Lane. There are still so many unanswered questions. Hopefully it gives us some answers to Leslie's kidnapping the day of my birthday party."

"What if it isn't helpful? What about other people's memories? Are you planning on watching those too?" Thomas asked. His voice held an angry edge that I hadn't seen before. He folded his arms and waited for a response from Jenson.

"Look, I'm only trying to help. Hannah and Kate approached me." Jenson threw up his hands as if to protect himself from any further blows.

It was obvious Thomas didn't trust Jenson. Maybe he would start to see that Jenson was trustworthy once he got to know him.

"Calm down. We can talk about that part later." I spoke to break the tension. "Let's get back to how we plan to get the key card from a guard."

"Well, we could incapacitate one of them with our fists," Jenson joked.

While Mom just rolled her eyes, the joke flew far over Thomas's head and instead was met with more distrust and accusations.

"What's with the violence? Is that always the answer for you or did you learn in prison?" Thomas asked.

"I was in federal prison. Plenty of guards, so I was hardly getting into fights every day. It was a joke, man. Chill."

Thomas grumbled under his breath but kept quiet.

"Look. Leslie came up with a decent, nonviolent idea to get rid of the guards. Let's hear it from her, okay?" I asked, trying to placate

Thomas and Jenson. Boy, did I sure hope this wasn't a mistake to bring them together. I wondered if it would be better with Kate as a buffer since she has known Jenson longer. "Go on, Les. Tell them your idea."

"I thought we could drug the guards. They take breaks every four and a half hours to get a drink and a snack. If we put something in their drink, we could wait until they pass out, and then lift the key card off of them."

"What kind of drug?" Jenson and Thomas asked at the same time. Maybe this wasn't a mistake after all if they were on the same wavelength.

"Rohypnol," Leslie stated, trying to use the scientific name to break the "I am a little kid" vibe.

Chancing a glance, I peered over at Mom across the room. She looked disgusted with this whole idea. I knew she wanted Dad out of Memory Lane, but I could tell that involving her children—even if I was "technically" an adult now—was bothering her.

Thomas laughed and Jenson scoffed.

"Do you mean roofies? Where are you going to get roofies?" Thomas asked.

"We haven't figured that part out yet. But it's perfect because it should knock the guards out long enough for us to steal their key card and get into the storage room."

"That's all well and good, but how are you going to both plant the device and get Uncle Robert out at the same time? Are they even in the same location?" asked Thomas.

"I was thinking about asking Kate for the blueprints so we could be sure."

Not a split second went by before Mom jumped in. "Absolutely not," Mom emphatically stated. "You are not to disturb Kate right now. Her Mom just died. She doesn't need this drama right now."

"She might welcome the distraction. Besides, I'm not asking her to come. We just need the blueprints."

"What makes you think she can get them?" asked Jenson.

"She has worked there, and it's her Dad's Memory Lane. They should be easier to get than plans for the Memory Lane when we were out of state."

Leslie joined in the conversation again. "She might even be able to draw them for us if she can't get us a copy. Didn't you say she told you where to find Thomas after you guys were separated?"

"That's a fair point. She may not even have to steal them for us."

"I forbid you to ask Kate!" Mom shouted.

All of us stopped and stared at Mom. I don't think she meant to yell, but tensions were high and there was a lot riding on this plan. Dad could be killed in a few days if we didn't figure this out.

Thomas changed the subject. "Do you think Kenneth has any roofies? I know we asked him to get us Covert Listening Devices. Even if we never used the CLDs since things went differently than we planned, he might be able to help."

"Not a bad idea. I can contact him."

"Who's Kenneth?" Mom and Leslie asked in near unison.

"I'll explain later."

"How about you explain now?" Mom demanded. "We all deserve to know the people involved in this plan."

I looked at Thomas surreptitiously. There was no getting out of this explanation.

Mom gave me a stern look. "Hannah, I mean it."

"He's just someone that owes me a favor. Kinda like how Jenson got involved through Kate by owing her a favor."

"And he has drugs?" Mom narrowed her eyes at me while Leslie tried to avoid making eye contact. I was in trouble and we both knew it.

"He also has other equipment we might need. Like CLDs." My explanation fell flat.

There was a pregnant pause as Mom took in a deep breath.

"Thomas. Leslie. Jenson. I need a moment alone with my daughter."

The three of them couldn't leave the kitchen fast enough.

"We'll be in the living room if you need us," said Thomas as he ushered Leslie and Jenson out of the kitchen.

"You're involved with drug dealers?! Who is this person? How do you know him?"

"Relax, Mom. He's a guy I know from high school."

"So that makes it okay? Has our family not been through enough? Seriously, I can't believe you right now. You are acting like a child!"

"You're still treating me like one!" I retorted.

"And how does Thomas know about him too? Did you drag him into your drug-riddled life?" Mom accused. *You would think there would be some understanding since I brought back Leslie alive, but all Mom could see was what was wrong.*

"It's not like that. Kenneth leads The Wild Ones. He's not a drug dealer."

"Oh. That makes me feel better. A rebel leader for teens." Mom angrily crossed her arms while rolling her eyes at me.

"Do you want to get Dad out of Memory Lane or not?" I asked.

"Of course I do. But not at the cost of my eldest daughter doing drugs and breaking the law repeatedly! I don't even know you anymore."

"I'm not doing drugs!" I yelled, louder than I intended. I sighed. "I just want to ask him if we can buy some roofies to stop the guards and get Dad out of Memory Lane safely. This is for our family. You have to see that, Mom," I pleaded. I could feel the tears brimming below the surface but I refused to let the tears fall.

"I know that, but how do you know someone that sells roofies in the first place?"

"He has connections, Mom. He isn't dealing drugs, he just knows where to get them. That's the only reason I even thought to contact him earlier this summer. I needed a Covert Listening Device because I thought we would use it to get into Memory Lane." I wiped a stray tear away from my cheek and continued trying to plead my case to Mom.

"Actually, it's still not a bad idea to have some CLDs handy so we could listen to what is going on inside before running in blind like last time."

Mom nodded in agreement. "I think you might be right. I don't like the invasion of privacy that CLDs bring, but I think they will be necessary to get us into Memory Lane during a time when the guards are unaware."

"The Memorizers had a bunch of CLDs being delivered to them when Thomas and I were in the truck with Brad. Should we try and get some from them instead? Antoine knows Dad and that we have memory retainment."

It hurt to think Mom needed to be convinced that I wasn't a bad person. Deep down she had to know I wasn't, but I could see how this was a lot to take in all at once.

"It's too risky," Mom said. "That would involve even more people that we don't even know are on our side. Right now, our sole focus is on getting your Dad out of Memory Lane. Figuring out what happened to Leslie from Kate's downloaded memory is a nice bonus but we don't need it."

"Agreed. Are you okay if I contact Kenneth?" I asked, just to make sure Mom was completely on board.

"I don't love it, but it's a necessary evil right now."

"Okay. Can we bring the others back in now?"

Mom nodded and I yelled for Thomas, Jenson, and Leslie to make their way back into the kitchen. They peeked their heads around the corner and I knew they had been listening in.

"So," I said to fill in the others. "We think we need some CLDs and Mom and I agree that we need to ask Kenneth about the roofies at the same time."

"What's the range on a CLD? How close should we be?" asked Thomas.

"A really good one should let us hear the guards about half a mile out," replied Jenson.

I whistled, impressed.

"What are we going to do about locating where Dad is being held inside? Still don't want us to bother Kate?" I asked, turning to Mom.

She turned to Leslie. "Do you think you could draw the layout from memory?" asked Mom.

"I can try."

"It's settled. Why don't you work on that, and I will contact Kenneth?" I suggested.

"What should Thomas and I do?" asked Jenson.

"Well, if things go our way and we get Dad out of Memory Lane, the whole family is basically going to be numero uno on the wanted list. So I think we should leave the country." I turned to look at Thomas. "Still think you can make us all fake IDs?"

"I think I can arrange that."

"Woah, hold on," said Jenson. "I didn't agree to that."

I laughed. "No offense, because you've been super helpful, but the fake IDs are for my *family*." I stressed the word so he would understand I meant blood relatives.

"Is Kate getting one?" he asked.

"I haven't asked her. I'm not sure she will want to leave the country with everything going on with her Mom's murder."

Jenson thought for a moment, and then asked Thomas, "How are you making these IDs, anyway?"

"Someone else is making them. I don't know enough to make them look legit and stand up to scrutiny."

"You trust this person? Will they scan into the system like real IDs and driver's licenses do?"

Thomas mustered a shrug. "I hope so."

"I could help, you know," Jenson offered.

"I'll keep that in mind," Thomas mumbled.

With a couple steps in the works, I took my phone out and sent a message to Kenneth asking if he had any CLDs. I figured I could ask about the roofies later when I met him.

Thomas took out his phone at the same time to contact his person for IDs while Mom went to go grab Leslie a piece of paper to draw the layout of Memory Lane. I watched as Leslie drew the front entrance, an area for the memory rooms on the side, the elevator, the memory storage room, and then a room she called "KP."

"What's KP?" I asked.

"Kid's Program. That's what they always called it."

"It sounds like StoryTime at the library instead of a cruel organization that kidnaps children to test them."

Leslie shrugged and continued to draw. She was actually getting almost all parts of Memory Lane down on paper. I still had to remind myself that she had lived there for four years. When she was done, she let Mom and me see the finished product.

"I don't see anything that might be where Dad is located," I pointed out.

"I'm not sure about that part."

"Maybe Kate knows more…" I trailed off, pretending to be thinking.

"Don't push me, Hannah. I already told you, don't bother her right now."

"Just thinking aloud, Mom." I glanced at Leslie's drawing again, tracing the hallways we'd walked on our last trip, and there, almost small enough to miss, was a blank area that didn't make sense. "Wait, what's that?" I asked pointing to an empty space.

"I'm not sure. It was a door I passed once or twice when I wasn't supposed to be out, but it wasn't labeled so I never knew what was in there."

Closing my eyes, I thought for a minute about being at Memory Lane and then it clicked. It might be where that janitor's closet was that Kate let me into. The same one with the secret passage to the other side of the facility where Thomas was prisoner. *Could that be where they were holding my Dad?* It was so dark you could barely see the step in front of you and I was wandering around in the dark trying to find Thomas the first time I was at Memory Lane. There was a real chance that doors to other rooms existed in that passageway. It would have been easily missed in the panic. Mulling over every inch of that hallway created a new question. *Why did Kate know about that area in the first place?*

"Guys, I think I have an idea where that door might lead."

"Are you going to share with the class?" asked Jenson.

"When we were at Memory Lane last time, Thomas and I got separated when Kate came to get me. I had to find my way back to you," I glanced at Thomas before continuing. "Kate led me through a janitor's closet with a tunnel that connected to another part of the facility."

"Why would there be a tunnel?" Leslie asked.

"Who knows. They kidnap and experiment on children. A super-secret passageway in a tunnel doesn't seem too far off. But I think that might be where they are keeping Dad."

"What about the part with the jail cell that you and I were in?" asked Thomas.

"He could be there too. There's no real way of knowing unless we contact him."

"We still don't know if that is safe. I don't trust that it's really him unless we are talking to him on the phone," said Mom.

My phone trilled, interrupting all of our thoughts.

I glanced down. It was Kenneth.

"Well, good news. Kenneth has the CLDs and I can pick them up tonight."

"Did you ask about the roofies?" Leslie asked.

"Not yet. Better to ask that one in person."

"Are you going alone?" Mom asked. "I think Thomas should go with you."

Glancing sideways, I looked over at Thomas and silently asked if he was okay with that suggestion. He nodded. I smiled and was reminded about our time at Memory Lane. I was lucky to have a cousin who was willing to protect me at all costs.

"What do you want me to do while you and Thomas are off getting 'supplies'?" Jenson asked with sarcastic air quotes.

"Figure out a way into Memory Lane without all of us getting caught or killed," I said. "And, Jenson, no fires this time."

Jenson smirked. "No fires. Cross my heart."

Chapter 4

Our plan was taking shape and I left the house with Thomas in tow. We climbed into Mom's car and my fingers nimbly keyed the address Kenneth had texted me into the touch screen, then punched the auto drive. Feeling a sense of calm for the moment, I sat back to relax. I needed some time to breathe instead of focusing on the road.

"How are you holding up, Hannah?" Thomas asked gently.

I'm sure he could see the dark circles under my eyes, but I responded anyway. "I'm fine. Just tired."

"How's Leslie settling back in?"

"She's okay. She is still having nightmares that end with her in my bed, but I can't complain. I never thought I would see her again. Getting her back is something I would never have dreamed of." *She can sleep in my bed forever if it means that I never have to lose her again.*

"Have you gotten her to really talk about her time at Memory Lane?" Thomas prodded.

"She tells me bits and pieces, but I don't want to push her." I changed the radio station to something a little more upbeat to distract me. The notes of a familiar tune played through the car as the scenery whizzed by the car windows. How many times had we driven down this road for family vacations or to head to school? I glanced out the window as we passed the high school and I couldn't help but feel nostalgic for a minute. The building looked more inviting somehow with its chipped brown paint and double doors leading into the main office. The front was lined with maple trees and a sidewalk that was really only wide enough for three people at most. It used to be so crowded in the mornings.

A memory flashed in my mind and made me smile. I remembered being called into the principal's office one time when my friends and I made shirts protesting the disgusting lunch food. The school didn't take too kindly to us wearing the shirts to convince other students not to eat lunch at school. It was a whole ordeal. Mom had to come up to school and she wasn't happy. I got grounded for a week after that incident. I guess I was always willing to stand up for something when I thought it was important.

"We will get Uncle Robert back from Memory Lane. I promise you." Thomas's voice, interrupting my thoughts, held a finality to it, a hope that I could only dream to have. Despite his tone, Thomas sighed. "I'm tired of all this. I need us all to be a happy family fighting over who will host the July 4th picnic."

I scoffed, turning my head to stare out the window. "That's a lofty promise, Thomas. You don't know what will happen in the future." *No one does.*

"If we can get your Dad out and then get those IDs, we can start over. We shouldn't have to run from Memory Lane forever. They have done enough damage to our family to last several lifetimes. We deserve to be free of it."

"Let's focus on one thing at a time."

Thomas nodded and then changed the station to something else.

"Hey! I was listening to that!" I shouted. "War Machine takes me back to when things were simpler."

"War Machine is overrated."

Grabbing my chest, I gasped in mock shock. "Blasphemy! Better not let Kate hear you say that."

"I'll say it to her face. You know I always hated them."

This moment, the simple playful banter, made me smile. It pulled me back to simpler times when all that mattered was music, family, school, and hanging out with my friends. It hadn't been that long since I had turned eighteen and I already had so many problems, thanks to Memory Lane. Absentmindedly, I continued to stare out the window as the car drove us to our destination to meet Kenneth. It stopped at a red light, and I turned to Thomas.

"Have you talked to Gill at all?" I asked.

Thomas winced. It was such a small gesture I almost didn't notice it.

"Nope."

"Should we VidChat with her?"

"For what?" asked Thomas.

"I don't know. Just to keep her in the loop. She did help show us around The Memorizers as much as Brad did, if not more."

Thomas nodded but didn't respond. He stared out the window and avoided my gaze.

"Do you not trust Gill?"

"Honestly, I don't really trust anyone at the moment that isn't related to me."

"That's harsh, Thomas."

"Is it? Well, it's the truth," said Thomas.

"Look, I know that we still don't know who poisoned you, but I think Jenson, Brad, Gill, and Kate are useful to us."

"Just because they are knowledgeable doesn't mean they aren't dangerous. People lie, Hannah."

"Yes, people lie. But not all liars poison people. Gill and Kate seemed really concerned when they found out you were poisoned. The only person I haven't heard a peep from is Brad."

"Okay, to be fair, I sort of forgot he existed until about thirty seconds ago."

"He seemed genuine when he told us his reason for joining The Memorizers and he willingly drove us there without any issues," I reminded Thomas.

"I'm just not ready to rule him out as a suspect."

"Fair enough. Look." I pointed off in the distance. "We're here." The car rolled to a stop on the side of the street. We were parked in front of a house that had the distinct look of being abandoned. The windows were boarded up with rotting wood. Trash was littered everywhere, and it looked as though no one had been here in years. There were rusted cars that were definitely not the kind that could *auto drive* you anywhere. The roof was missing shingles and the paint was peeling off the siding. There was an "I told you so" moment buried here. Maybe Mom was right after all. I was suddenly very glad that I had Thomas with me.

"Does Kenneth live here?" asked Thomas.

"No idea. This is the address he sent."

"Well, we better get a move on. I don't want to be here any longer than we have to," said Thomas. His eyes were wide as he opened the passenger side door and climbed out of the car. Despite my misgivings, I followed suit and then locked the car. As Thomas walked toward the dilapidated house, I got a chill and a shiver ran down my spine. I had a bad feeling about this.

"Thomas, wait—" I started to say when a car alarm went off in the distance, making me jump.

Thomas turned around to face me. "What? Having second thoughts?"

"No. Are you?" I stood my ground and walked in front of Thomas up the creaking steps to the front door. Sitting on either side of the front stoop was a potted plant and a ceramic frog; both were broken. It spoke deafening volumes about the place we were in.

Knocking on the door, we waited to see if Kenneth or anyone else would answer. Several uncomfortable seconds passed when Thomas looked at me. "Are you sure this is a good idea?" Shrugging, I turned my head back toward the door again to knock louder. Before my hand could knock on the door I heard footsteps on the other side. With far more force than was needed, the door was yanked open abruptly.

"Yeah?"

It was a guy I didn't recognize.

"Is Kenneth home?" I asked, trying to maintain my composure.

The guy inside the house was clearly annoyed by my presence. "How should I know?"

Well maybe because you are inside the house and have eyes? I thought to myself.

"Do you know where he might be? I was told to meet him at this address."

"I'm not his keeper."

Thomas stepped in when he sensed we were getting nowhere with this person.

"Can we come in and look for him?"

The guy in the house narrowed his eyes. "You could be trying to rob us. Why would I let you in?"

"Look, we have an appointment with Kenneth. If you could just—" Before I could finish my plea, a familiar voice spoke up.

"Hannah?" Kenneth appeared in the hallway and started walking toward the front door when he saw me. "T-dog, let them in."

T-dog? What kind of name is that?

Kenneth walked over and moved T-dog out of the way. He shook both my and Thomas's hands and then ushered us inside. The front entryway that led to the living room was actually clean and well-kept. I guess outside appearances aren't everything.

"Y'all follow me," Kenneth said.

Thomas and I walked through the living room, down a hallway, and then into a back bedroom.

"Have a seat." Kenneth gestured to the bed.

I glanced at Thomas. He didn't make a move to sit on the bed, so I remained standing.

"We're good, thanks."

Kenneth shrugged. "Suit yourselves."

Eager to get home and get closer to setting Dad free, I got straight to the point. "So, you have CLDs?" I asked.

"Of course I do. Do you think I would have brought you all the way out here for nothing?" He smiled. "What do you have to trade?"

"Can't we just pay in cash?" Thomas asked.

"You can. But I prefer new customers bring me vintage electronics. It helps us build mutual trust."

Damnit! I knew that. A few weeks ago, when I was originally going to meet up with Kenneth, I found an old iPod Nano to trade. I did not remember to bring it. *Stupid, Hannah.* "What about a gold pocket watch?" I asked, hopeful.

Kenneth seemed to mull over his decision for a minute before responding.

"Perhaps. Let me see the watch."

Before I reached into my pocket, I was startlingly aware of the weight of the old pocket watch that had been passed down for generations. Sometimes it takes losing things before you can get back the things that matter most. Reaching into my pocket, I ran my thumb across the filigree that was carved across the top. No greater beauty than what had been carved by hand so many years ago. Holding out my hand, I offered the gold pocket watch to Kenneth. Thomas looked at me in horror, like he couldn't believe I was getting rid of a family heirloom that easily. Glancing back, I gave him a look that said, "Mind your business."

Kenneth ran his fingers over the pocket watch, inspecting it. He pressed the button, and the front cover sprang open as if it was new, and the second hand ticked away. It was good quality and old. No one used these anymore, yet I hoped it was enough to win Kenneth over so he would allow us to purchase the CLDs we needed.

"It's a good start." Without a second thought, Kenneth placed the watch in a box with other old collectibles. "A CLD will run you $150 in cash but with this watch I'll sell you one for $100."

This was an entirely new game, and I glanced over at Thomas, searching his eyes, wondering if Kenneth was taking advantage of us. How was I supposed to know how much a CLD really was? Thomas seemed to shrug, which I took to mean that I should agree to the trade.

"We'll take it."

"Awesome. Wait here," said Kenneth. He stood up to get what I assumed was a CLD. As soon as he was out of earshot, Thomas turned to me.

"Do you have $100?" Thomas asked, his voice laced with panic.

"I do."

"Where did you get that kind of money?"

"Don't worry about it."

Just as Thomas was about to lecture me, Kenneth returned with a small package in his hand. He sat down on the bed as he tossed the package to me. All this trouble over something so small. Handing it over to Thomas, I reach into my back pocket to give Kenneth the cash. After I paid, Thomas nudged me.

"What?" I whispered.

"You know, ask him about the other thing," Thomas mumbled under his breath. For trying to be discreet, he was sure failing miserably.

"What other thing?" Kenneth asked, narrowing his eyes.

"Other than CLDs."

"Like what?" Kenneth asked again. We could both see that Kenneth's confusion was only growing.

Thomas jumped in to save me from any more embarrassment. "She wants to know if you sell drugs. Pills."

This did not help me avoid any further embarrassment. Quite the contrary, in fact, I now felt like we were buying heroin, or worse!

Kenneth's mouth grew into a full Cheshire cat grin. "Nope, but I can point you to the right people." Standing up, Kenneth led us through the house into another bedroom. There was another guy, and this time, he was playing an immersive virtual reality game. Kenneth knocked on the VR headset like it was the same front door we knocked on to get here to see him.

"Larry!" he called.

Taking off his headgear, Larry struggled to focus on the three of us standing in front of him. "This better be good," he said.

Kenneth introduced us. "This is Hannah," he said while nodding in my direction. "She's looking to buy from you."

Larry perked up at the mention of business and took his simulator gloves off. Shaking my hand he asked, "What can I do for you?"

"Do you sell roofies?"

He paused for a minute and looked at me and Thomas. He was puzzled.

"I'm not one to judge, but it's not usually a girl asking to buy roofies from me."

"It's not for us, we're using them to—"

Larry put up a hand to cut me off. "Look, I don't need to know. How many do you need?" he asked.

"Well, probably at least two," I replied, thinking about whether we would need to drug more than one guard.

"They are $50 a pill."

"Give me two of them."

He nodded and I reached into my pocket again to give Larry money this time. All the while Thomas looked at me like I had grown a third eye. I could tell he was worried about where I was getting all this money and the amount of money we had spent today on CLDs and roofies. Hopefully it was worth it in the long run.

With our transaction complete, Larry handed me two little white pills. I pocketed them and Larry nodded, and put his virtual reality equipment back on. I guess we were done here. Kenneth motioned for us from the hallway to follow him. I turned around and left the room with Thomas.

We made our way back through the house toward the front so we could leave and get this plan set into motion.

"Thanks for helping me out, Kenneth," I said.

"No problem. I look forward to working with you in the future. I can get you a larger amount of CLDs and other equipment if you bring me antique electronics."

"Noted." I reached for the doorknob, opened the door, and stepped out. Thomas followed behind. As we walked down the steps toward the car, Thomas asked what I know he had been dying to ask me for a while. "Hannah, where did you get all that money?"

"Mom gave it to me."

"Aunt Linda had that much cash just lying around? I find that hard to believe," Thomas replied, accusatory.

"Well, she must have sold some stuff to get it. I didn't ask."

Thomas reached for the car door and climbed in the passenger side. As the door slammed shut, he turned to me.

"Did you steal money from your parents, Hannah? I want the truth."

"No! How could you think that?!"

"I'm thinking a lot of things right now."

"I can't believe you think I would steal from my parents after everything we've been through." I turned away from Thomas to stare out the window as I started the car and put it on auto after punching in my home address. It was like getting sucker punched. Thomas didn't believe me. He was like my best friend at the moment. We went from the joking car ride on our way here to accusations of theft on the way back. Memory Lane was the enemy that tore families apart and they were working so hard at creating rifts and cracks in mine.

"I'm just saying that's a lot of money. Sorry for jumping to conclusions," Thomas apologized.

"It's fine."

Thomas nodded and we fell into an uncomfortable silence.

The car bumped along the road, making its way back to the false safety of home. Glancing out of the corner of my eye, I could see Thomas fidgeting.

"So, do you think one CLD is enough for what we need to do?" Thomas asked, throwing me an olive branch.

"Should be. I guess it depends on the range. I bet Jenson knows more." Hearing Jenson's name made Thomas scowl. Despite Thomas's distaste for him, he had come through in more than one pinch and I knew we could trust him.

"So how soon can we get those fake IDs made?" I asked next.

"Probably within a week."

"How many can you get?" I asked, mentally going through all the people I wanted to have one.

Thomas shrugged. "Depends on the amount of money we have."

"Well, how much does one ID cost from your guy?"

"I don't know. I will have to ask."

"You aren't very forthcoming with info currently. What gives? I thought this was your area of expertise?"

"I honestly don't know. I've never needed fake IDs like this before. I'm just friends with him. We've never discussed his side business."

"If you say so." I paused, thinking. "Is Aunt Nicole on board with leaving the country?" I asked.

Thomas shrugged. "I haven't really thought to ask her."

"Good grief, Thomas. She's going to freak."

"Probably, but unless she wants her son to be on the run forever, she'll have to deal."

He was right. Through it all, he still had stuck by me. Despite the accusations of theft earlier, he had even agreed to come with us to leave this place and all that Memory Lane touched. It made me smile. "Thanks for your support through all of this. I appreciate it."

The car turned onto my street and rolled to a stop in the driveway. It parked itself, and then Thomas and I got out. As we walked to the front door, I could hear Leslie yelling through the walls.

"I hate you!"

Unlocking the door, we walked into a scene that I hadn't witnessed in about five years. Leslie and Mom were facing each other, and Leslie was screaming. *Boy, I did not miss that.*

"I would rather you hate me, than for you to be dead!" Mom yelled back.

"What's going on?" I asked, interrupting their fight. I hoped they would notice Thomas was with me and calm down out of embarrassment.

"Leslie still seems to think that she can come with us to Memory Lane to rescue your father. I am not putting her in danger," said Mom, glaring at Leslie.

"And Mom," Leslie spat out the name like it was evil, "seems to think that I am just going to sit here at home and twiddle my thumbs while you guys break Dad out of Memory Lane."

"We're back to this?" I asked.

"It's your sister's life! I'm not through talking about it!" Mom yelled back.

"Hey, I'm not the bad guy here," I said, putting up my hands.

Mom's expression softened for a moment, and she turned toward Leslie.

"Look, I just want you alive and safe. Hannah too." She pointed toward me and wiped some stray tears off her face.

"Should I come back later or…" Thomas trailed off, clearly feeling awkward.

Leslie sighed. "I just want to be accepted as someone that has a say in this family."

The weight of that statement was heavy, and I couldn't imagine how Leslie felt. She was kidnapped and taken away from us, experimented on for years, and then came back to us through pure accident. Honestly, I wouldn't feel like I fit in anymore if that was my story either.

"You do have a say. I just also realize you are still a child and Memory Lane already took advantage of you once. I won't let that happen again," said Mom.

"Want to be in charge of picking out our fake names for the IDs?" I asked Leslie, trying to lighten the mood.

"As long as you don't get to veto it," she replied. Leslie had crossed her arms over her chest and she had the most sarcastic smirk on her face. She expected me to say no. Well, I could be anyone. *Bring it on, little sister.*

"It's a deal." I smiled back at her. She returned the smile and that was the thing that I had missed the most while she had been dead.

"Have you heard from Jenson?" asked Mom.

I shook my head no. "Not yet. But we got the CLD and the roofies."

"How much did you spend?" Mom asked, narrowing her eyes.

"Not too much," I replied sheepishly.

Thomas's eyes looked all around the room, avoiding Mom.

"Uh huh. We'll pretend that you guys aren't hiding something from me."

"I'm going to put this stuff down in my room. I'll be back," I said, while walking toward my bedroom. Thomas followed me.

"I thought you said she gave you money?" Thomas asked me as soon as we got to my room.

"She did." I placed the CLD and the roofies on my nightstand, so I knew where they were when we needed them for the rescue mission.

"Then why was she asking how much?"

"Maybe she wanted to know if there was change," I suggested, casually.

"Hannah, what's going on? Why are you being so evasive?"

I paused. "It's not a big deal."

"What's not a big deal?"

I sat down on my bed and avoided Thomas's gaze.

"Well?" he asked.

"What I spent today was Mom's savings. Everything she has."

"What!?"

"She knew we needed money to make things happen so we could get Dad out of Memory Lane and leave the country."

"Hannah! You spent all the money your family has right now?"

"I figured once we leave the country, I can get a job to help. My parents can get new jobs too."

"This is banking a lot on the IDs working out." Thomas ran his hands through his hair and took a seat on my bed. He was nervous. I could tell.

"You don't think the IDs will work out?" I asked.

"I'm not sure. I just think a lot could go wrong."

"Well, don't think that way. Stay positive." I smiled at him, reassuringly.

"You're awfully chipper."

"What can I say? I think it's time that things work out for once. Karma owes us."

Thomas scoffed. "I think you are confusing reality with movies."

"Lighten up. I have my sister back. I'm about to get my Dad back from Memory Lane and I will no longer be a fugitive soon. It's a good time to be alive. Sue me for trying to be positive."

"I'm glad you're so sure of all this. We will need all the good Karma we can get considering the crap we've started the last few weeks."

"Come on." I slapped Thomas's leg playfully. "Let's go downstairs and see what's going on with Leslie's names for our fake IDs."

"I hope she picks a ridiculous name for you. Something like 'Moon' or 'Rain.'"

A full laugh escaped as I followed Thomas out of my room. "If being called 'Rain' for the rest of my life gets me away from Memory Lane and allows me time with my family, then let it pour."

Chapter 5

"You have got to be kidding me! That's your plan?" I asked Jenson with no lack of hesitation and frustration in my voice. Despite the fact that most of the things we did at this point were crazy, this just seemed too far-fetched.

Trees and cars flew by swiftly past the car window as we drove home. We had waited to discuss the plan until we dropped off Leslie with Aunt Nicole. She went semi-willingly, though I am not sure you could call it that since she gave me and Mom the silent treatment all the way there. Deep down, I was sure Leslie knew her staying behind was safer, but I knew it sucked to be left out. Especially since she knew more about these compounds than we did. Tonight, we were busting Dad out of Memory Lane.

"Pretty much," Jenson replied.

Glancing toward Thomas, who was sitting in the back seat of the car next to Jenson, I could see in his silence that he had his thinking face on.

"I think it could work." Thomas nodded in agreement with Jenson.

"Did you both lose your brains?" I asked.

"Hannah. Don't be rude," Mom said from the driver's seat.

"Well, come on, Mom!" I practically shouted. "That plan will never work." I shifted back to facing forward in the passenger seat. It was easier to stare out the window at the changing scenes than worry about what would happen if something went wrong tonight. There couldn't be any mistakes.

Jenson's plan involved less fire than the last time we broke into Memory Lane. Still, it required a lot of things to go right. He wanted to impersonate a Memory Lane guard and just bring the three of us into restricted areas. He was completely sure that no one would question him while wearing their ridiculous uniform.

"What happened to 'chipper, hopeful Hannah'? Can we bring her back?" Thomas asked.

Turning around, I shot him a dirty look. "Shut up, Thomas."

"Look. If you've got a better plan, let's hear it," said Jenson, throwing up his hands in frustration.

He was right and I knew it. Worse than that, I hated that he was right. I knew his plan was better than nothing at all.

"Riddle me this then, Sherlock. How we are going to get a guard's uniform and badge?"

"You didn't let me finish telling you that part of the plan," said Jenson. "Since you have the roofies, I figure we drug the guards and then steal the uniform and key card."

"How are you planning to get close enough to drug them? The guards aren't exactly walking around the lobby of Memory Lane," I asked. Frustration saturated every word. I had to calm myself down. There was no time for emotional outbursts. If we were going to get Dad out of Memory Lane, I was going to have put aside my racing heart and focus.

"We cause a scene," Thomas said.

Jenson nodded. "Exactly."

"What, are you guys best friends now?" I asked, annoyed. Rolling my eyes so hard I practically fell into the back seat.

"No, just thinking about this the same way."

Mom finally spoke up, and I could hear the wheels in her head turning. "Hannah, I think this could work," said Mom as she pulled onto our street.

Thomas agreed with Mom. "Yeah, you've gotta admit. This plan is better than what you and I came up with last time."

"Last time I got into a memory room, so I call that a success," I retorted.

"And we ended up as fugitives," Thomas fired back.

"Are you seriously bringing that up right now?"

Thomas shrugged. "Well, it's true."

"Calm down. This only works if we are tactical and not driven by our emotions. Let's regroup inside," said Mom as she stopped the car. We all got out and made a beeline for the kitchen. Tossing her purse to the side, Mom grabbed the blueprint plans from the kitchen counter that Leslie had drawn from memory.

As Mom spread out the blueprints, I pulled up a chair and started looking at the detail that Leslie had added. We could see the front entrance, the memory rooms, and the back entrance. There was the KP location Leslie mentioned where the kids were kept most of the time. There was one spot that drew my attention and, with the information we had, I believed it might lead to the secret passageway where I thought Dad was being held.

"Look." I pointed to an area that was just a blank space on Leslie's blueprint. "That's the closet where I went through the passage that led to over here where the jail cells were."

Thomas and Jenson leaned in to look at what I was pointing to.

"How do we know that the random blank wall you pointed to is the right spot?" asked Thomas.

"You don't. You'll just have to trust me." I smirked at both of them. "Much like I have to trust you" —I pointed to Jenson — "on your part of the plan that involves stealing the uniform and key card from the drugged guard."

"She has a point," Thomas chimed.

It was Jenson's turn to roll his eyes. "Whatever you say."

"What time are we doing this tonight?" I asked.

Everyone shrugged.

"No one has any idea?!" I asked, slightly annoyed.

"You guys are the ones that have actually been to Memory Lane before," explained Mom.

"Well, I know, but still. Maybe we need more info about the guards' shifts at night. I want to be sure we can put the roofies in their drinks."

"What did Leslie say about when they go on breaks?" Thomas asked.

"I think she said that they go on break every four hours or so, but I have no idea when they start their breaks," I said.

"What time are we planning to break out your Dad anyway?" asked Jenson.

"Probably around midnight. The last time we went around nine and it was okay but there were still quite a few people in the building. Both customers and guards. If we go later, I think the possibility of running into less people is better."

"But if we go when there are less people, won't that make us more conspicuous?" Mom asked.

"Possibly. But I'm thinking that all of us shouldn't go at once. I think we just need to send in Jenson to drug the guards and then come get the rest of us so we can get Dad out."

"How is Jenson going to get to the guards to drug them? Don't you have to be escorted back to a memory room?" asked Thomas.

"Yes. That wasn't my part of the plan," I said and then shrugged.

Jenson spoke. "I think if I demand to go to a room they might let me back there."

"I'm pretty sure they will arrest you or just escort you outside," said Mom.

"What if the three of us caused a scene in the front lobby?" suggested Thomas. "The guards would have to respond to the call for security."

"How does that help?" I asked. "We want the guards docile enough so Jenson can drug them and then steal the key card."

"We could pickpocket the card," suggested Jenson.

"But don't we still need the uniform?" I asked.

"Yes. Dang. This is impossible. We are just going around in circles. I'm not sure this will work." Jenson went silent, as if in thought.

"So you finally see the stupidity in your 'genius' plan?" I said to Jenson.

"It's not stupid!" Jenson said, defending himself. "I'll admit it's not a foolproof plan, but it's better than the fire that got out of hand last time." He looked down for a second, as if ashamed.

"This isn't going to work if we just yell at each other. We have to refocus," Mom explained. "Think. How can we get the roofies into the drinks of the Memory Lane guards, get the key card, and then get the uniform all without being noticed?"

Her question was followed by what felt like the longest silence ever.

"Don't all talk at once," said Mom, sarcastically.

"Whatever we do, it has to involve you and Jenson," I said while pointing at Mom. "Thomas and I can't be seen inside Memory Lane if we want to get past the front. We're still fugitives."

"What if we used that to our advantage?" said Thomas.

"How so?" I asked, curious.

Thomas sat in a kitchen chair and took a deep breath, as if bracing himself. "What if we used me as bait?"

"Wait. What?!" Mom and I said at the same time. "No!"

"Why not?" he asked. "The guards will rush to the front where I'm at and that means you guys can go toward the back and get to where the memory storage rooms are."

"But if the guards are going to the front to apprehend you, they won't be in the back near the storage room for us to drug them. I don't see how this helps," I said.

Thomas shook his head no. "You didn't let me finish. I won't stick around long enough for them to arrest me. I will make them chase me for a while. Then when they can't get to me, you guys go into the building and wait for them to calm down and relax near the memory storage room. That's when you roofie them."

"That all sounds good, but how can you be sure you will outrun them? And won't it be obvious to the people in the front lobby that we are just traipsing through Memory Lane to the back area?" I asked, still skeptical of Thomas's idea.

"I might not be able to outrun them, but hopefully it's enough of a distraction for you guys to get past the people in the front lobby. They are just desk clerks anyway."

"I'm not sure your Mom would like the idea of us using you as bait, Thomas," said Mom. "Frankly, I don't care for the idea either."

"And who says the guards will come back into the building? What if they just continue to pursue you?" asked Jenson.

"Good point."

The three of us were silent for quite some time, all of us thinking.

What worked last time? I remembered that Kate was going into a memory room like a normal person. The problem we had was Jenson's out-of-control fire. "We could just have Jenson ask to go into a memory room and then have him drug a guard on his way there," I suggested.

"Just casually roofie him while walking by?" he asked. "You make it sound so simple. How do you suppose I do that?"

"I'm not seeing a whole lotta options here."

"What are the rest of us doing while Jenson is drugging the guard?" asked Thomas.

I shrugged. "Waiting for the signal."

Jenson let out a suppressed chuckled. "What am I, Batman?"

For a moment the tension was broken and we all relaxed just a little.

"What signal?" Mom asked.

"Whatever we want it to be."

"What if Jenson misses the guard's drink with the roofie? What if there is no drink?" asked Thomas.

Mom interrupted the questions between Thomas, Jenson, and me. "Look. I don't care if you hit the Memory Lane guard with a two-by-four. I just want him knocked out so we can get the uniform, key card, and then get Robert out of there."

A thought occurred to me and I turned to face Mom. "What if you ask to visit Dad?"

"How does that help?" Mom asked, confused.

"While they are taking you to visit Dad, Jenson can drug the clerk at the front desk so we can get past her to the back where the other guards are. All he has to do is charm her and provide her with a cold beverage."

Mom nodded for me to continue.

"Since it will be late, there shouldn't be much activity back there other than guards in the hallway near the memory storage room, which we need access to anyway."

They all stared at me, unsure.

"I'm betting there is only one guard posted back there at that time, especially since another one is preoccupied with taking Mom to see Dad."

"I'm still not following how we will drug the other guard near the storage room. Didn't you only get two pills from Kenneth?" asked Thomas.

"Hang on. I'm getting to that part." I paused for dramatic effect while their eyes were all on me. "I have a wig from Halloween about three years ago."

"Get to the point!" Jenson practically shouted, clearly impatient.

"I can pretend to be a new desk clerk bringing the guard his nightly drink. It will be the same drink that was already roofied by Jenson. We can add another roofie to it for good measure. The wig is so the guard won't recognize me."

Mom had concern written all over her face. "That sounds dangerous, Hannah."

"Thomas and Jenson will be right behind me to back me up. They can help me get the guard's uniform off and take the key card."

"What if the other Memory Lane guard doesn't want to take your Mom back to visit your Dad?" asked Thomas.

"Then she causes a scene until he has to throw her out."

Mom looked deep in thought. "I don't know. There are still a lot of things that could go wrong with this. And besides …" she paused and stood up to go get a drink from the fridge. "You never said how I'm supposed to get Robert out of Memory Lane by myself."

"Once we have the key card and plant Jenson's device, we'll be able to meet you with his key card access. It will have to be fast though. I'm not sure how long a roofie lasts on a fully grown man."

"But how are we actually getting your Dad out of Memory Lane? We can't drug everyone, and something tells me that he will be surrounded by security."

"I'm hoping that Jenson dressed as a Memory Lane guard will be enough to convince the other guard where Dad is being held that he can go on break. I'll hang back until Jenson is in control. Then we use the key card and get Dad out."

"You make it sound so simple."

"It won't be perfect, but I think it could work." I looked over at Jenson, apologetically. "Sorry I called your plan to steal the uniform dumb. I actually think that it will help us out the most. Are you sure your device will allow us to download all memories from any Memory Lane?" I asked him.

Jenson nodded. "Yeah, that shouldn't be a problem."

Good. I was anxious to see what Kate remembered about the day Leslie was kidnapped.

Leaning on the table, my hands spread across the blueprints, and feeling very much like a secret agent, I asked everyone, "So, are we good?"

The three of them nodded in agreement at the same time.

"Make sure you eat up and save your energy. We're leaving tonight at 11:30 p.m."

"What should we wear?" Mom asked.

I chuckled. "Dark clothes. Anything really. You don't have to dress like a ninja. That might be more suspicious." I turned to Jenson and asked, "Do you have the device on you, Jenson?"

"Yeah. I'm ready to roll in t-minus four hours."

"I'm starving. What's for dinner?" asked Thomas.

"Is food all you think about?"

"Being a fugitive makes a guy hungry. I never want to live like that again, so I eat food whenever I can."

"We don't have much, Thomas, but you are welcome to anything in the pantry or whatever the InstaFood panel can make. I don't think we have meat, though," Mom said, while standing from her chair at the table. She headed toward the pantry.

As I watched her and Thomas rummage for food, I stole a glance at Jenson. He was here helping us when he didn't have to. I felt a rush of guilt for being so oppositional.

"Thanks for agreeing to help us. I know you barely know me and my family. It means the world to me, and I know my Mom and Leslie appreciate it too."

Jenson smiled. "No problem." He walked over to the InstaFood panel and searched through the menu options we had available in our inventory. I stood behind him to see what sounded good. The options I could see were a salad, rice, pasta, or a peanut butter and jelly sandwich.

"What are you gonna get?" I asked him as he looked through the menu.

"Probably some pasta." He punched the buttons and waited about fifteen seconds for his food to come out. It was steaming fettuccine with alfredo sauce. My stomach growled. I didn't realize I was that hungry.

"Can you make that two?" I asked him.

"Sure." Jenson punched in the same buttons and waited for the InstaFood panel to produce the food for him. He handed me the plate of pasta and we both sat back down to eat.

I watched Thomas and Mom go to the panel to get some food as well. They both came back to the table with bowls of rice with vegetables. Looking around the table, I realized that none of us had any utensils. *Easiest problem I will solve all night.*

"I'll get some forks," I said as I went to the drawer next to the sink.

My last thought before sitting back down to dig into my alfredo was, *Don't worry, Dad. We're coming to get you.*

Chapter 6

"Can't you be still! You're making me nervous," Thomas told me.

We were standing a short distance from Memory Lane. Close enough to feel that surge of adrenaline beginning to take over. We were just waiting on Jenson.

"How can you be still since we are about to break into a secure building as wanted fugitives? Besides, I'm just excited to get my Dad back and get away from Memory Lane for good," I chided.

"You have the roofies?" asked Jenson, walking up to our group. It seemed he was all business now. No casual hello, just a check of the final pieces of our plan. He met us here at Memory Lane so he could get whatever drink we were going to drug and give to the girl at the front desk.

I nodded, "Yeah. You got the device and the beverage?"

Jenson nodded back and patted his front jacket pocket, indicating where the device was.

He looked at my blonde hair and smirked. He reached out a hand to flip a stray curl from my shoulder, "Nice wig," he said, chuckling. It was just the moment we needed to break the tension.

"Shut up," I said, playfully slapping his hand away.

In his other hand was the iced-mocha-whatever that he must have bought at a local coffee shop. I was actually surprised one was open at this time of night. Standing just fifty yards from Memory Lane's front door, the full weight of what we were about to do hit me. Thinking about Mom, Dad, and Leslie who we had just gotten back from the dead hit me like a ton of bricks. I really needed this plan to work. There were so many questions running through my mind but the one that stood out the most was, *Is Dad okay?*

Receiving a text on a phone no one even knew existed created a new depth of worry that made this whole plan a necessity. I knew Mom was worried too; she just hid it better. Adults are always better at hiding their feelings. *Will I get better at hiding my own feelings as adulthood looms at the edge of my world?* Mom interrupted my thoughts.

"What time is it?"

"12:03 a.m. It's go time," replied Jenson with a twinkle in his eye.

Without holding back, I sighed loudly. "You are a little too eager to break in somewhere again. I thought hackers liked to hide behind their computer screens and steal information, not physical things or people."

Jenson shrugged. "Guess I'm weird."

Thomas poked my shoulder. "Hey. What happened to that CLD you got from Kenneth? Did you bring it?"

My stomach sank. *Was that part of my job? Did I just ruin everything?*

I shook my head no and my shoulders sagged.

Even in the dark, Thomas could see the color drain from my face. "It's not a big deal. We can still make this work. I just know we went through the trouble of buying it, and it would make things easier if we could listen to the Memory Lane guards before going in and hoping they aren't aware of where we are."

"I could run to your house and get it," suggested Jenson. "Do you know where the CLD is?" he asked.

My mind flashed back to when we were making the plans in the house and I pictured myself putting the CLD down on my nightstand and then later grabbing it when getting ready to leave…

"Wait!!" I exclaimed, relief flooded over me as I reached into my back pocket. "Here it is!"

"No way! You actually did bring the CLD?" Thomas exclaimed.

"Yeah, I thought I left it on my nightstand, but it's in my back pocket. I must have forgotten that I grabbed it in all the excitement." I held it out for all of us to look at. "Can we use it from here?" I asked Jenson, since he had used one before and was the "expert" among us.

"We should be able to. Let's turn it on and see what the range is."

Jenson took the CLD from my hand and pressed the little button on the side. It beeped and he pointed it at Memory Lane.

The four of us listened intently, hoping that we would be able to hear inside without moving much closer.

Silence.

"Maybe we are doing it wrong?" I suggested.

Jenson shook his head. "No, we should be in range. There's no way it's totally silent inside Memory Lane." He fiddled with the CLD a little more and then walked about twenty feet closer to the building before trying again. I could tell he wasn't having any luck.

Jenson walked back to where we were standing. "They must have a blocker up against CLDs and other devices so that people can't hear what's going on inside the building."

"Man, I'm sorry. That would have made things a lot easier," said Thomas.

"It's fine. We had honestly forgotten about it until now. We'll just save the CLD for another time," I replied tucking it back into my pocket. "Who knows, maybe we can use it once inside. For now, back to the plan. Mom, you go in first. I think we should hang back a few minutes, so they don't think our group is together."

Mom turned to make sure we were all paying attention. Worry was strewn across her face and all three of us could tell this was not a moment for jokes. "All of you, this is serious. Please be careful. I'll see you inside in a little while." She leaned down to kiss my forehead.

My heart rate sped up as I watched as Mom walk into the building, a place that had caused my family so much pain. I squared my shoulders, lifted my head and with my hands on my hips, turned to face my crew. "You guys ready for this?"

"Yup. Let's go ahead and put the roofies in the drink now so they can dissolve and we are prepared." Nodding, I turned to Jenson as he removed the lid from the iced beverage. My curiosity got the best of me and I had to ask, "Do roofies have a taste?"

Jenson snorted, "No. That's sorta the whole point." Jenson dropped in the roofie, stirred the drink with the straw, and then replaced the lid.

"Oh yeah. Makes sense. How's my wig look? Is it on straight?" I asked Thomas.

"Yeah, it's fine. I wouldn't know it was you unless I heard you talk. I think it should work for what we need. Hopefully, no one looks too closely."

"Do you think it's been long enough since we sent in your Mom?" Thomas asked.

"I don't know." I shrugged. "Probably."

Jenson looked at the time on his phone. "It's 12:23 a.m. Been about ten minutes since your Mom walked inside. I say we go ahead."

"All right. Let's do this."

The three of us walked toward Memory Lane. I took a deep breath. *Please let this work.*

Thomas and I neared the entrance and hung back. I made sure we were out of sight but close enough to still see Jenson go through the doors. We found a large bush off to the side that had a good shot of the front desk.

"This is going to kill my knees," I complained to Thomas, while crouching low.

"You'll survive."

We both watched as Jenson sashayed up to the girl at the desk. She looked young and blonde. Perfect age for flirting. Jenson placed the drink on the counter and gestured with his hands. The girl smiled and brushed her hair behind her ear.

"I wonder what he is saying," said Thomas.

"I honestly don't want to know," I replied while rolling my eyes. "I just want it to work."

Jenson pushed the drink toward the girl, and she reached for it. I watched her take a drink through the straw. Thank goodness she fell for his flirting. Now we just had to wait for her to keep drinking and for the roofie to take effect.

"Ow! You're standing on my foot!" I whisper-yelled at Thomas.

"Sorry! I'm just trying to see what's going on," he replied.

Watching Jenson and the girl continue talking, I could tell she was enjoying the conversation. *How long does this usually take? Was this the normal length of time it took for the drug to take effect?* I glanced the opposite direction to see if anyone was trying to enter the building. That would cause a problem because they would see the girl pass out. I didn't see anyone approaching from the outside, so I went back to look at what was going on inside with Jenson and the desk clerk.

"Look, I think she's starting to act weird," said Thomas, breaking me out of my thoughts.

Looking back, I caught the girl just as she grabbed her head and started to shake it lightly as if trying to see why her vision was blurred. Jenson grabbed her by the shoulder to support her as she looked at him. She looked disoriented, even from where Thomas and I were standing. He moved the drink out of the way as she listed to the side. Her head fell into her arms, which Jenson gently placed on the counter. He turned around to look at us and gave us a thumbs up and a goofy smile. It worked!

Thomas and I stood up from our crouched position and walked through the entrance. I adjusted my blonde wig as I approached the front counter where the girl was passed out.

"I can't believe that worked," I said.

"We better hurry before someone comes and finds her like this and us standing here," said Jenson. He grabbed the drink from the counter and passed it to me. I was going to pretend to be a desk clerk and hand the drink to the other guard. Thomas and Jenson grabbed the young receptionist and brought her into a cleaning closet near the women's restroom. I worked on getting her uniform off while they looked the other way. No reason we can't give her some privacy even if we are stealing her clothes! I finished putting the uniform on and walked out of the closet between Jenson and Thomas so they could see me. I closed the door and hoped there wouldn't be any cleaning maintenance tonight.

"How do I look?" I batted my eyes for comedic effect. Jenson laughed but Thomas was too serious to join in. I grabbed the drink from the counter; it was time to go.

"Thomas and I will wait in the men's restroom. We'll meet you by the storage room in about fifteen minutes. You think that's enough time?" Jenson asked.

"Judging by how long the roofie took to hit our receptionist, it should be. Unless something goes wrong," I replied.

"Good luck," Thomas said, as he and Jenson walked toward the restroom on the other side of the desk and down the hall. I had to go to the right and toward the back rooms. Then, according to Leslie's drawings, the memory storage area should be a branch off that hallway. As I walked toward the rooms with the iced drink in my hand, my thoughts drifted to Leslie with Aunt Nicole. I hoped she was okay. I knew she would be worried and probably feeling left out, but once this was over we would all be together and burning rubber to get as far away from Memory Lane as possible.

I walked through the hall at a steady pace, working to give off a look that said I belonged and was supposed to be there. Seeing a sign that said "Memory Storage" with an arrow pointing to the right, I veered off that direction and without fail ran face first into a Memory Lane guard.

"Whoa. Slow down there," the man said. He looked to be about thirty-five with a beard and intense brown eyes.

I stammered out an apology, trying to regain my composure. "Sorry I —"

"Where are you going in such a hurry?" he asked.

"Nowhere. I'm one of the new night desk clerks and I thought you guys could use a beverage." I smiled and held up the drink as a peace offering and hoped he bought my lie.

A smile spread across his face. "Well, that was really nice of you." He grabbed the drink from my hand and took a long sip.

"Can I get a tour?" I asked, innocently. "This is my first shift." I was trying to stay in the area longer so I could make sure he would pass out back here.

"They didn't give you the employee tour when you went through orientation?" he asked, taking another long drink.

"Well, yes, but it was rushed and I think there are places they missed. What about the storage rooms?" I asked and pointed in the direction I was headed.

"Oh, that's off limits to desk clerks. Memory Lane guards and officials only," he replied, his voice taking on more of an authoritative tone.

"Darn. Guess I'll have to wait then." I smiled back at the guard hoping that he would let me hang out with him for a minute while the drug unknowingly worked through his system. "So how long have you worked for Memory Lane?" I asked, initiating some small talk, and hoping he would take the bait.

"About two years. It's good money," he replied.

"Tell me about it. I needed to be on my own and away from my parents. They are way too controlling." I twirled the hair on my wig and tried to sound more like a whiny teenager.

"I remember those days. Needing out of the house so bad —"

The guard stopped speaking abruptly. He dropped the drink and clutched his head as the drug began to hit.

"Sir? Are you okay?" I asked, faking concern.

"I don't—" he struggled to form the sentence.

"Sir, do you need help?"

"What's going on? What did you do to me?" he asked while grabbing my arm. His grip was firm but only for a moment as he began losing control of his muscles. I backed away and he took a step forward to try to grab me again but instead lost his balance. I let him fall on his knees while I looked behind me for Thomas and Jenson. *Had it been long enough? Were they coming to help? What would I do if this guard didn't pass out!?!*

"I'll kill you!" the guard mumbled at me while leaning against the wall now. He was trying to support himself rather unsuccessfully.

"I don't think you're going to do anything to me for a while," I said, while smirking.

The guard looked at me with anger and frustration in his eyes, unable to shake off the feeling of the drug. *Good thing I put both roofies into that drink.* They were doing exactly what they were supposed to do.

"Hey. Is he out?" I heard Thomas whisper behind me. He must have been hiding around the corner.

"Almost," I replied. I watched the guard struggle to stay awake before finally succumbing to the effects of the drug. He was out like a light. He leaned to the side against the wall and I kicked his shoe for good measure to make sure he wouldn't wake up as we undressed him. *Well, that sounded creepier than I thought it would. Don't think about that again!*

Motioning for Jenson to come over to where I was standing with the passed-out guard, we got to work. "Here. Hold his badge and key card," I said as I removed them from his shirt. I passed them over to Thomas. We had to work fast because I wasn't sure how long he would be completely unaware.

Jenson removed the guard's outer shirt and I thanked whoever it was that day that made the guard put on an undershirt. I did not need to think about what we were doing any more than while we were doing it.

"Go try the key card on the memory storage room door," Jenson told Thomas since he was holding the card.

I watched as Thomas headed down the hall a few doors away to try the key card. Jenson continued to undress the guard, now taking off his pants. The guard was wearing boxers so it wasn't as awkward as it could have been. Jenson took his own jacket off and then put on the Memory Lane shirt. He grabbed the badge and clipped it to the shirt. "Hello, Roy," I said, teasing.

To give Jenson some privacy while he dressed in the middle of the hall, I turned my attention back to Thomas. He put the key card into the door and he pushed it open. Success! I couldn't believe that it actually worked. Thomas smiled at me from down the hall and walked into the memory storage room.

"Hurry up, dude, so we can go see inside the storage room. That's not something anyone outside of Memory Lane gets to see," I said to Jenson.

"I'm going as fast as possible," he replied while struggling to put on the pants. The guard was quite a bit taller than Jenson, so he was trying to roll the pants up a little so they didn't drag on the floor. He zipped them up, and then buttoned the outer shirt. He looked passable as a Memory Lane guard, if not a little young. "Come on," Jenson said. "Let's move Roy somewhere that isn't the middle of the hallway."

I grabbed his legs while Jenson grabbed his arms. We shuffled awkwardly down the hall toward the memory storage room.

"Man, he's heavy," I said to Jenson.

"Tell me about it," he huffed back.

There was a small closet to the left of the memory storage room, and I dropped Roy's legs so I could see if the door was unlocked. It was not. "Hey, Thomas!" I called so he could hear me. "We need that key card."

Thomas came out of the storage room and into the hallway and passed me the key card. The door he came out of automatically shut behind him. Immediately I realized the little closet did not have a key-pad entry so swiping the card was useless. We needed an actual key.

"Great. Now what?" I asked both Jenson and Thomas.

"We could put him inside the memory storage room. We need to move out of this hallway before someone comes along or Roy here wakes up," suggested Jenson.

"Agreed."

We were short on time and needed to get to where my parents were fast. I hoped Mom was able to find Dad without any issues. "All right. Move then."

Jenson and I waited for Thomas to unlock the memory storage room again and then grabbed Roy to bring him inside. Thankfully he continued to stay passed out for the time being. We placed him just inside the door to the right, leaning up against the wall.

Out of breath, I turned to Thomas and Jenson. "What now?"

Jenson reached for the device inside the jacket that was no longer on his person. "Hang on," he said.

Thomas and I watched as Jenson went back into the hall to grab his discarded outfit. He brought the clothes into the memory storage room with him and dumped them into a trash can nearby after grab-bing the device needed to download the memories.

Taking it all in, I marveled at the room we were in. It was larger than I imagined from the outside, and it was filled with at least twelve rows of computers each containing five CPUs. They were all on and running. There was a monitor at the end of each row as big as a TV screen. I wondered if Memory Lane workers and guards ever watched the memories they received from people.

"Are these all connected?" I asked Jenson, completely clueless to how computers worked. I walked down the first row of computers, taking in all the lights and the sheer number. It certainly looked impressive.

"Yes. On a network."

Jenson picked a computer in the middle of the second row to attach his device to.

"Why that one?" I asked, curious.

"Less conspicuous," he replied. "If it's on the end, they are more likely to notice a foreign object on the CPU. The second row is also not as visible from either the door or the back of the room."

"Makes sense. Is that everything you need?" I asked him.

"Yeah, the information will be downloaded off-site."

Thomas interjected. "Are we just leaving the guard here?"

I shrugged. "I mean, I don't really see how we can put him any-where else. We need to go before the roofie wears off."

Thomas nodded. "Right."

The three of us left the room and made sure the door closed and locked behind us. As we made our way down the hallway, I pulled out the plans that Leslie had drawn of Memory Lane. According to the map, we needed to take an immediate right and then another right until we got to the storage closet that I believe led to the secret pas-sageway that would take us to the other part of the facility where Dad was being held. I hoped this was correct. I hoped that Jenson in a Memory Lane guard uniform and me in a wig was enough to be left alone and mistaken for people that actually worked there.

"Take a right up here," I said while pointing ahead. We followed my lead since I had the map. Just as we turned the corner, I ran smack into a guard. *Does no one around here watch where they are going?!?*

"Watch it!" he said while continuing to walk the way he was headed.

He didn't seem to care what we were doing in this area. I bet if he wasn't in such a hurry, he would have questioned why three young people were back here, but I wasn't going to draw attention to us any more than necessary.

As we continued to draw nearer to the secret passageway, my phone vibrated. I took it out of my pocket to see who it was. Kate was trying to chat with me. I didn't have time to answer the call, so I let it ring.

I checked the hand-drawn map again. "Turn right ahead. The door we need should be up here."

Jenson and Thomas followed me down the hallway.

My phone rang again. If it was Kate, she would just have to wait. I had to rescue Dad right now. I took it out of my pocket and looked at the screen. Kate had texted me.

> **KATE:** where r u?
> **KATE:** i need u
> **KATE:** i think my Dad killed my Mom
> **KATE:** call me now
> **KATE:** hannah????

Chapter 7

Frozen in the moment, I had stopped walking toward the secret passage. The blueprint hung loosely in one hand and my phone held my gaze in horror. Jenson and Thomas bumped right into the back of me.

"Hannah! What's wrong with you?" Jenson asked to get my attention.

Thomas stepped in front of me and gently touched my shoulder. "Is everything okay?" he asked.

"It's Kate." That's all I could get out. Turning my phone screen, I showed him her text messages. It took a minute to process what he was reading.

"What makes her think that?" he asked, shocked.

Tears stung the back of my eyes, and I hoped this wasn't true for Kate's sanity. "No idea."

"We need to move out of the middle of the hallway," said Jenson, reminding us that we were on a time crunch. "Your Mom is waiting for us and we need to get a move on."

I nodded and we walked the rest of the way to the door that I suspected was the one with the secret passageway behind it. As we approached, Jenson opened the door and scanned the hallway to make sure no one saw us. The three of us walked inside and closed the door behind us. I reached for the light and as my eyes refocused from the dark I could see it was the exact same room as before. The janitor's closet. I was right!

"What are you going to say back to Kate?" asked Thomas.

"I don't even know where to begin. But we have more pressing things right now."

"What happened to Kate?" asked Jenson, concern flooding his voice.

Thomas ignored Jenson and continued, "If her Dad killed her Mom, Kate could be in real danger right now."

Jenson gasped. "Killed her Mom? What!?"

"Everyone just stop!" I yelled, louder than I intended. "I need to think."

I looked back at the panicked messages on my phone. Kate sounded desperate. We had to finish this before I could do anything to help.

HANNAH: i will meet you in an hour
HANNAH: dont do anything till I get there

That should give me enough time to finish what we started here at Memory Lane and then make sure that Kate was safe and taken care of. Satisfied with that choice, I turned my attention back to Jenson and Thomas.

"I told Kate I would meet her in an hour. Let's get going. There's a wall here that I went through before which leads to another part of the facility."

Moving the mop bucket and cleaning supplies revealed a small door. It was nearly invisible to the naked eye. Lifting the small latch, I pushed hard. The secret door gave way silently, as if it was created to muffle sound. Poking my head out, all I could see was inky blackness. The last time I was here it was extremely dark too. This time I reached for my phone and turned on the flashlight.

"Come on," I said to Thomas and Jenson. I crawled through the small door in a crouched position and landed on the concrete, dusting myself off upon landing. Thomas came through the door next. He barely fit since he was so tall. Jenson was last to make it through and he reached back into the janitor's closet to close the secret door.

"Which way?" asked Thomas. I could barely see his face in the faint light of my phone. Kneeling down, I opened the map that Leslie had drawn and illuminated it with my phone so I could read it.

"Looks like we need to go that way," I said pointing to our right.

Thomas turned to face the direction we were headed. "Lead the way."

"Is there a reason we are using this dark, dirty passageway to get to your parents when I am wearing a Memory Lane uniform?" asked Jenson as we trudged through who-knows-what filth.

"You are more than welcome to go back through the door and walk through the hallways flashing your badge. But we can't help you if they question why you are wearing Roy's badge. Thomas and I also can't walk through the hallways nonchalantly anyway." I said, pointing to myself and Thomas, "Fugitives, remember?"

Jenson paused for a moment, as if contemplating what he was going to do. "I'll just stick with you guys. Easier than trying to meet up later."

"Glad you decided to keep slumming it here with the little people," I said, turning Jenson around so we could continue walking.

"Hold the phone up higher so I can see what's in front of me," whined Thomas.

"I made this journey already without any light AND I was alone. Quit complaining. We aren't trying to draw any attention to you, big baby," I teased.

"Hrmph, well I don't like stepping in things I can't see."

"When did you become so high maintenance?" I asked Thomas.

"Shut up."

"Both of you shut up. I think I see a door or something up ahead," said Jenson.

"Let me check the map," I replied. I stopped walking and brought the phone's light over the drawing so I could see where the door back into the halls of Memory Lane was located.

"I think you're right," I said. "That's the door we need."

"Everybody remember their roles?" Thomas asked us.

I nodded and adjusted my wig. This thing was itchy. "Yeah. Let's go."

The three of us went through the door one by one. Coming back into the main building, I let my eyes adjust to the light that Thomas had turned on since he went through the door first. We were in a room similar to the janitor's closet. There was a filing cabinet that was empty and some other miscellaneous items.

"Which way now, Hannah?" asked Jenson.

I consulted the map. "Looks like we need to go to the left once we get into the hallway."

Jenson nodded and then adjusted the badge on his uniform. "Well, here goes nothing." He led the way with Thomas and me bringing up the rear. As we walked through the halls, we saw no one. So far, the plan seemed to be going well. We took a right when the hallway branched, and I noticed a sign on the wall that said, "High Risk Visitors." *What does that mean? Is my Dad considered high risk?*

There was a door that led to the "High Risk area" that Jenson swiped his badge to get us into. It worked like a charm. Thank goodness 'Roy' had enough clearance to access pretty much every part of Memory Lane. As we entered the new area, there were two guards down the hallway who glanced in our direction quickly and then returned to what they were doing. One of them did a double take when he saw me and Thomas.

"Hey!" he shouted. "What are y'all doing back here?!"

Thinking fast, I pretended to be a prisoner fighting Jenson as a Memory Lane guard. "Let go of me!"

Thomas looked to see what I was doing and then followed my lead.

"You can't keep us here!" he yelled at Jenson.

"Do you need help, sir?" asked the other guard to Jenson.

"No, I can handle them," he replied to the other guard. "Move it!" Jenson grabbed my arm hard and pushed me forward. "You too. Let's go," he said to Thomas.

"This is crap! I want my phone call!" yelled Thomas as the three of us walked down the hallway. I'm sure we were a sight to behold. Two teenagers and a Memory Lane guard yelling at each other.

"You think he bought it?" I asked Jenson and Thomas as we got farther away from the other guard.

"Seems like it," replied Jenson, while looking over his shoulder to be sure.

"Are we getting close?" asked Thomas.

I looked at the map again. "I think so. It should be just another right and then a left."

"Good. I'm ready to get out of here."

As we approached our destination, I saw the holding cells where Thomas and I were the last time we were here. Memories flooded my mind with all the things that went wrong. It seemed like so much had happened since then. I remembered Kate and her text to me about her Dad being her Mom's killer. I hoped she was safe for now and that we could figure out what was really going on.

I saw the door we needed on our left.

"Here we go," said Jenson. He swiped Roy's badge and it granted us access. The three of us walked through the door and I immediately saw Mom standing off to the side talking with Dad through a glass wall. There was a two-way speaker she was using to have a conversation with him. A Memory Lane guard watched my parents with a look of disgust on his face.

Jenson spoke first to the fellow guard in the room. "Hey. I'm here to relieve you."

The Memory Lane guard and both of my parents turned around at the sound of Jenson's voice.

"Who are you?" asked the guard, accusingly.

"Your relief. I also have two more prisoners to add here," Jenson replied dismissively while pointing to me and Thomas.

"Have I ever met you before?" questioned the guard.

"I don't know. Are you trying to date me or go on break?" Jenson sounded annoyed.

Fear was rising up and I prayed the guard would leave us alone already so I could talk to Dad. I caught Mom's eye and hoped the guard didn't notice that we knew each other.

"What'd they do?" the guard asked.

"I didn't ask. I'm just the person delivering them where Mr. Wesley wants them."

The guard nodded. "Fair enough." He moved toward the door and turned back to speak only to Jenson. "Give them the special treatment." He waggled his eyebrows and then laughed as he reached for the door handle and left the room.

"Thank God. I thought he would never leave," I said running over to where my parents were standing. "Dad? Are you okay?" I asked into the speaker.

"You have to press the button, Hannah. Otherwise, he can't hear you," Mom said. She looked as though she had aged ten years in the time since she had walked into Memory Lane on this rescue mission.

I pressed the button and then spoke into the speaker again. "Are you okay, Dad?"

"I'm fine. It's so good to see you," Dad replied while smiling at me.

"So, are we just gonna stand here and watch you guys talk?" asked Jenson.

"Chill, dude. They haven't seen each other in ages. They're just catching up," defended Thomas.

"I just don't know how long we have to get him out of there and leave the building unnoticed. They can chat later."

Mom nodded in agreement. "Yeah, we have been here too long already. Let's get a move on."

"Does that door open with my badge?" asked Jenson.

Mom looked at the locking mechanism on the glass partition separating us from my Dad. "I have no idea. Let's try it."

Jenson walked up to the mechanism and scanned Roy's badge. The scanner beeped and he tried the lock.

We all waited impatiently hoping that it would unlock and we could just leave. Nothing happened.

"Now what?" I asked.

Jenson looked at the lock closer and tried the badge again. "Hey, there's a hole here on the side. Like for a key."

"A key?" I asked, confused. "Do you have one on you?"

Jenson searched Roy's shirt pocket and his pants pockets. In the back pocket he found a small weird-shaped key. "Here goes nothing," he said.

I watched as Jenson put the key into the small hole, turned it, and then scanned the badge. The mechanism beeped, and then turned green. We all heard the latch on the other side of the door unlock.

Dad jumped and then reached for the door on his side. He pushed it open and then walked through. He grabbed Mom into a giant hug while tears streamed down her face. I joined the hug and tried to hold back my tears. It was so good to see Dad again.

"Look guys. I hate to do this, but we gotta go," Jenson said.

I pulled back from the hug and wiped the few stray tears that escaped.

Dad looked over at Thomas. "You doing okay?" he asked him.

"I should be asking you that," replied Thomas.

Dad smiled and looked over at me and Mom. "I can't complain, honestly."

It occurred to me that Dad didn't know the whole story about Leslie and how we had her back. He was in for a shock in just a little bit. We had to get out of Memory Lane unscathed first.

Jenson poked his head out of the main door to see if the coast was clear.

"Are we just going to walk out with my Dad like nothing is weird?" I asked.

"Do you see another exit?" Jenson asked.

I looked around and saw no other options. I didn't like this. The five of us walking around together would look too suspicious.

"Should we split up?"

"What is it with you and splitting up?" Mom asked, annoyed.

"Five people just walking around is too suspicious. Traipsing around the halls of Memory Lane is going to draw attention to us trying to get out. Besides, the clerk and the guard we drugged are probably awake and looking for us now."

Dad gasped. "You drugged people?!"

"It's a long story. Besides, it worked, didn't it? We made it to you."

"We didn't have another way," Mom said, reaching for my Dad's hand and linking her fingers in his.

Thomas made a move toward the door to exit the room. "Why don't Jenson and I go one way and the three of you go another way. That way all of us aren't captured."

Jenson nodded in agreement. Mom looked at me and Dad and silently asked if we were okay with that.

"I guess we can meet by the car?" I suggested.

"Sounds like a plan," replied Jenson. He and Thomas left the room.

I turned to my parents. "You guys ready?" I asked.

Both of them hugged me. Dad looked down at me, "Let's get out of here,"

The three of us walked toward the door and I peered into the hallway to see if anyone was coming. We turned the opposite way from Thomas and Jenson, and I realized how good it felt to have my parents with me this time. Even though I was legally an adult, I still felt like a kid sometimes. It was easier to let someone else be in charge and not have to make every decision. We came to a hallway with a fork in it.

"Which way?" Mom asked.

"I'm pretty sure the front of the building is to the right," Dad replied.

I trusted him to know since he was housed here at Memory Lane for so long.

"What's our story if we run into a guard or someone that questions why we are back here?" I asked as we walked through the hallways.

"Tell them we're lost?" Mom suggested.

"This is not the time for jokes, Mom. There is a high possibility that—"

I was interrupted by the loudest alarm known to man. I immediately grabbed my ears to protect them and watched my parents do the same thing.

"What is that?!" I yelled. I couldn't even hear myself over the sound of the blaring alarm. I hoped my parents could read my lips. The three of us looked at each other and started running through the halls now. If there was an alarm going off, it was probably because we were about to get caught.

I ran through the hallways like I imagined a high school track star would. Not that I ever was one, because running was gross, but I didn't have time to dwell on how much I hated to run. I turned left and glanced backwards to make sure that both Mom and Dad were keeping up with me.

We approached the hallway that was attached to the lobby area and I paused to get a good look at what we were dealing with. *Where are Thomas and Jenson?* I hoped they made it out okay.

I could see that it was teeming with Memory Lane guards and policemen. The Memory Lane guards were yelling at the police, telling them to get out and this was a business matter, not a law enforcement matter. *Are we under arrest?* I began to wonder if there was something bigger going on here, when I caught movement out of the corner of my eye. Near the front entrance, the automatic double doors slid open, but there was no person walking through them. The police and the Memory Lane guards in the lobby stared at the doors like they had just seen a ghost.

One brave guard approached the door and looked both ways outside to see if there was anyone around. When he decided the coast was clear, he came back into the lobby.

"Must have been a fluke," he said.

The double doors slid open again. No one came through. This time, I watched as the police officer stepped forward to investigate.

"Hey!" the Memory Lane guard called after the officer. "You don't have jurisdiction here unless we give it to you!" The guard followed him outside to see what was going on.

I couldn't see from my vantage point, but there was definitely something fishy about the doors opening on their own more than once. *Could it be Jenson and Thomas?*

"There's a bomb!" yelled the police officer. "Everybody run!"

A bomb? I looked over at my parents to see what they wanted to do.

The guards in the lobby and the other officers ran behind the front desk for cover. The officer and guard that had gone outside to check out the doors and found the bomb, dove behind the nearby bushes where Thomas and I hid earlier.

"Back away!" yelled Mom as she took off running down the hallway away from the front lobby. She grabbed my hand and dragged me with her. I felt Dad running next to me, ducking for cover as well. About a minute passed before I heard the loud boom and felt the ground under my feet shake all the way from the front of the building. Rubble and smoke from the blast crept down the hall my parents and I were crouched in.

"Where did the bomb come from and who could have set it?" I asked, while covering my mouth and nose with my shirt. It was already getting hard to breathe.

"No idea," Mom replied.

I coughed. "Do you think Thomas and Jenson got out okay?"

Mom grabbed my hand to comfort me. "I hope so."

The alarm was still blaring throughout the facility. I had a feeling I would have some permanent hearing loss after tonight.

"How do we get out now?" I asked.

Dad spoke first. "I think leaving through the front is out."

I nodded. "Maybe the side or the back? This place backs up to the woods. It's how me and Thomas were able to escape last time."

"I think we need to move now. We can't let them find us. It will be easier to leave in the chaos," Dad said.

Mom and I stood up while holding hands. We began to follow Dad back through the halls and toward another exit. Any other exit was fine with me. I just wanted out. The alarm's noise was starting to settle in my bones. We walked down another hallway and took a right. There was an exit sign with an arrow pointing straight ahead. As we approached, I saw that the door was marked as "Emergency Exit Only." I think the bomb and Dad as an escaped prisoner qualified as an emergency. There was a warning on the door that read, "Alarm Will Sound" but I didn't care. It couldn't be worse than what we were dealing with now.

I pushed the door open and we were met with the cool night air. There were a few steps to walk down, but other than that, there was no one around on this side of the building. Mom and Dad followed me down the steps as we tried to orient ourselves. I could see police lights to our left, meaning that was probably the front of the building.

"That has to be the front," I said, pointing in that direction. "Where do you think the others are?" I asked.

"I don't know, but we need to get your Dad out of here," Mom said, desperately.

"Let's go the other direction," Dad suggested.

Mom and I nodded and followed him around the other way toward the back of the building. There were woods in that direction. I really hoped we could avoid going through the woods. I did not need another repeat of what Thomas and I dealt with last time.

As we walked around the building, I hoped that we were able to avoid the Memory Lane guards, police, and anyone else enough so that we could get to the car and get the hell out of Dodge. I was walking in front of both my parents when I heard a whispered call.

"Hannah!"

I stopped in my tracks.

"Who's there?" I whispered back.

"It's me."

"Thomas? Where are you?" I asked into the darkness. Mom and Dad had stopped behind me to see what was going on.

"Behind the bush to your left."

I looked over, and sure enough, there were Thomas and Jenson hiding in the bush, crouched together.

"Thomas!" I yelled, a little too loudly.

He jumped up and hugged me and Mom.

"We were so worried that you guys got caught in the blast," Mom said.

"No, we were already outside when we heard the boom. Are we headed to the car?" asked Thomas.

I nodded. "Yeah, if we can escape the guards and the police."

"Let's go. We can take the long way around and avoid the front of the building."

The five of us walked away from the building, crouching in the darkness, staying closer to the surrounding woods so that we could avoid being seen.

With the chaos dying down, the next crisis called my name.

"So, what are you going to do about Kate?" whispered Thomas to me and Jenson. My parents were behind us because they were holding hands. I guessed they had missed each other. Gross.

"I'm meeting her soon," I said, while looking at the time on my phone. It had been a little more than an hour, and I had a few missed messages from Kate asking where I was.

ME: i'm coming. promise. jenson & thomas r coming too

My phone dinged again.

KATE: hurry

"She sounds pretty desperate," I told Jenson and Thomas. "We need to hurry."

The side street where the car was parked came into view from where we were walking near the woods. I could see the police lights reflecting off of Memory Lane in the distance. They were probably still investigating where the bomb came from.

"So, who do you think planted the bomb?" I asked Thomas and Jenson.

Jenson got really quiet and avoided my gaze. *Is he hiding something?* We all approached the car and stopped before getting in. "Where did you park?" I asked Jenson.

"Just a street or so over. I'll meet you at your house."

I nodded. "Hurry. We need to meet Kate." I closed the car door after climbing into the back seat with Thomas. Jenson headed to the street over while Mom got into the driver's seat and Dad sat up front. It seemed strange to me since Dad usually drove. I shrugged it off, as there were too many things going on and right now, I was just glad we all made it out.

Mom started the car and pulled away from the curb where we were parked. She drove away from Memory Lane, and relief washed over me. We did what we came to do, we had gotten my Dad out and everyone we brought with us made it back in one piece.

Thomas tugged on my shirt to get my attention and as I leaned over while he whispered, "I need to talk to you about Jenson."

Chapter 8

Mom pulled into the driveway and, before she could come to a stop, Thomas and I jumped out of the back seat.

"Where's the fire?" Mom yelled while turning off the engine.

"We're meeting Kate. There's some stuff going on with her," I said. I kept my explanation vague on purpose. I wanted more information before I told my parents anything about her Dad in relation to her Mom's death.

"Okay, well don't be gone long. The sooner we discuss the IDs and when we are leaving the country the better."

I nodded.

Thomas and I stood in the driveway for a moment, and I checked my phone for the time. "Where's Jenson?"

Thomas looked down the street to watch for Jenson's car. "He said he would be here. Let's give him five more minutes. Not everyone speeds like Aunt Linda."

The car slowly backed out of the driveway. Mom rolled down the window. "We're going to pick up Leslie. Meet you guys back here."

Dad still looked unsure of Leslie being alive. He also asked on the way home if it was even safe for us to be there. I assured him that we had taken care of distracting the Memory Lane guards and the police by making them think we were all over the country, but he still seemed uneasy. Leslie being alive was still new to him but I think it would sink in for real when he got to hug her. I nodded to my parents and waved as they took off for Aunt Nicole's house.

As we scanned the street for Jenson to arrive, I turned to Thomas. "All right, spill it. What's wrong with Jenson?"

"He set the bomb."

"What!!?! How? When?" Shock was an understatement. *Where did Jenson get a bomb?!?*

"When we split from you guys, we went back through the front lobby area and the desk clerk was awake. She was frantic trying to figure out how we were in the back and what happened to her clothes during the missing time. She was calling for Memory Lane guards when we went through the double doors and started running."

I interrupted Thomas's story. "Get to the point. How did he even have a bomb?"

"I'm getting there. We were tired since it was late and decided to just hide in the surrounding bushes on the side. That's when Jenson told me he had a back-up plan."

I looked at Thomas impatiently, urging him to continue.

"He showed me the bomb from inside the pocket of Roy's uniform. It looked like a pen. I don't know how he made it or if he bought it, but it was a bomb."

"Are you sure it wasn't something he found in Roy's clothes when he changed?"

"Yes. He said it was something that he brought."

I shook my head in disbelief. "And he just threw it at the doors?"

"Pretty much. When the police arrived, that's when we knew that there was going to be trouble. He claimed he was using the bomb as a distraction so you and your parents could get out."

"That might be true," I replied.

"Yeah, but a lot of people were probably hurt in that blast. People might have died that we don't even know about. Think about how crazy it is that Jenson was willing to blow up the place so we could escape."

"He's loyal to the cause."

Thomas rolled his eyes. "There's loyal and then there's downright nuts." He motioned down the street to an approaching car. It was Jenson.

"He's dangerous, Hannah. We need to be careful."

I nodded and then made sure I wasn't talking about it anymore when Jenson pulled into my driveway.

I opened the passenger door and motioned for Thomas to get into the back seat.

"Where are we meeting Kate?" asked Jenson.

"The lot behind the old mall."

"What mall? I'm not from here."

"Just let me punch in the address," I replied. I pushed in the numbers and the street name on the panel on the dashboard. I noticed that Jenson wasn't using the autopilot setting.

Jenson looked at me while driving. "So, what's your plan if Kate's Dad, Gideon, really did kill her Mom?"

"I guess she can stay with my parents."

Jenson shook his head. "And you don't think Gideon Wesley would think of that and find her?"

I hadn't thought of that. Dang. I need a different plan.

"She could leave the country with us," I suggested.

"So now she's family?" asked Thomas. He sounded upset.

I turned around and looked at Thomas. "You would rather her life be in danger?"

"I didn't say that. But the more people we attempt to make IDs for and leave the country with, the more suspicious we become. Six people cannot just disappear without people asking questions."

"Let's just talk to Kate and see why she suspects her Dad."

Jenson drove us in silence for a while. As we approached the lot by the old mall, I looked around to make sure that we were alone and could speak freely. The only cars were driving past and not stopping in the lot. I still couldn't believe this place was still here. No one used shopping malls anymore because there was no need to actually go to the store and buy the clothes. It was much easier to purchase clothes online and have them shipped to you. Almost every mall in the lower states had been turned into something else or abandoned altogether. A few towns over, one of the malls had been turned into a school, complete with an indoor pool for swimming classes.

We pulled the car into the empty lot and I noticed that Kate was already there. She was standing outside of her car, looking nervous, fidgeting with her hands. I jumped out of Jenson's car before he had completely stopped the vehicle to run and hug Kate. She looked a mess. Her hair was disheveled, her makeup was smeared, and she looked like she had been crying all day.

Her Mom died; of course she's still crying. Stupid, Hannah.

"Are you okay?" I asked Kate after we pulled apart from hugging.

She sniffled and nodded yes. I could tell she was lying. I heard Thomas and Jenson get out of the car behind me, but I ignored them. "Why do you think your Dad killed your Mom?"

"I overhead a phone conversation between him and a Memory Lane guard. The guard told Dad that he needed the money the next day or else he would go public with the way Danielle died. It sounded like a threat."

"That doesn't mean your Dad was involved."

Kate wiped away some more tears. "There's also this." She reached into her back pocket and pulled out her phone. She showed me a screenshot of an email from her Dad.

Nathan,

You did an excellent job taking care of Danielle. The police are not a threat to us, considering I paid them off. She is no longer a security issue. The money we agreed upon will be wired to your account in about two days.

All the best,
Gideon

I handed Kate back her phone after showing Thomas and Jenson. "How did you get this?" I asked Kate, in disbelief.

"Dad accidentally left his email open while he was in the shower a few days ago. I went into his office to ask him for something else, and then I couldn't resist looking through his emails since they were right there on the screen. This was the top email in his inbox. Nathan's name caught my eye. He's worked at Memory Lane as a guard since the beginning, basically."

"I still don't understand why your Dad would do this," Thomas said.

"Beats me. I still can't believe he is the one responsible for my Mom's death. What am I gonna do? Where am I gonna go? How can I—"

I interrupted Kate's rambling. "Calm down. We're going to figure this out together."

Jenson spoke next. "Not to burst your bubble, but what can a couple of teenagers do against Gideon Wesley? He's got tons of money and admitted to paying off the police. We don't stand a chance."

I shot Jenson a look. "Not helping."

Thomas interjected to break the tension. "When was the email dated?"

Kate glanced at her phone to look at the screen shot. "Four days ago. That's only two days after my Mom died." She started crying again and I hugged her again.

"Can we follow an electronic trail of the money? That could prove your Dad hired someone to kill your Mom in conjunction with this email," said Jenson.

"I bet Dad is smart enough to know not to use one of his company accounts. He has plenty of off-shore accounts that are in fake names. They will never be able to trace the money back to him," Kate explained.

"Let me give it a try," said Jenson with a twinkle in his eye. Give him a hacking job and he was all smiles. "Do you know any of his fake names he uses?"

Kate shook her head no.

"That's okay. Everything leaves an electronic signature. I'll figure it out," Jenson said, reassuring Kate.

I still didn't trust him completely. I flashed back to what Thomas told me earlier about Jenson having a bomb as a back-up plan. I made a mental note to ask Kate more about him later.

"As far as where you are going to stay to get away from your Dad, just tell him you are staying with some girl friends," I suggested.

Kate looked unsure. "That's only a temporary fix, though. I need to get away from him for good."

"Didn't you say that you hardly ever saw your Dad because he was busy with Memory Lane? Will he even notice you are gone?" I asked.

"He's all about appearing to be a 'family man' at the moment. Keeping up appearances and all that."

"And?" I asked.

"And that means he's been tracking me and sending security guards with me everywhere I go. I convinced one of them to give me like an hour of time by myself so I could 'meet my boyfriend.' Speaking of …" Kate looked down at her phone to check the time. "I have to get back soon or my Dad will put out an APB on me."

"You're going back?" I asked, concerned. "I thought the whole reason you contacted me was because you wanted to escape your Dad. Are you afraid of him?"

Kate paused for a moment. "No. I don't think he would kill me. But I also never thought he would have my Mom killed…"

"Look, I don't think it's safe for you to stay at your Dad's house," Jenson said matter-of-factly.

"We aren't actually dating anymore, you know," replied Kate. "I don't need you to protect me."

Jenson shook his head. "It's not like that. As your friend, I think you should stay away from your Dad."

"I don't know if he'll let me."

I offered a way out. "Let's at least try. Go back home and plead with him that you need to see some of your friends for a girls' night. Talk about losing your Mom and how a 'girl just needs to be around other girls.' Don't make it sound like you are leaving for an extended period of time."

Kate nodded and turned back toward her car. "I'll text you later," she promised.

I watched as she got in her car and drove away. We would just have to wait and see what happened next. "Let's go back to my house, so we can talk about the IDs some more. They know Dad wouldn't endanger us in his escape so we should be safe at home, even just to talk through what to do next. Thomas, have you contacted your guy? I don't think we will be able to stay around here much longer, now that Dad has escaped," I said to Thomas.

"Yeah, he said he would meet me tomorrow as long as we paid him up front."

The three of us got back into Jenson's car and drove back to my house. As we parked on the street, I noticed that my parents were back. That must mean that Leslie was home. I couldn't wait to see her again. Part of me remembered a time when she was my "annoying little sister." All traces of that were gone since she returned from being dead for four years. I stepped out of Jenson's car and walked inside.

"We're back!" I called from the front entryway. Thomas and Jenson followed me into the kitchen, where my parents were sitting at the table. There was tension in the air so thick we could all feel it.

What's wrong? What happened?" I asked.

Dad's expression softened, and he looked at me with sadness.

"Where's Leslie?" I asked.

"She's in her room." Dad grabbed Mom's hand in support and then turned to us. "Thomas, can you guys please go in the other room for a minute? We need to speak to Hannah alone."

"Sure thing, Uncle Robert," Thomas replied.

I watched as the two of them went into the living room and then took a seat at the table next to Mom. "What's going on?"

"Hannah, your Mom had"—he paused, as if searching for the right word—"an episode in the car."

"It's nothing. I'm fine," Mom said.

"An episode? What does that mean?" I asked, looking to both of my parents for cues as to why they were acting so strange.

"She forgot that Leslie was alive. When we arrived at Nicole's house to pick her up, she had no idea why we were there," Dad explained.

"What? How is that possible?!"

"She remembered again once she saw her, but it took some convincing on my part that it was really Leslie."

"This doesn't make any sense. You haven't seen Leslie since she was dead, Dad, and now Mom is the one who forgets she is alive? She's been with us for weeks!"

"I'm fine, Robert. It was just a fluke."

Dad smiled at me. "Hannah, I need you to think very carefully. Have you noticed any signs of memory loss in your mother?"

"I'm right here!" Mom exclaimed. "I'm fine!"

I stared at both of them in silence, unsure of what to say.

"I haven't noticed any memory loss, Dad. Honest."

"See? I told you. I'm fine. It was a one-time thing," Mom said, trying to convince Dad. I started to wonder if she was trying to convince herself.

"If we're going to leave the country and assume new identities, we can't have you forgetting who we really are or who we are supposed to be. It could ruin everything," I pointed out.

This was not good. If Mom was going to have memory loss, now was not the time. She could put us in danger by saying our real names instead of our fake ones and blow our cover. I couldn't imagine leaving Mom behind and just going with my Dad, Leslie, and Thomas. That didn't feel right either.

"Have you told Leslie?" I asked.

"She sort of witnessed the aftermath of your Mom's confusion of seeing her alive at your aunt's house. I'm sure she figured out what happened."

"It won't happen again. I was just stressed and happy and worried and too many other emotions from rescuing your Dad," Mom said.

I smiled at her reassuringly. "It's fine, Mom."

Is it really fine, though? We do not need this right now.

"I'm going to check on Leslie," I said, standing up from my chair at the kitchen table. I walked up to Leslie's room and knocked on the door. There was not a reply from within so I opened the door cautiously and peeked inside. "Les? Are you in here?"

I found her on the bed crying. "Hey, what's wrong?"

"Nothing," she replied.

"We'll pretend that's real. Are you upset about Mom?"

Leslie turned to look at me with tears running down her face. "What if she forgets me completely?"

"I won't let that happen." I pulled her in for a hug. She fell against me and sobbed. I knew there would be something that would make her break down completely since returning to us mostly unscathed. There were clearly traumatic things that occurred over the course of four years, and I wondered when it would come to light.

"You can't promise that," Leslie said, while rubbing her face in my shirt. She had not done that since she was really little. This must be hitting her hard.

"We'll get through it as a family. Mom just got confused. It's probably just from the stress of rescuing Dad."

"She seemed fine up until she left me at Aunt Nicole's house. That was the first time we had been apart for a long time since..." Leslie trailed off.

"I know. We'll just make sure you're with her more to reinforce the memory that you really are back for good." I rubbed Leslie's back to comfort her and assure her that I was there.

Leslie nodded against my shirt and pushed away to look at my face. "I'm glad we got Dad back," she said.

"Me too. And I'm glad we got you back." I looked around Leslie's room and nostalgia hit me. Mom had left the room untouched since Leslie "died." She didn't want to disturb anything in the room in honor of Leslie's memory. I thought it was creepy at the time, but now I was thankful for it. The fact that there was still a bed and other furniture made things easier for all of us.

"Hey. What do you say to a sleepover in my room tonight?"

"Really? You sure you want your baby sister to annoy you all night?" Leslie asked, smiling.

"Yeah. It'll be like old times. But I won't kick you out this time. Let's go downstairs and get a snack," I said, pulling Leslie off the bed with me. Food could improve anyone's mood in my experience. As we walked to the kitchen, I saw Thomas and Jenson in the living room arguing over what to watch on the TV.

"Hey, come in the kitchen!" I called to both of them.

Leslie and I looked in the pantry for something to eat. There weren't many good snacks, but we could make do with some chips. They were fat-free and organic, but you couldn't get regular chips anymore. Not anywhere that I knew of. The guys came into the kitchen and we all stood around the table, except for Leslie who was sitting down with the bag of chips. My parents were sitting down too, waiting to see what everyone was doing in the kitchen. Jenson stole a chip from Leslie and began talking.

"What's the deal with the IDs?" he asked, with a mouth full of food.

"We should know more tomorrow. Meeting with my guy then," replied Thomas.

"Do I get one?" asked Jenson.

There was silence as we all looked at each other. Leslie ate more chips and I could hear her crunching.

Mom responded first. "It depends. We'll see."

I grabbed a few chips from Leslie's bag and popped them in my mouth. I stole a glance at Mom and tried to read her expression. "What's wrong, Mom?"

"I'm just worried because we are harboring several fugitives of Memory Lane and I think we need to leave the house soon. Like maybe tonight, just because they have already searched here before, doesn't mean they won't come back and check again."

"And go where? There's five of us plus Kate who I really don't want to leave alone right now," I said. I looked at Jenson to judge his reaction to me saying "five of us." He had to know I meant my family and Thomas. He continued eating chips from Leslie's bag. I guess he didn't care.

"Is Kate in danger?" Mom asked, narrowing her eyes.

I conceded. "Yeah, she believes her Dad hired someone to kill her Mom."

"What?!" Mom and Dad exclaimed at the same time.

"Call her right now. I don't want her anywhere near her Dad," said Mom, sternly.

I was glad she was taking this seriously. "But where are we going?"

All of us stared at each other, racking our brains for ideas of where to stay.

I looked over at Jenson. "Where are you staying? Do you have room for us?"

"I'm in a motel a few miles outside of town. It's one room. I guess we could get more rooms. Are you sure you all want to stay together? Memory Lane might be able to find you easier that way," he pointed out.

Leslie's eyes got very large at the possibility of being separated from us.

"I also think we need to get farther away than just a few miles outside of town. Especially me," Dad said.

I received a text on my phone and glanced down to read it.

I could feel my heartbeat faster inside my chest. "Whatever we do, we better do it quick. Kate just said that Dad's escape from Memory Lane is on the news. The bomb too. They are sending out guards to find all of us."

All of us stared at each other in shock. We should have known this was coming. It was dumb to think we would have more time and how foolish it was for us to come to the house at all. Leslie grabbed my hand from where she was sitting at the table. She squeezed it so hard, it hurt. I had just gotten my whole family back and now there was a strong possibility that it would all be ripped away from me. I squeezed Leslie's hand back trying to quell my own fears. We were so screwed.

Chapter 9

"Girls, go pack. We can't waste any more time," Mom ordered. We walked back toward our bedrooms.

"Where are we going?" asked Leslie as we walked down the hall.

"I don't know yet, but just make sure you stay close to me." I squeezed Leslie's hand. I didn't want anything to happen to her if guards came right now. "Just grab the essentials." She nodded and headed to her room to grab some clothes and I walked across the hall and grabbed a bag for mine. I put some jeans, a hoodie, some bras, underwear, a phone charger, and a toothbrush inside the bag. Looking around my childhood home, it hit me that after tonight, I might never see it again. I took in every inch of my room. There was no turning back. Finishing my packing, I quickly texted Kate and let her know that she needed to come right now. We were leaving. It was now or never if she wanted to get away from her Dad.

Her text back was lightning fast; she said she couldn't meet me right now but to tell her where we were going and that she would meet us there. *Even I don't know that yet.*

With nothing left to pack, I walked to Leslie's room to check and see if she was almost done. She had a bag in her hand and was standing in the doorway. Her eyes looked a million miles away. I guess she was ready. "Why was there a bomb at Memory Lane?" she asked. I forgot that she didn't know anything about what had happened while we were rescuing Dad.

"I'll explain later. I don't actually have all the details yet."

We headed back toward the kitchen and found Thomas and Jenson standing around.

"Why aren't you packing a bag?" I asked Thomas while setting mine on the table.

"My stuff is at my house. I don't want to attract the guards to my house with Mom there."

I sighed. "Hate to say it, but I think they will go looking for you there anyway."

"I know you're right. Still, I'm hoping Mom, or both of my parents, can meet us wherever we go tonight before we leave the country tomorrow. They should be able to bring me a bag."

"Where'd Mom and Dad go?" asked Leslie.

"To get their stuff packed," replied Thomas.

I smiled at Leslie. "Can you go see if they need anything? Please?"

She nodded and ran off to our parents' bedroom. Now I could get some answers.

"What's with the bomb, Jenson?" I asked. "We are a team; you can't make a decision like that without telling all of us. Someone could have been hurt."

He looked at me sheepishly. "I'm sorry, Hannah. I had to have a back-up plan. We couldn't risk being trapped inside Memory Lane." Jenson replied.

"It's not that simple," Thomas butted in. "What were you thinking? Bombs are dangerous!"

"I was thinking that we needed a better way out of the building and a distraction. I had a back-up plan. It's not a big deal," Jenson retorted to Thomas. "Did you have a better way to get out?"

Thomas's face was red with anger. "You could have gotten killed. Or gotten me killed."

Jenson crossed his arms in self-defense. "It worked, didn't it? No one was hurt. We couldn't have made it out without it!"

"That doesn't make it okay!" Thomas yelled.

"Keep your voice down, Thomas!" I said, pushing my way back into the argument.

Thomas dropped his voice to a harsh whisper. "What if it went off in your pocket?"

"Well, it didn't," Jenson replied. "Look, we got my device on the computer to download the memories. We got your uncle out of Memory Lane. Relax. We won."

"The guards are still after all of us. How is that winning?" Thomas asked angrily. "Maybe it's a mistake for you to be here."

"Are you blaming me? It wasn't my idea to break into Memory Lane in the first place."

"Everybody calm down," I said. *How do I diffuse this? Without Jenson, we may have never made it out of Memory Lane.*

Leslie came back into the kitchen with my parents in tow. They all had bags and were staring at the three of us, concerned at the angry stares and awkward silence between Jenson and Thomas.

"What's wrong?" asked Leslie. Before I could respond, Thomas made a decision that would affect us all.

"Nothing. Jenson was just leaving," Thomas responded.

What?!? "Thomas, are you sure—"

"Yes," Thomas said, cutting me off.

Without a word, Jenson turned from the kitchen and walked through the living room, Thomas trailing behind as if to make sure he left. Thomas was so angry you could see him just seething under the surface. I had never seen him so mad. It was like Thomas thought Jenson didn't care about anyone, including himself. Sure, something could have gone wrong with the bomb, but we were already in danger. I didn't want to think about what could have happened if Jenson hadn't set off that bomb. I thought about Leslie being left alone without a family if we had been captured. How would we have been able to tell her what had happened? Jenson saved us. If it weren't for him, Leslie would be alone. She spent the last four years at Memory Lane not knowing what happened to us and, no matter what, I wouldn't let that happen again.

I was shaken out of my thoughts by Thomas appearing back in the kitchen.

"Everyone ready? Thomas, did you call your Mom?" Dad asked.

"Not yet. I thought I would call her when we get wherever we're going."

"Sounds good. I'll go start the car," Dad announced, walking toward the driveway through the front door. It was strange and surreal being together. Almost like we were going on a family vacation instead of fleeing the country as fugitives.

Mom looked at both me and Leslie. "Are you guys ready for this? Nothing will ever be the same again after today."

I smiled at her. "As long as we are together, I don't care." I grabbed Leslie's hand again to remind her that I was there. She squeezed it back.

"Let's get a move on then," Mom said.

Leslie, Thomas, and I followed her through the living room and to the front door so we could load the car with our bags. I turned back to relish in one last look at the house I grew up in. So many memories with friends and family at holidays and birthdays took place in this house. I would cherish them forever. I promised myself not to forget them even more now that Mom apparently was feeling the effects of ALD-87 more severely than the rest of us, who had no memory loss.

"Hannah? What's wrong?" asked Leslie from the driveway.

"Nothing." I gave myself one last glance and shook off the feeling of loss as I walked away from my childhood home for the last time.

****

"This is where we're staying?" asked Leslie with disgust in her voice. I couldn't blame her for her response. The motel looked like something from a horror movie. Layers of paint peeled in all directions, showing the evolution of colors it had been painted in the years since its construction. The numbers of the rooms were faded and almost indistinguishable. Derelict cars were haphazardly parked in spaces, sometimes far too close to the car next to it. The banisters were bent and hung loosely, certainly not something you would want to lean on for support. It clearly wasn't fancy.

"It's only temporary," I reminded her.

Leslie looked at the motel again and turned up her nose. "It looks like it hasn't had people in it for a hundred years."

"That's the point, Les," I said. "No one will notice us here."

Dad opened the driver's door. "It's late and we are all tired. I'll get us some rooms and maybe we can get some rest," he said with a heavy sigh. He got out, shut the door, and headed toward the office.

We got out too and stood around the car, bags in hand and waited for Dad to return with the room keys. I felt vulnerable just standing out in the open. Instinctively I grabbed Leslie's hand. Just having her close by afforded me some comfort. Finding her in Memory Lane re-played over and over in my mind and I squeezed her hand. I can't lose her again.

"Did you get Aunt Nicole on the phone?" I asked Thomas, trying to distract myself.

"Not yet. I'll call her in a bit once we get the rooms and get settled."

Dad walked back from the office and opened the car to grab his bag. "Rest is just a moment away. We're in three rooms on the side. Rooms seven, eight, and nine." He dangled the keys in the air, and they made a strange sound bumping against each other as if it was the sound of potential peace. So much had happened in the last few hours that I felt like my senses were heightened. Every sound reverberated through me and I wondered if rest was even possible. He tossed one to me and another to Thomas.

"Can we afford all these rooms?" I asked, concerned about our money situation. I knew that I had already spent so much on the roofies.

"You know you don't need to worry about that stuff now. Plus, they are really cheap." Dad smiled at me and I felt more at ease. He was always in control and that's what made me feel safe. I was glad he was out of Memory Lane and that we were all together again.

"Come on, Les, you'll be with me," I said tugging her along with me. We had the key to room eight, right in the middle of my parents and Thomas. I grabbed my bag and started to walk toward the side of the building with Leslie in tow. The place we were staying was called The Greenleaf. Everyone here knew about the stories of this motel. It was a sleazy place people patronized to do unmentionable things and hide it from their significant others or parents. There were stories of people who came here for drugs and just never left. A shiver ran down my spine. There were just too many things to process right now. I hoped the sheets were at least clean.

The door to room eight looked older than me. The paint was flaking off and if it weren't for the fact that room seven and room nine were more readable, I wouldn't be sure I was trying to get into the right room. I unlocked the door and threw my bag on the bed nearest the door. Leslie took the bed that was closer to the bathroom and away from the door. I needed to be in between her bed and the door in case anyone tried to get inside. She sat on her bed and bounced up and down a little bit, testing the mattress.

"Does it feel okay?" I asked.

"It's lumpy but not terrible," she replied. Leslie looked down at her hands and I could tell she was just as restless as I was.

"Come on, let's go next door and see what Mom and Dad are doing," I suggested.

I locked the door behind us as we walked out. Leslie knocked on our parents' room and waited for them to answer the door.

"Come in," Mom said, while gesturing to the beds. The layout was the same as our room so there wasn't even a table to sit at. We would have to sit on the floor or on the bed. I chose the bed nearest the door and sat down. The mattress was lumpy just like Leslie said. I probably wouldn't be getting much sleep tonight.

"Where's Thomas?" I asked.

"He must still be in his room," Dad replied.

"Why did you get me and Leslie a separate room? The four of us could have shared," I pointed out.

Dad shrugged, and made air quotes to drive home his point. "I just figured since you're a 'grown-up,' you might want more space." I laughed a little, feeling the slightest break in the tension. "Plus, isn't Kate coming? You can sleep here if you want to. It doesn't matter to us." Grateful for the offer, I still felt like Leslie and I would be fine in our own room. The only person missing from our motel room gathering was Thomas.

"I'm gonna go get Thomas. Be right back," I said, jumping up. I headed out the door and, in less than twenty steps, I knocked on Thomas's door.

"Open up. It's me," I called.

Thomas was on the phone when he opened the door. He ushered me inside.

"I am not leaving Hannah, Mom!" Thomas yelled into the phone.

Raising my eyebrow in confusion, I stared at Thomas. *What could he mean by that?*

"Can you please just meet us at The Greenleaf with a bag of clothes at least? And my phone charger?" Thomas asked into the phone.

My aunt was shouting on the other end of the line but I couldn't make out what she was saying. By the sound of it, it didn't sound like she was agreeing with his suggestion.

"Can we discuss the details of that when you get here? I'm in room nine. I love you, Mom." Thomas reluctantly hung up the phone and dropped down on the mattress nearest to the door. "Man, she was not happy," he sighed.

"Is she bringing your stuff?" I asked.

Thomas nodded and ran his hand through his hair.

"What's wrong?" I could tell that he was unhappy or worried about something.

"Mom doesn't want me to leave the country with you guys."

"Why not? She has to know we can't stay. Does she know that she's invited too?"

"Yeah, I told her that we will figure out a way to get all of us a fake IDs and passports, but she thinks it's all too dangerous." He rolled his eyes. "As if we weren't already stuck in the danger zone anyway."

"Does she think running from Memory Lane forever is safer?"

Thomas shook his head and shrugged. "Who knows? I'm hoping to change her mind when she gets here."

"How much are these IDs gonna cost?" I asked.

"A lot. My guy will give us a discount, but it will still wipe out everyone's accounts, I'm sure."

"Maybe that's what your Mom is worried about," I said, thinking out loud. "Maybe my parents have an idea."

"Doubtful. We'll have to see," said Thomas.

"No sense in guessing. Let's regroup in my parents' room. Come on," I said, while gesturing with my head to the motel room door. Thomas audibly sighed and I could tell he was worried and frustrated. He grabbed his room key and locked the door behind him as we walked two doors over. I knocked on the door to room seven and waited for someone to answer.

Mom opened the door and ushered Thomas and me inside. She peeked her head out and I could tell she was trying to see if there was anyone around who looked suspicious. Considering how sketchy this motel was, I thought everyone looked suspicious. Leslie was sitting on the bed flipping through the TV channels. "Move over," I said, while she made room for me on the bed.

"Anything good on the TV?" I asked.

"Pfftt. No. Just trying to decide on the least annoying thing to watch."

"What did your Mom say?" Dad asked Thomas.

Thomas shrugged. I could tell he wasn't ready to dive into what had just happened over the phone. "I told her where we were staying. She said we can talk about everything when she gets here," he replied.

Dad smiled. "Looking forward to it."

"Are we going to eat something?" Leslie asked.

Mom laughed for a moment and nodded. It felt like the past few years had never happened. We were together again. "Yeah, we'll figure that out after your Aunt Nicole gets here."

"Where's Jenson?" asked Leslie, looking around the room. "Is he coming too?"

Thomas and I exchanged a glance.

"He might. We'll see," I said.

Leslie looked from me to Thomas. "Did something happen?" she asked.

Leslie wasn't dumb. She had certainly learned to read people while she was in Memory Lane and she could tell that there was a reason Jenson wasn't currently with us.

"I'll explain later. Promise," I told her.

Now we just needed to find out if we were going to be able to get Kate away from the danger at home. I took out my phone and sent a VidChat to Kate to let her know that we were at The Greenleaf Motel and to meet us here as soon as she could. A few minutes later she let me know she was on the way. With everything going on, I was anxious to discuss what really happened with her Mom's death. Kate was my best friend and I just had to find a way to keep her safe. I didn't trust Gideon Wesley one bit.

"Kate's on her way," I said aloud to everyone. "I'm sure she'll bunk with me and Leslie for tonight."

"What time is the meeting tomorrow for the IDs and passports?" Mom had been managing the particulars and I am sure she was concerned about getting these done and getting out of town as soon as possible.

"Around noon. He's supposed to message me when he is ready," replied Thomas.

"Do we all need to go?" asked Dad.

"Tomorrow we will find out the price and then arrange the payment. Once he has that, I think he will need to take everyone's picture to create the fake IDs. We will need them to look as authentic as possible."

Mom looked worried. We had spent so much money to break Dad out of Memory Lane and now we had to figure out how to pay to start our lives over somewhere else. "How much money are we talking about?"

"He hasn't told me yet. But his old price used to be $500 per ID."

"How do you know this guy anyway?" I asked.

"He's sort of a friend of a friend," replied Thomas.

"Is the $500 per ID the discounted price?" I asked.

"Not sure. I'll see what he says tomorrow. We are asking for a lot of IDs, you know. They have to look real enough to pass government scrutiny."

Our conversation was interrupted by a knock on the door. We all turned our heads to look as Dad walked over to window. He peered carefully through the curtains to check if it was safe to answer. It was my aunt Nicole. Feeling confident that we were reasonably safe, Dad opened the door to welcome her in. She rushed in and ran straight to Thomas to pull him into a hug. "Are you okay?" she asked. I had never seen Aunt Nicole so worried, though to be fair, we broke into Memory Lane twice and were wanted fugitives. She had quite a lot she could worry about.

"Yeah, Mom. I'm fine," replied Thomas. "Did you bring my stuff?"

Aunt Nicole nodded. "Yeah, it's in the car." She looked to Dad. "Robert," she said. "It's good to see you again."

"Where's Dad?" asked Thomas.

"He isn't coming. He has to work. Besides, we really don't think you should leave the country."

There was a collective gasp in the motel room.

"What do you mean? Why not?" I asked.

My aunt Nicole sat on the bed farthest from the door. "I just don't think it's safe."

"Do you understand that Memory Lane will always be after us?" Mom asked. "It's not like we are just being dramatic."

"I know that, but I want Thomas here with me," Aunt Nicole replied.

"You can come too! Memory Lane has no problem killing you or Uncle John if you remain in the country. They will find you. Just look at what happened to Danielle Wesley…" I said, suddenly trailing off. I feared I had said too much.

"Her death wasn't caused by Memory Lane," Aunt Nicole said.

"Do you really believe that, Nicole?" Mom asked. She sat down on the bed next to her sister. "I have seen things in the past few weeks since Hannah and Thomas broke into Memory Lane that have made me question everything Memory Lane stands for. You can't deny that they have too much control. They sent guards after our children. These people have no morals and will stop at nothing to get what they want."

"It's more than just that," said Aunt Nicole, her eyes downcast. "I don't think I can afford the IDs for me and Thomas." She looked ashamed to admit it.

Mom smiled and rubbed her sister's shoulder. "We'll figure it out. All of us. Together."

My aunt Nicole sighed. "You are all just ready to give up everything you've ever known and flee to another country?"

Leslie leaned forward to face Aunt Nicole and answered her question before any of us could chime in with a response. "Remember how I 'died' four years ago? You all buried me, mourned me, and yet I was with Memory Lane the whole time. They performed tests on me to try to make me forget things. The more I said it wasn't working the harder it got. They hated that I remembered my family. Eventually, I had to pretend that their experiment was working so they would stop leaving me in isolation. So they would feed me and stop trying to beat me into submission. So yeah, I'm more than ready to leave the country to get away from Memory Lane," she said matter-of-factly.

The silence following Leslie's confession was deafening. Without a second thought, I walked over to where Leslie was sitting on the other bed and wrapped my arms around her and squeezed, hoping I could help her feel even a little bit safer. When I looked up we were both crying. This was the first time that she gave specifics about something that happened over the course of the four years that she was away from us.

"Oh, Les, I'm so sorry they put you through that!" Tears filled Aunt Nicole's eyes. "They are terrible people for experimenting on a child."

Leslie brushed away a stray tear and sniffled. "Not a child … children. There were lots of us. If we weren't struggling with memory loss then we were stolen away from our families and treated like science experiments." Leslie sat a little straighter; sharing more of what happened there seemed to be helping her feel safe enough to share more.

My aunt spoke again to the whole room. "Do we have a plan? If we do this, where are we going to stay? Canada? Do we have a house or anything lined up? I don't have enough money for all of that."

"We could go to Mexico," I suggested. "Aren't things cheaper there?"

Dad nodded. "Hannah has a point."

"I don't care where we go, as long as we are all safe," Mom said.

There was another knock at the door. Everyone fell silent again. We may have been at a middle-of-nowhere motel but that didn't mean that Memory Lane wasn't still searching their hardest to find us. Peeking through the curtains the same way Dad did, I could see Kate's small frame. She had lost weight since her mother died.

Quickly, I unlocked the door and pulled Kate inside. She hugged me so tight, and I could tell she was still unsure what was happening, "Hannah, it's good to see you again."

"I'm so glad you are safe," I said, returning the hug. Kate stepped sideways and politely waved to everyone, setting her overnight bag on the floor.

"Sit down anywhere, Kate," Mom offered.

"Are you okay?" I asked.

Kate nodded but I didn't buy it.

"I'm going to order some food. I know Leslie is just 'dying' of starvation," interrupted Dad. He rolled sarcastic eyes at Leslie, and she responded with a replay of her fainting skills from earlier. He laughed and asked, "Is everyone okay with pizza?"

We all said yes as I handed Dad my phone so he could order the pizza. He walked outside the motel room and closed the door. Sitting next to Kate, I took her hand and asked her, "Does your Dad know you're here?"

She shook her head no.

"Good, let's keep it that way."

Everyone was looking at Kate with pity. It was the same look people gave me when Leslie died four years ago. I hated it. I promised not to do that to Kate.

"Where's Jenson?" asked Kate.

"It's a long story," I replied.

Kate looked around the motel room, confused. "Did something happen?"

"I'll explain later," I said.

"How are you, Kate?" Aunt Nicole asked. She was clearly trying to lighten the mood but we also hadn't had the chance to explain to her why Kate was here instead of at home.

Kate shrugged. "I've been better."

Wasn't that the understatement of the year for us all!

Dad opened the motel room door and came back inside. "Pizza should be here in thirty minutes. Hope everyone likes anchovies."

"Eww! You better be joking," Leslie exclaimed.

Dad chuckled and sat down on the other bed.

Kate's phone rang from her pocket and her eyes grew wide. She showed me the screen. It was her Dad calling.

"Answer it. Act casual. He probably has no idea where you are," I said.

Everyone in the room held their breath and kept quiet so Gideon wouldn't hear.

"Hi, Dad," answered Kate.

The sound of yelling could be heard in the entire room and I gestured to Kate to put it on speaker phone so we could all hear what he had to say.

"Do you think I am stupid! I know you're at The Greenleaf Motel with the Healys. I am sending someone for you right now. You will not run away from me in the middle of an investigation!" Gideon yelled.

It was my turn to panic. What were we going to do now? Gideon Wesley had a lot of resources and would stop at nothing to get Kate back. She was a liability to us, but I couldn't justify leaving her. Especially since Gideon most likely had Danielle Wesley killed.

"I have no idea what you're talking about, Dad," Kate replied, shakily.

"Don't lie to me! I tracked you to their motel."

"But I—" began Kate, trying to explain.

Gideon's voice interrupted. "And you're completely crazy if you think I'm letting you leave the country with people that broke into my facility—twice!"

How did he know our plan? Was he listening? I looked to my parents for guidance, but they were just as dumbfounded as Kate and I. A million questions ran through my mind. Did we need to rethink everything? How powerful was Gideon Wesley?

Gideon's voice lowered slightly. "Listen, I know Hannah is your friend. I won't harm Hannah and her family if you come back home without a fight, Kate. You have fifteen minutes to decide."

Chapter 10

The motel room was deathly silent. The mere seconds since Kate's Dad's declaration felt as though they dragged on forever.

"Dad?" Kate's voice, echoing through the motel room, was filled with panic. "Hello?" She stared at the call that was no longer connected. Without saying goodbye, he had hung up the phone.

Everyone in the room stared at each other in disbelief.

"What now?" I asked.

Mom stood up straighter and I could see that something had changed in her. Since we had broken into Memory Lane, she had grown more courageous, like a lioness who senses danger to her cubs. "Well, obviously we can't let Gideon take Kate. We need to go somewhere else now," she said with urgency. She walked up behind Kate and put her hands on her shoulders.

Don't worry, Kate, we aren't going to just let you get taken back to God knows what kind of danger!

"Where? We can't get IDs until tomorrow," replied Thomas.

Kate started crying. It only took a moment to feel as though everything we had worked for to get here was falling apart.

"This is all my fault. I'm so sorry. My Dad tracked me here and now I put all of you in danger." She brushed the tears off her cheeks with her shirt sleeve and tried to stop crying.

"We don't blame you, honey," Mom said, trying to comfort Kate.

"I'll just get out of here," Kate stated abruptly. "Then you guys can leave the country and not have to worry about Memory Lane ever again." There was a panic in her voice that no one could ignore. She was afraid. I couldn't blame her for that fear. I was afraid for her, knowing that her Dad had her Mom murdered. Something was very wrong at Memory Lane and we all needed to get as far away as possible and quickly.

"Hold on a minute," I said to Kate. "Let's think about this. I don't want you with your Dad. He's bad news."

"But he will arrest you guys if I don't agree to his terms right now. If he was willing to have my Mom killed..."

"What about going to The Memorizers?" Leslie asked.

I turned to look at her. "What?"

Leslie spoke again. "The Memorizers. They are underground and they took you and Thomas in before." She said like it was the most obvious thing in the world to suggest.

"Does your Dad know about where The Memorizers are?" I asked Kate.

"I don't think so. That's where I was before when I ran away from him and he never tracked me down."

"This might actually work as a temporary solution," said Thomas.

"Hold on," Mom interrupted. "How do we know that we can trust The Memorizers? They poisoned Thomas."

I put my hands up to silence Mom from going into more details of why she distrusted The Memorizers. Thomas's Mom was already beyond worried, we didn't need to add more fuel to that fire. "Fair point, Mom. But Antoine knows about Dad's special memory situation, and he seemed to respect our family. He let us stay in a sector above where everyone else starts out. We don't have a lot of options and we have no time to choose."

Mom still seemed uneasy. "Why can't we just find another motel and have Kate dump her phone?"

"We can't run forever. Leaving the country was supposed to be a more permanent solution to get away from Memory Lane. Besides, Gideon knows about me and Thomas," I stressed.

"The Memorizers aren't even in the same state," Dad pointed out. "Are we going to hitch a ride there? I don't think we should use any of our cars; it's too easy for us to be tracked."

"Whatever y'all decide to do, Thomas and I are leaving," said my Aunt Nicole with finality. "Come on," she said and grabbed Thomas's arm.

"Mom, wait—"

Aunt Nicole was panicking like an animal trapped in a corner with nowhere to go. "Now! I don't want to be a part of this!"

Mom stepped up and grabbed her sister's arm. "Nicole, calm down. We can all stay together if we think about this carefully."

Ultimately, I believed that Aunt Nicole knew Thomas was in danger, but she was letting that fear and anxiety get the best of her.

"Kate's Dad is coming now. You have no plan except to put my son back in the hands of the very people that poisoned him!" my aunt yelled. "I won't allow that to happen again. We're leaving."

I looked at Thomas with fear and sadness in my eyes. After everything we had been through together at Memory Lane, how could it all end here?

"Can we just talk about this for a minute?" I asked my aunt.

"What is there to talk about? We aren't leaving with you guys. I have to do what is best for my family." Aunt Nicole tightened her grip on Thomas, swallowing as she glanced toward the door.

Tears were falling from my eyes and I did nothing to stop them. How did things turn out like this? My aunt didn't trust us to keep Thomas safe, Kate's Dad was going to capture and kill us all if we didn't do what he said – but even worse in my mind was that they could take Leslie away to Memory Lane again. I felt helpless.

My aunt apologized. "I'm sorry, Hannah. I really am."

Leslie jumped from the bed and ran to hug my aunt. "Aunt Nicole, you can't leave us! We need you and Thomas!" she sobbed.

A move like that was out of character for Leslie, and it made me wonder what she was planning. I decided to play along.

"Yeah. You're the one that let us escape from those guards when we were at the restaurant. We couldn't have made it out of there if you weren't willing to stand up to them."

"I got shot for it!"

Mom interrupted. "Is that what this is about? You're afraid of getting shot again?"

"No! I'm afraid of the Memory Lane guards killing my son because he tried to help *your daughter* escape. I'm afraid that Thomas will get hurt or worse," Aunt Nicole fumed.

"That's unfair!" Mom yelled.

"It's unfair for Thomas too!"

"I'm right here," Thomas said between gritted teeth. "I'm an adult and I can speak for myself."

Emotions were running too high and things were getting out of hand. We didn't have much time.

"We've already wasted five minutes talking about what we are gonna do. We need to do it before something happens to Kate," I said with urgency.

Kate looked at me. "I want to go with you guys but I also don't want to put all of you in danger." Her voice wavered and she clutched my hand. She hung her head, ashamed at not wanting to be a martyr.

"We have been running for so long now, it can't be any worse than having the guards after us," I said plainly.

"Hannah! Don't say that!" Mom yelled.

I shrugged. "Well, seriously. It's just our life now. We get to choose how we see this, and for now, this is the only way we get to live. We keep running."

"Do you really believe that?" Mom asked.

"Yeah, I guess."

The motel door slammed closed and before I could say another word, Thomas and Aunt Nicole were gone. I ran to the door and rushed to the banister.

"Thomas!" I yelled.

He turned around and faced me.

"How will we keep in touch? What if we need you for the fake IDs?"

My aunt sighed and spoke for Thomas. "I'm not sure it's a good idea for us to be texting or VidChatting with you anymore. We need to keep our distance. Sorry."

A sob tore through my throat and I ran the rest of the way in order to catch Thomas in a suffocating hug. The seconds passed slowly, but I caught my breath and forced myself to calm down. We didn't have enough time for me to be emotional. "I guess this is goodbye."

Thomas squeezed me before he pulled out of the hug. "Yeah."

"Thanks for everything," I said. "I mean it."

"No problem. That's what family is for." Thomas smiled sadly. "I wish things could be different."

"Me too," I replied.

I heard the motel door open again. It was Leslie. She must have come to see where I went.

"Hannah? Are you leaving too?" she asked. She sounded scared of my answer.

"No, I'll come back inside in a minute," I reassured her.

Leslie took a long look at me and then nodded her head before walking back inside the motel room.

"I'll miss you, Aunt Nicole," I said.

"We'll miss you too, sweetie. Be safe."

She turned away and pulled Thomas with her. The last thing I saw before wiping away my remaining tears and going inside were the taillights of my aunt's car. We really were on our own.

The air in the room was heavy and somber. Kate stood off to the side of the bed awkwardly. She looked like she didn't know if she was coming or going.

"So, The Memorizers then?" I asked, bringing back up the plan to stay with them.

"With Thomas gone, we have no way of getting the IDs, so I think staying with The Memorizers is our best option," Mom chimed.

"Are you coming?" I asked Kate. "It's now or never."

Kate looked at me and my parents, as if asking for permission.

"I don't want anyone else to die because of me or my family," she said.

"We will protect you," Dad replied.

"You can't guarantee that."

"We can try."

"Come on," I said to Kate, putting my arm around her shoulder. "It will be like old times."

She forced a smile and then nodded her head.

"It's settled then. We need to get going," Dad said.

"What about the pizza? I'm still hungry," whined Leslie.

"We can take it to go," Mom said.

"How are we gonna get there? My Dad will track the car I'm in and I'm sure he can track yours too," Kate pointed out.

"We will have to trade cars along the way," Mom stated, as if this was an everyday occurrence.

"You mean steal a car?" I asked.

Leslie shrugged at the suggestion like it was no big deal. "It's not like we haven't done it before."

Criminals. Memory Lane had reduced all of us to petty criminals that were in a race for our lives. What happened to being a normal teenager who worried solely about hanging out with my friends and staying away from my annoying, overbearing parents? Boring was not in my vocabulary since I got to have adventures and defy death on a regular basis.

There was a knock on the door and all of us froze. Dad moved to look through the window curtains while the rest of us stayed completely silent. *Was it Gideon Wesley? Memory Lane guards? The police? Someone worse?*

Dad broke the tension. "It's the pizza guy."

The rest of us let out a collective breath, Dad opened the door and greeted the man. "Good evening."

The pizza man passed the pizzas over to Dad. "It's $34.56."

He paid the man in cash and told him to keep the change. Closing the door, Dad turned around with the boxes of pizza.

"I remember someone saying they were hungry…"

"Yes!" Leslie and I shouted at the same time.

"We need to leave, Robert," Mom said with warning in her tone.

My stomach growled. "Can't we eat for a minute?" I asked.

She shook her head. "It isn't safe for any of us here. We have already wasted too much time. Kate's Dad could be on his way here right now. It's time to get out of here. You guys can eat in the car. It may be a bit before we switch cars so you can eat and maybe even get a little rest. It has been the longest night."

She was right, as she usually was. Everyone agreed and grabbed their bags. Kate left her phone on the bed inside the room my parents had rented. We would get her a cheap one later. Leslie climbed in the back seat of the car and Kate and I slid in beside her. "Are you sure you're okay leaving your Dad?" I asked.

Kate shrugged. She looked so lost. "I guess."

It's hard to lose one parent, but to lose both so close together and for frighteningly different reasons would be too much for anyone to bear. Wrapping my arm around her shoulders, I gave her a side hug hoping to help her feel just a little better.

"Pass the pizza!" shouted Leslie to Mom sitting in the front seat.

"Here," Mom said as she passed a box back to me and Kate. "Share. And try not to make a mess." Mom narrowed her eyes at us, accusingly.

I nodded and opened the box. Pepperoni and green olives. My favorite. I grabbed a slice and then waited for Leslie and Kate to each grab one.

"So good," I said while biting into a slice.

Dad started the car and drove out of the motel parking lot. I thought about contacting Gill or Brad, but I decided to wait until we got closer and switched cars. I didn't necessarily trust them completely and the less people who knew about my family coming to see The Memorizers, the better. I stole a glance at Leslie and smiled. She was happily eating her pizza and didn't seem to have a care in the world. I couldn't blame her. She had both of our parents, me, and Kate by her side. That was a far cry from what she experienced the last four years without any of us.

As happy as I was for Leslie and my family at the moment—aside from the fact that we were still running from Gideon and the rest of Memory Lane—my heart ached for Kate. I couldn't imagine one of my parents having the other killed for any reason. She also didn't have any siblings to lean on during this difficult time.

"Hey, gimme another slice," said Kate, knocking me out of my thoughts.

I opened the box and watched as she got another piece of pizza. "So, how far are you planning to drive until we 'borrow' another car?" I asked my parents.

"Far enough to get away from Gideon Wesley, I guess. We'll know when it's time," Mom replied.

Kate looked down with guilt. "I'm sorry. This is all my fault," she said.

"Stop blaming yourself. Everyone here made choices. There's no one at fault here," said Mom. She was trying to make Kate feel better.

I smiled at Kate comfortingly and offered her another slice of pizza.

I turned my head as a police car with its lights and siren turned on pulled into view of us.

"How could they possibly have found us?" I asked. My heart was beating hard inside my chest.

"They may be chasing someone else," Dad said while looking in the rearview mirror at the fast-approaching police car.

"Are you going to pull over?" Mom asked. "I don't want anything else to go wrong."

The police car changed lanes and zipped past us.

I released my breath. "Guess the police weren't after us," I said.

"We're all on edge right now with everything that's going on. It's normal to be paranoid," Mom said.

I nodded and leaned back a little in my seat. I wanted to be in another car right now so we could be incognito from Memory Lane guards and the police. At least for a little while. We drove for at least thirty minutes before getting just outside of town. I looked at the windows of the backseat to see where we were.

"I'm not seeing a lot of unattended cars that we can steal," I said.

"Maybe we should consider taking a bus," suggested Leslie.

"There are no buses anymore. You know that, Les," I replied.

Leslie looked back at me, confused.

My heart sank for just a second, assuming that Leslie had forgotten something thanks to the effects ALD-87.

"What? Since when?" she asked.

"Since two years ago. Memory Lane decided that buses were cesspools for germs and that only the poor used them anyway, so they weren't necessary for most of the country anymore. They put in above-ground trams in most major cities on the east coast to connect businesspeople."

Leslie looked shocked. "What about school buses?"

I was starting to really worry about why Leslie didn't know about any of this happening.

"School buses are still around, but only in small towns. You didn't see any of this on the news or hear anyone in Memory Lane talking about it?" I asked.

"When I was taken, they isolated all of us kids. We were kept in the dark about anything happening outside in the real world. They basically kept us in a bubble to torture us," Leslie explained.

"I'm so sorry, Les," I said, while giving her a side hug. "Sometimes it's hard for us to understand how disconnected they made all of you from the world."

Leslie smiled at me. "It's okay. It's not your fault." She shook her head. "Man, I can't believe buses aren't a thing anymore. What do the trams look like?"

"Here," I said, while taking out my phone to look up a picture of the tram in New York City. It was solid white and looked similar to a bullet train. There were windows but the tram moved so fast, I couldn't understand why people would want to look at the world zipping by. As far as I knew there were only two stops it made from one major city to another. There were no platforms for people to enter or exit in between metropolises. I passed my phone over to Leslie so she could see it.

"Whoa. It looks fancy," she said. "Does it run all day?"

"I think so, but I'm not sure. I've never been on one, if that makes you feel any better."

Leslie nodded slightly and then passed back my phone as it received a text.

It was Jenson. I rolled my eyes as I opened up the message to see what he wanted.

JENSON: i found something on my device from memory lane's computers. ur gonna want to see this
JENSON: it's from kate's memory

My heart started beating louder inside my chest. I nudged Kate in the shoulder to get her attention.

"Look at this," I said, while showing her my phone and my text exchange with Jenson.

"Whoa, I wonder what it could be?" asked Kate.

"Who knows?" I replied. "I mean, it's a little late now anyway. We aren't even close enough for him to show us what he saw in your memory."

"True, but maybe he could meet us at The Memorizers?" suggested Kate.

I sighed. Thomas was worried about Jenson being involved at all. Could I trust him to keep the people I loved safe? What about the bomb? I knew it got us out of Memory Lane alive, but what if someone had been hurt?

"I don't know if that's a good idea," I said apprehensively.

"You don't think they will take him in? I thought The Memorizers were trying to grow their numbers and fight Memory Lane?"

"It's just that I don't need everyone and their Mom to know where we went. Truthfully you should be worried about that too, with your Dad looking for you and my family."

"That's not fair!" Kate shouted. The tension in the car was thick and the weight of the last twenty-four hours seemed to press down on all of us. Kate had never yelled at me like that before. Not even in our most heated fights. After all we were doing trying to get her safely away from her Dad!

Mom turned around to face us from the front seat.

"Calm down, this is going to be a long drive and everyone is tired," she said, trying to settle us down.

"I didn't say it was fair," I said. "Is anything fair about running from your Dad so that he doesn't murder us all?"

Kate gasped. "Are you serious?!"

"Isn't that exactly what we are doing right now? Just calling it like I see it."

"Hannah! That is uncalled for," Mom said. She looked at Kate. "I'm so sorry, Kate. Memory Lane has taken a lot from Hannah. I know you understand that more than anyone else could."

I scoffed. "I meant every word. Who created Memory Lane, hmm? It was Kate's Dad."

Dad pulled the car over. He knew we needed some space to work this out and he didn't want that space to cause a car accident.

"You're the one responsible for your family's problems!" Kate shouted. "You broke into Memory Lane. That's illegal. It's no one's fault but your own. If you hadn't done that, Thomas would never have become a fugitive or gotten poisoned. If you didn't have to go to the waterpark for your thirteenth birthday, maybe Leslie would never have been kidnapped!"

Kate might as well have slapped me across the face. I stared, mouth agape. This was my best friend. How dare she tell me everything was my fault? Didn't she know the guilt was already eating me alive? Anger and resentment bubbled inside me and I snapped.

"Get out! I don't want you with us anymore. How dare you say that!"

Hot, angry tears rolled down my face. I shoved at Kate and tried to push her out of the car.

Kate opened the car door and jumped out. In seconds, Mom got out of her seat to go talk to Kate. Leslie just stared at me, trying to hold back tears. How did this escalate so quickly? Everything was fine twenty minutes ago. I couldn't help but blame Jenson. He was the trigger for the fight between me and Kate. How could I fight over something I wasn't sure how I felt about? Jenson saved our lives. I was letting Thomas's doubts override what I had already known. Without Jenson, we may have never made it this far.

"I know you're mad at Jenson, but you have to remember that he did help you get to me. No questions asked. That has to count for something," Leslie pleaded.

"I know he helped me find you and he helped us get Dad out of Memory Lane, but Thomas has a point in that his actions could have gotten people hurt. Mom and Dad included," I explained to Leslie.

"What did he want anyway?" asked Leslie.

"He said he had some information I needed to see about what was in Kate's memory of the day you were taken from the waterpark."

"You mean there might be answers?!" Leslie couldn't contain the curious excitement at learning about the one day she couldn't remember.

"I guess so, but I don't think—"

"You don't think what? I want to know why this happened to me. You don't think I have wondered for years 'why me?'"

"Don't you start being angry at me too," I replied.

Dad turned around to face me and Leslie in the back seat. "We all need to take a few minutes and calm down. Everyone is running on no sleep and emotional fumes."

"I want to know what was in Kate's memory. I deserve to know," Leslie stated calmly.

"I don't think that's a good idea, Les," I said.

"You don't get to make that choice for me, Hannah."

The door opened to the back seat and Kate slid back in the car. I stared at her as Mom got back in the front seat.

"Some things were said. There will be time for apologies later. Let's just focus on finding a car to make it to The Memorizers in one piece. Okay?" Mom asked.

The three of us nodded silently and with that, Dad started the car again and pulled back onto the road. I couldn't even look at Kate. *How could she blame me? Did she really believe that this was all my fault?* How would we ever get back to the friends we were before? Part of me couldn't see how things would ever be the same between me and Kate again.

Chapter 11

One day you wake up and realize that you have made the choices that have led you to exactly where you are. We were fugitives and that meant adding more crimes to our list just to survive. It was time to steal a car.

"If I give you five dollars will you go steal the clerk's car keys from the back?" Dad asked. He was talking to a man loitering outside of a gas station.

"What? Why would I do that?" asked the man. He was unshaven, his clothes were dirty, and he looked to be homeless.

"Because five dollars is five dollars," Dad replied.

The old man seemed to consider Dad's offer. I looked on from inside of the car with the window rolled down. We had scoped out the place and it seemed that there was a possibility of taking the owner's car which was parked in the back. If we could get the keys, it wouldn't be that big of a deal. I couldn't believe that was a justified explanation for stealing a car, but I knew the past couldn't be changed.

The plan was to get the keys, take the clerk's car, and then have Mom drive our car a little ways down the road so we could leave it stranded and hidden.

The man was arguing with Dad. "What are you gonna do with the keys?" he asked. "I should get more than five dollars for helping you steal a car!"

"Keep your voice down," Dad said to the man. "I don't have a lot of cash. What if I buy you some food?"

The man seemed to think about what my Dad was offering him. "I want beer too," he said.

Dad smiled and nodded his head. "We have a deal," he said, while shaking the man's hand.

Dad came back over toward the car and told all of us to get out so that the store was more crowded. If we could get a bunch of us in the store with the homeless man, it wouldn't be as suspicious when the clerk's keys were stolen.

I opened my car door and Mom did the same. Leslie and I climbed out from one side while Kate got out the other side of the back seat.

"Remember to act casual. Just pick out snacks and then head toward the front so I can pay for it," Dad said.

I nodded and walked into the store with Leslie in tow. She was my shadow again. For a moment my mind blinked back to a time when she was little, and I was annoyed at her mere presence. I chided myself inwardly for being so selfish then. I hated that she wanted to be with me all the time. Now, I had to admit that I didn't find it annoying anymore. Perhaps it was losing her and spending four years living in the land of regret at how I didn't appreciate her the way she deserved. Having her alive and with us again was a gift, and one that I wasn't giving up. Keeping her close now meant that I knew where she was at all times. It was a small comfort and I was hanging onto it for dear life.

We headed for the chips and candy while Mom went to the refrigerated drinks. I was vaguely aware of Kate in the store somewhere, but I was trying not to pay attention to her so I wouldn't get mad all over again.

"Here, take these," I told Leslie while handing her a bag of chips. They were multigrain and not my favorite, but it was better than nothing. Finding 'good' junk food was almost impossible these days. Leslie nodded and took the chips while eyeing the chocolate candy. Mom came up behind me and Leslie and looked at what we were getting. She nodded in approval and added some sour candy to our stash.

Her eyes kept darting over to where the homeless man was. I was worried that Mom would draw attention to what was happening with the owner's car keys by glancing repeatedly in that direction.

"Relax, Mom. It will be fine," I told her.

Dad nodded in our direction, signaling that we needed to head to the front to pay for our stuff. I noticed that the old man was heading over toward the back room marked "Authorized Personnel Only" but I quickly focused on the task at hand. Leslie, Mom, and I headed over to the front counter where the clerk was busy on his phone. We placed our snack items on the counter while Mom added the cold drinks to our purchase. Dad put the beer on the counter and the clerk barely batted an eye. He acted like we were bothering him with our purchases.

"Can we also get twenty dollars on pump three?" Dad asked, while taking out his wallet.

The clerk sighed and then got up to ring up our items. The old man came back from his mission to get the clerk's car keys and briefly nodded to signal that he was done. He went over to the beef jerky and grabbed a pack so that he wouldn't be suspiciously just hanging around inside the store.

"That will be thirty-three forty-five," said the clerk. "The pump's ready for you."

"Can we get a bag?" Mom asked.

The clerk sighed heavily and then reached below the counter to grab a bag for all of our snacks. He threw them in and then handed them to Mom as Dad passed the cash over. The clerk made the change and handed it to Dad while the rest of us left the store. Dad grabbed the beer and then followed us outside. I got in the car and watched as the old man paid for his jerky and then came back out of the store. Dad met him off to the side.

"Did you get the keys?" Dad asked.

The man nodded. "Did you get my beer?"

Dad handed him the beer and then held out his hand for the keys. As the exchange was made, I couldn't help but think that was too easy.

"Hey!" yelled the store clerk. Dad and the man both looked in the direction of the clerk. He had come outside. This was it. I held my breath, waiting for the other shoe to drop and for us to be arrested.

"There's no loitering here! Leave the premises now," shouted the clerk.

"Okay, we're going," Dad said, holding back a sigh of relief.

Our homeless accomplice nodded and he and Dad parted ways. Seeing that the "crowd" was dissipating, the clerk went back inside.

Dad came back over to the car and asked if we were ready to finish what we started.

"You mean are we ready to break the law some more?" I asked.

Leslie chuckled. "At least our lives aren't boring."

"Touché," I replied.

Mom slid into the driver's seat of our car while Dad walked toward the back of the store where the clerk's car was. We pulled out of the gas station parking lot and drove away. I hoped Dad was able to steal the car okay and that nothing bad happened to him on the way to meet us.

"How far are we gonna drive?" Leslie asked, leaning into the front seat.

"Until I feel like we got away with stealing the car," replied Mom.

"Is that Dad behind us?" I asked. I had turned around to check and see if he made a clean exit from the back of the gas station.

"Looks like it," Mom said, glancing in the rearview mirror.

I breathed a huge sigh of relief.

Fear and stress were at a high point so we kept driving in silence for about another ten or fifteen minutes. Kate was looking out the window in the back seat, facing away from me. With everything going on, the last thing I needed was to fight with my best friend. When we left the motel, it was a relief to have her with us. We could keep her safe and I could have her beside me for this strange adventure. Instead, I was grateful that she was looking away because I didn't know what I would say to her if we even had the chance to talk.

Mom pulled the car over at a rest area along the highway. It was time to ditch our trusty family car and put as much distance as we could between us and Memory Lane. This was the perfect location. People wouldn't question a parked car at a rest area for a good long while. Sure, it would let Memory Lane know that we drove through this way, but it would be days before our vehicle was reported found. Dad pulled into a spot near us and we all got out of the car and grabbed our bags from the trunk. There were two other cars parked in the area that we were in, but there were no people in them. The rest stop looked abandoned and that was just perfect for us. The four of us walked over to where Dad was parked in the clerk's car, threw our bags in the trunk, and got inside.

The car was smaller than ours, so the backseat was cramped. It was not really made for five people, but it was better than walking all the way to The Memorizers. Leslie squeezed in between Kate and me to act as a buffer. Mom turned around to face all of us in the backseat.

"Everyone settled?" she asked.

We silently nodded and Dad pulled us out of the rest stop and back onto the highway.

"That was almost too easy," said Leslie.

"We need to put as much mileage in between us and that clerk as possible," Dad said.

****

There is no telling when I fell asleep. We had been awake for a solid twenty-four hours and during the drive I had passed out. We must have been driving for several hours before I was shaken awake by

Leslie. We weren't driving anymore, and I wondered how long we had been parked.

"Hannah, something is wrong with Mom," she said with panic in her voice.

"Wait, what? What's wrong?" I asked sleepily. Sitting up, I tried to shake off the sleep. "What happened, Les?" I looked around the car and realized that Les and I were the only ones in it. *Where did Mom and Dad go?*

"She started freaking out about me being here. She forgot me again." Anguish threatened to push Leslie into a full-blown panic attack and I couldn't let that happen. "She started yelling at us about Kate being in the car, then she shouted that someone was trying to trick her or that she was drugged or something. Hannah, I don't know what to do anymore."

"Slow down, Les. Where is she now?"

"She ran off down the road. Dad went after her."

"Where's Kate?" I asked.

"Standing outside the car. She keeps pacing. It's strange, but she looks guilty. Like she knows something. I don't know, maybe I am just being paranoid," grumbled Leslie.

Wow, how could I have slept through all of that!

Pushing the car door open, we got out and went around to the front of the car where Kate was standing. "Which way did my parents go?" I asked her. What Leslie said before rang in my ears. *She looks guilty.* I shook it off. We had more pressing things to get through right now.

She pointed in the general direction in which they'd gone and Leslie and I took off walking that way.

"Did Mom seem angry?" I asked Leslie.

Leslie nodded. "A little. Mostly confused."

"It's the memory loss. I wonder why it's affecting her so badly now."

"There's Dad," I said, pointing just up ahead.

We walked faster to meet up with him. "Where's Mom?" I asked.

"She isn't feeling well right now. I didn't want to make it worse, so I gave her some space. She is sitting on a rock up ahead. She just needs a few minutes."

The fear was rising in me and without thinking I shouted, "What does that mean? We can't split up!"

"It means that your mother is very confused right now and I don't want to upset her more. Please take Leslie back to the car and wait there," Dad said, very calmly.

"I don't think that's a good idea, Dad. This is the second big episode of Mom forgetting. Something is wrong. Why is it so sudden and so much time lost? It doesn't happen this way. It is a little bit at a time, not whole chunks of someone's life all at once!" I exclaimed.

Leslie squeezed my hand in solidarity.

"I don't know, but we can figure it out when we get to The Memorizers," Dad replied.

"I think she needs a hospital, Dad. This is serious."

"You don't think I know that!?!" Dad shouted. He sighed and ran his hand through his hair, closing his eyes. In less than twenty-four hours Mom's memory began to fail, my friendship with Kate was on rocky footing, Thomas was gone and I didn't know if he was safe. It was too much. Now we were sitting on the side of the road with a stolen car and I had no idea what might be taken away from us next.

I took a step back with Leslie.

Dad looked remorseful for yelling. He looked so much older than I remembered him. Memory Lane had stolen so much time from us and yet here we were, still battling for the little bit of time we had scraped together.

"I'm sorry, I just got you and Leslie and your Mom back. Now I feel like I am already losing your Mom again. It hurts so much to see your Mom this way. The way I saw so many others when I was working at Memory Lane. Now we are just trying to get away and start a life free from this chaos and nothing is going the way we planned."

To say I could relate to all that Dad said was an understatement. Breaking into Memory Lane, not once but twice, had taken its toll. None of that mattered now, though. We had to keep going. "I know, Dad. The only way we can get through this is to work together so we can all stay together. I already had to say goodbye to Thomas. Please don't make me say goodbye to you or Mom too," I pleaded.

Understanding flashed across Dad's face and he reached out and pulled me and Leslie into a hug. "You grew up on me. You have your Mom's wisdom, that's for sure. Thanks for the pep talk, Hannah. You are right. We have to stay together. Let's go get your Mom," he said as we walked down the road a little bit.

As we approached, I saw Mom sitting on the rock off the side of the road with her knees up against her chest. She looked like she had been crying.

"Mom?" I called, hoping she wouldn't be too scared to answer.

Her head darted up and her eyes widened when she saw Leslie behind me.

"Go away! This is a mean trick!" she yelled. Mom looked so small and frail sitting on the ground. Her eyes were wild as though she was a wild animal that had been cornered by a predator. Every time I thought I couldn't hate Memory Lane more, something always happened. We were finally a family again and now Mom's very memories were being stolen from her.

"Mom, it's me. Hannah. Dad's here too," I said, trying to leave Leslie out of it for a minute. I slowly inched my way toward her, making sure my movements were smooth and calm. If I could just sit next to her, I knew I could comfort her enough for us to keep going. To get her to someone who could help.

"I know who my daughter is, thank you very much," Mom replied, sarcastically. She sounded angry and scared, though she sat up straighter and seemed to want me to come and sit down.

Slowly I closed the gap between us and took a seat next to her on the road while Leslie hung back a little bit.

"Are you okay, Mom? What's going on? Talk to me," I said, trying to keep it light.

"None of this makes any sense," she replied.

I grabbed her hand. "What doesn't make sense?" I asked.

"Everything is all wrong," she mumbled. "Why Leslie is here. Why Kate is here."

"It's okay. Can you tell me what the last thing you remember is?"

Burying her face in her hands, Mom started crying. "I don't even know anymore," she said. *How far gone is she this time? Will we be able to get her back?*

"It's not your fault. It's ALD-87. We can fill you in on what you forgot." I gestured to Leslie to get her to come over to where Mom and I were sitting on the side of the road. Mom looked apprehensive, yet I could see in her eyes a glimmer of hope. "Leslie is here because I rescued her from Memory Lane a little bit ago. She never died four years ago. She was kidnapped by Memory Lane guards."

"It's true, Mom," said Leslie, nodding along.

"But we attended her funeral..."

"I know, but I promise; it was all faked by Memory Lane. We only just found out about this. No one is tricking you now. Leslie is real and she is alive and perfect." I smiled at Leslie.

Leslie chuckled. "I don't know about perfect, but yes. It's me, Mom."

"You're alive?" Mom asked in awe. Tears streamed down her face as she reached forward to touch Leslie's cheek. Once she knew she was real, she pulled Leslie into a hug.

Was this going to happen every few days with Mom and Leslie? Hours? I wasn't sure that we would be safe ever leaving the country if Mom couldn't keep it together long enough. Seeing a small amount of progress made to ease Mom's mind, Dad chimed in.

"I hate to break up this reunion, but we really need to get going."

For a second, I forgot he was there with us. Leslie and I helped Mom stand up and she wiped her tears on her sleeve. She looked a little better and if that was all we could ask for right now, it would have to do. Our broken little family of four walked toward the stolen car. I suppose it was ours now. Kate was leaning against the outside of the car. Her mind looked a million miles away.

"What is Kate doing here?" asked Mom. "And where is our car?"

Oh boy. "Mom, it's fine," I assured her. "She's riding with us to meet with The Memorizers. We borrowed this car so we can get to The Memorizers faster."

The confusion never lifted from Mom's face, and I knew from loved ones we had seen go through this that explaining things over and over could now be our new normal. "You guys are talking? Since when?"

"Since we rescued Leslie. I promise, it's fine. Let's all just get in the car." I couldn't think of anything else to do except keep reassuring Mom that everything was normal and fine, even if it wasn't.

We all got into the car as Dad started driving toward our destination again. Mom still looked uneasy around Kate but seemed to be dealing with Leslie's revelation better.

"What if The Memorizers don't take us in?" asked Leslie.

"Why wouldn't they? They know me and Dad."

"Yeah, but there are five of us now. We might draw too much attention this way."

"I think it will be fine. They are pretty accommodating. Besides, they need us. I feel like they are building resistance against Memory Lane. The more people on The Memorizers' side, the better," I said.

"I guess you're right," replied Leslie.

"I won't let anything happen to you," I reassured her. Leslie held out her pinky and knowing what she needed, I looped my pinky around hers. "Promise?" she asked.

Leaning forward, I set my forehead on hers and squeezed her pinky with mine. "Promise."

She smiled back at me and then nudged me to look at Kate sitting with us in the back seat.

What? I asked with my eyes.

Leslie mouthed, "Talk to her."

I rolled my eyes. Kate could talk to me just as easily as I could talk to her. This friendship, or whatever you wanted to call it, was a two-way street.

Leslie nudged me again. She clearly felt strongly about my relationship with Kate, but she also wasn't here for four years. She didn't understand how broken we had become. How we barely managed to become friends again and now we were just as fractured as before. Leslie didn't live through all the hurt and pain of losing a sister and a best friend at the same time.

Sighing, I decided to appease Leslie and start off the conversation with some small talk.

"So, is anybody hungry? Want to stop and get food?" I asked everyone in the car.

Leslie rolled her eyes. She and I both knew that is not what she meant for me to ask.

"Not really," Mom replied.

"I'm fine," Dad said.

"Nope," muttered Kate.

So much for small talk.

"Well, then how about we listen to some music?" I suggested.

My suggestion seemed to stick and Mom turned on the radio and hunted for a song. She settled on some pop song and left it there for all of us to listen to. When your world feels like it is falling apart, pop music is a bit too much. Though it may have been too upbeat for the tension in the car, we all would have to admit it was better than silence.

Dad changed the station after the song ended to music that was a little bit older, and I immediately recognized War Machine. Kate and I used to love them. Kate's head perked up when she heard the song.

"Dad, turn it up!" I said, excited.

Kate and I both sang along to the War Machine song that was on the radio. It was just like old times. For a few minutes, it felt like four years ago when things were right in my world. I had Kate and Leslie by my side and my favorite singer on the radio. Kate and I were both laughing, and my parents looked at us from the front seat like we were crazy.

As the song ended, I settled back down in my seat. Kate glanced over at me and for a moment, I felt like she wanted to say something. The moment passed as we continued to drive down the road, inching ever closer to The Memorizers and farther away from Kate's Dad.

Chapter 12

"Are we there yet?" Leslie moaned. I couldn't blame her. It felt like we had been driving forever. When you are a fugitive and driving a stolen car, time just seems to slow down. You would think running away from everything would be faster.

The sun was setting outside of my window. I had taken a few naps already, bored as I was, but I felt ready to drift off again as the sun dipped below the horizon, a deep blue following closely behind. Hundreds of stars were peeking through the night sky, revealing just how far away we had gotten from the city. I glanced at Leslie, trying to remember if she had ever gotten to see a sky full of stars, but she was still pouting toward Dad.

Old advertising billboards revealed peeling posters that had long been abandoned, and I could see a few derelict buildings to my right. As we passed these empty businesses with their boarded-up windows and faded paint, something familiar began to come into view. Inconspicuous to someone just driving by was a dilapidated, wooden fireworks stand. *We had finally made it.* "Pull in here, Dad."

"Here?" Dad looked unimpressed, seeming to doubt the abilities of this organization.

"The Memorizers are underneath a fireworks stand?" Mom asked, unconvinced.

"Yes, just let us handle this." I motioned for Dad to park the car near the front of the fireworks stand.

He pulled the car into the dirt parking lot and got out. I followed suit and we walked up to the counter as if we were there to purchase fireworks for some grand family vacation.

"Can I help you?" The guard's "uniform" wasn't much, but his languid demeanor suited his current role as fireworks attendant. We would see how quickly that changed when he knew why we were here.

"We are here to see Antoine," Dad responded.

Instantly the guard's tone changed to one with authority and his gaze turned steely. "And who are you?" The guard looked past Dad and me to the car and then his eyes landed back on my Dad, uninterested.

"Robert Healy."

The guard's eyes went wide as he straightened his back. "Is Antoine expecting you?" he asked carefully.

"Don't think so. Suffice to say we do need a safe place to stay." Dad forced a smile at the guard, hoping that he would let us through.

"Sir, I've been here before. My name is Hannah Healy. I came with Brad last time and I spoke with Antoine. He knows me." You could see understanding flash across the guard's face as he realized the level of importance that stood before him. No doubt he had seen the news about Dad being broken out of Memory Lane.

The guard nodded, reaching for his walkie-talkie. "This is Gaines. Transfer me to Antoine. This is a level three communication alert." There was some static and a pause, then some more static. "Yes, Hannah Healy and her Dad Robert are here to see you, sir. The whole family is. How would you like me to proceed? Over."

There was silence as we listened to see what Antoine or whoever the guard called decided to do about us. Leslie had climbed out of the car and grabbed my hand. Her palms were sweaty, and I could tell she was on edge. No doubt as nervous as the rest of us.

There was static on the walkie-talkie and the guard nodded along. "Over, sir." Leslie smiled at the response, appearing to understand what the garbled noise meant.

"I will need to check you all for weapons, but once that is clear you guys are going straight to meet Antoine," said the guard.

Dad motioned for everyone else to get out of the car and grab their bags. The guard searched each bag thoroughly and patted each one of us down to make sure we weren't hiding anything. Once we were cleared, he pointed to the door at the back of the fireworks stand. "You remember where to go?" he asked.

Kate and I both nodded.

"Head inside and open up the trap door. Once you get to the bottom of the stairs, follow the hallway and there will be another guard stationed at the underground entrance. He'll take you to Antoine. I wish you all the best of luck." The guard dipped his head in a respectful nod, stepping aside to let us through.

Dad took the lead and we followed. He opened up the trap door and held it open for everyone to walk through. Everyone walked through first and as I was walking through, Leslie's hand still firmly tucked in my grasp, she paused and jerked me to a stop.

"What's wrong?" I asked her.

"I have a bad feeling." She shuddered, letting go of my hand to grip her arms. Her face held fear that I hadn't seen since the day we rescued her from Memory Lane. She would not move any closer.

"Why?"

"I can't explain it." She tried to shake it off. "It's probably nothing; don't mind me." She tried to walk forward again, but I stopped her.

"Mom," I called to get her attention. "Wait."

"What's wrong, Hannah?" she asked, popping her head back through the trap door to look at me and Leslie.

"Leslie doesn't want to go in."

"What? Why? We aren't leaving her alone!" Mom looked at Leslie with worry, even though she still seemed unsure about her youngest daughter.

"I know, I wasn't suggesting that. Why don't you guys go on ahead with Kate? She knows where to go. We will catch up. Let me talk to Les," I suggested.

Mom, still overwhelmed by her memory struggles and the pure exhaustion of forty-eight hours with very little sleep, held no fight. "Okay, but don't take too long. We will see you inside," she said.

Leslie and I watched as they walked down the stairs. For a moment, I heard Thomas's words ringing in my ears. I was standing in the park, planning to meet with Kate after her dead silence for four years. "Hannah, I hope this is all worth it," Thomas had said. I looked down at Leslie and knew that I would do everything all over again to be standing here with her. *It has to be, Thomas,* I thought. I wished he could have been here, beside me for all of this. Just like before. Instead, I would have to be the strong and brave one, especially for Leslie.

I set the trap door closed and sat down on one of the benches meant for stocking fireworks. Pulling Leslie down next to me, I kept both of her hands in mine. "Okay, tell me what's really wrong," I said.

"The last time you and Thomas were here with Kate, Thomas got poisoned. How do we know who we can trust?"

"I really don't think Kate would have poisoned him and then spent all this time with us," I said.

Leslie raised her eyebrow at me. "You're defending Kate?" she asked.

"I can be annoyed with her on a different level and still feel in my gut that she didn't harm Thomas."

"Well, someone here did," Leslie pointed out.

"Are you worried that it would happen to you?" I asked. Staring down into her fear-filled eyes, I had to remind myself that no matter what she had been through, she was still just a little girl.

Leslie nodded sheepishly. "Or to you, or Mom and Dad. I just made it back to you guys. I don't want anything to happen to y'all."

I squeezed her hands. "We know to stick together this time. Besides, we might not be here very long," I replied.

"I also think Gideon is tracking Kate another way than her cell phone," Leslie admitted to me.

"What? How?"

"I don't know. He could certainly afford the technology to implant a chip in her or something. Kate could be leading him right to us. You wouldn't believe all the crazy technology we saw over the years of being at Memory Lane. He already had his wife killed. I doubt he would think twice about killing you. Or me."

"We can protect you," I explained.

Leslie shook her head in mild defiance. "You can't know that. Not for sure."

"I'll die trying," I said.

Leslie started sobbing. I pulled her into a hug and tried to soothe her. *How much pain would my family have to endure before Memory Lane would leave us alone?!?*

"That's what I'm afraid of!" Leslie shouted. "Do you have any idea what it's like to be told over and over that your family is dead and that you meant nothing to them?"

I brushed her hair from her tear-stained face. "No, I don't. But I do know what it's like to believe that your sister is dead for four years. That wasn't a picnic either. What Memory Lane did to you or any of those kids was not okay. I spent too long believing you were dead, and I won't let anyone take you away from me. Ever again. I love you, Les."

She wrapped her arms around my neck and hugged me and all at once I was standing in front of the apartments where we had found her. Leslie sniffled. "Thank you, Hannah." She smiled at me for a brief second.

"Ready to go inside?" I asked, holding out my hand.

Leslie nodded. She grabbed my hand as we slowly walked over to where the trap door was behind the fireworks stand counter. We descended the steps into the darkness, and I let my eyes adjust to the low lighting underground. A few hundred yards later, I saw my parents and Kate waiting for Leslie and me. We caught up to them and all walked toward Antoine's room with the guard showing us the way.

Leslie was quiet as she took in the sights around her. I remember being in awe of the size of this place. I couldn't believe that The Memorizers had such an organized system. As we passed the dining area, Leslie scooted closer to me. There were people eating and others playing cards at the table. A wave of sadness came over me when I thought about how Leslie had become scared and distrustful of people. She was never that way before she was taken by Memory Lane.

A few minutes later, all of us arrived at Antoine's dwelling—his word for his room, not mine—and waited as the guard knocked on the door.

"The Healys are here, sir," said the guard.

The door opened and I made eye contact with Antoine. "Hannah," he said. "It's good to see you back here." He smiled at me. "How's Thomas?"

That sent off all kinds of red flags to me. Why did Antoine care how Thomas was if he wasn't the one who poisoned him?

Antoine scanned all of us and paused when he saw Dad. "Robert!" he exclaimed while shaking his hand. "Come in, come in. Have a seat."

I saw the bean bag chairs and glanced at Leslie and Kate to see if they were going to sit in them. Neither of them made a motion to sit down. Mom looked uneasy about it as well. We had important things to discuss and I felt like the bean bag chair was a little too casual for what was going on with my family right now.

"Would any of you like some tea? It's hot," said Antoine.

All of us shook our heads.

The guard was awkwardly standing near the door and looked anxious to leave.

"You may go," said Antoine to the guard.

As soon as he left the room and the door was closed, Dad started talking. "Is my family safe here?" he asked Antoine.

Antoine smiled and sipped his tea. "Of course."

I wasn't so convinced.

"Do you have room for all of us here?" Mom asked. "We don't want to split up."

Antoine nodded yes.

Dad leaned against Antoine's desk where he was drinking tea. "Gideon Wesley is after Kate and us by extension. Can you protect us?"

"Why is he after her?" asked Antoine.

"You guys don't get the news down here?" I asked.

"We do, but it's usually on a delay," replied Antoine.

"Pretty sure my Dad had Mom killed," said Kate matter-of-factly.

There was silence in the room except for Antoine sipping his tea. It was starting to make me mad. Didn't the man have emotions?

Kate looked annoyed as well. "So can you protect us from my Dad or what?"

"That shouldn't be a problem," replied Antoine.

"Does he know about this place?" asked my Dad.

"I don't think so. Only people directly involved with the resistance against Memory Lane know. Unless we have a leak, of course," said Antoine nonchalantly.

"A leak? You don't trust your own people?" I asked.

Antoine's eyes narrowed. "I can't know everything."

"There is no system? People just come and go as they please?" Mom asked. "That sounds dangerous."

"That system is what let your family in here," pointed out Antoine.

"Can we all stay together?" Leslie asked in a quiet voice.

I turned to look at her to assure her that at the very least I would bunk with her.

"Sure. Pick whatever sector you like," said Antoine.

"I thought we needed to start out in the red sector since that's the lowest?" Kate asked. "That's what you made me do last time."

Antoine put down his tea and folded his hands. "I think Robert and Hannah and, dare I say it, Leslie deserve better than the red sector, my dear."

Mom looked upset. "What does that mean?"

"It means your daughters and husband are special," Antoine replied.

"We are not splitting up!" Mom shouted.

Antoine remained calm. I swear he was on drugs. Nothing ever seemed to faze him. "I didn't suggest that your family split up. I am merely recognizing the importance of memory retainment that seems to be abundant in their genes."

There was an awkward silence as we all looked at each other. I knew from the last time we stayed with The Memorizers that Antoine knew about my memory retainment as well as Dad's. But I didn't think he knew about Leslie's abilities as well. *Just how much did Antoine know? Could he be trusted with that information?*

"Thank you for your kindness," Dad said.

Antoine waved him off like it was no big deal. "We can discuss jobs tomorrow. Let's meet back here at 9:00 am," said Antoine.

We all agreed and then left the room together.

"What sector do we want?" I asked as we walked down the hall away from Antoine's dwelling.

"I think we should stick with a mid-level sector, so we don't call attention to ourselves," Kate said.

"How are we going to make this work anyway?" asked Leslie. "There's an odd number of us."

"Your Dad and I will be in one room and then you girls can share another," suggested Mom. "Let's hope that they have two rooms near each other."

"Which color sector are we going to? I want to lie down," said Leslie.

"I think yellow is just fine," I replied.

We all headed off in the direction of the main atrium where food was served for meals and looked around at the entrances to the different sectors. The setup of The Memorizers came back to me as I got my bearings. The entire underground compound was several floors deep and it was set up like a giant bicycle wheel. While I wasn't sure what may have been located on the other floors, this one was set up so that the spokes of the wheel were each a hallway. Each hallway was a different color.

I spotted the yellow sign and led the way through that hallway. There were definitely rooms available but there were none next to each other. The best we could find were two rooms that were diagonally across from each other and about four doors apart.

We passed a few people in the hallway as we searched for rooms. They stared at us and for a moment I was nervous that we had been spotted by someone who recognized my face as a fugitive of Memory Lane. I had been running for so long, no doubt I wouldn't be hard to recognize. Then I remembered that these people should, in theory, be on the same side as us. Leslie nudged me to get my attention. "Come on, Hannah. Our room is over here," she said while leading the way. Kate and I followed her into the room and noticed right away that this room was bigger than the one that Thomas and I stayed in before. This room had a sitting area with an overstuffed couch and matching footstool and another one of the famous bean bag chairs that Antoine seemed to be known for. Across from that was a dual desk set up with pens and a table lamp. At the far end of the room were two sets of bunk beds with pillows and blankets. Gone was the musty odor of the motels we had stayed in on our way here; instead it was warm, dry, and clean. There was also a bookshelf and it made me chuckle when I noticed that a lot of the books were older, just like I complained about last time.

"You can have the top bunk if you want," I told Leslie.

She smiled at me and climbed the ladder immediately to get onto the bed. "This isn't bad," she said while bouncing a little to test the mattress." Pulling the blankets back, Les climbed under the sheets and relaxed.

"Good, because it's about as safe as it's gonna get for a while," I replied.

Kate walked over to the other set of bunk beds and sat on the bottom bunk. There was still a hint of annoyance when I thought about the things she said to me earlier in the car, but I was feeling a little better, considering.

"What are you thinking?" I asked her, trying to make conversation. If we had to share a room, might as well break the ice again.

"Just thinking about how surreal and crazy our lives are," she replied.

"Lucky us," I said dryly.

"Have you contacted Gill?" she asked.

"Not yet. We probably should since we are here now," I replied.

"Are you sure you completely trust her?" asked Kate.

I glared at her. She was one to be talking about trust right now. "I mean, I think she can help. That has to be good enough."

I pulled out my phone and texted the last number I had for Gill, letting her know that I was back.

I looked back over at the bunk bed that was mine and Leslie's and noticed she was out like a light. She had been through so much and it felt like we had done nothing but run since I brought her home. Now, she was sleeping peacefully. She must be exhausted.

My phone buzzed. Gill had sent me a return message. She wanted to meet in the recreation area.

I looked over at the bed where Leslie was sleeping and tried to decide what to do about meeting Gill. On the one hand, Leslie was asleep and she probably wouldn't even notice that I was gone. On the other hand, if she woke up and I was missing from the room, she would freak. I didn't want to do that to her. I contemplated waking her up, but I knew she needed the rest.

"Would you mind staying here with Les while I go talk to Gill?" I asked Kate.

"Sure. No problem. I'll tell her you will be right back if she wakes up."

"Thanks."

I left the room and went in search of the recreation area. I made my way through the yellow sector's hallway and out into the main food area. It was loud and busy with people lining up for a meal. My stomach growled but I ignored it and kept walking away until I saw the sign for the recreation area. As I entered, Gill was sitting on the couch.

She jumped up when she saw me. "Hannah! I'm so glad to see you! Where are Thomas and Kate?" she asked.

"Kate is in the room and Thomas isn't here. His Mom forbade him to come," I replied.

"Is he at least alive?" asked Gill.

I forgot that we never filled her in on what happened after I left with Thomas. "Yes, he's fine. The arsenic had no lasting effects after he woke from his coma."

Gill looked confused. "Arsenic?"

Her reaction was actually telling me quite a bit about who might have poisoned Thomas. Gill wasn't a suspect at the top of my list anymore.

"Yeah, I know it's weird. But that's what the doctor said was in his system. It was scary for a while, but he pulled through. I think that's why my aunt didn't want him to come back here. She's scared that he might be in danger."

"And I thought my life was nuts," said Gill.

"Tell me about it," I replied.

"So why is Kate in the room?"

"She's with my sister."

"You have a sister?" asked Gill.

Man, we really didn't get a chance to tell Gill anything before Thomas was poisoned. *How could I sum up the story of Leslie without sounding like I was making it up or crazy?*

"Yes, I have a sister. It's complicated. Let's leave it at that," I said.

151

"Your relationship is complicated?"

"Not really what I meant," I replied.

Gill seemed to move on. "Fair enough." She sat back down on the couch. "So, what brought you and Kate back to The Memorizers?" she asked, making conversation.

I took a seat on the couch next to Gill and looked around to make sure that no one else was in earshot. "Kate's Mom died. We think her Dad hired someone to have her killed."

"What?!" Gill looked shocked.

"Yeah, and did I mention that Kate's Dad is Gideon Wesley?"

"No way. You think he is capable of murdering his own wife?"

"At this point, I'm not ruling anything out," I replied.

"How's Kate handling this?"

I sighed heavily. "She's scared and sad and angry and every other emotion you can imagine. I feel bad for her. Your parents are supposed to be the people that you can count on the most in life. I guess it's not true for everyone," I said.

"It's not. And Kate needs you right now. With her Mom dead and her Dad…" Gill trailed off.

"I know. But I also need to make sure that my family is safe. Gideon is after us too."

"Understandable," said Gill. "Are you joining The Memorizers or just hiding out?"

"Not sure yet. I need to talk to my parents and see what they want to do. The original plan was to leave the country and go to Canada but we think Gideon could find Kate there."

Gill hesitated for a minute. "I hate to say this, I really do, but I think Kate's Dad will find her no matter where she goes. Are you sure he would hurt her? Wife and daughter are two very different things."

"I don't think Kate wants to stick around with him to find out."

"Fair point," said Gill.

Behind me, I heard the door to the recreation center open and Leslie screaming my name. "Hannah!"

I whipped my head around just in time to be plowed into by Leslie. She was frantic and crying. "It's okay, Les. I'm here. You're safe," I reassured her.

In the next moment, Kate hurried into the room. As I hugged Les close while she sobbed into my shoulder, I looked over at Kate. "What happened?" I asked.

"She woke up and started screaming about you being dead. I think she had a nightmare."

I nodded and continued to console Leslie. *Would our lives ever be peaceful again?*

Chapter 13

Dinner was quiet as we all gathered to eat. Leslie had calmed down from her nightmare, but she wouldn't leave my side. I watched as she picked at her food. I know it wasn't the tastiest, but it was better than the gas station food we had been eating as of late. "You need to eat, Les," I said nudging her shoulder.

"I'm not hungry," she replied.

"Just take a few bites then," I suggested.

Leslie kept her eyes on her plate, pushing the food from one side to the other. I knew Leslie was still scared and worried. I was too.

"How long are we staying here, Mom?" I asked.

"Not sure yet. We'll have to see what happens in the next few days," she said.

I looked over to Gill. "How delayed is the news here?"

"A day or two usually. Why?" she asked.

"I was just wondering if there was any word on Kate's Dad or if he reported her missing."

"We can check the internet if you want. I think I have some saved up time," Gill replied.

"That would be great. Thanks," I said.

Kate was sitting across from me and I saw her put her fork down for a second. "What if I don't want to know?" she asked in a small voice.

"You don't want to know if your Dad is looking for you?"

"I would rather just pretend he didn't exist," she said. Her face was downcast, and she looked so small and lost in that moment. Despite everything my family had been through, I still couldn't wrap my mind around being hunted by my own Dad while still grieving the loss of my Mom. Scared if I was found and worse, missing them despite the pain and fear. I couldn't imagine feeling that way about one of my parents. Sure, they were annoying at times, but I knew they still loved me and wanted the best for me.

"Okay, we don't have to look," I told Kate.

Despite my reassurance to Kate, I made a mental note to tell Gill later that I still wanted to look up where Gideon Wesley was and what he was doing regarding Kate. My family was involved in this too, and I didn't want to be surprised later down the road.

My phone buzzed in my pocket, and I looked to see a message from Jenson flash across the screen. Honestly, I was surprised I could receive a message in this bunker in the first place. I knew he was desperate to talk to me about what he saw in Kate's memory and I needed to know what happened the day that Leslie drowned. With her by my side, putting together what happened that day almost seemed harder.

"Who's that?" asked Kate since she saw me looking at my phone.

"Jenson," I replied.

"Are you going to answer him?"

"Maybe later," I said dismissively.

"So, what job did you have last time you were here?" asked Mom.

Pausing to finish the bite I was chewing, I put down my fork. "I helped serve food. It was pretty easy."

"I wonder other jobs they have. Maybe adults have different jobs," said Mom.

"I'm sure there are other things they need done around here," said Dad. "We'll figure it out."

"What's the real plan though?" I asked. "We can't stay here forever."

"Why not? It's safer than our house," Mom asked.

"I'm just worried that we will eventually be asked to officially join the resistance. Are we ready for that?"

Leslie spoke for the first time in a while. "I know I am." Her voice held a resolve that was reserved for those who have lost everything. She had plenty of reasons to want to see Memory Lane destroyed. Four years stolen from her, from all of us. I knew she had a real reason to be upset and want to fight back. I suppose we all did.

"Do all of you feel that way?" I asked. "What about our plan to leave the country? I don't know if I want to hide forever or be fighting for my life over and over."

"Maybe we should ask Antoine about joining officially when we ask about a job tomorrow," suggested Kate.

"That's not a bad idea," Mom pointed out.

Dad caught my eye and looked at me apologetically. He could tell that I wasn't completely on board with us fighting with The Memorizers just yet.

"Let's give it a few days and then we'll vote on it. All of us. As a family," said Dad.

"That works," I said, feeling a little bit better.

Truthfully, I was sad that Thomas wasn't here to join us as a part of my family. He had sacrificed a lot to come with me and protect me from Memory Lane. He didn't have to do any of that. I felt like we owed it to him to at least protect him and his parents now. It was my fault that he was involved in all of this and it was killing me that he had to deal with the consequences on his own.

"Can I go back to the room?" asked Leslie.

She hadn't really eaten, and she looked beyond tired. It had been a long day for her, and the nightmare earlier didn't help.

Mom looked at Leslie. I could see her studying the exhaustion on her face.

"Of course, try to get some rest." Standing up, Mom gave Leslie a hug and kissed her forehead.

"Yeah, I'll go to the room with you. Give me one sec," I said.

Snagging the last few bites of my dinner, I stood up to walk Leslie back to our room. "See you guys in the morning in Antoine's room for our job meeting," I said.

Leslie and I walked out of the atrium and into the yellow sector until we arrived at the room.

"You okay?" I asked.

She shook her head no, and plopped herself on the bottom bunk. "Hannah, I think I remembered something from my nightmare," she mumbled.

"Really, do you want to talk about it? It's okay if you don't." I sat down on the edge of the bed next to her. She looked so tired.

"I want to. I don't want to feel crazy anymore. Maybe if I tell you, it can help me remember more."

I nodded to her, trying my best not to make her feel pressured. More than anything I had wanted to know what happened to Leslie while she was in Memory Lane. Maybe we could begin to piece things together now.

"There was a set of rooms they kept us all in. We had bunk beds and desks and a small bookshelf in each one. They didn't let us have a lot." Leslie wiped away a stray tear and I pretended not to notice. I waited for her to feel comfortable enough to go on. One day, Memory Lane would pay for what they did to my sister.

"The guards came to get me for testing one day. They would always force us to take this pill to make us tired. I think it was to make it where we struggled less. I hated how it made me feel because they always told me things I knew weren't true. Things like you had died. I didn't want to feel confused, so I figured out how to hide it in my cheek and then spit it out when no one was looking. We started walking down the hallway and I was looking through the windows to see who was there or what might be happening. Right before we got to the testing room, I looked through the last window and it was who I saw that got me into trouble. It was Kate. I yelled her name; I banged on the glass with my hands, and she looked right at me. She saw me, Hannah. It's hard to remember anything after that. I know the guards yanked me away from the window and someone gave me a shot. Why didn't she help me, Hannah? I don't know if we can trust her..."

How do you know if a nightmare is just a nightmare or if it's a memory? You don't. Looking into Leslie's face, I could see the confusion there. If she really saw Kate, why wouldn't Kate have helped Leslie? Instead of adding clarity to Leslie's time away, it added more questions.

"It's okay, Les. We know to be careful who we trust. No matter what, it's you, me, Mom and Dad and of course, Thomas."

"You believe me, don't you, Hannah? It didn't feel like a dream. It felt real."

I reached down and hugged Leslie as hard as I could. "Of course, I believe you, Les. We are going to figure all of this out. Okay?" It was a reassurance that I struggled to give. *Would we figure it all out?* For Leslie, my answer seemed to soothe her and she smiled and laid down on the pillow again. For a moment, she finally looked peaceful.

While Leslie was lying down, I let my mind wander. Was Kate in a room at Memory Lane and saw Leslie and never told me? If she was, why would she let me believe Leslie was dead? Was Leslie just having a nightmare and it wasn't a memory at all? What about the strange text from Jenson? What did he mean? How would Kate feel about Jenson and I knowing what she saw in the memory room? What if it was something bad? Would it change the way I felt about Kate? I hated feeling like I had to decide about a memory that wasn't mine, that was Leslie's dream to begin with. Too many things were happening. I finally had Kate back after losing her the same day I lost Leslie. Regardless of all of it, Kate's Dad was still a dangerous man and I still wanted to know if what Kate saw in the memory room would help us figure out who kidnapped Leslie that day four years ago.

Sometimes it felt like it happened a lifetime ago, and other days it felt like Leslie was taken from us yesterday. Having her back with us helped to stop the overwhelming grief, but there were still moments when I couldn't believe the things we had been through as a family. To get answers, we needed Kate.

Kate walked into the room and I looked up as she entered. I made a silencing motion with my finger over my mouth and pointed toward Leslie so that Kate knew to keep it down.

"Did you talk to Jenson yet?" she whispered.

"Nope. I was actually about to ask you if you were sure about us really looking into your memory. It is private for some people," I said.

"I know, but I did it to help you with Leslie. So whatever I remembered is important," Kate replied.

"Thank you for that. I appreciate it." I smiled at her so she knew that I meant it.

I pulled out my phone from my pocket and texted Jenson back. The phone buzzed a few minutes later due to slow service underground.

JENSON: so does that mean u wanna watch the memory?
ME: yeah i guess
JENSON: r u guys already with the memorizers?
ME: yeah
JENSON: how do we meet?
ME: u come here we can't leave
JENSON: i'll need a few days
ME: ok

I showed Kate all the texts from Jenson on my phone and she nodded in approval.

"So, how are you holding up?" I asked Kate, testing the waters a bit since our huge argument.

"I'm okay, considering."

The elephant in the room grew larger as I checked on Leslie in the bed. She was still asleep. I decided to just come out with it first.

"Do you think your Dad is going to find you and have you killed too?" I whispered.

"It's a possibility. I think my Mom found out about something she shouldn't have known. That's the only thing I can think of. I don't see Dad as the jealous type if she cheated on him. That's more my Mom's thing."

"Do you think she cheated?" I asked.

"I have no idea. I didn't really ask too many questions. I just stayed out of the way. The less I was around, the better."

What a sad existence. I felt bad for the way that Kate's life turned out since the time we stopped being friends.

"Look, Hannah. I really am sorry about what I said earlier. I don't really think Leslie's death was your fault. There's no way any of us could have known what would happen that day at the water park," Kate said.

"Thanks." I gave her a small smile.

The truth was, I had been blaming myself every day for the last four years so Kate didn't say anything that was completely untrue. It was my birthday and we did leave Leslie alone for enough time for her to be taken.

"I'm also sorry for the things I said about your Dad," I offered.

Kate looked down in shame and picked at her nails. "Thanks, but you're mostly right. I'm not really his biggest fan right now."

A heavy silence fell over the room.

"It's still early. Want to go to the rec area and watch TV or something?" asked Kate.

"Nah. I think I'm just going to lie down. I'm pretty tired. You go ahead though."

"Alright. I'll be back later," said Kate, closing the door behind her.

As Kate left the room I went to the bottom bunk and laid down to rest my eyes. The next thing I knew I was shaken awake by Leslie.

"What is it?" I asked, still half asleep.

"There's a man outside our room. He knocked on the door and asked for you," Leslie whispered. She looked scared.

"What? Who?" I asked, sitting up straight. My heart was racing.

"I have no idea," she said.

I checked my phone for the time. It was only 8:32 p.m. I hadn't been asleep that long and it was late, but not too late for someone to visit if it was urgent.

I motioned for Leslie to stay in the bed as I tiptoed quietly to the door.

"Who's there?" I asked.

"It's me, Brad."

I opened the door quickly. Brad looked the same as the last time I saw him here with The Memorizers. He was still wearing a cap and I smiled at the memory.

"Hey, Brad. How are you?" I asked.

"I'm alright. How about you?" he asked.

"Tired. How did you find out I was back?"

He shrugged. "People talk. Where's Thomas?"

My face fell for a second and I winced. "Not here this time."

"Bummer." Brad attempted to come into the room, but I blocked him with my arm across the doorframe. I wasn't comfortable with him around Leslie, and I honestly wasn't sure if he was the one who poisoned Thomas or not.

"Is something wrong?" Brad asked when I blocked his attempt at entering the room.

"It's late. And my sister is here. We can talk tomorrow if you want."

"Message received. I'll see you at breakfast," Brad replied.

I watched as he walked down the hallway and around the corner. I closed the door and turned back to face Leslie on my bed. "Scoot over," I said.

She made room for me on the bed and I got under the covers.

"Who was that?" she asked.

"Someone that helped me and Thomas last time."

"You don't trust him," Leslie said matter-of-factly. I guess she could tell that I wasn't one hundred percent sure about Brad at the moment.

"I don't know who we can trust anymore," I sighed.

"Where's Kate?" she asked, settling in on my pillow and yawning.

"She went to watch TV. She'll be back later, I guess."

I nudged Leslie as she dozed off. "Do you want your own pillow from the top bunk?"

She didn't reply because she was already asleep again. I put my arm around her and settled in for the night. I hoped that my presence could protect her from the nightmares she was prone to lately. It certainly worked when she was little.

A few hours later, I heard Kate come in through the door. I rolled over to see what time it was and made myself comfortable again. Leslie was still sleeping in my bed. At least she wasn't having a nightmare.

"Sorry, I didn't mean to wake you," said Kate as she got ready for bed.

"It's fine. Goodnight," I replied.

"Have you ever thought about what happened to the other kids in the program with Leslie?" asked Kate.

I opened one eye, annoyed that she was trying to carry on a conversation with me when I clearly was trying to remain asleep.

"What?" I whispered, so Leslie wouldn't wake.

"Well, I mean, there were several of them. Maybe even more in other states. We need to get them away from Memory Lane for good."

Now fully invested in what Kate had to say, I sat up and carefully wiggled my way out from underneath Leslie's arm that was across me. I walked over to Kate's bed across the room. "I agree that we need to protect the kids, but how can we do that?" I asked.

"I think The Memorizers could help," said Kate.

"We don't even know if they are actually ready to fight Memory Lane."

"They seem ready to me. I'm ready to be done with them for good."

A sad smile crossed my face as I realized what this meant for Kate. She wanted peace of mind and the whole situation with her Dad to be finished. She wanted closure.

"Look," I began as gently as possible. "I agree that The Memorizers stand for putting an end to Memory Lane. And I'm sure they would be on board with protecting children, but realistically we need more information. We need to talk with Antoine and see what the manpower of The Memorizers really is and how we would logistically make this work."

Kate looked sure of herself. "I don't want to wait. I can't sit around waiting for my Dad to find me while kids are being tortured. They don't deserve that."

I nodded to show Kate that I was listening. "I completely agree. But we can't tackle this on our own. I've tried that multiple times and it hasn't ended well. We need to involve adults that we trust."

"And we trust Antoine?" Kate asked.

I sighed. "For now."

A beat of silence passed. "You need to sleep. We can discuss this further in the morning," I said while yawning.

Kate nodded. "Goodnight."

I walked back over to the bottom bunk and climbed back in, trying not to wake Leslie. She scooted over automatically as I settled under the covers. I smiled to myself as I closed my eyes to go back to sleep. I guess some things never changed.

****

"So you're saying that you have one thousand people willing to fight against Memory Lane?" Dad asked.

We were meeting with Antoine as a family. Leslie and I were occupying the bean bag chairs while Kate sat on a stool to the side of Antoine's desk.

Antoine spoke calmly. "Yes, Robert. About one thousand Memorizers have committed themselves to loyally fight for the cause."

"Do you have weapons? A strategy?" Dad continued.

"We do have weapons if absolutely necessary," stated Antoine.

"What does that mean?" Mom pried. She sounded irritated. "If you seriously think you will beat Memory Lane with sunshine and flowers, you are crazier than I thought."

"Linda!" Dad shouted.

"Well, I am not putting my whole family in danger for some hippie who thinks that the ultimate power is love. That will never work with a company that tortures people and whose founder hired someone to kill his wife."

Kate sucked in a breath.

"Mom, calm down," I said.

Antoine stood up and slammed his hands on his desk. "I will not be talked down to like this!" he shouted.

I had never heard him get mad like that before. Mom wasn't incorrect in what she was saying, but her approach was a little off. She tended to get upset when talking about her family. I loved her for it most of the time.

Always the peacemaker, Dad put up his hands and stepped forward. "Why doesn't everyone just calm down."

"I'm going to get something to drink," Mom asserted as she left the room.

She walked across the room and tried her best not to slam the door as she left. It was easy to understand why she was mad at Antoine. He clearly had a point of view on how to deal with Memory Lane that was on the gentler side which Mom disagreed with. When you put together the atrocities Memory Lane had caused it didn't seem as though a peaceful option was possible. They kidnapped children and ran tests on them to see if they had memory retainment so that they could isolate the gene that caused it and remove it from people. It was all related to money and control. Sickening. They deserved to be shut down and tortured themselves for what they did to Leslie and the other kids. Not to mention what they did to Dad all those years.

"Can I have the same job as before—serving food?" I asked to break the tension in the room and change the subject.

"What?" asked Antoine. He was clearly caught off guard.

"I'm just here to find out about what job I can get. I'll leave the war strategy to the adults," I said.

Dad chuckled and shook his head. I got my sense of humor from him.

"I don't care what you sign up for," said Antoine. "I need a minute alone with your father."

"We'll be outside then," I said while rising from the bean bag chair. It was not a graceful act and took longer than I meant it to. Kate followed suit silently.

Leslie, Kate, and I walked out of Antoine's room/office and waited in the hallway. I could hear raised voices but couldn't really make out what was being said. It sounded like Antoine was madder than Dad. I mean, he was just insulted by Mom so I couldn't blame him. My biggest fear was Antoine saying that my family was no longer welcome here. What other options did we have if The Memorizers wouldn't let us stay?

Chapter 14

"Where did Mom go?" asked Leslie.

It was the perfect excuse to leave. I just couldn't stand in the hallway any longer while Antoine and Dad argued. "Come on, Les. Let's go find somewhere else to be," I said. I grabbed Leslie's hand as we walked out of the blue sector and toward the atrium with Kate in tow.

"I'm not sure. Maybe she's in her room," I suggested. "Do you want to go look?" Leslie made a face that made it clear that was not appealing to her at the moment, so I let it go. A man approached me from behind while I was facing Leslie and tapped me on the shoulder. I flinched before turning around.

"Hey, Hannah."

"Oh Brad! You scared me," I said, grabbing my chest.

"Sorry, I didn't mean to."

"I'm glad you're here anyway," I said, dropping my voice to a whisper. "I wanted to talk to you about the logistics of a revolt against Memory Lane."

Honestly, I still didn't know who I could trust, or if I could trust Brad, for that matter, but I needed to gather intel about weapons available to The Memorizers. Who better to ask than Brad? It seemed like he would know, considering the last time Thomas and I were here,

Brad was delivering a bunch of CLDs to Antoine. He had to know *something*.

"Whoa, those are some big words for an eighteen-year-old girl," said Brad.

Rolling my eyes, I chided, "Don't patronize me. I just need information. Do you want to help or not?"

"I don't know how much help I'll be, but I can tell you what I know. Let's go to my room," said Brad.

I turned to look at Kate and she shrugged. "It can't hurt." I grabbed Leslie's hand and the three of us followed Brad to his room. Leslie seemed wary of Brad and stuck to my side like glue. Once the door was closed to Brad's room, I jumped straight to the point.

"What kind of weapons does Antoine have?" I wasn't here to chat.

Brad looked taken aback for a moment. "Weapons like what?"

"Guns. Heavy artillery. Anything to help fight against Memory Lane."

Brad shook his head. "I'm not in charge of weapons. You need to ask Sergio. He's your guy."

I studied Brad for a moment. *Was he telling the truth?*

I decided to drop all pretense and ask Brad about the CLDs that I saw last time. "So why do The Memorizers have so many CLDs? Who are y'all listening to?" I asked.

"Important people," replied Brad.

Well, that was helpful. I rolled my eyes again.

"Memory Lane?"

Brad stared at me with a look that said he wasn't going to elaborate any further.

"Look," Brad began. "I'm under strict orders not to mention anything about the Covert Listening Devices The Memorizers use. I literally can't tell you or else they will kill me."

"Why would The Memorizers hide the fact that they are listening to Memory Lane? That doesn't make sense. Unless you guys are listening to your own people…" I let my voice trail off as I considered that possibility.

The look in Brad's eyes told me that I was correct. The Memorizers were listening to people in their rooms and throughout the facility. So much for getting away from government overreach.

"Is Antoine listening right now?" I whispered.

Brad nodded yes.

I made a motion with my hands to signal that I wanted pen and paper. Brad looked around in a drawer and found me some. I wrote down my next question while Leslie and Kate looked on.

"What do they do with the recordings of what people say here?" I asked Brad on paper.

He took the pen and wrote his response. "I have no idea."

"Can we fight Memory Lane if The Memorizers don't even trust their own members?" I wrote next.

Brad took the pen again. "Not likely."

"Just great. Now I feel violated," I said aloud while throwing down the pen and paper notepad.

Every conversation I had with my parents, Kate, or Leslie had been recorded without my knowledge. Antoine already knew about the memory retainment Dad, Leslie and I experienced, but I didn't need him to know everything. Some things were just private.

"Hannah, are you okay?" Leslie asked.

"Yeah," I replied. "Just processing all of this."

Kate grabbed the pen and paper and wrote down a question to show to Brad. "Do you have access to the recordings from the CLDs?"

Brad shook his head no.

Kate wrote again. "Do you know how to get it?"

Brad took the pen. "The audio files are stored in Antoine's room. He has them in a safe."

"Code?" Kate wrote.

"I don't know it," Brad responded on the paper.

Kate wrote again. "Who is the closest person to Antoine? Would they know the code for the safe?"

"My best guess is Sergio. He's been here the longest and he's in charge of the weapons," Brad wrote.

"Well, I guess we know who we have to talk to next," I said. "Thanks for your help, Brad."

Kate, Leslie, and I walked out of his room. I began to wonder how much we really knew about The Memorizers and what they stood for. Yes, they hated Memory Lane and wanted to stop their control, but at what cost? *Are The Memorizers just the lesser of two evils?*

I contemplated our predicament while we headed back to our room. "We need to find Mom and Dad and tell them what we know," I whispered to Leslie. She nodded in agreement.

I began to wonder if Gill knew about the CLDs The Memorizers were using to spy on their own people. She was a runner that went on missions, but did she know what supplies she was picking up? Did she know Sergio? I had so many questions that I wanted answers to but knowing that CLDs were in our rooms and throughout the facility, I felt like there wasn't a safe place to talk anymore. Communicating through written messages would suffice for now. I could text Gill without being in the same room as her if there wasn't paper around. We could make this work, we just had to be more careful.

I pushed open the door to our room and sat down on the bottom bunk. Leslie came and sat next to me while Kate took a seat on her bed.

"Well, this morning just got interesting," said Kate.

"Tell me about it," I replied.

I got up to look through the bookshelf in search of paper to write on. We didn't have a notepad in our room like Brad did. I browsed through the books and decided that I didn't mind defacing a book that was so old no one would care that I used the margins to write notes in. I could throw the paper away when we were done. I settled on a copy of *Harry Potter and the Order of the Phoenix* and took it off the shelf. I hated classic literature and Harry Potter was precisely that. I opened it up and was shocked to discover a CLD inside the book. The majority of the pages had been cut out to fit the CLD inside. I motioned to Leslie and Kate so they could come see too.

The three of us stood there in awe as we realized why there were so many rooms with old books in them. It was an easy way to hide a CLD and listen to everything in the room. Most people didn't read anymore so it was not likely to be discovered. There was also a chance that our room happened to have a CLD in a book, and that other rooms had them in other places so people didn't pick up on a pattern.

I dropped the Harry Potter book and walked over to my parents' room to see if I noticed the same thing. Leslie and Kate followed behind me. As we entered, I scanned the room for the bookshelf. I made a beeline straight for it and the three of us started looking through all of the books for a CLD. I had made it through three or four books before I heard Mom's voice behind me.

"What's going on?" she asked.

"Mom! Hold on a second," I replied.

I dropped the book I was currently holding and walked over to Mom to take her hand. She had a confused look on her face but followed me back to my room while I led her. I showed her the Harry Potter book with the CLD inside and she gasped.

"Is that what I think it is?" she asked.

I nodded and closed the book. We walked back over to Mom and Dad's room to find Leslie and Kate still looking through books. They shook their heads indicating that they had not found another CLD. I motioned to Mom that I wanted a pen, and she looked around the room until she found one in the desk drawer.

Grabbing a book I had never heard of off the bookshelf, I wrote down what we knew about the CLDs from Brad and how we found the one in the Harry Potter book in our room.

Mom took the pen and wrote "Where else did you look in here?"

"Just the books so far," I wrote back.

The three of us began moving chairs around to see if we could figure out where the Covert Listening Device was in my parents' room. While we were looking, Dad entered.

"Did we lose something?" he asked.

Mom waved him off and continued looking behind the bed and desk.

"Well, tell me what it is we are looking for. Maybe I can help," Dad said.

Without a word, I walked over to him and held up the book that Mom and I wrote messages inside of so he could read about the CLDs. He had a look of disgust on his face and started looking through places in the room to find the CLD. After several minutes and no luck finding anything, I sat down on one of the chairs. I grabbed the book we were writing in and wrote, "Maybe not every room has one?"

Mom took the pen and wrote back in the book we had already defaced, "No way that's true."

Shrugging, I gave her a look that said I was out of ideas.

I wrote back to her that she should keep looking and that I was going to find Gill and find out what she knew. Mom nodded and Leslie followed me out of the room. Ever since I found Leslie, she had become my shadow again. Despite that big sister complex, I had to admit it felt good to be needed again. As we weaved through the halls of the yellow sector, I pulled out my phone to text Gill and find out where she was. It took a few minutes for her to respond. Leslie and I arrived in the atrium and found an empty table to sit at. Breakfast was over and lunch wasn't going to be served for a little while.

> **ME**: u busy?
> **GILL**: packing for a mission. what's up?
> **ME**: in ur room?
> **GILL**: yea
> **ME**: ok im coming to u
> **GILL**: ok

"Hey Gill," I announced as we reached her room. "Can you look at this for me?" I asked. I wanted to keep my question as innocuous as possible so The Memorizers didn't suspect anything was amiss if they were listening. I had to assume they were listening at all times. I texted Gill what was going on with the CLDs and asked her if she was aware of them being in the rooms.

When the text went through, she gasped and shook her head no immediately. I had to assume that she was telling the truth. Her reaction seemed too genuine to be faked. Gill texted back "where?" and started looking around her room. I pointed to the bookshelf and then explained to her that was where Leslie and I found the Covert Listening Device in our room. We all walked over to the bookshelf and started looking through the books to see if the CLD was placed inside one like it was for us.

After several minutes of looking through the books and not finding anything, we moved to start looking at other places around Gill's room. There was no CLD attached to any chair or behind the desk. Leslie tugged on my hand and pointed to the bed where Gill's suitcase and clothing were spread out. My eyebrow rose in question to Leslie and she indicated that she thought the CLD might be under the mattress.

I nodded in agreement and motioned to Gill to move her belongings and lift the mattress. Leslie and I helped put Gill's suitcase and other clothes on a nearby chair. The three of us lifted the mattress and feasted our eyes on a CLD. I guess this meant that there was probably a CLD in every room here with The Memorizers. I picked up the CLD and went to turn it off so we could have a real conversation without being overheard.

"Wait!" said Gill. She pulled out her phone and texted me.

GILL: don't turn it off or destroy it. if the CLD stops transmitting sound they will think there is something wrong & replace it

ME: good point
GILL: so now what?
ME: we r gonna have to talk in code or text now
GILL: not the worst thing

A sudden thought came to me about the audio recordings that Brad mentioned. I wondered if there was discussion in a room in range of a CLD when Thomas was poisoned. Could I steal the recordings and maybe figure out who was responsible?

ME: do you think antoine has a CLD in his room?
GILL: doubt it
ME: yea, prob true
GILL: well im still gonna pack
ME: ok we'll leave you to it

Leslie and I left Gill's room and headed back to where our parents and Kate were still looking for the CLD in their room. I wondered if they'd had any luck.

"Hey, you doing okay?" I asked Leslie as we walked through the atrium again.

"Yeah, I'm fine."

I didn't really believe her but I also didn't want to pressure her into talking right now. This revelation about the CLDs was a little overwhelming. It felt like we couldn't do anything without being overheard. I stopped in the doorway to my parents' room where Kate and Dad were sitting on the bed looking upset.

"Where's Mom?" I asked Dad.

"She went to look into getting some time on the computer," he replied.

"What's wrong?" I asked Kate, while taking a seat next to her.

Kate handed her phone over to me so I could read a text. It was from Gideon Wesley.

DAD: I know where you are. Don't make me come get you.

"How on earth…." I began before showing the phone to Leslie so she could be let in on the news.

Kate wiped away tears and shrugged. She grabbed her phone back and typed a message to me. This was slightly more convenient than writing in old books. The service down here was spotty due to us being underground. Sometimes it took too long to send the message and it wasn't worth the wait when the message was urgent.

> **KATE**: im so sorry hannah. this is all my fault
> **ME**: its not i promise. i blame ur Dad
> **KATE**: we have to leave again because of me
> **ME**: its okay i didn't love this place anyway

Kate chuckled half-heartedly through her tears. "Now what?" she asked aloud. Dad sighed and shook his head. That usually meant he was out of ideas as well.

> **ME**: how did he find u?
> **KATE**: idk hes good i guess
> **ME**: i think he put a tracker in u
> **KATE**: like a chip?
> **ME**: yea
> **KATE**: i wouldnt be shocked
> **ME**: dont worry we'll figure this out

At that moment, Kate's phone died and she set it aside on the bed. I looked for the book that Mom and I were using earlier to communicate with. I found it along with the pen on the chair near the desk. I wrote, "Are you sure your Dad really knows where you are?" Kate shrugged. I made a mental note later to destroy evidence of these book conversations on paper before we left The Memorizers. Whenever that may be.

I wrote again. "Maybe we should get him to actually say where you are to prove it."

Kate took the pen from me and wrote, "I don't think that's a good idea. It might give away my location for real if he is tracking me through this phone."

"Good point," I wrote back.

Leslie took the pen from me and wrote, "did you guys find the CLD in here?"

Kate pointed to a picture frame that was hanging in an odd direction on the wall. I got up to check it out and when I moved the picture out of the way, there was the CLD staring back at me in all its glory. Man. Three out of three rooms that we checked had CLDs in them. There was a high possibility that all of them did. The Memorizers had invaded everyone's privacy without their knowledge. I wasn't sure that was any better than what Memory Lane did to people.

My head was spinning with all of this information. I grabbed the pen from Leslie and furiously wrote, "I want to get into the safe with the CLD recordings that Antoine has. I think we can figure out who poisoned Thomas." I showed what I wrote to Kate and Dad.

"That sounds dangerous," Dad whispered. "Antoine is very protected here."

"I don't care. I will not let him do this to people without their knowledge. He's no better than Gideon Wesley or Memory Lane!" I shouted.

Kate looked down in shame.

"Sorry, I didn't mean it that way."

Kate looked up at me and smiled briefly. "You did. I don't blame you for feeling that way about my Dad, not anymore." Her tone was bittersweet.

Kate grabbed the pen and wrote in the book. "Is Jenson still coming? Do we have an update on his arrival?"

I shook my head no and then wrote that I would find out. More than ever, we needed Jenson to get those CLD recordings from Antoine. Thomas may have been worried about having Jenson here, but Thomas wasn't here to help. Without him, I just needed someone else that I knew I could trust. Jenson had saved our lives so many times and while his methods might have been questionable, we were still alive. That was enough for me.

Dad took the pen this time and wrote something for all of us to see. "While we wait for Jenson to come, we should all keep our jobs here and carry on as normal. We don't want to draw attention to ourselves and get thrown out before getting the evidence against Antoine. Once we have it, we can tell the rest of The Memorizers what was going on under their noses and let them decide what they will do with the information."

I grabbed the pen next. "Does that mean we are forming our own resistance against Memory Lane and The Memorizers? Are we ready to be leaders?"

The four of us looked at each other. Millions of thoughts ran through my mind, and I could only imagine what everyone else was thinking. Leslie was still just a kid, but she had been through so much with Memory Lane kidnapping her. She wanted to stop them and everything they stood for. Dad had a lot taken from him, thanks to Memory Lane, so I knew he didn't have a problem fighting them. The Memorizers gave us a place to stay but also couldn't be trusted, thanks to the CLD devices they planted in every room. My family had no one else to rely on but each other.

The person I was worried about the most—as far as going along with us leading a separate resistance against Memory Lane and The Memorizers—was Kate. We were fighting her Dad. The last of her family. She had to be conflicted. The room was silent minus the sound of pages within a book flipping and the shuffling of the pen from one set of hands to another.

"We need to ask Mom," Leslie wrote in the book.

She had a point. There was no way we could decide to take on two entities without full support from everyone in our circle.

"We'll ask her when she gets back," I wrote.

Everyone nodded and agreed.

Dad wrote in the book again. "Are we all one-hundred percent sure about this? It's a huge undertaking."

"I'm in," I said aloud with confidence.

"Me too," said Leslie.

"Me three," replied Kate.

"Let's do this then," Dad said with solidarity.

Chapter 15

Work, eat, and sleep. The rhythm of The Memorizers. Sitting at the table eating dinner, I leaned over and whispered to Kate, "Jenson should be here tomorrow." She nodded and took a bite of her potatoes. The less people who overheard who was coming and what we were planning, the better.

After Mom got back, she agreed to join us on our crusade to destroy Memory Lane and The Memorizers. She didn't take too kindly to being spied on through CLDs. Most people didn't. That's why they were illegal.

I stole a glance at Leslie to make sure that she was eating her dinner. She had eaten some of her carrots and a bite or two of chicken. It wasn't much, but I would take it.

"I'm serving the breakfast and lunch shift tomorrow," I said aloud, wondering if any of the others had been assigned a job yet.

"Good," said Dad.

"What about me? Am I getting a job?" Leslie asked.

Mom smiled at her. "Oh, sweetie. I think you're a little too young."

"Hey, other kids my age are helping out though. I don't want to sit in the room and do nothing while all of you are working," she replied.

There was more to Leslie's complaint than the unfairness of everyone else having a job. She didn't want to be alone in the room.

"Want me to see if you can help me on my shifts?" I asked, trying to reassure her.

Her face lit up and I could almost see her posture relax. "Yes please."

"I'm sure we have some fifty-pound sacks of potato flakes that need to be carried into the kitchen area. If I remember correctly, you bench like two-eighty, right?" I teased.

"Yeah, that sounds easy enough," Leslie quipped, smiling at my joke and flexing her muscles to prove she had what it took to move the potatoes. Glancing around the table, I could see a small smile on almost everyone. It was the closest thing to a normal moment we had had in a long time. Part of me wished we could stay in this moment forever. Just like Kate wished she could forget her Dad, I sometimes wished we could just forget the whole world. It just wasn't possible until we all were safe.

"Have you seen Gill since the revelation?" asked Kate. You would think we were secret agents from one of those classic books on the shelves of our rooms here. Communicating in secret with the pages of old books and creating code names. Since we found the CLDs, Kate had taken to calling our discovery "the revelation."

"Last I heard she wasn't going on the mission she was scheduled for. Something about her loyalties changing," I said.

"That's good," replied Dad. "It means we might have more people on our side than we think."

Finishing off my chicken, I stood up to clear my plate. "I'm getting more water. Anyone else need anything?" I asked the table.

"I'll take dessert," remarked Mom. She cracked a wry smile.

I sighed audibly. "I would give anything for a piece of cake." Grabbing my trash and cup, I headed to the trash can and made a beeline to get more water. Looking around the room, I couldn't help but think about each person sitting at all the tables. They had no clue they were being monitored all the time. What would they do when they knew what was happening? I shook my head to break free from the *what ifs* and walked back to the table.

"Well," said Mom as she stood from the table. "It's time for my shift. See you all in the morning." She had been assigned to do overnight inventory. It was a crap job, but we couldn't afford to be picky.

"Have fun," Leslie and I said simultaneously. Leslie and I both looked at each other and broke out into laughter.

"I'll try," replied Mom, winking at the two of us. As she walked toward the storage area, I watched her until she was out of view, then turned my attention to Dad.

"So, what are you going to do while Mom is working?"

"Research. I want to find out everything I can about Antoine and The Memorizers. The more information we gather, the better chance we have of fighting them and Memory Lane."

"What about your job?"

"It starts in the morning. I'm mopping the recreation area. I feel like I'm a seventeen-year-old kid at his first job again, but I guess it could be worse. I could be a fugitive," said Dad. He winked at me, letting me know that he was joking. At least my parents had kept some of their humor through all of this.

"Come on," I said to Kate and Leslie. "Let's go find Gill. See you later, Dad."

The three of us rose from the table while Dad stayed and finished eating.

We walked over to where the recreation area was first and ran into Brad.

"Hey, how's it going?" I asked.

"Looking for another person to go on a mission with me. You game?" he asked.

He needed someone else because Gill had backed out. Honestly, I was curious what happened on these missions, but I couldn't leave Leslie right now. There was no way she would be okay with that.

"I don't really think I'm ready for that just yet, but thanks for the offer," I said.

"Can I go?" asked Kate sheepishly.

"Doesn't Antoine have to approve who goes on missions?" I asked Brad.

"Usually he does, but he said this was a special situation and that I could choose," replied Brad.

That sounded fishy to me. "Excuse us," I said while grabbing Kate's hand and moving away from Brad momentarily. Leslie followed.

"Are you sure you want to go with him?" I whispered to Kate.

"Yeah, it can help us figure out what The Memorizers are really up to. I need to start helping instead of just causing problems."

"Whoa. I never said that."

"You don't have to. I can see it written in all of your faces," said Kate.

"That's not true!" shouted Leslie.

"Les, keep your voice down," I said, reminding her that CLDs were probably present as well as other listening ears.

"Listen, I should go with Brad so we can figure out what is going on. It's also harder to find a moving target," Kate replied.

The issue with her Dad finding out where we were was weighing on her heavily and I knew she needed a way to feel useful, so I conceded. It was true that Kate going with Brad could be useful. It was her decision regardless. I wasn't in charge of her life. I couldn't stand when my parents tried to control me and I shouldn't be doing it to other people.

"Okay, Kate. You should go with Brad."

Kate smiled at me. "Thanks, I'll go tell him."

I watched as she walked back over to where Brad was and told him that she would go on the mission with him. They spoke a few moments, then Brad nodded and walked away. When Kate returned, she filled me in on the details.

"He said we leave tonight and should only be gone for a couple of days."

"Sounds easy enough. Did Brad say what you would be doing?"

"Nope. I think he wants to keep it a secret until it's too late for me to back out."

"And you're sure about this?" I asked her one last time.

Kate nodded.

Lowering my voice again, conscious of the CLDs everywhere in this place, I moved us away. "I'll keep you updated about what Jenson says when he arrives. Do you want us to wait to watch what he saw from your memory?" I asked.

Kate thought for a moment and then said, "Honestly? It's up to you guys. I don't care either way. If it helps you work through what happened to Leslie, then I'm all for it."

"Thanks. I appreciate that."

"I guess I'm gonna go get ready to leave. I'll see you guys in a little bit." With a small wave, she turned and left.

I glanced toward the TV area and decided to kill some time. Leslie and I walked over to one of the couches and sat down. There was a guy on the other end of the couch already watching some national news channel. It said "LIVE" but it was clearly from two days ago because the date was showing in the upper right-hand corner. Settling in, I watched the commercials playing mindlessly. Leslie was sitting right next to me but leaning against the arm of the couch.

Once the news lady came back on the screen I leaned forward to listen. She sat at the news anchor desk with her news copy ready to address the camera. "Authorities are not sure what caused the malfunction of memory rooms in Memory Lanes across the country. They were inoperable for at least six hours. Our own Matt Stevens is on location to speak with Memory Lane about this breach."

The screen cut to a Memory Lane facility I didn't recognize. One that must be in another state. The news anchor was standing in the rain holding a microphone with a man wearing a suit bearing a Memory Lane logo standing beside him. Maybe a guard. I leaned a little closer to the TV.

"Yes, Vicki, Memory Lane is on high alert since the malfunction led to a breach into their database. Memory Lane is hiring officials to investigate what happened. Sir, what can you tell us about this breach?"

"Well, Mr. Stevens, there appears to have been a breach in the database that stores the memories. Memory Lane wants to assure the public that no memories were lost. The memories were accessed for a total of fourteen seconds but then the hacker was kicked out of the database. We have very sophisticated security measures in place just in case something like this happens."

"Sophisticated. Yeah, right," I scoffed under my breath.

"Serves them right," Leslie huffed.

Was this breach caused by Jenson or were other people getting more rebellious against Memory Lane? It was highly doubtful that NO memories were stolen during the fourteen seconds. Someone accessed memories and I intended to ask Jenson about it when he got here tomorrow.

The interviewer tried to pry more information from the guard in true reporter style. "Can you guarantee that the memories accessed were not tampered with or seen by a person that isn't authorized to do so?"

"Memory Lane is confident that no memories were accessed during the fourteen second breach. There simply wasn't enough time," said the guard on the TV screen.

"When will Mr. Wesley be available for comment?" the newscaster asked.

At the mention of Gideon's name I leaned a little closer, not wanting to miss a thing. If the Memory Lane guard actually told the truth, maybe that would give us a clue to where he was. The guard paused and looked like a deer in headlights for a split second before answering.

"He is busy with a new product coming out soon for all of our Memory Lane customers. It will debut in four days! It's a surprise."

"Well, that is exciting and unexpected. Can you give us any kind of hint on what it might be?" asked the reporter.

"Nope, my lips are sealed," replied the guard.

New product, yeah right! There is no way Gideon Wesley was too busy to give a comment when all of his Memory Lane facilities suffered a data breach and malfunction in the memory rooms. Something fishy was going on and Gideon was in hiding for some reason. I needed to tell Kate about her Dad before she left with Brad tonight.

"Come on, Les. Let's go tell Kate what we just heard about Memory Lane." We both stood up and walked back to our room in the yellow sector and found Kate sitting at the desk.

"Everything okay?" I asked, closing the door behind me.

"Yeah, I'm just thinking. What's up?" asked Kate.

With the conversation open, I reached for another book from our shelf so that I could write down what Leslie and I saw on the news. Kate deserved to know that her Dad was unreachable at that time according to the news. Kate handed me a pen and I began to explain what we saw.

I handed the book and the pen back to Kate so she could read what I wrote. "Are you sure this is true?" she asked aloud.

I nodded my head yes and then told her that I was sorry.

She picked up the pen and then wrote to me, "Who do you think is responsible?"

I took the pen and book and wrote back, "I don't know. The first person I can think of is Jenson but there might be others that are capable of the same thing."

Kate nodded in agreement and then wrote in the book again so I could see. "What about my Dad? He should be pursuing the people that did this."

I shrugged and then motioned for Kate to give me back the pen and book. "That's what is weird to me. They interviewed a random guard instead of your Dad or someone else higher up. Do you think Memory Lane could be involved in the breach somehow?"

"I wouldn't be shocked, honestly." Kate wrote.

"What is their end game?" I wrote back.

Kate shrugged and wrote, "Your guess is as good as mine. It's time for me to leave and meet Brad. He said we should be back tomorrow night." She placed the pen and the book on the desk and stood up to leave. "See you when you get back," I said, hugging Kate.

"Be safe," said Leslie.

Kate smiled at both of us and left the room, closing the door behind her.

"Do you really think she'll be okay?" asked Leslie. She was biting her lip, which meant she was worried.

Rather than add fuel to the fire of listening ears, I grabbed the pen and book again from the desk. "I'm worried about her Dad finding her, but there's nothing I can really do to stop her."

Leslie nodded and then laid down on the bed.

"Are you tired?" I asked her, while laying the book and pen on the desk.

"A little. There's nothing to do here," she whined.

"Well, I know this place isn't a fancy mansion, but at least you're back with us," I said while smiling down at Leslie.

"I miss my friends," she replied in a small voice.

My heart sank. Leslie didn't really have any friends because she was presumed dead for four years and hadn't really had any time to make new ones since we found her a little bit ago. I guess it had to be hard to only have a big sister and parents to talk to all the time.

I sat next to her on the bed and held her gaze. "I know you do. I wish we could fix that but unfortunately that isn't an option right now."

Leslie bit her lip again. "I know. It just sucks sometimes."

"I'm sorry. You really are getting the short end of the stick, huh?"

Leslie said nothing while I wiped a stray tear off her cheek.

"I wish things were different. I really do. It will get better when all this is over. I promise."

"You don't know that for sure," Leslie said through tears.

Pulling her close, I hugged her just as tight as I could. There was nothing worse than seeing your baby sister cry and she had been doing a lot of that lately. I wanted my happy-go-lucky, annoying kid sister back. I knew there was no way you could just wave a magic wand and undo four years of trauma and torture, but I wished there was something small I could do for her to make things a little easier.

"Get some rest. Things always look better in the morning. Besides, we'll have something to focus on when Jenson gets here tomorrow," I said.

Leslie agreed and made herself comfortable on my bed.

"Hey, aren't you going to move up to the top bunk?" I asked, teasing.

"I'm too tired," she replied and snuggled closer.

Smiling to myself, I covered her with the blanket. My thoughts wandered to how Dad's research was coming and how Mom's night shift was working out as I drifted to sleep right after Leslie.

****

"I have to go serve breakfast, Les. Are you going to wake up and come with me?" I asked a still-sleeping Leslie the next morning.

"Yeah. I'm up."

"Your eyes are still closed," I replied.

One eye opened the slightest amount as she looked at me. "Give me five minutes."

"I don't have five minutes. I have to leave now," I said. I walked away from the bed and started to make my way over to the door.

"Fine, I'm coming," Leslie said while jumping up.

"Glad to see you're awake," I replied while reaching for the doorknob.

Leslie grumbled something in response that I didn't quite catch but I loved that she was her typical grumpy-morning self. On the way to the atrium, we passed our Mom. She looked really tired.

"How was work?" I asked.

Mom rubbed her eyes. "Fine. I'm going to lie down. I'll see you guys later. Is Les staying with you?"

I nodded and then Leslie and I continued to the atrium. When we arrived, we saw the same guy, George, from the last time when I had kitchen duty. I never officially told anyone that this was the job I picked, but I figured they could use the help. I didn't want to be late and make a bad impression.

"Hannah? What are you doing here? Last I heard you left when your cousin got sick," said George.

"Yeah, well, I'm back now. Need any kitchen help? This is Leslie," I said while nodding in her direction. "Can she help too?"

"I mean, I guess she can if she wants. I don't want her serving though. She's too young. People will think we are condoning child labor," he said while half-chuckling.

"Thanks. Do you need me this morning or would you rather I wait until lunch?" I asked.

"You can serve this morning. My main breakfast server is sick."

"Cool. Thanks," I replied.

"You remember where the stuff is?" he asked.

I nodded and walked behind the serving line to the back where the aprons were stored and the food was made. Leslie followed. I grabbed an apron and hairnet from the stack and looked at the bags of powdered grits and eggs. "Want to help me mix these?"

Leslie turned her nose up at the bags but agreed to help anyway.

"Powdered eggs?" she asked.

"Well, The Memorizers don't exactly have chickens down here. Think about how many eggs we would use for breakfast everyday if they were real. It isn't cost effective," I replied.

"I guess I hadn't considered that before," she said while grabbing the opposite side of the bag and lifting. We hoisted the bag of powdered eggs onto the counter and I looked around for a scoop. The directions were on the side of the bag. The recipe called for eight scoops of the mix to 16 cups of water. Seemed simple enough. I looked around the counter space for a scoop that we could use while Leslie grabbed one of the long metal serving pans to put the eggs and water in.

"Is there a spoon we can use to mix the eggs?" she asked.

"Yeah, I think they are on that other counter over there," I replied.

I found the scoop and started adding the eggs and water to the metal pan. Leslie came back with a spoon for mixing and waited for me to finish adding the eggs and water. She mixed the powdered egg mixture (I had to admit it did look gross) while I got the other empty pan ready for grits.

After fifteen or so minutes, George came back and got the powdered egg pan to take to the front. "Are you almost ready? We need you out here to serve," he said.

"Yeah, the grits need more time though," I replied.

George looked annoyed. "I'll finish those. You get out there," he said firmly.

I walked out to the serving line and saw a slew of people. Everyone must be hungry. We still had about eight minutes until breakfast officially started, but with people standing there, the pressure was on. I glanced to see if there was a stack of trays at the start of the line and noticed that we could use some more silverware.

"Hey, Les. Bring me some forks and spoons please," I called to the back room.

No response. "Leslie? Hello? We need silverware," I said loudly.

I waited another thirty seconds before I officially started to panic. *Where did Leslie go?* I ran back to the kitchen storeroom and my heart sank. Leslie was in the corner of the room on the floor, crying with her knees drawn up to her chest. George looked panicked and confused as he tried to approach her.

"Get away from her!" I yelled.

"I didn't do anything!" he shouted back.

I approached Leslie calmly and started to speak to her in soft tones. "Hey, Les. It's me. You're safe."

"It's not real. It's not real. It's not real," Leslie repeated to herself over and over. It was like a mantra. She was trying to convince herself of something.

"Leslie? It's me, Hannah. Can you look at me?" I asked softly.

Leslie buried her face into her knees and sobbed even louder. She covered her ears. "Not real. Not real. Not real."

"What isn't real? I'm real, Les. So are you. I promise," I said, still trying to make her see that she was fine. As fine as she could be in the midst of a panic attack.

"Should I get someone else or..." said George.

I shook my head no. "What happened?" I asked him, trying to keep the accusatory tone out of my voice.

"I asked her how she knew you and instead of answering me, she dropped the pan she was holding and started freaking out. I didn't even touch her, honestly. Is she going to be okay?" George asked.

Unable to think of a response, I turned my attention back to Leslie.

"Nothing is going to hurt you. You're safe," I repeated, hoping to break through whatever trauma she was experiencing right now. I gently placed my hand on her back and rubbed in slow circles, hoping that it might trigger a feeling of safety since my voice wasn't working.

Leslie immediately looked up at me as if the fog had lifted from her eyes and threw her arms around me. The weight of her hitting me in my crouched position landed us both on the floor.

"Hannah! You're alive!"

I felt tears soaking through my shirt. Sobs wracked her body, and she was shaking as she struggled to pull in the next sob-filled breath.

"Shh, it's okay. I'm right here," I told her, while still hugging her.

How was I ever going to be able to fix this?

Chapter 16

Our room door opened and Mom walked in, worry lining her face. She must have heard about the commotion in the kitchen earlier. "How is she?"

"She's resting. Finally." I rubbed my eyes and stretched. This was all starting to take a toll on me. If this was how I was feeling, I couldn't imagine how Leslie must feel.

Mom walked farther into the room and took a seat on the desk chair. "Has she said what happened?"

"Not yet. I don't want to pressure her into anything right now. She was so scared."

"I'm glad you were able to get through to her. It sounds like a panic attack or a vivid hallucination. I wonder what caused it," Mom said.

"Could it be that our lives are screwed up?" I commented dryly.

Mom lowered her voice to a whisper. "Should we be having this conversation aloud?" Her brow was furrowed in worry, and I understood her concern, but I just couldn't tiptoe around this anymore.

"Yes! How can we ever be free of this if we keep hiding from it? I need to get to the bottom of this for Leslie's sake. For all of us to heal and start to move on." I glanced at my phone. It was only 9:00 a.m. but it felt like I had been running on pure adrenaline for days. I was so tired of everything getting screwed up because of Memory Lane. Even breakfast turned into a fiasco, the repercussions of Memory Lane and their crimes always butting into my life.

The room went silent, and the only sound was the peaceful breathing of the sleep that Leslie desperately needed. I checked my messages and VidChats to see if Jenson had contacted me. There was still nothing new, only the text from Jenson before breakfast saying that he was still making good time and should be here tonight. He said he had a surprise for me that he guaranteed I would like. Truthfully, not a whole lot mattered right now except helping Leslie through whatever this was and getting the hell away from The Memorizers and fighting Memory Lane. The number of people I could count on was dwindling day by day.

Leslie stirred on the bed, and I reached out to soothe her by placing my hand on her back. Her face was scrunched in pain, and my heart skipped a beat thinking about the nightmares she must be suffering. No part of me could imagine what was happening inside her mind. We still had no idea what had happened while she was a prisoner.

"It's okay, Leslie. You're safe with me," I whispered into her ear.

She continued moving around for a few seconds, but then seemed to calm down after that.

"Where was this Hannah when Leslie was younger?" I looked up to see Mom watching me with a smile on her face.

"She slept in my bed many times when she was a toddler." Despite my defense, there was guilt in my voice. How much had I missed because I was wrapped up in my own world?

"I know, I was teasing," replied Mom. She walked over to the bed and carefully sat down so as not to disturb Leslie. I watched as Mom took Leslie's hand and, without warning, started silently crying.

"My precious baby girl, I never wanted this for you. I am so sorry we failed at protecting you. If I could, I would give anything to go back and change what happened," Mom whispered to Leslie's sleeping form.

"It's not your fault, Mom," I whispered back.

"How can it not be? I'm her Mom. It's my job to protect you both."
She wiped her tears away with the hand that wasn't holding Leslie's.

"I know Leslie doesn't blame you for her being kidnapped," I said.

"Like that matters," Mom scoffed. "She doesn't have to. I blame myself every day for not believing that she was alive all this time. For accepting what the coroner said when she was pronounced dead." Mom paused and then looked me in the eye. "At the very least, I should have believed you, Hannah. You always felt that her death didn't make sense and you tried to learn everything you could about that day. I should have seen that you weren't crazy for insisting that something else was at play. I'm sorry."

Well, that's an apology I never expected to get.

"Honestly, it's fine, Mom," I said.

She smiled back. "How did you and your sister turn out so well?" Mom asked.

"Our real parents must have been amazing," I replied, pushing her with my shoulder. For a moment, things felt just a little lighter.

Mom chuckled. "Have you talked to Kate?" she asked, changing the subject.

"Not yet. I'm hoping no news is good news."

"She should be back tonight?"

I nodded yes. "And I think Jenson should be here then too. It's a party."

"Hopefully he has good news" said Mom.

"We'll see."

"I'm going to go lie back down. Wake me up if Leslie needs me." Mom released Leslie's hand gently and headed to her room, closing the door softly behind her.

I settled back down on the bed and watched over Leslie as she slept. Deep down I wanted to fix what was broken. Her stolen childhood made me angry at Memory Lane and it took everything in me not to just march down there myself and blow it up. Every Memory Lane across the country. *Maybe Jenson had the right idea.* As I lay there, I began to think about all that was going on with Leslie and how she was a liability to us right now.

She was struggling to connect to reality, thanks to the tests that Memory Lane performed on her. It would give her away as a child from the program and potentially get her kidnapped or arrested. I shook my head trying to lose the image of her being taken again. I couldn't let that happen. As it was, Memory Lane was looking for her anyway, since she was technically missing from their program in the first place. The sooner that Jenson got here and Kate was back, the sooner we needed to start figuring out our plan to end Memory Lane. I didn't see how The Memorizers could be a part of that.

The bed shifted beside me and I looked over to see Leslie waking up.

"Hannah? Why are we in bed?" she asked.

I sat up a little bit so I could read her emotions better. "What do you remember?" I didn't want to overwhelm her right now.

"It's all kind of fuzzy. I was in the kitchen with you mixing some eggs and then I woke up here."

"You don't remember talking to George?" I asked.

Leslie shook her head. "Why? Did something else happen?"

"You're fine," I said, while rubbing her shoulder. "You just got scared in the kitchen for a little bit."

"I did?"

I nodded yes. "But you're fine now. There's nothing to worry about," I said, trying to keep my tone light. I wasn't sure if she was ready for all the details.

"Am I forgetting stuff like Mom now?" Leslie asked.

"I don't know."

"Hannah, I'm scared. What if Memory Lane permanently messed me up? I don't want to start forgetting other stuff." Leslie started silently crying.

I hugged her. "Shh, it's okay. We'll figure it out together."

Leslie sniffled and pushed out of my hug.

"You sure you don't remember being in the kitchen with George?"
Leslie shook her head.

I looked into her eyes to see if she could handle the truth. I decided that keeping a secret from her about what I witnessed her saying wasn't worth her well-being. Maybe something would come back to her if I told her about what happened.

"Hannah, just tell me," she said.

I sighed. "You were seeing something. It's like you were somewhere else. You kept saying that I wasn't real when I tried to talk to you."

"That doesn't make any sense."

"It doesn't have to make sense at this very moment. Maybe it will come back to you later. You don't have figure it out right now."

Leslie nodded, but still looked ashamed of what happened. "I'm sorry I'm so messed up," she said, her eyes downcast. She was wringing her hands and I could see how she was struggling just to piece together the moment.

I gently pulled her chin up and made sure she was looking me in the eye. "Don't you even start that. This is not your fault."

"But I—"

"No, Les. This is the fault of Memory Lane. No one else."

Leslie seemed to agree but stayed quiet.

"I need you to say it out loud. Please. For me," I said.

"This is not my fault," Leslie repeated.

"Say it like you believe it," I said.

"This is not my fault," Leslie said, with more confidence.

Smiling, I patted her on the shoulder. "Good. Make sure you repeat that to yourself if this happens again."

"Are you in trouble for not helping with breakfast this morning?" Leslie asked, changing the subject.

"Nah, it's all good. I have the rest of the day off."

My phone buzzed and I glanced to see who the message was from.

KATE: dude. this is big.

ME: what?

KATE: can u talk?

ME: im with leslie

KATE: she ok?

ME: for now. i'll explain later

ME: what time r u coming?

KATE: brad says around 7 tonight

ME: ok see u then

Leslie tried to read the messages over my shoulder but she looked really tired and was squinting her eyes to see. "Everything okay with Kate?" she asked.

"Yeah, she has something to tell me later."

Leslie nodded and closed her eyes.

"You still tired?" I asked her.

"Yeah. I don't really know why. I went to bed early last night."

"You've had an eventful morning. Why don't you rest here while I see if Dad found anything while researching last night?" I suggested.

Leslie's eyes shot back open. "No. I'll come with you," she said forcefully.

"I really think you could use the rest, Les."

"I want to come." Leslie sat up and hopped off the bed. "See? I'm awake."

"If you're sure—" I started to say.

"I am. Let's go," she replied, grabbing my hand and pulling me toward the door.

I followed Leslie out of our room and closed the door behind me. As we walked down the yellow sector hallway, I remembered that Dad said he had a cleaning job this morning and that was where he probably was. A man ahead of us in the hallway didn't move out of our way in enough time while we tried to pass, and his shoulder bumped into Leslie.

"Sorry, miss," he said.

Leslie froze. She stared straight ahead and looked terrified. She looked as though she was in another world.

I got down to her level to look her in the eye and gently grabbed her shoulders.

"Leslie, hey. Look at me. We're in the hallway. You're fine," I said. The color had drained from her face and her arms were limp at her sides as she remained unblinking and catatonic.

She was breathing really fast and bordering on a panic attack.

Where was this coming from? This was unlike Leslie. She was a brave kid who didn't care what anyone thought of her. I had witnessed her taking control of the situation with Devon when I rescued her from Memory Lane earlier in the summer. She didn't care that the guards would hurt her, only that Devon was younger than her and needed protecting. Where was *that* Leslie?

"Listen to my voice. You're safe, Les."

I felt a crowd gathering around us since we were in the middle of the hallway. There were whispers and murmurs about Leslie, but I ignored all of it. All at once, Leslie suddenly blinked, her breathing leveled out and the color returned to her face. She then looked at me like nothing was wrong.

"What's wrong, Hannah? Why are we standing here?" She looked around to see a crowd of people staring.

"You tell me," I said.

The crowd began to leave, seeing that nothing exciting was going to happen. I moved Leslie to the side of the hallway so they could get through.

"What happened before in the kitchen area happened again. You froze and couldn't move. It was like you weren't seeing what was around you for a few seconds."

"Why does this keep happening?" Leslie asked. She was on the verge of tears.

"I don't know but we'll figure it out together," I said. I hugged her and we continued walking down the yellow sector hallway again. We made our way to the atrium which was fairly empty since it was after breakfast but before lunch. I grabbed both of us a table for a minute so Leslie could fully compose herself. She looked okay now but I wanted to make sure she was really okay. The two of us sat and people-watched for a little while before I broke the silence.

"Do you think Dad is cleaning in a sector or in the recreation area?" I asked.

"No clue. Maybe we should check the rec area first?" suggested Leslie.

"Sure, let's head that way," I said.

As soon as we got up, I heard my name called from the other end of the atrium.

"Hannah! Wait up!" Dad called. I turned to see him walking quickly toward us, bucket and mop in his hands.

"We were on our way to see you," I said.

"Why? Is something wrong?" he asked, narrowing his eyes at both me and Leslie.

I decided that Mom could tell him what was going on with Leslie later. "No, we just wanted to see how your research turned out," I said.

"Nothing to report really. I didn't have anything specific that I was looking for. Antoine has done a good job of keeping everything about The Memorizers off the internet."

"What about Gideon Wesley? Any new developments about him looking for Kate or being charged with his wife's murder?" I asked, keeping my voice low.

Dad shook his head. "Not that I saw."

Leslie started fidgeting while she stood next to me.

"Are you okay, honey?" Dad asked her.

"Yeah, I'm good, Dad," she replied. Leslie paused for a little bit and started picking at her nails, as if she was nervous about something.

"Has there been any update about the other kids that were in the program with me?"

"I didn't see any new information, but I also wasn't really looking for that," replied Dad.

"I just wondered if they were all okay."

"We'll make sure we find out soon," I promised Leslie.

She nodded but seemed a little disappointed. I had a feeling that it was because these attacks where she spaced out and didn't hear or see us were new and scary. Surely if it was happening to her, she wanted to know if it was happening to the other kids too. I had to remind myself that Leslie was almost new to our family again. She spent the last four years living a different life with other people and learning the way things worked with them. Even though none of that was her choice, she still had to do whatever it took to survive.

"How'd breakfast go?" asked Dad.

Leslie turned beet-red, embarrassed. It was an innocent question to change the subject, but Dad had no idea what had happened with Leslie this morning.

"It was fine. Uneventful," I lied. Leslie could tell Dad in her own time and in private if she wanted to.

Dad smiled. "Good, I'm glad."

"Well, I guess we'll let you get back to cleaning," I said.

"See you guys later." He walked off with the mop and bucket in his hands.

With nothing better to do, and some time to kill before Jenson and Kate arrived, I decided to see what Gill was up to today. "Come on, Les. Let's go find Gill," I said, walking in the direction of her hallway and sector.

The two of us approached Gill's room together. I knocked and waited for the door to be opened. Gill was a huge mess. Her hair was disheveled and the room looked like it had been completely torn apart. There were clothes strewn all over the bed and the floor. I could see the tear tracks on her face.

"What happened?" I asked.

"I've been kicked out of The Memorizers," she said.

"What? I thought they let everyone in?"

Gill wiped the tears off her cheeks and snorted. "Yeah, I did too. Apparently, I violated their policy," she said.

I stepped into the room now and closed the door. I motioned for a pen and paper to write on so we could have a conversation without The Memorizers listening to us.

Gill grabbed a book from the shelf and handed it to me. There was a pen on a shirt that was lying on the ground. I picked it up and wrote, "What policy did you violate?"

Gill responded by writing, "having a brain to think for myself."

I wrote back, "explain."

Gill took a deep breath and began writing. "I found a CLD in the rec area last night after pretty much everyone had gone to bed. I whispered into the CLD that I was onto their little game. Then this morning they came and dragged me out of bed and into Antoine's office to ask me what I meant by my comment."

I gasped as I read what Gill wrote. Leslie shifted beside me so she could read what was written too.

"What did you tell them you meant?" I wrote.

Gill grabbed the pen from me and frantically wrote her explanation. "I said that it wasn't fair that they were listening to people without consent. I told Antoine to his face that he was no better than Memory Lane and that's when he told me to get my stuff and leave."

This was bad.

"Are you sure Antoine won't have you arrested or killed for what you know?" I wrote.

Gill looked upset at that possibility. She took the pen and book back to respond. "He might. Which is why I can't tell you where I'm going. In fact, you probably shouldn't be seen with me once you leave this room."

I hated to ask my next question while Gill was so upset, but I had to know what else she told Antoine. I had to make sure that my family wasn't in any more danger.

I held out my hand for the pen and wrote, "Did you tell Antoine anything else? Did you tell him that my family knows about the CLDs in the rooms?"

"I'm not an idiot!" she shouted aloud.

"Sorry, I had to ask," I said.

I wrote in the book again. "Do you have the means to get another phone? Are you planning to stay in contact with me and Jenson and Thomas?"

Gill shrugged and said, "I'll figure something out."

Leslie looked pensive for a minute, and then said, "Can I ask you something?"

Gill nodded yes.

Leslie took the pen and book from me and wrote, "Why say something now? Why not just wait until we could all leave together?"

Gill thought for a minute and then wiped the tears off her cheeks. She was clearly still upset by everything that had transpired. After all, she had been here with The Memorizers much longer than my family and I had. She took the pen from Leslie and wrote again.

"I couldn't sit by and watch my friends have their privacy invaded. They don't deserve that. Everyone deserves to have freedom."

"But don't you deserve to have somewhere safe to stay? Don't we all?" I wrote back.

"I'll be okay," she wrote. "I can look after myself."

Gill put the pen and book down on the desk and reached into her pocket. "Oh, and another thing. I brought you something from Antoine's office."

Gill placed something very small in my hand. It was a tiny plastic bag with white powder in it. When I turned it over, I read what the bag contained: Arsenic.

Chapter 17

My heart pounded in my chest so loud and fast I was sure that everyone else in the room could hear it. "What?" I asked. "How?"

Gill grabbed the pen and book again. "It was in a box by the door. He was storing it with his tea bags of all things."

How could such a small thing cause so much damage? Lifting the bag to the light, the powder inside could have been anything. Baby powder, flour, and yet this tiny bag was capable of taking a life. It had almost taken Thomas's. Putting the bag of arsenic in my back pocket, I grabbed the pen.

"But how did you get it without him seeing?" I wrote back.

Gill smirked while grabbing the pen back from me. "I knocked over a bunch of stuff on my way out like a child throwing a tantrum. They made me clean it up and I swiped the baggie."

I let Leslie look at what had transpired to catch her up on our silent conversation. "Does this mean that Antoine is the one who poisoned Thomas the last time we were here?" I wrote.

Gill nodded and then wrote back. "That's my guess."

"I'll kill him," I said aloud.

"Hannah, keep your voice down," whispered Leslie. She grabbed the pen from Gill. "Just because he had the arsenic doesn't mean he's the one that poisoned Thomas."

"It makes it highly likely." I wrote back. "Come on Les, let's go," I said, while grabbing her hand.

"Wait! Where are we going?" Leslie asked, confusion washing over her face. Before I could process it, my frustration got the best of me.

"To figure out what to do!" I shouted.

Leslie shrunk back for a second, as if scared of me.

Inside I cringed, immediately regretting my yelling. "I didn't mean to yell. I'm sorry. But can you please come with me so we can do something about this huge revelation?"

"What about Gill?" Leslie asked.

Bless this child. With all she had been through, the time lost, the pain that Memory Lane had inflicted on her and still, she was worried about someone else. Even when everything around us seemed to be falling apart. Looking down at Leslie, I smiled, squeezing her hand. Glancing back at Gill, I could only offer an apologetic gaze.

"I'm sorry, Leslie. I don't think there is anything we can do. Antoine has already made up his mind."

Gill walked over and crouched down to look Leslie in the eyes. "Don't worry about me. Things that are meant to be, find a way of coming to pass. We are friends, right?"

Leslie nodded. "This isn't goodbye. Promise."

It was exactly what Leslie needed to hear and she wrapped her arms around Gill's neck and hugged her tight. Once Leslie let go and Gill stood up, I hugged her tight too. Between Memory Lane and now The Memorizers, it seemed like the world was pulling us all apart.

"Take care of yourself and as soon as you can, let me know that you're okay," I said.

Gill nodded and I gently grabbed Leslie's hand and walked out of Gill's room for the last time.

"I think we should show Mom and Dad the arsenic Gill found," I told Leslie as we walked down the hall.

"Probably a good idea," she replied. "Are you going to tell Thomas?"

"Don't you think he deserves to know who poisoned him?" I asked. Leslie nodded.

"How are you going to contact him?"

"Not sure. We'll figure something out."

We arrived at the atrium and started to walk through when Leslie came to a dead stop. Her glassy expression had returned, and it seemed she was having another one of her episodes. She stared into the distance at an invisible enemy, the fear and terror on her face made my stomach drop. Squeezing her hand, saying her name over and over again and trying to reassure her that she was fine did nothing. It was as if she was in another world. One we couldn't see and the monsters there couldn't be fought against. Looking around, I was glad there weren't many people in there right now to bother us.

"Les, it's okay. It's me, Hannah. Come back to me. You're safe, I promise," I said, trying to mask the shaking of my voice and speak in low, calm tones.

"Is she okay? Does she need help?" asked a voice from the atrium. Out of the corner of my eye I saw a man approach us to see what was going on.

"She's fine. Leave us alone," I said.

"I was a psychologist up until about five months ago," said the man. "Are you sure you don't want me to help?" he asked.

Leslie continued to stare straight ahead. I put my hand on her shoulder when she started to cry and whisper. "Not real. Not real. Not real," she said, on a loop.

"Yeah, I've got her," I replied to the man. I attempted to block his view of Leslie while she was in this state.

"Leslie, look at me. You're safe," I tried again.

The man reached over my shoulder and grabbed Leslie's arm. That seemed to do the trick and Leslie came out of her stance and screamed. "Ahhhhhhhh!"

"Don't touch her!" I yelled.

The man backed away, but continued to stand nearby. I tried to keep him in my sight while making sure Leslie was okay.

"Are you okay?" I asked Leslie, rubbing her shoulders to get her to focus on me.

She nodded yes and then her eyes got really wide at something behind me. I turned around expecting more drama and was pleasantly surprised to see Jenson.

"You're here early!"

"Yeah, we made good time," he replied, reaching over to give me an awkward side hug.

"We?" I pulled back and looked at Jenson, eyebrow raised in suspicion.

"Remember the surprise I mentioned?" Jenson asked.

I nodded my head.

"Follow me," he said.

The man that was standing near Leslie and me while she was having that episode continued to stare at us. It was obvious enough for Jenson to notice.

"Dude, what is your problem?" Jenson asked, a note of strong protectiveness in his voice.

"I don't have a problem. I was just making sure this young lady was alright," he said, while motioning to Leslie.

"She's fine," I said, drawing her a little closer to me. This guy was freaking me out. I'm sure he meant well, but he had overstayed his welcome at this point.

"I think we've got it from here," Jenson said with finality.

"If you say so," said the man. He walked away from us shaking his head. Once the stranger was out of sight, Jenson relaxed and returned his attention to me.

"Come on, let's go see your surprise!"

Looking down at Leslie, I had to make sure she was really okay. "You sure you're good?" I asked her one more time.

She nodded and we started to follow Jenson to wherever he was taking us. After the rough time we just had, not only was my curiosity piqued, but I was ready for something that didn't feel like life or death.

We arrived in the recreation area and I let out a squeal. "Thomas?!"

He was standing at the pool table and turned around when I said his name. Rushing over to him, he looked almost back to normal. As if the poisoning was just a distant memory. I could still hear the beeps of the hospital machines and see his lifeless body covered in wires as we waited to find out what had happened.

"Hannah! It's good to see you! And Leslie!"

We walked over to where he was and I grabbed him in a hug. It felt like I hadn't seen him in forever.

"How are you here? Why are you here? Is something wrong?" I asked in rapid-fire fashion.

Thomas chuckled and hugged Leslie. "One question at a time. Let's go sit down for a second," he said.

We walked over to sit on the couches when I remembered our current situation with The Memorizers listening to our every word.

As all of us sat down, I held up a hand to stop Thomas from talking before he said too much information. I pulled out my phone and typed out a message to Jenson so he could read it and know what was going on with the CLDs and The Memorizers listening to everyone.

After I finished typing, I showed the message to Thomas while Jenson read it on his phone. Both of them looked very unsure and confused. Jenson began typing.

JENSON: since when?
ME: since always I guess
JENSON: are you planning 2 stay?

ME: probably leaving soon. tryin 2 get a feel 4 who would come w/ us & start a new group
ME: and who would remain loyal to the memorizers & antoine

Thomas grabbed Jenson's phone to type out a question.

JENSON: i thought antoine was a peacemaker?
ME: u can be anti-war & still spy on ur people. it's just in bad taste
ME: speaking of bad taste...gill helped us find something out about antoine u aren't going 2 like
ME: tbh i don't like it either

The phone was passed around to fill in Jenson and Leslie so that no one was left out of the conversation. I inwardly rolled my eyes at how annoying this whole situation was, thanks to Antoine spying on everyone. Taking a deep breath, I thought about how I wanted to tell Thomas about Antoine having arsenic at his disposal. It wasn't one hundred percent the smoking gun we needed, but it was probably as close as we were going to get. I looked at Leslie for her opinion on telling Thomas. She smiled and gave me the go-ahead with a quick nod.

Thomas looked at me expectantly and waited for me to type in my message.

ME: gill found arsenic in antoine's office

Thomas's eyes got very wide and he stood up from the couch immediately.

"Where are you going?" I asked aloud, following him.

"To give Antoine a piece of my mind!" shouted Thomas.

People in the rec area stopped what they were doing and stared at me and Thomas.

"Charging in there is not the answer!" I yelled back.

Thomas dropped his voice down to a stage whisper. "The man poisoned me! I am not going to let him get away with it!"

The other people had started going about their business again, giving Thomas and me some privacy to continue our conversation.

I grabbed Thomas by the shoulder to get his attention for just a minute. Once he turned around, I held up my phone again and typed so Thomas could see.

> **ME:** i know you want to go bash Antoine's head in. i do too. but u just came back 2 me & i don't want u to get carted off in a gurney or a stretcher again. can we just settle down and figure out what 2 do together? i haven't even told my parents yet

Thomas grabbed my phone and typed back.

> **ME:** but he's spying on his own people and tried to kill me!

I took back my phone to respond to Thomas and tried to calm him down.

> **ME:** i know. that's why we r trying to rally some followers & leave this place to fight memory lane on our own. it will happen in time

Thomas ran his hand through his hair. He had been here for five minutes and already the frustration had reached critical levels. Despite the call for vengeance, he reluctantly nodded.

"Okay."

We walked back over to where Leslie and Jenson were sitting on the couches. "Let's go to the room so we can talk a little more privately," I said.

They all agreed. Leslie stood up to grab my hand as we walked to our room. Jenson and Thomas brought up the rear.

"Where's Aunt Linda and Uncle Robert?" asked Thomas.

"I think Mom is sleeping since she worked a night shift, and Dad was working, the last we saw. He should be back in their room soon. They will both be happy to see you, I bet."

Opening the door to the room, I immediately grabbed a book and a pen from the shelf. I explained to Thomas and Jenson that we would use this method to talk to each other because it was faster than typing, since the messages took forever to send sometimes. Leslie took a seat on the bed and I sat down next to her. Thomas opted to stand while Jenson took the chair.

"So my first question for Jenson is this. Did you have something to do with the breach at Memory Lane a few days ago?" I wrote.

Jenson grabbed the book and read, then winked at me while passing the book back.

"I'll take that as a yes, then," I wrote. "Did you download information during that breach of Memory Lane?"

Jenson read my question and then grabbed the pen to write back. "Of course. I have it stored on a laser flash drive that we can view at any time. I don't know that I would look at the information here with The Memorizers since they are spying all the time."

"Can you summarize what you found?" I wrote back, now getting frustrated. *Why couldn't he just give me a straight answer?*

Thomas chuckled at the exchange between Jenson and me. He clearly already knew about all of this and was enjoying watching me squirm.

"It's not funny!" I said aloud.

Jenson hesitated for a second before deciding to write down what he took from Memory Lane during that short download and interruption of their services. He wrote for a solid minute or two and then passed me the book with a look of "are you sure you want to see this?" written on his face.

I quickly grabbed the book and held it out so that Leslie could see too. He had written a few sentences detailing what was in the breach. "I found an anomaly with the children that Memory Lane were running tests on. Kids like Leslie. They may have implanted something in all of the kids."

"What?! There's no way that is true," I said while jumping off the bed. Leslie sat on the bed, frozen.

"Keep your voice down!" whispered Jenson.

"I need to see the information!" I said back.

"We shouldn't look at it here, Hannah," reasoned Thomas.

I hastily grabbed the book and pen again and wrote out a question while standing next to Jenson.

"Are you sure all of the kids were implanted?" I wrote.

Jenson looked resigned as he wrote out his response. "I have information on twelve children. Leslie's name was on the list."

NO. Just no. This couldn't be happening. Leslie didn't deserve any more of this pain. Tears silently began to fall down my face and I made no effort to brush them away. I walked back over to where Leslie was sitting on the bed. *Why couldn't the nightmare that was Memory Lane just be over already?*

"Les? Are you okay?" I asked.

She continued to stare straight ahead. The time in between her episodes was getting shorter and each time it seemed the episode lasted longer and got worse in how Les responded.

"Not again!" I cried out.

Thomas looked concerned. "Has she been doing this a lot?" he asked. Ignoring his question, I dropped to the floor to see Leslie's face and look into her eyes to see if I could get her to connect that I was here.

"Can you hear me, Leslie? You're safe. You're with me," I said in soft tones.

I turned to look at Thomas. "Yeah, a lot lately. But only since the last day or so," I replied.

Jenson tapped me on the shoulder to get my attention. He handed me the book, having written something as I worked to bring Leslie back to this moment. I took a second to read what he wrote.

"Look, I know this isn't a good time, but I think Memory Lane has turned on the implants in the kids. That's why she has been spacing out like this."

"What?!" I asked, shocked. There was no time for further explanations because Leslie finally came back to us.

"Hannah?" asked Leslie. She was disoriented and confused again upon regaining awareness. "What's going on?"

"Hey, there you are. Don't worry, you're okay. You just spaced out again," I told her, trying to keep my voice even. She didn't need anything else to worry about.

Leslie shifted uncomfortably, noticing that all eyes were on her.

"Why are all of you staring at me like that?"

I smiled at her to make light of the moment. "Jenson and Thomas just have bad manners. Don't sweat it," I said.

Leslie's glance went from uncomfortable to cautious in a microsecond. She looked at all of us to try and see what was really going on. "You're lying, Hannah. Something is wrong. I can tell. What are you hiding from me?" she asked.

Looking up, I glanced at Thomas and Jenson for help. Was Leslie ready to hear that there was a possibility of an implant in her brain that Memory Lane had control over? On the other hand, I didn't think it was fair to keep the information from her.

With a deep sigh, one that even I couldn't mask, I conceded to telling her everything we knew. At least if she knew what was happening, it might give her some comfort when she came out of the episodes.

"The important thing to remember is that everything is going to be fine," I said in my calmest voice.

Leslie rolled her eyes so hard that honestly I was surprised she didn't fall over. "That's comforting," she said. *If sarcasm runs in the family, then you could know we were sisters just by that.*

Several beats of silence passed as I searched for the words. *How do you tell your NOT-dead-anymore sister that there is more grisly news about what had happened while she was trapped at Memory Lane for those four years?*

"Just tell me already," Leslie whined.

Picking up the pen, I found a page that had plenty of blank space to tell her everything that we knew. "Well, you know how you've been spacing out lately and then coming to with no recollection of why you freaked out or what happened?" I wrote.

She looked at the book and then nodded.

"It seems that Memory Lane has something to do with that," I explained in writing.

Leslie took the pen and wrote back to me. "What? How?" Her expression was full of questions. Questions I knew that I didn't have very many answers for.

I gave her a reassuring smile and took the pen back and wrote more. "Jenson found out that Memory Lane put implants in all of the kids that were in the program. They are using those implants to control the kids."

Leslie looked upset. You could see her trying to puzzle things out with each bit of additional information. "Are you sure we all have one?" she wrote. She looked hopeful and it made my heart sink to know that I couldn't offer her the reassurance that they didn't put one in her too.

Grabbing the pen and book, I took a deep breath and wrote the truth. "Jenson said your name was on a list of kids that have an implant." Before I could hand her the book I hastily wrote my apology. *How could I have let all of this happen? Why didn't I protect her during my stupid birthday party!?!* "I'm so sorry, Leslie. I wish I could go back in time and make sure this never happened."

Leslie's expression went from one of horror to one of outright anger. "So now I'm a danger to the whole family!" Leslie screamed, her frustration and fear exploding as she broke down and began to cry.

"We don't know that!" I shouted back.

"Everyone, calm down," Thomas interjected.

For a moment, I had forgotten that Thomas and Jenson were in the room. I knew that anger and frustration were not going to help us fix whatever was happening with Leslie. Jenson grabbed the pen and book from me.

"We don't know that they are tracking your location necessarily. We just know that they're turning on the implant probably to test it. It is obviously making you stop seeing what's really in front of you. You're sure that you have no idea what happens when these episodes occur?" When he was finished writing, he passed the book directly to Leslie.

I read what he wrote over her shoulder.

Leslie shook her head no, then started to cry even more. "Why is this happening to me?" she asked, her voice sounded hopeless and for the first time since we had gotten her back from Memory Lane, my fearless baby sister looked as though she was ready to give up.

I pulled her into a hug and just let her cry. This was a lot of information to get in a very short amount of time and as her little body sobbed against my shoulder, I could feel her tears wetting my shirt. What more could Memory Lane take from us?

"Can you guys catch up with us later? My parents' room is across the way. I'm sure they will be happy to see you both," I said. "And Thomas? I still want to know why and how you are here, so don't think I am letting you off the hook."

Thomas forced a smile and Jenson nodded, as they closed the door and left us alone.

How could I fix this? I hugged Leslie harder and promised her that everything would be alright. She continued to cry and I held her close to me.

For four long years, we thought she was dead. We finally find out the truth, we get her back from Memory Lane and now this. Deep down, I wasn't so sure that I could keep that promise. An implant from Memory Lane? My mind raced back and forth to the worst possible scenarios. Knowing they had control over the kids that were with Leslie and that they could control the kids and even force them to go back to Memory Lane against their will, all because of the implant. What was the purpose of controlling kids? Maybe another possibility was Memory Lane had changed the kids' memories. Giving the kids false memories of their time in the program. *Would we have to remove the implant? Could we? Would it kill her?* That last thought sent a cold shiver down my spine. I couldn't lose her again.

"Take it easy, Les. It will be okay," I said, I ran my hand reassuringly down her hair while shushing her.

My phone vibrated and startled me. When I bent down to see who it was, Thomas came rushing back into the room.

"Don't tell my Mom I'm here!" he yelled.

Raising my eyebrows in mock accusation, I glanced down to see what he was talking about. Sure enough, there was a missed call and VidChat message from my Aunt Nicole.

"I sort of figured you escaped without her knowing," I replied dryly. "She's not dumb, Thomas. Aunt Nicole can put two and two together to figure out where you are."

"I know, I just need her to sweat it out for a little longer. It serves her right anyway," Thomas fumed.

"That's ominous. What do you mean?" I asked.

Thomas sighed, "I'll explain later. It's a long story."

Everything seemed like a long story lately. *Why can't our lives just be simple?* I nodded. "I'm holding you to that."

Thomas returned to my parents' room and I focused my attention back on Leslie. She was calmer but still seemed so tired.

"You okay?" I asked.

She nodded and wiped her tear-stained cheeks on her sleeve.

"You know, you are one of the strongest people I know, Les," I encouraged.

Nothing will make you feel more powerless than when someone else is in control of those you love. Memory Lane had done enough damage. I had to find a way to fix this. That meant I really needed some answers from Jenson. What were the implications of Leslie's implant? We could not continue to live in fear of Memory Lane controlling her from afar. There was a gnawing worry in the back of my mind. Why were they testing the implants now? Assuming they put the implant in the children at the beginning of the program, why wait four years to test it? It didn't make any sense. Unless they were testing it all along unbeknownst to the children.

"Hannah?" Leslie asked.

"Yeah?"

"What if Memory Lane turns on the implant again and I am forced to go back there?"

"None of us will let that happen," I said without hesitation.

"It happened before," Leslie said, quietly.

"I wish I could go back in time and change it, but I can't. Besides," I said, while hugging Leslie tighter. "We know what to watch out for now. Four years ago, we had no idea anything like this would happen."

"That's true," Leslie conceded, hugging me back.

My phone vibrated and I saw that it was a text from Kate. She was back from her mission with Brad.

"Let's go meet Kate. She's back," I said.

Leslie nodded and we both stood up from the bed. As we walked out of the room and closed the door, I heard raised voices coming from my parents' room.

What now?

"That's not true!" Mom shouted.

"Sorry to say it, but your sister isn't perfect, Aunt Linda!" Thomas yelled in retort.

What's that all about? Thomas doesn't normally speak to my Mom that way. I wondered what happened to cause him to be so rude.

"Come on, Les. We can deal with that later," I said. We walked down the yellow hallway and toward the atrium to meet with Kate. She said she had big news to share and the only thing I hoped was that it was good news. I didn't think any of us could take much more news that was bad.

Chapter 18

Hustling down the hallway, I scanned the faces of different groups of people talking. Kate was supposed to have gotten here and was waiting for us near the cafeteria area. Spotting her just as she was walking toward me, I rushed up to hug her and find out what she learned while she was gone.

"So what is your big news?" I asked, pulling out of the hug to make sure she was okay.

She looked fine, all things considered. Lord knows anything could have happened while she was out "running errands" for Antoine.

"Not here," she said, rolling her eyes. She must have had something that we wouldn't want all of Antoine's "ears" to hear. She gestured for us to follow her back to our room.

"Where's Brad?" I asked.

"He's debriefing Antoine on the trip."

Well, that's ominous, I thought to myself.

Walking up to our room door, Kate practically pushed us inside as she closed the door behind her. Without losing a single second, Kate immediately grabbed a book off the shelf, sat down at the small desk and began writing in the margins. *How many books had we defaced now just trying to have a shred of privacy in this place?* Leslie sat down on the bed while I continued to pace the small space. I was far too nervous about what Kate had to say to sit down. Kate wrote for a minute or two and then passed me the book. I walked closer to where Leslie was so she could read it too.

"When Brad and I left to deliver supplies, we turned on the radio for tunes, news, whatever came on. Something to break up the silence. Most of the drive was uneventful, but on our way back we heard a news broadcast about Memory Lane. They are starting mandatory memory screenings next week. Everyone over the age of five years old will have to go to a Memory Lane and be scanned into the system."

Mouth agape, it took me a second to regain my composure. It wasn't that I couldn't believe that Memory Lane would do this, it was more that I didn't understand why everything bad had to happen all at once! I grabbed the pen and sat down at the desk to write a response.

"They can't be serious. How is that legal? What even is a memory screening?" Scribbling my question, I widened my eyes to try to make Kate understand how scary this all was.

Kate grabbed the book from me and began scrawling words furiously. "As far as we can tell, they are just scanning your brain into the system. Sort of like an ID for every person. It's just a guess though." She looked at me, handed me the book and shrugged her shoulders. Scanning what she wrote, I wrote back.

"Any idea what Memory Lane is planning to do with the screening?"

Kate's written reply was short, and her expression spoke volumes. "Nothing good." Kate rested the pen and the open book on the desk.

As Leslie read the last few messages her expression changed to one of serious concern. She picked up the pen and book to write out her own question. "What if people refuse?"

Kate audibly sighed, looking resigned to what she would write next. "The radio said that everyone had five days to comply. They also said they would use the last census information to review who had been compliant. People who don't willingly get their brain scan will be arrested and be scanned against their will."

"What?" I shouted. Startled, both Leslie and Kate looked at me and motioned to the book. "Sorry, I just don't even know what to say."

Picking up the book and pen, I began to write what I was thinking. "How is this not the definition of communism? Don't people remember history?"

"They have more supporters than not, and I doubt Memory Lane cares," wrote Kate. There was very little space left on the page, but I wanted to make good use of it. Finding a mostly clear spot, I asked, "Have there been any protests against this?"

Kate nodded and spoke aloud. "Some, but not many. Most people are just complacent because they don't care anymore."

Flipping the page, I wrote in all capital letters, trying to get my inner screaming to reach both Kate and Leslie. "WE HAVE TO STOP THESE SCREENINGS! There is no way the vast majority of this country is okay with this! Memory Lane is brainwashing people!"

Leslie tapped me on the shoulder and gestured for the pen. Writing below my words, she wrote, "What if they're implanting adults now and calling it a memory screening?"

"I wouldn't put it past them." I said out loud, my voice dripping with disgust. Kate looked confused and grabbed the book and pen.

"Implanting?"

Sighing, I looked at Leslie. "Do you want to tell her or should I?" I asked aloud. I could see Leslie mustering all her strength to share what Memory Lane had done to her. She was so much braver and stronger than she could ever know.

Leslie took a deep breath and flipped the pages of the book until she came to one only half filled with typed story. Smiling, I nodded a small yes to let her know that I had her back.

"Memory Lane put some kind of implant in my brain. We don't know why, all we know is they have been testing it or turning it on. I space out, and Hannah has trouble getting me to come out of it. It makes me forget where I am. We just found out about this from Jenson," Leslie wrote. Kate's hands covered her mouth in horror. Leslie and I could see the immediate guilt that washed over her face. It couldn't be easy for her knowing her Dad did that to Leslie.

"I apologize this has happened to you. I didn't know that my Dad could do anything like this. I am so sorry, Leslie. I hope you can forgive me for not being able to help you!" Kate said as her voice cracked through the tears. Leslie hugged Kate tightly, showing her that she didn't blame Kate for what had happened.

"It's going to be okay," Leslie whispered. "It has to be."

As Kate pulled out of the hug to wipe her tears, I grabbed the book to tell Kate more of what Jenson had found. "It seems Jenson caused the breach at Memory Lane a day or two ago while gathering information about these chip implants. Other kids in the program got them too."

Kate grabbed the pen and wrote a question. "Why start messing with the implants now?"

"We don't actually know when the chip was implanted. Leslie doesn't remember getting it, so we assume all the kids were knocked out when it was put in their brains. Jenson should have more info. We can go see him now," I wrote back.

I looked over to Leslie while Kate read what I wrote. "Are you okay to talk to Jenson? We can wait if you aren't ready," I asked her aloud.

Leslie nodded and then got up from the bed. Kate placed the book back on the shelf, making sure it was closed so that no one could read our conversation should they come into the room while we were gone. We headed next door to my parents' room where I hoped Jenson and Thomas were still waiting. If they wandered off, this conversation would only prolong the inevitable. The door was slightly ajar and I pushed it open slowly.

"Knock, knock," I said while entering.

Thomas and Jenson both glanced up from where they were sitting on the bed. M Dad was sitting in the chair and Mom was pacing.

"Thomas?" Kate said in disbelief. "What are you doing here?"

"Hello to you too, Kate," he replied wryly.

Mom huffed. She was clearly still angry. "Why don't you fill Hannah and Kate in on why you're here, Thomas?" She narrowed her eye and looked at Thomas with disdain. "Leslie, let's go find somewhere else to be. I don't want you to hear this."

"What?! I deserve to be here just like everyone else!" Leslie pleaded.

"Leslie, listen to your mother," Dad calmly instructed.

Why were they still treating her like a baby who wasn't old enough to know what was going on? Out of all of us, she deserved to know the most! I sighed. "With all due respect, Mom, I'm just going to fill Leslie in later, so she might as well hear whatever it is straight from the source."

Leslie smiled at me, looking vindicated.

"You don't get a say in what Leslie gets to hear," Mom lashed out at me.

"But—" Leslie began.

"Nope. I won't have it. Now come on, let's go get a snack or something," Mom said while pushing Leslie out the door.

Leslie turned to look at me with pleading eyes. "It's okay, Les. Just go, I promise to fill you in."

After they left, I crossed my arms and rolled my eyes. "What is so horrible that Leslie can't hear?" I demanded.

Grabbing a book from the shelf, I took the pen from the desk and added to my statement, "She has an implant in her brain, for goodness sake!"

Thomas motioned for the pen and book and began writing. "My Mom cheated on my Dad with one of The Memorizers. That's why she was so against me coming here with you. She didn't want me to find out."

I showed what Thomas wrote to Kate and then replied. "What? Aunt Nicole? No way that's true!" I wrote back.

Thomas looked angry as he wrote back to me. "It is. My Dad has proof."

"But how? And when?" I wrote.

Thomas looked disgusted as he grabbed the pen to explain. "It first happened in May. She met this guy online and then they decided to meet up. My Mom apparently had a second phone no one knew about since then. My Dad found it and read through her texts with this guy and that was all the evidence he needed."

I took a minute or so to read his explanation and my eyes grew wide. "Buy why? I thought everything was fine between your parents?" I asked back.

"So did I. People can hide a lot of things behind closed doors," Thomas wrote.

Kate took the pen from Thomas. "I'm so sorry," she wrote.

Dad looked at Thomas apologetically. He looked like he wanted to say something and then changed his mind and stayed silent.

"How are you feeling with all of this?" I asked Thomas aloud.

"Honestly, I'm angry. But also, sad. It's just all confusing because it came out of nowhere," he replied.

Kate wrote again. "And we are sure that the person your Mom was with was a Memorizer?"

"What does that matter? She cheated on my Dad!" Thomas wrote back.

"Maybe your Mom will join The Memorizers now that her secret is out. You said she didn't want you coming here because you might discover her secret. Things unfolded in a different way, so maybe she will come around and join the cause," wrote Kate.

Thomas grabbed the pen out of Kate's hand quickly. "I'm not ready for that," he wrote.

I placed my hand on Thomas's shoulder to show him I supported his decision. It was his Mom. He could decide if he wanted her here or not.

Jenson took the pen this time. "Why don't we all regroup? What did you guys come in to talk to us about?" he wrote.

Kate and I looked at each other. I gave her a signal to go ahead and explain since she is the one who heard it on the radio. She wrote for a bit and then took some time to let both Jenson and Thomas read it.

"What?! That cannot be legal!" wrote Jenson. He passed the pen to Thomas, who wrote, "What the heck is a memory screening?"

I shrugged and took the pen back. "I don't know what the screening is, but we can sure try to guess knowing what they did to Leslie. We may be close to having an uprising against Memory Lane on our hands soon. Too many people will fight this."

Jenson didn't look convinced. "You sure? I actually think people on the whole are pretty compliant with whatever Memory Lane says," he wrote.

"The Memorizers aren't. And their numbers are growing," I wrote back.

Thomas looked angry when he wrote something in response. "Considering Antoine may have tried to poison me, and what is happening with my Mom, I don't know that I can support The Memorizers."

I looked at Thomas and squeezed his shoulder in support. "I understand. No one blames you for that," I said out loud.

Jenson took the pen and began writing again. "So, what's the plan? We need one fast because I still need to show everyone what I collected the other day from my hack of their system."

"We need to fill in your Mom before we do anything," said Dad.

I forgot for a second that he was in the room.

"I feel like we are back at square one with all of this," I wrote in the book, then held it up for everyone to see.

Dad shook his head in defiance and grabbed the pen and book from my hand. "That's not true. We've learned how to fight back. We've learned how to stick together as a family."

"Did you see how Mom left? I'm not sure that's enough anymore," I said aloud. Kate squeezed my hand in support.

Before Dad could respond, a distant wail began to sound outside the room. We all looked up at the same time to turn toward the sound.

"What on earth was that?" I asked.

We all walked toward the door and opened it to find out what was happening. The sound increased in intensity and we could see it must have been some kind of warning system. More and more people started running down the hall in panic. The intensity of the siren was increasing and soon the hallway was engulfed in sound. WEE WOO. WEE WOO. WEE WOO. WEE WOO.

I covered my ears because it was so loud.

Looking up and down the yellow hallway, I saw a siren in the far corner. *Has that always been there?* I wasn't sure if the siren was new or if I had just been oblivious. To be fair, I wasn't exactly hanging out in the hallway all the time.

WEE WOO. WEE WOO. WEE WOO. WEE WOO.

People continued to run past our door toward the atrium.

"Should we follow?" I yelled at Thomas, Dad, Jenson, and Kate to hear myself over the noise.

Thomas shrugged.

Kate looked scared with her wide eyes.

Jenson looked confused.

Without waiting, I made an executive decision to follow the people. We didn't know what kind of emergency could be happening and moving toward the atrium had to be better than standing here, going deaf by the siren in this hall.

Joining the throng of people proved chaotic as people knocked into us from all angles while running.

"Watch out!" I yelled.

WEE WOO. WEE WOO. WEE WOO. WEE WOO.

"What's going on?" someone asked me when we reached the atrium.

I shrugged and made sure to find Dad and the others so that I wouldn't get separated. Spotting Thomas's head from behind, I made my way over and stood by him. "When is this noise gonna stop?" I asked, still trying to shout above the siren's call.

He shrugged.

Jenson and Kate stepped in beside me.

"Where's Mom and Leslie?" I shouted to Kate.

"What?" she yelled back.

It figures she couldn't hear me over the panic and the noise in the atrium.

"Hannah!" a panicked voice shouted.

Turning around, I saw Mom running toward me. We embraced for a minute before I looked again to see if Leslie was with her. My eyes grew wider as I didn't see her appear. Panic welled up inside me as I frantically searched the sea of faces for Leslie.

"Mom, where's Leslie?" I yelled, trying to be heard over the siren.

"She was right behind me…" said Mom, while craning her neck to see around all the people.

The siren continued to blare.

WEE WOO. WEE WOO. WEE WOO. WEE WOO.

"You lost her?!" I shouted, my voice filled with anger and fear.

Jenson and Thomas both turned to look at me with determination in their faces. "We'll find her."

Just as they started to leave our group, the siren stopped. The silence was eerie as everyone was no longer talking and shouting.

"Attention!"

Pretty much all of us turned to face the direction the voice came from.

It was Antoine standing on a table in the atrium. Brad was standing near him off to the side and I started to wonder what was really going on. None of this made any sense.

"Attention all Memorizers! The siren you just heard is a way of communicating to the whole facility. It means we have been breached and that we must move to a secure location."

Mass chaos broke out as everyone began shouting questions all at once.

"What?!"

"How is that possible?"

"Where is the secure location?"

"Is there a traitor among us?"

The questions from people immediately surrounding me were all I could make out through the noise.

Antoine held his hand up to silence the crowd. It worked. *Was he a god to these people?*

"I know you have questions right now. I wish I could answer them but it is in our best interest to act swiftly and silently so that we can reach the other location safely."

"Where is it?" a woman from the front asked.

A man followed up her question with one of his own. "How can all of us travel together?"

"This makes no sense!"

"You can't treat us like this!"

This was all happening too fast. I had the same questions, but all I could think about was finding Leslie. She had to be lost in this crowd somewhere, and what if she had spaced out again and she was standing catatonic in this sea of people? I started to weave my way through the mass of people since they were all standing still and facing Antoine.

"The secured location is in Alaska. There is an underground compound for The Memorizers there. I have already been in contact with the head of operations at that facility and they are prepared to take in two hundred of us with no questions asked," said Antoine, calmly.

"Two hundred! That's not even half of us!" I heard a man shout.

People yelled "Yeah!" in agreement.

"Isn't it dangerous to tell us where we are going if someone is a traitor here?" someone else shouted.

"How are we getting there? Won't it be suspicious if we all travel together?" a woman from the back of the crowd asked.

"How were we breached? It had to be someone from within!" yelled another woman.

The crowd was in an uproar. Everyone started shoving and pushing and fighting, trying to see who was responsible for the breach. I felt someone grab me from behind and I turned around to hit them when I realized it was Leslie.

"Oh my God! I'm so glad you're okay!" I exclaimed, pulling her into a hug. I looked down into her face and could see she was afraid.

"Hannah, its Mom!" Leslie was yanking my hand to pull me through the crowd.

"Les, what's wrong?" She looked panicked. Before I could finish asking what had her so upset, a booming voice interrupted us all.

"Silence!" shouted Antoine into a voice amplifier. It looked like a regular microphone but instead of just making your voice louder, it projected a hologram-like image above the crowd. This wasn't the first time I had seen the voice amplifiers, but they had only been on the market maybe six months. *How did he get his hands on one of those?* Since Antoine spends all of his time underground with The Memorizers, he must have ordered it online or had it brought here to him.

Everyone in the crowd stopped yelling and shoving and looked up at the hologram of Antoine's head. "Listen to me. There is no need to panic. The breach of The Memorizers has only given away our location, not our numbers. Memory Lane has no idea how many members we have. We can still make this work by going to the secure location in Alaska. Unfortunately, we only have room for two hundred Memorizers at that location. The rest of you will have to scatter so that we can remain vigilant and fight Memory Lane."

"How will we decide on the people that go?" asked a man from the crowd.

The hologram image spoke again. Honestly, it was weird seeing Antoine in real life and in holographic form at the same time. "It will be based on your color sectors. Blue, yellow, and black can come to Alaska. Details of this will be discussed in the next hour for those of you this applies to. The red, orange, and brown sectors will have to disperse throughout the country. We will provide each of you with a walkie-talkie to communicate with us. The channel you are looking for on the walkie-talkie is channel eight."

The crowd was angry again and I pulled Leslie close to me. Stretching myself up on my tiptoes, I craned my neck to see if I could find my parents, Thomas, Jenson, or Kate. We had to decide what to do from here.

"What is there to communicate with those of us you are leaving behind?" a woman asked. "Are we just pawns in your game? You're no better than Memory Lane!" she shouted.

"Yeah!" the crowd agreed.

The Antoine-hologram spoke again from above. "I would like those of you that cannot come to Alaska with us to still fight for The Memorizers. We can use all the help we can get in the movement against Memory Lane."

"Movement? I thought this was a war..." I said aloud so only Leslie could hear.

"This is insane. There's someone among us who gave away this location. Who's to say the same thing won't happen again in Alaska?" asked a man from the crowd. I recalled seeing him in the yellow sector hallway, but I didn't know his name.

"I assure you the person in question that caused the information leak has been taken care of," said Antoine matter-of-factly.

Leslie tapped me on the shoulder, and I crouched down so she could whisper in my ear. "Do you think he means Gill? She wouldn't have done this! Gill was removed and then this happens. It's too much of a coincidence. Antoine has it all wrong!"

"You're right, Gill wouldn't have given away the location. We need to find everyone else and talk about whether or not we want to head up to Alaska," I whispered back.

"Everyone now has half an hour to gather their belongings and clear out. I think Memory Lane guards are headed this way within a few hours. If you are in the yellow, blue, or black sectors, follow me to the recreation area so we can discuss how we will travel to Alaska.

Thank you for leaving this atrium in an orderly fashion," Antoine said. He turned off the voice amplifier and his hologram faded away.

Immediately people started running to leave the atrium. *So much for not panicking.* I maintained my grip on Leslie's hand as we just tried to follow the crowd of people. I still hadn't been able to find out what had Leslie so upset. Looking around I could see there was no way I was going to find anyone in this mess. I headed back to our room and hoped that they would come up with the same idea.

Someone shoved past Leslie and knocked her hand out of mine.

"Watch it!" I yelled, while grabbing her hand again and tightening my grip to continue forward. Leslie and I had just made it back into the yellow hallway when I heard someone call from behind me.

"Hannah!"

As I turned around, I realized it was Thomas. I moved over to the side of the hallway to let some people pass.

"You found Leslie! But where are the others?" Thomas asked.

Without responding, I ushered the three of us into my room and closed the door.

"I don't know," I said, finally responding to Thomas's question. Before I could say another word, Leslie started yanking on my hand.

"Hannah, Mom lost her memory again!" I felt the blood drain from my face. It had been so long since the last time this happened that I completely forgot she was starting to lose her memories. *Why did this have to happen now?!?*

"We got halfway down the hallway after the argument about Thomas and she just freaked out. She saw me standing there with my hand in hers and she let me go. Like I was a ghost. I tried to talk to her, Hannah, really I did. Mom just wouldn't believe me. She just kept repeating that I was dead and asked where she was. Then she took off down the hall. I ran after her but lost her around one of the hallways and then the alarm went off. I didn't know what to do so I just went looking for you!" In a single breath, Leslie had rushed through what had happened. She sucked in a gasp of air.

"Do you know where she is now, Les? Did you see her in the crowd at all?"

She shook her head no. This facility was huge; there was no way we could just go look for her. I had to hope that this memory lapse would pass like the others, and she would make her way back here. "Do you think Jenson, Aunt Linda, and Uncle Robert will come back here?" Thomas asked.

"They should. At least Dad and Jenson will. Hopefully they found Mom. How do you feel about Alaska?" I whispered to Thomas.

"Well, I think it's smart to go toward Alaska because it's close to Canada. Our plan was to go there in the beginning and that could be our way out of this mess," said Thomas.

I nodded, contemplating what that really meant. So many unanswered questions. *How would we get there? Are we actually staying with The Memorizers? Was this even a good idea with Leslie's chip and now more memory lapses from Mom?*

"Do you think the information leak was done by Gill?" Leslie whispered to Thomas.

"That would be my guess, but honestly it could be anyone. Heck, it could have been Antoine. I don't trust that guy as far as I can throw him," replied Thomas.

"I don't either," I said.

The door opened and all of us turned to see who it was. It was Jenson. I motioned for him to close the door so that people in the hall or wherever else wouldn't be able to listen in. Without asking what he thought, Jenson chimed in, "If we're sticking with The Memorizers, we need to decide soon," he said.

"Where are my parents?" I asked. "We should probably decide as a group what we're doing."

"They were speaking with Antoine about Alaska, I think," Jenson replied.

The door opened again — *Seriously? Was there a sign on the door that said, "Come on in"?* — and I looked over to see Brad.

"What are you guys doing in here? Why aren't you meeting with the other people going to Alaska?" he asked, confused.

"We're still deciding on some things," I replied.

"What is there to decide?"

I looked from Jenson to Thomas and back to Brad.

"I need to talk to my parents first," I explained.

Brad started pacing in the room. "Well, you better get a move on. Things are happening fast. Truthfully, I think people in The Memorizers are going to start freaking out soon about the mandatory memory screening from Memory Lane. Most people here haven't seen that on the news yet because they don't always check the internet or the TV for news. They're in for a rude awakening when they get back above ground."

"Yeah, Kate told us earlier what was going on. None of this is good, but how does going to Alaska help avoid the memory screening? Last I checked, Alaska is still a state in this country and still ultimately governed by Memory Lane," I said sarcastically.

Brad sighed and leaned in so we could all hear. Speaking in a low voice, he said, "We're not really going to Alaska."

Chapter 19

"What does that mean?" I furrowed my eyebrows.

Brad put a finger over his mouth to silence me. Leslie reached for a book from the shelf, giving him a pen without skipping a beat. Brad quickly began writing to explain what was really going on. He scribbled on the paper for several minutes, and we just had to wait in silence. When he finished, he shoved the book back in my direction. Everyone leaned over my shoulder, peering down at the book.

"Antoine is going to hide out in northern Michigan. He's paranoid that The Memorizers' location in Alaska has an alliance with Memory Lane, and that the leader there told the guards that we are on our way. He thinks it's a set-up," Brad wrote.

"This is giving me a headache." I rubbed my temples, trying to think of a way around this. Things keep getting worse, and honestly, one day of boring would be a vacation at this point.

Thomas wrote out a question in the book. "So, who is leading The Memorizers here if Antoine isn't going to Alaska?"

Brad took the pen back, this time scribbling vigorously. His handwriting looked even worse than before. The letters were exaggerated with strange curves that I could barely make sense of. Squinting at the paper, I finally pieced together a few comprehensive sentences. "That's what the meeting is about right now. Antoine is asking for several people to lead smaller groups of people. It would look suspicious if we all left on the same transportation to Alaska."

Stealing the pen from Brad, I wrote my own thoughts. "I think people will notice that Antoine is not with his group of Memorizers." *Does no one else feel like it's too suspicious?*

Brad, smiling eerily, offered his explanation. "He'll be traveling with a very small, select group of people. Me included. If I asked, I could even get you guys in too."

I gritted my teeth. "So you're okay to sit back and watch all of these other people get led into a trap while you and Antoine run away?" Brad jolted, looking up with confusion.

"I'm inviting you!"

"That doesn't make it right!"

Jenson sighed. "Hannah's right, Brad. There's no way we're going along with this. I would rather be forced to do a memory screening than be a part of this little *charade*." Brad frowned, looking hurt.

Thomas clenched his fists and turned away from Brad. "This is disgusting. I can't believe you even suggested that!"

"It wasn't my idea!" Brad ground his jaw, pinching his eyebrows with a look of fury. "I just thought you guys wanted to fight Memory Lane as much as we do. Clearly, I was mistaken." He turned to leave the room, reaching for the doorknob.

"Wait! Hang on just a minute."

Brad stopped and turned around.

Grabbing the book, I took a deep breath and wrote, "Explain to me how you and Antoine going to Michigan continues the fight against Memory Lane. I really do want to try and understand the purpose behind losing two hundred Memorizers."

"That's confidential information, only available to those that are signed up to go with us," Brad wrote confidently.

"Really, dude?" I swore out loud. As if keeping information a secret was grounds to suddenly want to join this faux rebellion.

Brad looked smug and crossed his arms.

Thomas rolled his eyes. "You can just go, then."

Brad frowned, but ultimately left the room, slamming the door like a petulant child behind him.

"What's his problem? Who brings up all that crap and then doesn't even explain what it means?" Jenson asked as he ran his hands with frustration through his hair. "Honestly, I can't stand him."

Thomas and I looked at Jenson; neither of us ever totally trusted Brad. Now I could clearly see why.

"I know he brought you here to The Memorizers and that kept you safe for a while but he's a jerk. Seriously," Jenson said, irritably.

"We never knew if we could trust him before. Honestly, I am glad he showed his true colors now. We need to tell my parents about this. We should try to find them." Before we could leave the room, I turned to see Leslie, frozen in place and staring at the wall. My stomach dropped. *We do not have time for this right now. Don't panic, Hannah. Of course, they would trigger the implant right now. I should've expected this.* Taking a deep breath, I prioritize my sister.

"Les? Can you hear me?" I gently touched her arm. "Come back to me, Les. We need to go get Mom and Dad so we can leave." I used a soft tone, getting on one knee to look up into her eyes.

She was repeating a phrase over and over, but it was so quiet that I couldn't make out the words. My heart beat heavily. I leaned in, trying to catch the phrases.

"Must not go ... Must not go to…"

Panic was rising in my chest, like the walls were closing in on me. With all my will, I pushed the panic down. Maybe I could get her to answer me. "Must not go where?"

Leslie was still staring straight ahead with a blank look on her face. When I waved my hand in front of her face, she didn't register the movement at all, she just continued to stare wide-eyed without blinking at the wall. I glanced worriedly at Thomas and Jenson, waving my hand again just in case. If she doesn't wake up soon …

"Les? Come on. It's me, Hannah. You're safe, I promise," I told her.

Thomas and I locked eyes, concern apparent on both of our faces. We didn't have time to wait on Leslie to come back to us. We needed to leave this place for good, one way or another.

Leslie continued to repeat the phrase "Must not go to..." over and over. As we waited for her to come back to us mentally, she suddenly started to walk toward the door. Without realizing what was happening, Leslie opened the door and walked into the hall. Her walk was very slow and robotic.

"Leslie!" I threw myself after her in a rush. "Where are you going?!" I struggled to contain my panic and concern. *We need to leave now.*

She continued to awkwardly walk down the length of the yellow hallway, and I jumped in front of her, spreading my arms out to block her. "Leslie," I said again, urgently. I gently approached her, grabbing her shoulders with soft hands. I knelt down to look up into her eyes again.

"Les, can you hear me? It's Hannah."

As if she could tell I was holding her back, her legs were trying to continue walking around me and I grabbed her shoulders firmly to keep that from happening. I scrunched my nose, tears building from the frustration and anger at all that was happening. Everything was going wrong. I took a calm breath.

I looked up to see Thomas and Jenson running to catch up to us.

"What's going on?" Thomas asked anxiously. "Why is she walking away from us?"

"It has to be the chip. They must be calling the kids to go somewhere," I guessed.

I turned to Jenson. "Do you have access to the chip information that you collected? Can you turn her chip off?" I asked frantically. Jenson frowned.

"I have the information, but I don't have the capabilities of deactivating the chip from a remote location," Jenson explained.

"Well then what good are you?!" I shouted, clenching my fists and staring at Leslie with tears welling up in my eyes.

Jenson jerked back, surprised by my outburst.

"I'm sorry, Jenson, I just don't know what to do." Tears slid down my cheeks. "How do I help her?"

"Hannah?" Leslie asked. She had just come out of the trance, and relief flooded into my heart. "Why are we in the hall?" She frowned, and I knew that it would only take her a moment to puzzle it out. I tried to subtly wipe my eyes with my sleeve. *Now isn't the time to cry, what am I doing?*

"We followed you out here. What do you remember from the last few minutes?" I asked.

"There was a phrase in my head that was repeating over and over. It was very annoying." She watched as I stood up to my full height again, and Jenson looked at my reddened eyes with a sigh.

I kept my hands on Leslie's shoulders to hide the tremors from my panic and tried to focus on our mission.

"What was the phrase, Les?"

"Must not go to Michigan," she replied blankly. "Do you know what that means?"

Thomas and Jenson looked at me with wide eyes. *Does that mean that Memory Lane knows about Antoine sending The Memorizers to Alaska while he heads to Michigan?*

"Why is Memory Lane preventing the program kids from going to Michigan?" I asked aloud to the others.

"Beats me," said Thomas.

I swallowed. I looked at Leslie again, finally releasing my hands from her shoulders as I completely composed myself. "Let's go find Kate and Mom and Dad."

Since the atrium was at the center of this whole complex and connected to most of the other areas, we walked there first. As we approached, I could see people pushing, shoving, and attacking others without remorse. It was complete chaos, and I wrapped an arm around Leslie instinctively as we got closer to the violence.

"The meeting for people going to Alaska, where is it?" I shouted at Thomas over the noise.

"I think they were meeting in the rec area," suggested Thomas. "But that's just a guess."

I craned my neck to look over the crowd of people. "Where's Kate?"

Leslie pushed closer to my side. This was a lot of people acting erratically, and truthfully, I was nervous. We didn't know what these people were capable of, and they'd already seemed to go straight into the path of violence. I wasn't sure what would come next.

"Surely she wouldn't still be in this crowd," Jenson yelled over the noise.

As I looked for Kate, a million thoughts raced through my head. *Why are these people still here, fighting? They know that Memory Lane is coming soon. They also know who was already pre-selected to go to Alaska. They can't change their color sector now, so what is the point of beating each other up about it? Why are The Memorizers so trusting of Antoine? Why are they so desperate to follow him across the country?*

I looked up to see Kate sprinting toward us from the recreation area.

"Hannah! Where have you been? Is everything okay?" she asked, wrapping me in a hug.

I squeezed her once, before pulling out of the embrace. "We're fine. Where are my parents? Were you in the meeting with them?"

She pulled me and Leslie away from the fighting in the atrium, leading us off to the side of the yellow hallway. Thomas and Jenson followed. "Yes, they were right behind me. We were headed back to the room to grab some stuff so we could leave."

"Leave? We're going with Antoine?" I asked in disbelief.

"Let's talk in the room," she replied.

"Hannah!" I heard someone call from behind me.

Turning around quickly, I saw my parents. A wave of relief passed over me. Mom looked fine, as though nothing had happened. In this moment, it didn't even matter. We were finally all back together and could decide as a family what our next course of action would be.

We hugged, and I nearly melted in my parents' arms. You never know how much fear is driving you until, for a moment, it stops. Tears stung my eyes for the second time that day in knowing that at least for now, Mom and Dad were okay.

"You guys holding up okay?" Dad asked.

"Yeah, I guess." I let myself linger in their arms for a moment before awkwardly pulling away.

Dad ushered us all down the hallway and back to his room. As soon as all of us were inside, we closed the door. For a moment, I held my breath, anxious to hear my parents' input on this whole thing.

Dad looked resigned. "So, we think it's best to go our separate ways from The Memorizers. Kate's Dad is still looking for her and with The Memorizers' location now compromised, we just don't see how it can get any better if we stay with them."

"Don't you want to have all the information first?" Jenson asked impatiently.

I turned to glare at him. I agreed with my parents. I didn't trust Antoine or The Memorizers for that matter.

Mom sighed. "What information? We went to the meeting with Antoine. He has a caravan getting ready to head up to Washington state, and then a ferry will be arranged for people to continue to Alaska. He's trying to avoid Canada if he can help it."

"We should go with them!" said Thomas, suddenly. "That's our way into Canada!"

All of us turned to look at Thomas in shock.

"You want to go to Alaska?" I asked.

Thomas grinned slyly. "I didn't say that."

"You literally just did," I pointed out.

Thomas looked smug. "No, I said that we should go with The Memorizers and then go on toward Canada. That's our way out of the country."

"But Memory Lane knows that Antoine isn't really going with The Memorizers and that he's headed toward Michigan," Jenson pointed out, scowling.

"Exactly. Which means that the Memory Lane guards won't expect people in Alaska."

Mom had a look of consternation on her face as she thought about what Thomas had to say. "I'm not sure that's true. I think Memory Lane must know most of the plan, or even the entire thing."

"What are we planning to do about Leslie?" I interrupted. Both my parents and Thomas looked at me. "We can't let Memory Lane poke around in her head forever. Is it safe for her to go to Alaska?"

"I'm right here, you know," said Leslie, irritably. She hated that we were always talking about her as if she wasn't in the room.

"Hannah has a point," said Mom.

"I would like to put as much space in between me and my Dad as possible," Kate said softly.

I gently squeezed her shoulder in support. "We know. Don't worry."

Leslie looked around the room and opened her mouth several times to say something and then changed her mind. Sometimes children could see through all the unnecessary things and make the most obvious choice. "Why don't we take a vote?" she finally asked.

"That's an excellent idea!" Mom cheered.

"All those in favor of going with The Memorizers toward Alaska?" I asked.

Thomas, Kate, Leslie, and Dad raised their hands.

"All those in favor of going our own way?" I asked after everyone who voted put their hands down.

Mom, Jenson, and I raised our hands.

"That settles it then," I sighed, but conceded. "We're going to Alaska." Making eye contact with my parents, I made sure to emphasize what needed to happen next. "So, who is going to tell Antoine and Brad that we aren't joining their 'special group' going to Michigan?" I asked.

"I'll go tell him," Dad chimed. "Everyone else, get ready to go. We're meeting above ground to figure out who is going in what car."

We all nodded simultaneously in agreement.

"Wait, there are cars already waiting for The Memorizers? How did Antoine manage that?" Thomas blurted.

"In the meeting, Antoine said the cars are about three miles west of here at a junkyard full of cars. Antoine knows the guy running the place. He promises that there are unregistered working cars in the back," explained Mom.

"So, we're walking three miles today, to a car that may or may not work based on what was told to us by a guy we can't trust?" asked Jenson, disgruntled.

"Looks that way," said Dad. "It's not ideal, but we'll have to deal with it for now."

"How far are we actually planning to go with The Memorizers?" I asked.

Mom thought for a minute. "Probably until everyone gets on the ferry in Washington. I think we'll just disappear and hope no one questions it," she said.

"I still think we need to figure out how we're getting into Canada," said Thomas. "We will need IDs and passports, among other things."

"Fair point," Dad replied.

"Didn't you have a 'guy' that could make us IDs?" Mom asked.

Thomas nodded. "I'll have to VidChat him later to see if he can ship them to us when we get to Washington. It should take us a few days to get there anyway," he said.

"Sounds good. We'll keep an eye out for something better, but I think your guy is going to be our best option," Dad said.

There was still one more thing we had to plan for. Taking a deep breath, I tried to swallow the awkwardness in my throat. "There's something else we need to talk about before going above ground." I nudged Leslie to encourage her to ask about her place in all of this.

"What do we tell people if I space out again because Memory Lane is controlling the chip in my head?" Leslie asked. "I don't want y'all to get kicked out of the caravan but I also don't want to be left alone," she added in a small voice.

"We'll tell them it's none of their business," stated Mom.

"And if I can't resist the urge to listen to the chip?" asked Leslie, timidly.

"We won't let that happen," I replied, reaching out to take her hand so she knew with absolute certainty.

Leslie gave me a small smile. "Thanks, Hannah." She squeezed my hand, and I knew I would do whatever it took to keep that promise.

I glanced over at Jenson. He looked like he was concentrating really hard about something. "I just had another thought. Who is the leader of this caravan of cars and people heading to Alaska, since Brad and Antoine are headed elsewhere?"

"Why does there have to be a leader?" Mom asked. "Why can't humans just come together and work toward a common goal?"

"I don't know what 'kumbaya world' you live in, but people can't be trusted to work collaboratively in a group without a leader these days. Most people are followers," replied Jenson sardonically.

"No need to get hostile," said Mom defensively.

Thomas looked Jenson right in the eyes and they stared at each other for an uncomfortable amount of time as we all watched. "Are you volunteering?" Thomas challenged.

"To lead?" Jenson chuckled. "Absolutely not. We just need to know who to steer clear of once we get going. If we become too chummy with the leader, they will be suspicious when we disappear in Washington."

"How do you know so much about the way people will act?" asked Dad, genuinely curious.

"You learn about the way people really are in prison. The time I spent there for illegal hacking taught me a lot about the human condition. Even in prison there is a hierarchy of leaders in groups. Listen, I'm not proud of what I did, but I refuse to be a victim of my circumstances. I can only get better by learning from my mistakes. Learning means not repeating them by being a sheep."

Mom's eyes went wide, but she seemed to appreciate his honesty. If I was honest with myself, there were times I often forgot that Kate told me Jenson served time in prison for hacking. He seemed so helpful all the time and willing to do whatever we needed. A lot to ask of someone's ex-boyfriend.

"Here's an idea," Dad suggested to the group. "Let's just join the group and then see who comes out as a natural leader. We don't have to appoint one. Other people might have someone in mind. I agree with Jenson, the lower profile we keep, the better."

We all nodded in agreement and finally left the room. We had wasted enough time talking about what we were going to do instead of actually doing it. As we wandered into the hallway, there were shouts and screams all around. People were still going crazy. I grabbed Leslie's hand to keep her close to me. All of us walked anxiously through the atrium and main tunnel to head up to the surface.

There was a line of people waiting at the above ground exit and it was mass chaos on the ladder. People were shoving and pushing each other to get out. Leslie looked at me, her eyes wide with fear, and I gripped her tighter to me. *I knew there was a limited number of people that could go to Alaska, but I thought that was already decided by the color hallway we were housed in? It's not like we could change that now.*

"Get out of the way! I'm going with The Memorizers no matter what Antoine says!" a man yelled from the bottom of the ladder. I watched in horror as he pulled out a gun and started shooting it in the air erratically. I ducked and immediately dragged Leslie down with me and shielded her with my body to make sure she wouldn't be hit by a bullet. Her body was aggressively shaking as I held her against me, and I prayed that God would protect us from any more. *Hadn't we been through enough?!?*

Screams and shouts erupted as the man continued to shoot. Bodies fell off the ladder and as the shots continued to ring out, even more people were running away from the exit. Mom shouted my name and was frantically looking for me and Leslie.

"Mom!!" I shouted just as Mom locked eyes with me. Relief spread across her face when she saw that I was covering most of Leslie's body with my own. She reached down to grab my hand and pull Leslie and me around the corner.

The screaming and shouting continued as people pushed and shoved their way through the crowd trying to get away from the man who continued to shoot. The acrid smell of gunpowder filled the air. *How many bullets were in his gun?!?*

Dad came running up behind Mom at the same time Kate and Thomas did. "Everyone steer clear of that exit. That guy has gone crazy!" shouted Kate frantically.

"Wait, where's Jenson?" I asked. "He was right next to Leslie and me before the shooting started."

Thomas and I peeked around the corner toward the ladder to see if Jenson was over that way but he was nowhere to be seen.

The smell of blood was metallic in the air and just as it seemed as though the first shooter ran out of bullets another man took out his gun and started firing back at the original shooter. *Where were these people getting guns?!? Did they always have them?*

The hallway was filled with sounds of children crying, and people coughing and choking. Mothers lay at the feet of their kids, weeping and screaming that their babies had been shot. *How could Antoine not have known that telling people to fend for themselves would cause chaos?*

Hugging Leslie tighter, I worried about what we would do next, when suddenly Jenson came running up to our group. He was out of breath, and his pale face was dotted with sweat.

"Where'd you go?" asked Kate, sounding relieved that he had found his way to us.

"I was trying… to help some people… get away from… the man with the gun," he stammered, wincing. Something was very wrong.

"Are you okay, man?" Thomas asked, his eyebrows knitted with worry.

Before Jenson could answer, he tried to take a deep breath, one that drained the rest of the color from his face as he rocked on his feet and fell to his knees. He grabbed at his side, as a red spot began to soak through his shirt and covered his fingers with blood. Jenson looked down with his last bit of energy before falling the rest of the way to the ground. My eyes grew wide as I grasped the severity of what was happening. Jenson had been shot.

Chapter 20

The chaos around us faded into the background as time slowed down. "Jenson," I gasped. Relinquishing my hold on Leslie and handing her over to Mom, I dropped down to the ground.

The red spot on Jenson's stomach increased in size tenfold as blood leaked onto the floor. Lifting his shirt, I looked for an exit wound. If he didn't have a hole on his back, the bullet could still be inside. Thomas dropped to the floor and gently tried to turn Jenson on his side so we could get a better look at what we were dealing with. No exit wound. Sighing, I checked Jenson's breathing; it was there, but sounded labored. His skin was pale and sweaty, yet he seemed to be shivering at the same time.

"Jenson, can you hear me?" I asked him, while lightly gripping his shoulder. The puddle of blood Jenson was lying in was growing and with it my worry. We couldn't lose Jenson!

No response.

Leslie took off her jacket and handed it to me. "Put it under his head, Hannah."

"Maybe it's the blood loss; he could be unconscious from that or the pain. I'll call 911," Thomas said as he took out his cell phone. He walked a few steps away so he could tell the emergency operator what happened and that we needed medical assistance now.

Someone grabbed Jenson's hand and I glanced up to see that it was Kate. Her face was drawn with worry.

I took a moment to look at each face crowded around Jenson's bleeding body, and I saw fear in each one. It seemed as though nothing would ever go our way.

Dad took off his sweatshirt and handed it to me. I stared at him blankly with my eyebrows knitted in confusion.

"Press it on his wound. The pressure should stop the bleeding," he explained.

"Oh! Right," I said while nodding. How did I forget something so fundamental to stop the bleeding?

As soon as I pressed Dad's shirt into the wound, Jenson opened his eyes and gasped.

I winced along with Jenson. "Sorry, but I have to control the bleeding," I said.

"Warn a guy next time," Jenson said between short breaths. He tried to force a smirk and, honestly, seeing his sense of humor peeking through made me feel a little better. Maybe he would be okay.

"Why do people act like getting shot is no big deal in the movies?" Jenson asked, and it made me smile down at him.

"I thought you were a big tough guy," I joked, hoping to keep his mind off of the bleeding.

My senses were returning, and I could still smell the gunpowder in the air, and the metallic scent of blood. There was more shouting and I glanced up from Jenson's wound to see people rushing toward the ladder again. It was then I realized that there were no more gunshots. The commotion at the ladder was due to the man with the gun being subdued. People were back to racing to get out of the compound.

People are crazy, I thought to myself as I shook my head.

"The ambulance is on its way," said Thomas, breaking my thoughts. "I made sure they sent several since who knows how many people have been shot."

"Did they say how long they'd be?" I asked, tension rising in my throat.

"Just about six minutes," Thomas replied.

It felt too long. I could feel the heat from the blood that was slowly soaking Dad's shirt. It was so much blood. I forced a smile despite the rising fears and made sure to keep pressure on his wound, "Hear that?" I asked. "Help is coming."

Kate squeezed his hand in reassurance and Jenson attempted to give a thumbs up with his other hand, but he was struggling. His blinks were getting longer and I feared that he would go unconscious again if we didn't keep him awake. I seemed to remember that was an important part of treating someone with trauma involving blood loss.

"Hey," I said, while slightly shaking Jenson. "You have to stay awake. Talk to me about something."

"How's the weather?" he asked, smirking and wincing at the same time. His eyes closed briefly and I shook him awake again.

"I'm serious, Jenson. You gotta stay awake," I said.

There was more commotion around us as more people started climbing up the ladder to exit the facility. A woman came up to where we were all kneeling because we were blocking the walkway. I didn't really want to move Jenson at the moment because keeping pressure on his wound seemed to be slowing down the bleeding. I didn't need him to get any worse.

"Is he okay?" the woman asked, while leaning over my shoulder to take a closer look.

Mom jumped up and tried to block the woman's view. "He's fine," she said matter-of-factly. "We already called for an ambulance."

"I used to be a doctor," replied the woman. "Are you sure you don't need help?"

I looked from Kate to Thomas and then to Dad. *What were the chances of there being a medical doctor here among The Memorizers? Could we really trust her to help?* I raised my eyebrow to ask what Dad thought as a form of silent communication.

He shrugged in response.

"We're fine here," said Mom. I guess she decided we didn't need the woman's help after all.

The woman looked resigned, but then turned around and walked toward the ladder so she could exit. There were less and less people around us as more people continued to leave. Good, we didn't want an audience right now.

"So, tell me about the information you found regarding the kids in the program," I asked Jenson.

He opened one eye and then cocked one eyebrow. "Now?" he whispered.

"Now's as good a time as any," I replied.

Jenson coughed and then winced hard as it pulled at the muscles in his abdomen. I glanced down to see little droplets of blood at the top of his shirt.

Was he bleeding internally? I asked myself.

"Hey, easy there," I said in my calmest voice possible. I didn't want to alarm him.

Kate caught my eye and we exchanged a glance that said coughing up blood could not be good.

"I'm thirsty," said Jenson, his voice raspy.

I sighed. "I know. The ambulance will be here any minute and I bet they will give you something to drink," I said.

"The program originally started—" Jenson began. He was cut off again by another coughing fit that produced more blood coming out of his mouth.

"I'll go get him some water," said Leslie, rising from her place by my side. I thanked her silently and then saw Mom go with her.

Turning my attention toward the ladder, I heard a commotion again as the paramedics arrived. They were trying to come down the ladder as others were still attempting to climb up.

"Out of the way!" someone yelled.

I watched as people moved and several paramedics made their way into the room.

A woman shouted frantically "I need help over here! My daughter has been shot!" One of the paramedics ran over to help her while another scanned the room for other people with injuries.

"Over here!" Kate yelled, as she got up to grab someone and bring them over to help.

"Hannah," Jenson whispered. His voice was raspy and barely audible. Leaning closer, I put my ear near his mouth to better hear him. What he said next, I will never forget.

"Be careful. Trust no one."

My blood ran cold. "Jenson, what do you mean?" I begged. He coughed again, and closed his eyes as two paramedics made their way over to where we were. Just having them here eased some of the pain growing in my own chest and I breathed a huge sigh of relief.

"What do we have?" asked the paramedic.

"He's been shot in the stomach," I replied. "Please, hurry."

The paramedic saw the bloody shirt that was pressed into Jenson's wound and lifted it slightly.

"Nice job keeping pressure on it," he said. "My partner and I will take it from here."

His partner was already shoving Kate out of the way so she could monitor his breathing.

"Has he been unconscious?" she asked. I glanced at her name tag while moving away so she could work on Jenson. It read "Holly." Holly pulled scissors from one of the many utility pockets on her pants and cut open Jenson's shirt.

"Not long. We made sure to keep him talking almost the whole time," I told Holly. She continued to put other sticky things onto his now open chest and abdomen.

"What are those for?" I asked, feeling anxious about Jenson's condition.

Thomas gave me a look that said, "Stop annoying the lady so she can do her job."

I rolled my eyes and kept probing Holly for information. Her partner was scanning the stickers she had placed on Jenson's chest. There was a readout that popped up in the air above his stomach displaying his vitals. There were a lot of numbers that meant nothing to me. Holly and her partner shared a glance when the numbers came up. *Were they concerned already?*

This equipment they were using was new. I hadn't seen fancy readouts like that before. When Thomas was poisoned, they didn't use monitors like these.

"To keep an eye on his heart rate and other vitals. Now stop asking questions. I need to pressure dress his wound to keep the bleeding controlled," Holly said.

Her partner pressed on Jenson's abdomen, and he winced.

"You don't have to hurt him," I said, slightly angry.

Holly gave me a pointed look. "I know he's your friend or whatever, but you have to let us do our job, okay? We are going to do our best to keep your friend stable to get him the help he needs," she stated.

Nodding, I gave Jenson a small smile to let him know that we were all still there for him. Then I rose and stood off to the side so the paramedics had more room to work.

"Who's going in the ambulance with him?" Thomas whispered to me, Kate, and Dad when we were slightly out of earshot.

"I hadn't even thought about that yet," I replied. In my head, all I could think about was staying with Jenson. He had saved our lives more than once and he had found information about Leslie that no one else had been able to get. He was the one who recognized Leslie with the other children. If it hadn't been for Jenson, we would never have gotten Leslie back.

Before I could volunteer, Kate spoke up. "I'll stay with him."

"But what about your Dad and his quest to bring you back home? If you go to the hospital with him, he'll find you for sure. That's how Memory Lane found Thomas and me last time," I said. "Besides, I can go with him. I am not as recognizable as you are, Kate."

Kate thought for a moment and then spoke again. "I think I'm just going to have to take that chance. None of y'all can stay with Jenson if The Memorizers are leaving for Alaska soon. You have to go with them if you want to get to Canada."

"The Memorizers can't be the only way to get there. Canada can wait," I replied. "I'll go with you and Jenson."

Holly and her partner started maneuvering Jenson onto a stretcher. Jenson was clearly in pain because he was moaning and breathing heavily again. They slid the solid board under his side and then laid it flat so he rested on it. Then both paramedics lifted him into the air. It did not look like an easy task, and I was glad it wasn't me trying to do it. Holly and Doug—I finally got a good look at her partner's name badge—began walking toward the ladder again while carefully pulling Jenson on the stretcher.

"What hospital are y'all taking him to?" asked Kate, walking forward to catch up with the paramedics. I followed closely behind her.

"Whatever is closest. He's pretty critical, so he'll be moved into a room right away. He'll likely need surgery to remove the bullet," said Holly.

My eyes went wide at that proclamation. *Would Jenson be okay?*

"Hannah!" called Dad. "Wait up!" He moved briskly toward where Kate and I were walking beside Jenson's stretcher. I stopped so Dad could catch up while the paramedics and Kate continued toward the ladder for the exit. *How were they going to get Jenson up the ladder on that stretcher?*

Dad touched my shoulder lightly and made sure I was looking him in the eye before speaking. "I don't think you should go with Kate to the hospital. It's too dangerous."

"But I—"

"Listen to me for a second. This is all too close. I don't want any of us separated. I don't even think Kate should go with Jenson."

"You want us to abandon him?" I asked, defensively.

"He's an adult."

I made a face and I was about to retort back when Dad stuck his hand up to stop me.

"I want our family back. You, Leslie, and Mom are more important to me than whatever else is going on. It's my job to protect all of you. If that needs to extend to Kate, then so be it. I will not let Memory Lane ruin our lives any longer," he said.

"Kate and I are adults too, Dad," I replied. "If it wasn't for Jenson, Leslie wouldn't be here and neither would you!" I almost shouted.

"I respect that. I really do," said Dad. "But I honestly think we need to go to Canada to escape this mess with The Memorizers and Memory Lane. We can send someone for Jenson once he is safe to move."

Mom and Leslie walked up to where Dad and I were standing with a glass of water in hand.

"Where'd everyone go?" Mom asked.

"The paramedics are here, and they have Jenson loaded up to take to the hospital," I said, pointing to the ladder. As we all looked over, I noticed that they were attempting to push him up the ladder on the stretcher and it didn't look like it was going well. He slid down the ladder a few steps, crying out in pain at the jolted stop.

I winced along with Jenson as they attempted to bring him up the ladder again. This time, I saw a third set of hands reach down from above ground and three other bystanders gathered around the stretcher. They pushed as a group to get it up the ladder, finally pulling Jenson out of view. Kate followed behind the paramedics and another group of people who had been waiting to use the ladder to escape the building.

Resigned to staying with my family, I grabbed onto the ladder and started walking up it slowly. I had to make sure that Jenson was okay first.

"Hannah! Wait!" called Dad.

"I'm not leaving with him," I replied angrily, without turning around. "I'll be right back." I continued walking up the ladder while everyone else stayed behind.

Squinting in the sunlight, I stepped up to look for any sign of Kate and Jenson. As I turned to the left, there were several ambulances parked just outside of the fireworks stand on the dirt road. Kate was standing by one of them and I hoped that was the one that Jenson was being loaded into.

"Kate!" I called as I ran to catch up to her.

She turned around at the sound of my voice.

"How's he doing?" I asked.

Kate shrugged. "I don't know. He seems to be okay for now," she replied.

Leaning over, I glanced into the open ambulance doors to peer inside. The paramedics were almost done loading the stretcher into the back. As the stretcher clicked into place, Holly and Doug began connecting the wires and monitors to Jenson and started an IV of fluids. He looked so small and pale. *He had to be okay, he just had to.*

"Are you going to ride with him?" I asked Kate.

"I think so."

"My Dad doesn't think that's a good idea," I told her, quietly.

Kate thought for a moment. "We just can't leave him. How will we know if he is okay if no one goes with him? I don't really want him to be alone," she replied in a small voice.

"Me either. If it wasn't for my Dad, I would be right there with you. Just don't give them his real name or yours. Make sure you keep the door of the hospital room cracked at all times so you can try to listen in to the nurse's station conversations. Keep us as posted as you can."

"Understood," Kate nodded, "You stay in touch with me too. As soon as he can be moved, we will try to get to where you are."

"Hannah!" called Leslie from behind me. "Don't leave!"

I turned around just as she ran up to me and hugged me around my middle.

"Hey, Les, I'm not leaving. Just making sure Jenson is okay and that Kate knows what to do to stay as safe as she can," I cajoled. Stroking her hair lightly, I tried to soothe her a little bit. I hated seeing her like this.

Why was Leslie out here anyway? I told Dad I'd be right back. Knowing them, they sent her out here to make sure I wouldn't leave. It didn't take a genius to extrapolate the reason she came running up to me. Guilt could be an incredible motivator.

"Which one of you is coming?" asked Holly, leaning out of the still open back door of the ambulance. I heard her partner, Doug, slam the driver's side door.

Kate and I exchanged a glance. "Kate is," I said before she could say anything. "Stay safe," I told her.

Kate nodded and then stepped up into the back of the ambulance. I looked down at Leslie and back into the ambulance at Jenson. Part of me wanted to go, but I also knew that this was not the time to leave my family. The Memorizers were relocating, with their "fearless" leader Antoine off doing whatever he needed to keep himself safe like the coward he was. Not to mention that Memory Lane was still searching for Thomas and me and of course Leslie and the other kids in the program. This was where I was needed. Kate could handle taking care of Jenson.

"Hey, when Jenson pulls through, ask him about the program," I yelled to Kate over the sound of the ambulance engine roaring to life, hoping that she would know what I meant. I hated to ask at a time like this, but we needed answers about Leslie and this chip in her brain sooner rather than later. Jenson was the only one with that information.

Kate smiled at me and nodded just before Holly slammed the back door shut and the ambulance took off down the road.

Leslie pushed away from me and stomped back toward the fireworks stand, angry.

What was that all about? I followed her back to the ladder just as my parents and Thomas came through the underground hole.

"Don't ever make me do that again!" shouted Leslie, when she saw Dad. "It's not right to be used as a pawn to manipulate people! It's no different than what they did to me at Memory Lane!"

"What are you talking about, Les?" I asked. She glared at Dad, seething. I had never seen her so angry.

Dad rolled his eyes like it was no big deal. "We just wanted to make sure that you didn't decide to go to the hospital with Jenson. So, we sent Leslie out here to convince you to stay," Dad explained.

"Yeah, I saw right through that, Dad," I said, my tone flat and irritated. "Besides, I said I would be back, didn't I?" *How were we going to get anywhere if we couldn't trust each other's word?*

"You did," he replied. "But I wasn't taking any chances."

Another ambulance took off down the road after people were loaded into it. The chaos around us seemed to have died down a little. It felt as though an entire lifetime had transpired in the last hour. Thomas looked at me expectantly.

"Now what?" he asked.

"Well, I guess we're headed to that ferry in Washington," I replied.

Chapter 21

The midday sun beat down on us as we headed to the junkyard for a car Antoine promised would be capable of taking us to the ferry. The sun was so high that our shadows disappeared beneath our feet and once more, we found ourselves split up. Kate with Jenson headed to the hospital and the rest of us on the never-ending walk to nowhere. *I wonder what it is like to be a normal family that just gets up every day and does the same thing.* How many families had been torn apart by Memory Lane?

"Are we there yet?" Thomas whined. He sounded like a child stuck in the car.

"What are you, five?" I asked, turning around to look at Thomas.

Thomas kicked a rock in my direction and it bounced off my shoe. "I'm just saying."

Leslie and I glanced at each other, rolling our eyes at Thomas at the same time. I shook my head at Thomas's antics and childish tendencies, and continued walking. Our parents were in front of us a few paces, and other Memorizers were spaced out all around us. *Could we really call them Memorizers anymore?*

The walk to the junkyard for the cars was brutal. We were all tired, thirsty, and after everything that had happened at the compound, we needed some rest. This whole plan better work itself out. I didn't know if I could handle one more thing going wrong.

"Hannah?" said Leslie, trying to get my attention. "It's happening again."

Looking back, Leslie had stopped walking. On the surface she just looked a little sweaty. Other than that, nothing was visibly wrong with her. "What's happening again?" I asked.

"The world is fuzzy and there's a weird tingling in my brain," she replied.

Kneeling to look at her face more closely, I could see that glossy look like the other times she had one of the many episodes she experienced while staying with the Memorizers. "Have you felt this way before?" I asked her.

"Not that I can remember," she replied. Leslie rubbed her temples, as if she had a headache.

Thomas, who had been keeping up the end of our sweaty conga line, came up behind us. He looked worried as he studied Leslie and me. I leaned in closer to Leslie so that other people walking by wouldn't hear.

"Do you think it could be the chip?" I whispered.

Leslie nodded yes with teary eyes.

"It's okay, I'm here," I said, trying to reassure her.

"Help me move her out of the way," I said to Thomas. We ushered Leslie off the road. Unable to see anything happening around her, Leslie stumbled, and thankfully Thomas caught her. Once off the main road, I wanted to get as much information as possible to help her the next time this happened.

"Can you tell us what you see and feel?" I asked her.

"I can see my old room at Memory Lane. It's the same room they kept me in for those four years I was gone. It feels like I'm there right now."

"You can't see me at all?" I asked.

"Not at the moment. But I can hear you just fine."

Thomas's eyes grew wide. "That's freaky."

"Tell me about it," Leslie said.

My parents must have realized that we weren't behind them anymore because they suddenly came running up to where Thomas, Leslie, and I were crouched.

"What happened?" asked Mom in a panicked voice.

People began to slow down as they saw something must have been happening with us.

"Move along!" shouted Dad as he attempted to block their view of us.

"What's in your room?" I asked, feeling more at ease knowing Leslie could hear me. It made staying calm easier knowing she wasn't alone and trapped somewhere that I couldn't reach her. Watching Leslie with the blank look on her face while she was clearly somewhere else was bizarre. "Is there someone there with you?"

Leslie shook her head no. "It's just me," she replied.

"Does everything look the same as before?"

"Well yeah, I mean we shared rooms. I can see the two sets of bunk beds on the back wall. We usually had four of us in each room. Some of the blankets from the beds are on the floor."

"What's going on?" asked Mom. She touched my shoulder gently. "Is she having a breakdown or something?"

"Shhh! Not right now, Mom," I said, growling under my breath.

Mom backed away slowly and looked hurt and confused. She didn't seem to understand what was happening with Leslie and I didn't have time to explain it all to her. This wasn't about any of us, it was only about Leslie. Right now, my only focus was finding out what was happening to Leslie.

"Is there anything out of the ordinary in the room?" I asked.

Leslie continued to stare straight ahead without really seeing.

"It all looks the same. The beds, the blankets, even the pens and papers on the desks. There's a beeping noise now; I have never heard it before," she said, grabbing her ears to cover them. "It's getting louder."

Leslie shouted, even though she was the only one who could hear it. I was pretty sure that auditory hallucinations couldn't be stopped by covering your ears, though I wasn't going to tell her that. Glancing at Thomas, I saw he was sporting a matching worried look.

"Can you tell where the beeping is coming from, Les?"

Leslie turned her head from side to side, trying to hear where the sound was coming from.

"From the hallway. It's getting closer. I'm going to follow it," she said.

Follow it where?

"Tell me what you're seeing," I told her, trying to keep the panic out of my voice.

"I'm walking through the room and into the hallway where the beeping is. It's so weird. I walked over the blankets, and I could feel the bumps under my feet."

A few seconds of silence passed when Leslie gasped, her face twisted in fear.

"What?! What do you see?"

"There's a Memory Lane guard at the end of the hallway. He's asking me to come to him," whispered Leslie in a shaky voice. She sounded terrified.

"He can see you?!?" I asked her in shock.

Thomas whispered to me, "Well it's not like he can really take her anywhere. Leslie is here with us. It's only her mind that's back there with the guard."

I knew he was trying to comfort me, but I shushed him while I tried to listen to Leslie to figure out what was really going on. Was the chip projecting her body to Memory Lane or just her mind? This was next-level scary.

"Is he approaching you?" I asked Leslie.

"No, he's just standing there."

She reached forward and I grabbed her hand and squeezed so she could feel that I was still there. Leslie squeezed back. There was a relief knowing she could hear me and communicate what was going on, unlike all the other times her brain was hijacked by Memory Lane. *Was she learning more how to control whatever this was?*

"Don't go near the guard," I told her. "Turn around and leave the hallway."

Leslie's face looked confused for a moment.

"What's wrong?" I asked her.

"The door to my room is locked now. There isn't anywhere I can go. I can't get out of the hallway and away from the guard."

Thomas, my parents, and I exchanged a worried glance. How could something happening in Leslie's mind stop her from doing what she wanted? It was her mind. None of this made any sense.

People continued to walk past us, all heading for the junkyard to get a car and escape the coming onslaught of Memory Lane. The gravel crunched under their feet as they continued walking, and no one stopped to ask what was going on with Dad standing as an imposing sentry.

"Hannah, you have to help me! He's coming down the hall. He can't find me! He'll make me go with him!" yelled Leslie, panicked. Standing on the side of the road, we were in Memory Lane and a dusty street in the middle of nowhere at the same time. Leslie started visibly shaking as the fear of being taken back to Memory Lane overtook her.

I grabbed both of Leslie's hands, trying desperately to get her attention away from the guard inside her head. *How can I protect her from something I can't see?*

We watched as Leslie started backing away from where she was standing. Her fear was taking over her physical movements now as she tried to get away from the guard. Before I could grab her, she backed away and tripped, landing in the dirt. Startled, she blinked and squinted in the sun.

"Leslie?" I called.

She pushed herself up to a sitting position. "It's all gone."

I walked over to her. "You can't see it anymore?"

"No, the hallway, the guard, all of it disappeared. It's like they turned the chip off or something. I'm really tired," Leslie said, as she tried to stand.

"Here," I said, grabbing her shoulder. "You stay right there and I'll sit with you."

Mom and Dad inched closer to where Leslie and I were sitting. "How are you feeling, honey?" asked Mom. She looked older somehow. I knew all of this was hard on her too. Memory Lane just continued to take from my family. *There has to be a way to stop all of this!*

"Tired," Leslie replied.

Dad smiled at her while he kneeled down next to us. "It's okay. We can wait until you're ready to move forward again."

"Can you describe the guard?" Mom asked.

Leslie shook her head no. "He looked like all the other Memory Lane guards. Old and angry."

I exchanged a look with Thomas. "Old?" I mouthed at him. "How old, Les?" I asked.

"Like older than Mom and Dad," she replied.

That wasn't very helpful for identification purposes.

"Any other defining characteristics you remember about the guard?" I asked.

Leslie seemed to think for a moment. "Not really. I mean, he had an accent. Like a northern accent."

Well, that really narrows it down, I thought. "You're doing great, Les." I smiled at her.

"Had you met him before?" Thomas asked.

"I don't think so. I mean, I guess he looked familiar, but I'm not sure," Leslie said, yawning.

My parents exchanged a look that said they knew more than they were telling. Part of me wanted to know what it meant but I was too wrapped up in helping Leslie get to the bottom of this experience that I shrugged it off.

"We'll be right back," said Mom. She and Dad both walked back over toward the gravel road to talk about something they didn't want Leslie or me to hear.

"Do you want to keep going?" I asked Leslie when they left.

She yawned again and then seemed to think carefully about her answer. "I'm not sure I have a choice. Besides, once we get a car from the place, I can sleep in the back."

"You sure?" I gave her a reassuring smile and stood up. I needed her to know any answer was fine.

She nodded and then reached for my hand so I could help her stand up again. As we dusted ourselves off, I looked at her calm face. Despite being tired, she always pushed on. She had been forced to grow up so fast. My little sister was no longer little. She was growing into a fierce little woman. I had to admire her bravery. Her time in Memory Lane had grown a strength in her that was more than any of us would know or understand. She didn't want to be a burden on all of us even though she had to be terrified of Memory Lane having control of her head. Thomas looked at both of us and then motioned for us to get going just as my parents walked back over from their strange private conversation.

"You ready?" Mom inquired gently.

Leslie nodded and so did I.

All of us walked next to each other, with Leslie in the middle. It was as though silently we had created a cocoon around Leslie, to keep her safe. No doubt we were all feeling extra protective in light of everything that had just transpired. Other groups of people were about twenty-five yards in front of us as we continued to trudge along, looking for this junkyard car lot that supposedly was going to be the answer to our escape.

As we walked in silence, I thought about Jenson. Just thinking about what had happened, the gunshot wound, the blood, his coughing and the paleness of his skin created a heaviness in my stomach. *Was he okay? Was Kate? Would things ever be calm and peaceful again?*

Kate's Dad was insane, and the work Memory Lane was doing was disturbing and there was no doubt in my mind that if he found her, he would kill her. The fact that we had avoided him thus far was astonishing, and part of me wondered if Gideon Wesley was letting us be free of him for a while to mess with us. Like a game of cat and mouse. He was sick.

At this rate it didn't feel any better being with The Memorizers. I thought about Antoine and Brad—how, for their own selfish needs, they had abandoned most of the people who trusted them. The world didn't need more selfish people. The world needed more people who cared for others. We needed leaders who could care about the people they were leading. It all felt hopeless. America had become a place of mere survival since the famine of 2087. Humanity has always been greedy and selfish, but the famine truly brought out the worst in people. It didn't seem as though there was a way to go back to a time when we all tried to look out for each other.

"Look!" shouted Thomas. We all turned to see where he was pointing up ahead a mile or so. There was a line of five or six cars pulling out onto the road. *That must be where the car lot is. Finally!*

Seeing the junkyard gave us renewed energy, and the five of us walked briskly to the front entrance off the main road just a bit. Looking over the cars in the lot, I watched an older man and woman climb into a compact car. *Were they part of The Memorizers?* Maybe they were just an older couple looking for an older car that didn't have all the new fancy technology. Many of the older generation were uncomfortable with the self-driving cars of today and often looked for older models to be reminded of a time when they still felt in control. I couldn't relate. Driving was easy when the car did it for you. I didn't want to be in charge of anything anymore. Too many decisions had the ability to change the course of my entire life. I had been shown that over and over as of late.

"Let's see if they have something a little bigger for all of us," Dad said as we approached the guy who seemed to be the owner of all the cars.

"Hello, Antoine sent us," Dad stated, shaking the man's wrinkled hand. The man running this place looked as weathered as the cars parked here. His long beard was nearly all gray and he wore old jean overalls. His skin was covered in lines from a long life and the inescapable aging of time. If I ventured a guess, I would say he was about seventy years old, but Thomas always said that I was really bad at guessing people's ages. If I was honest, I always thought people were older than they actually were.

"Are you looking for something specific?" asked the man, smiling. Perhaps he was thrilled with all the business The Memorizers were giving him. None of us knew what kind of deal Antoine had made with this guy and part of me hoped he was getting a lot of money. This was dozens and dozens of cars that all of these people needed. My heart hurt knowing that many of these people had nowhere to go. They had made their home at The Memorizers compound. Where would they go?

"You got any vans or SUV-type cars we can use?" Dad asked, scanning the lot. Several of the cars to our immediate right looked like they wouldn't run at all. They were just there taking up space. They were missing front fenders, tires, hoods, mirrors, and the like. Who knew if they even worked in this kind of condition.

The owner typed something into his computer and smiled. "Yeah, I actually have one that would be perfect in the back. Follow me."

Dad walked away with the man and the four of us followed slowly behind, looking around the car lot more. Not only was this place so much bigger than it looked from the street, but it was also a wreck. It was few and far between that I saw a car that looked even halfway useable. Seriously, this place was a dump. Obviously, we couldn't afford to be picky, but would it do us any good if we just broke down on the side of the road in a few hours?

There was a noise off to my left as a car door slammed and a girl's voice said "OW!"

Instinctively, I pulled Leslie closer to my side.

"Who's there?" I asked, trying to sound confident and not terrified. It could literally be anyone. The owner's daughter, wife, or just a random homeless woman living in one of the junk cars.

There were dust and footsteps as the person crept out from behind the car. Thomas stood in front of me, Leslie, and Mom, prepared to fight off whoever this was. As she came into view, she looked much less threatening. Dirty from living in the junkyard and wearing torn clothes, she looked to be around my age. Maybe a little older. As she came closer to where all of us were standing, I felt Leslie shift even closer to me.

"Well, look who it is," said the girl.

The voice took a moment to register in my brain as I took in her disheveled appearance.

"Gill?!" I asked, in disbelief.

"The one and only," she replied, bowing and smirking. She looked as though she had aged years in the mere days it had been since we had seen her last. So much had happened in such a short time.

"Why are you here? How did you get here? Are you okay?" I asked in rapid succession.

"It's a long story. But I'm so glad to have found you guys."

As Thomas looked at me, I could see the skepticism in his eyes. I had the same questions. It didn't make sense that Gill would be here of all places. She wasn't even in The Memorizers compound when the alarm sirens went off and the plan to get us here unfolded. Was this really all just a coincidence?

More footsteps approached as the owner of the lot and Dad came back to where we were.

"We're all set with an SUV. Follow me to the back so we can—"

Dad abruptly stopped speaking as he took in Gill.

"Where did you come from?" he asked, clearly just as confused as we were.

"Gill was just about to fill us in on how she got here," I said, urging her with my eyes to tell us.

"You're trespassing!" shouted the owner, "Get off my property!"

Gill held up her hands in surrender. "Wait! I just wanted a place to sleep for the night. I didn't mean any harm," she explained, her voice wavering. Fear shone in her eyes as the color drained from her face.

"You can't be here!" yelled the owner. He pulled out a gun from one of his pockets and pointed it at Gill.

"Whoa!" Dad exclaimed. "Let's not get upset. Take it easy."

Without hesitating, I grabbed Leslie and shielded her with my body as best I could. She was shaking with fear and Thomas moved in front of me.

Gill had a wide-eyed look on her face as she kept her hands up in surrender and slowly backed away.

"Don't move!" yelled the owner. "I have a right to my own property."

"Sir, I really didn't mean any harm. Honest. I'll leave right now," Gill said in the calmest voice she could manage with a gun pointed at her. She continued to back away slowly with her hands raised, facing us as the owner glared at her. I tried to make eye contact with her so she knew that we would be waiting for her once we got the car. Gill nodded imperceptibly. I took that to mean she understood.

He fired a shot into the air, and we all jumped. Leslie was clinging to me while Gill dropped to the ground and covered her head with her hands.

The owner had a smug look on his face when he saw just how scared Gill was. "Consider that a warning! I won't be so nice next time! Get out of here, and don't you dare come back!"

Everyone stayed frozen in place and waited to see what the owner would do next. He seemed so nice and accommodating when we arrived and, in an instant, grew so angry when Gill appeared. I wonder if people had stolen from him before.

"What are y'all waiting for? Do you want to use the car or not?" asked the owner. He looked at Dad expectantly.

"Yes, of course," Dad stammered. There was a huge shift in tension while we all readjusted to the new vibe the owner was giving off.

We followed the owner back to the SUV he had shown Dad. Leslie followed close by me, clutching my hand. I was still wary of the owner with his gun. He could change his mind again and I didn't want to take any chances. "Okay, so I guess we're all set," Dad announced, trying to break the tension. "There's an SUV for us back here." He nodded in the direction of the back of the lot.

I saw the black SUV that was meant to be ours. It looked older, and if I guessed right, it didn't have the automatic drive option. *Manual it is,* I guess. Not that we could afford to be picky. It probably didn't have GPS either. That would complicate things a bit, but we would just have to make do. Leslie and I opened the back door on the driver's side and she climbed into the middle seat. Thomas slid into the backseat from the other side just as the owner smiled and told us to drive safe. I watched the owner walk back to the front of the junkyard and relief washed over me. At least we could get out of here now.

"Everyone ready?" Dad asked, looking from Mom to all of us in the backseat.

"Yes. Let's get going," Thomas said. We all nodded quietly, too disturbed by the last turn of events to speak. Exhaustion was setting in. Maybe now we could get some rest while we looked for a place to stay for the night.

Dad nodded and then slowly drove back to the front side of the car lot so that we could exit and hopefully pick up Gill.

"Do we have room for one more?" I asked my parents.

"It looks like there's a third row of seats back here," Thomas added, turning around to see what space we were dealing with. They were small seats, but Gill couldn't afford to be picky if she wanted to ride with us.

"Yeah, we can stop and pick up Gill. She will be safer with us and I bet she didn't get too far from the lot," said Mom.

As we drove down the main road, I spotted Gill walking slowly and kicking up dirt with her shoes. Dad pulled the SUV over and I pushed past Thomas so I could open the door and get out to talk to Gill. She had turned around to see our car pull to a stop.

"Gill! Wait!"

Her eyes met mine, and she looked wary.

"Come with us. We have some room and you will be safer with us than alone," I said.

"Are you sure it's not too much trouble?" Gill asked, looking down and fidgeting with her hands. She looked tired and lost. Carrying nothing but a small backpack of things with her, you could see that The Memorizers had taken everything from her. We knew more than anyone how she could be feeling right now.

"Of course! Don't worry, Thomas doesn't get a say," I joked, smirking at her.

She nodded and offered a small smile. She opened the door on Thomas's side to climb in just in time for Thomas to insert his foot directly in his mouth.

"Look what the cat dragged in," joked Thomas.

Gill's eyes went wide as she looked down at her disheveled appearance. Her cheeks darkened in embarrassment, and Thomas appeared to regret his words the moment he saw Gill's reaction.

"Thomas!" admonished Mom. "Enough. Get out so Gill can get in."

"I was only kidding," said Thomas, climbing out of his seat and folding it down so Gill could climb into the third row.

When she was settled, Thomas climbed back in, we closed the doors, and Dad started driving again. We were finally headed to the ferry and, God willing, we would get out of this country and away from Memory Lane for good.

Gill leaned forward in her seat so that her head rested on the backseat between me and Leslie from behind. "So, what'd I miss?"

"It's a lot. You go first," I told her.

Chapter 22

"You tried to steal his car?!" I asked Gill. My eyes went wide in shock.

"I needed a way out," Gill replied from the back seat, shrugging. "It's not like I knew that junkyard was filled with running vehicles for Antoine. If I knew that I would have taken one from the back of the lot and been far away from here by now."

"To be fair," Thomas interjected, "you and Jenson actually stole a car."

"What? That's not even the same thing!" I exclaimed, glaring at Thomas.

I looked over to see Leslie stifling a laugh behind her hand while I heard a full laugh from Gill. Frowning, I quit talking to prevent myself from saying something that I would regret. To say I was irritable would be putting it lightly.

"Calm down, everyone," Dad ordered. It felt like we had been driving forever. We were still driving, and it was way past dinnertime. The musty smell of the car from the junkyard combined with the dusty interior did nothing to make me want to stay in it any longer than we had to. At this point, everyone was hangry, not to mention tired beyond reason.

I crossed my arms over my chest like a petulant child, not caring if I looked grumpy. I needed sustenance and a bed—soon. Too long in the car, no food, the stress and worry over our lives, and the situation with Jenson and Kate was getting to me. It was nearly ten o'clock at night. Staring out the window, I saw only an inky blackness occasionally peppered with other cars.

"Are we going to stop soon? I need food," I told my parents as I picked at the peeling fabric of the seat. *How old was this car, anyway?*

"I second that," said Thomas.

I would kill for access to an Instapanel right now. No sooner had the thought crossed my mind when my stomach growled loudly. My stomach agreed.

"Yeah, we need to find a place to stay anyway," Mom chimed.

"I need a shower," said Gill.

I nodded in agreement. We all needed to shower, eat, and rest. I looked down at Jenson's blood, now dried on my pants and embedded in my nails. I needed a change of clothes, badly. Not exactly easy to blend in when you have someone's blood all over you. My mind raced back to the parking lot, the ambulance pulling away. *Was Jenson okay? Had Kate been caught?* I shook my head to free myself from the image of blood pooling around my fingers as I held Dad's shirt over the gunshot wound.

"How are we all gonna travel together as one caravan of cars? There's no way that will work forever." Thomas asked. It was a great question. I couldn't picture how that would work when I thought about the logistics of it.

"How many ferries could there possibly be in Washington state?" asked Mom.

Dad shrugged as if she had asked a simple vacation question. "I have no idea. We'll cross that bridge when we get to it," he assured her.

"I have to use the bathroom," said Leslie.

Mom chuckled and then shook her head. "This is giving me flash-backs to when we used to take road trips with Thomas and the girls. There was always something they were whining about…"

Dad laughed out loud, and it was such an oddly normal sound if you considered we were in a strange car running for our lives.

"Hey! I never whined," Thomas grumbled. "I was a great kid to take a road trip with."

I rolled my eyes. "Oh, please! Remember the trip we took to California when you and I were ten? You threw up on the side of the road because you were car sick from riding in the back seat. I distinct-ly remember you getting to ride in the front after that," I retorted.

Leslie giggled, and Gill rolled her eyes at both Thomas and me.

"That was *one* time!" defended Thomas.

"You said you were a great kid to road trip with. I was just trying to remind you how wrong that is," I shot back.

Gill made an unpleasant face and put her hand over her stomach. "I think I'm gonna be sick…."

I turned around quickly. "Seriously? You gonna hurl?" I asked her. "Dad, stop the car. Gill's not feeling well."

I studied Gill from my position in the car. She looked okay to me. Just dirty and tired.

Laughing at my expense, Gill smirked. "I'm fine. I was just sick of you and Thomas acting like children."

"That was not funny!" I exclaimed, reaching back to fake slap Gill's arm. For a moment, I really thought she was going to throw up.

"Don't make me turn this car around, kids," Dad yelled toward the backseat. He glanced in the rearview mirror to get our attention in the back. For a moment, we could have been any family on a trip to somewhere special with a car full of kids goofing around. "Let's get some gas and grab whatever we can here to munch on."

He pulled into a small convenience store that had only two gas pumps. The gas station sign was lit but the first letter no longer lit up. Instead of it saying the Shell station, it said hell station. Each window

had bars over it and at best it looked sketchy. There were no street-
lights, just the lights that emanated out of the windows and the sign
letting us know we had made it to hell. It would be almost funny if it
wasn't so fitting.

"Are you sure this is okay?" Mom asked, looking around.

"There hasn't been a store or a gas station for miles. I don't see
anything else around. We really can't manage a trip into a restaurant
either. Gill smells homeless and Hannah is covered in someone else's
blood. We are past the point of looking inconspicuous and we need to
keep a low profile with everything going on. Matter of fact," he said,
unbuckling his seat belt, "I think only one of us should go in."

There was a collective groan from all of us who had been trapped
in the car. *How were we going to even get enough food to carry if only
Dad went in the store?* There was no telling what the store would even
have that was edible.

"How are you going to carry enough snacks and food for all of us?"
I asked.

Dad seemed to be lost in thought for a moment as he stared out
the window.

"Fine. I guess me and your Mom will go in. What does everyone
want from inside?" He turned around to face us in the backseat.

All of us started requesting food at once.

"A sandwich."

"A hotdog."

"A slice of pizza."

"Whoa, whoa, I can't understand all of you at once," Dad said,
holding up a hand to silence us. "One at a time." Before we could speak
up Mom jumped in to stop another round of the food guessing game.

"Why don't we just go see what they have and choose for the kids?"
She took her seat belt off and opened her car door.

"I resent that. Most of us are adults," I mumbled under my breath
and slouched back into my seat.

"Oh for heaven's sake. You know what I meant," Mom chided.

"Sorry, I'm just tired and hungry. I'm sure whatever you and Dad get is fine." I rubbed at my tired eyes. With the car doors closed behind them, they headed toward the store to get gas and food. I watched them walk into the convenience store before nudging Leslie with my shoulder.

"Les? You okay?" Peering down at her, I saw that her eyes were closed. Her head had fallen onto my shoulder and her breathing had slowed.

She nodded but didn't speak.

"You sure?" I asked again.

"Just tired," she said, yawning. Her yawn was contagious and I felt that familiar feeling as I yawned too.

Pulling out my phone, I messaged Kate to try to get an update on Jenson. Just as I finished the message and set my phone back in my lap, I noticed headlights pulling into the parking lot. This wasn't a busy place and maybe I had become a scant paranoid, but when they parked next to us, I immediately leaned into the front seat to make sure the doors were locked.

Thomas gave me a look that said, *"What was that for?"*

"You never know what people are capable of," I stated matter-of-factly. We all watched as a man got out of the car and started to walk into the convenience store while texting someone on his phone. Before he made it to the door he turned around suddenly and stared right at me.

I shivered as chills ran up my spine.

What did he want?

"Are you guys seeing this?" I whispered to Thomas and Gill.

They both nodded and I pulled Leslie closer to me in case he tried anything. Looking past him into the store, I tried to find my parents, but the shelves were too tall for me to see clearly.

Unblinking, the man continued to stare at me. Finally, when Dad pushed the door open so he and Mom could exit the store, the door knocked into the creepy stranger. That in turn knocked some of the food out of Dad's hands and scattered it to the ground. Mom shook her head and headed to the car as Dad profusely apologized to the stranger. *Not your fault Mr. Creepyface was staring, Dad.* The man bent down to help Dad pick up the food. Mom got to the car and tried to pull on the door handle and noticed it was locked. She looked into the backseat with the standard Mom face of *Seriously?* I reached into the front seat and unlocked the door for her.

As she got into the car with the food she was carrying, she turned around to start dividing it up among us.

"Why did you lock the doors?" she asked, while passing back a sandwich to Thomas.

Before I could explain, Dad opened his door to get in the car.

"Why does everyone look like a deer caught in headlights?" he asked.

Mom grabbed the rest of the food Dad brought and continued passing it to the backseat for us. Grabbing some whole grain chips and a hotdog from her, I opened the chips and jammed a handful into my mouth. They weren't my favorite, but it was still something to eat and anything that would stop the painful growling could very quickly become my favorite.

"The guy you ran into was staring at me like a creeper. It was like he wanted to hurt me," I said through a mouthful of chips.

"Do you think he recognized you?" Mom asked, her tone changing to worried.

"Not sure." I shrugged. "He definitely didn't look like he was looking for a new best friend."

Thomas nodded in agreement.

Dad opened up a drink and took a swig. "Did he say or do anything other than look at you?"

"No, but I really think he would happily hand me over to Memory Lane or something." I took a bite of the hotdog and wiped my chin when I felt mustard drip all over it.

Dad climbed out of the car and filled up the gas tank. The stranger was still inside the store, and I was silently wishing the gas pump to finish. We had to get out of here before that guy came back. Put some distance between us and Crazy Guy!

What felt like an eternity passed before Dad finally got back in the car. Mom lovingly jammed a bite of sandwich into his face as he backed the car out of the parking space and pulled us back onto the main road.

A thought occurred to me as I ate more chips. "Do you think he's a former Memorizer? Like is there a chance we'll run into him again?" I asked.

"Possibly. I hope not," said Thomas. He took a bite of his sandwich and there was momentarily silence in the car as we all ate our make-shift dinner.

Gill chimed in next. "Yeah, he had a sinister look about him."

Dad drove the car for another half hour or so before I started to get sleepy. Leslie was already asleep against me and Thomas was bab-bling about something that I was only halfway listening to. He tended to chatter mindlessly when he was tired, though he never wanted to admit it. The low hum of the car and the lack of lighting on the main road made the perfect combination for sleep and I found myself doz-ing in the back seat. Just as that sweet bliss of rest was about to hit, my phone buzzed and jolted me awake. It was a VidChat from Kate. I glanced down to see the message before tapping on the video and watching the glowing holographic image appear with Kate's face.

Thomas and Gill leaned over to see the VidChat too for the update on Jenson.

Kate's voice filled the car as we all listened to her update. "Jenson is out of surgery and resting in a recovery room. The doctors said that the bullet hit his spleen so they removed it. Apparently, it is a relatively routine procedure according to the doctors and easier to survive than if one of his other organs had been hit. He'll have to take some pills the rest of his life because his risk of infection is greater now without a spleen, but I think that's better than anything else that could have happened."

The three of us breathed a collective sigh of relief.

"I'm glad he's doing okay. Have you seen him since the surgery?" I asked Kate's hologram.

"Not yet," Kate's face replied. Her eyes darted around, which made me think she was worried about something.

"Everything else okay?" I asked.

Kate's hologram nodded. "Yeah, I'm just tired. You guys doing okay? How far away did you get once you found a car?"

I yawned. "Been driving for hours. Just trying to stay awake long enough to find a place to crash for the time being. Hopefully you and Jenson can join us later," I said.

"Hannah," Kate's hologram said, while turning around to see the doctor right behind her, "I gotta go. I'll VidChat you later."

After she hung up, I turned to look at Thomas and Gill who were staring at me.

"What?" I asked.

Thomas chimed in. "Nothing. I just find it funny how—"

His words were cut off by the sound of crunching metal and the force of our car being thrown forward. Something had just crashed into the back of our car! My seat belt choked me and Leslie was jolted awake from the force of the crash. Dad swerved, fighting to maintain control of the car and keep it in our lane. Looking out the rear window, I couldn't see anything on the road. The closest set of headlights was far back in the distance.

"What was that?!" Thomas yelled from his seat.

Mom turned around to check on us. "Everyone okay?"

Before any of us could respond, we were hit again. CRASH. Thrown forward again, I held my breath to choke back a scream.

No way the second time was an accident! My heart was coming out of my chest as I thought about why someone would intentionally hit us.

Those of us in the back seat were thrown forward again as the car behind us smashed into us for a third time.

Leslie reached for me as Mom shouted at Dad, "This guy is crazy! Get us off this road!"

Our car jerked to the right as Dad tried to get away from whoever was trying to run us off the road.

The car sped up, pulling alongside us in the left lane. We all stared wide-eyed to see who was actively trying to kill us. My heart sank as I recognized the car.

"Isn't that the creepy guy from the gas station?" I asked Thomas and Gill.

"I think it is!" replied Thomas. "What's his problem?"

The other car sideswiped the driver's side mirror as he rammed into us again. I was thrown to the right at the impact and if it weren't for my seat belt, I would have likely hit my head on the opposite window.

"Dad! Get us away from him!" I shouted in desperation.

"I'm working on it!" he yelled back.

The car hit us again at full speed on the driver's side and this time, we were forced off the road. Instinctively, I reached for Leslie as our car started to spin out of control.

There was a collective gasp as all of us realized a second too late that the car was going to tumble. There was nothing I could do except hope that we all lived.

The car rolled twice, and then came to rest upside down.

For a moment, my vision was blurry, but as it cleared up I could see the roof of the car from my vantage point. Mentally I took note of any injuries and, aside from a pain in my shoulder from the straining seat belt, it didn't seem like anything was broken.

"Leslie!?" I called out. "Thomas?"

No response from either.

"Leslie!" I yelled again. "Answer me!" I reached out in the dark to pull on Leslie's shirt sleeve. I couldn't see her very well, but her hands were limply hanging down toward the roof of the car, she must have been unconcious. All of us were suspended by the seat belts that held us from being ejected from the car during the tumble. She groaned and then whispered something to me. "Why are you yelling?"

"Are you okay?" I asked her.

"Yeah, the world is just upside down and I can't breathe because the seat belt is choking me," she said while coughing.

I heard coughing from the front seat and then Mom spoke up. "Hannah! Leslie! Are you girls okay?" Her voice was raspy and frantic.

"Yeah, Mom, I think we're fine," I said, straining to talk.

"Thomas? Gill?" Dad rasped loudly toward the back. "You both okay too?"

Thomas coughed and replied, "Yeah." But he sounded like he was in pain.

Gill still hadn't said anything, and I could feel the panic rising in my chest again.

A million thoughts raced through my head. *Was she okay? Was she hurt? Unable to speak? Dead?*

Just as I was about to unbuckle and see what happened to Gill, there was the sound of crunching glass under boots and a sudden pounding on the driver's side window.

KNOCK. KNOCK. KNOCK.

Kneeling beside Dad's window was the guy from the gas station. He was the one who hit us. The seat belt strained against my weight, pulling me headfirst toward the roof of the car. *How were we going to get out of this?*

Hanging there upside down by the seat belt, I tried to crane my neck around to see what he wanted but even stretching my neck hurt my shoulder more.

"Open this door!" Crazy Man angrily yelled.. *The doors must still be locked! Otherwise this guy would have yanked Dad out of the car by now.*

Multiple scenarios flashed through my mind of what he could want with us. *Was he sent by someone? Did Memory Lane find us? Is he just some crazy person who's unhinged?*

KNOCK. KNOCK. KNOCK.

"Open this door!" the man yelled again standing up and kicking the glass window, shattering it and sending shards of broken glass inwards.

"Don't open the door, Dad!" I whispered from my precarious position.

Crazy Man crouched down and stuck his face in the driver's side window so that Dad could see him. He spoke again, but this time sounded calmer. "Look, mister, I don't want to hurt you. I'm looking for Kate. If you hand her over, I'll leave you and your family in peace."

Chapter 23

Leslie, hanging upside down beside me, was rubbing her temples. I could see the blood had rushed to her face, her eyes clenched tightly closed. My head was throbbing, and it was getting harder to focus on the man who had ran us off the road. It was getting harder to breathe by the second and I didn't know how much longer we could hang this way.

"Who's Kate?" Dad questioned.

Oh no! Dad must have hit his head during the crash.

The stranger narrowed his eyes. "You know, it's dangerous to hang upside down for too long. Your other organs begin to crush your lungs. It can kill you. I wouldn't lie to me, Mr. Healy. Tell me where Kate is and I'll be on my way. Simple as that."

"Sir, please! We don't know anyone named Kate! I'm just on a road trip with my wife and kids."

The man shook his head. "Listen, mister, your family wouldn't be the first I made disappear and probably won't be the last. Do you really want this desert to be where you and your family die?"

"No sir, please. You have to understand you have us mixed up with someone else. My name isn't Healy, and we don't know anyone named

Kate. My daughter's names are Bethany and Julie. My son is Nathan. Honest," Dad pleaded. "Please just let us go."

Fake names? I struggled to focus on what Dad could be planning. Spots were forming in my vision and the pressure in my head was getting worse.

The man sat back on his heels and considered what Dad said for a moment.

"I'm going to level with you because your family is in the car. Mr. Wesley was very clear on what I was supposed to do. Bring back Kate. I have no desire to hurt anyone else unless you refuse to cooperate."

"You hit us with your car and made us crash!" shouted Mom.

Mr. Wesley? Kate's Dad? I held my breath to see what the man's re-action would be. *Please don't let it get worse.*

"I hit your car to get your attention. That was just the tip of the iceberg," the man replied.

"How could you do this!" yelled Mom.

The man stood up and pounded on the door again. "Control your wife!" he shouted.

I could hear Thomas grunting in the back seat, followed by a click and a thud as I watched him fall down onto the car's ceiling with a moan. He shifted uneasily until he was more upright and fumbled around, trying to open the door.

"Thomas! What are you doing?" I yelled as he found the handle and pushed on the door, the top of the window dragging against the dirt as he shoved the door open enough to get through.

"Thomas! Don't!" Mom shouted.

As Thomas tumbled out of the car, I heard another voice from outside.

"Is everything okay?" a woman asked. *How did she get here?* In all the commotion I didn't even hear another car pull up.

"No! We need help! This man is trying to—" Thomas started.

"Shut up!" the stranger yelled. There was a clicking sound and a gasp from the lady. Oh no, he has a gun! *Think, Hannah, think!* I unbuckled my seat belt and fell onto the ceiling. I could feel bits of broken glass digging into my arms. I pushed that aside; I had to try to help Thomas.

"Hannah, no!" shouted Mom.

"Please stay here," I said to Leslie.

I crawled to the open door and climbed out of the car to see what was going on.

My eyes went wide as I saw the man pointing a gun at Thomas. The woman standing near our car had her hands up in the air. All the color had drained from her face, and she looked terrified. Tears were streaming silently down her face and I could hear her labored breathing from where I was standing on the other side of the car. I put my hands up and approached slowly, so that the man wouldn't be startled and shoot Thomas or myself.

"This is really simple. You tell me where Kate is and you don't die!" he yelled.

"We don't know anyone named Kate!" Thomas shouted back.

The man chuckled derisively and his face changed from angry to cruel and calculated. "Yeah, right. I know the old guy gave me fake names. I heard you all calling each other different names in the car. Stop lying to me," he growled.

Maybe I can lead him in the wrong direction.

Slowly, I walked around the car, and every nerve in my body felt alive. I could feel the stones beneath my shoes shifting with each step I took toward the man and Thomas.

"I'll tell you where Kate is," I spoke calmly. The inside of my chest was pounding with every heartbeat, but no one needed to know that.

The man jerked his face toward me and pointed the gun in my direction. I heard Thomas gasp when he saw me in harm's way. I put my hands up to show that I meant no harm.

"Why would I believe you?" asked the man.

"Because I just want to keep my family safe. Besides, do you really have a choice?" I asked, keeping my tone even, pushing down the panic rising up inside of me.

"I'm the one with the gun!" he yelled. He waved the gun back and forth, aiming it at me, then at Thomas and the innocent woman who had just stopped to try to help us.

"You'll never find out where Kate is if you kill me," I said, struggling to keep my breathing even. *Where was all this bravado coming from?* Locking eyes with the stranger, my mind raced. I had to come up with a believable place that Kate might be.

"I don't have time for this. Mr. Wesley has given me strict instructions and I am more than happy to take you in Kate's place as leverage if I have to!" he shouted. His tough-guy bravado was slipping away and panic was beginning to show on his face.

Just keep him talking. You can do this. "Okay, okay. Kate's in Tennessee with her boyfriend," I said, dropping my shoulders and trying to sound defeated.

"Hannah! No!" screamed Thomas.

Well done, Thomas! His reaction was perfect. It made it seem more likely that I was telling the truth.

The man started walking closer to me and aimed the gun more purposefully at my face. I felt my heart rate increase.

The stranger paused to consider if I was telling the truth. "That's a long way away from here. When did she leave? Why didn't she just stay with you?"

"We had a falling out. She left a while back. We couldn't agree anymore on what to do and it was too dangerous to let her stay, so..." I trailed off.

"I don't believe you!"

I shrugged, hoping to look nonchalant even though inside I was shaking with fear. "Believe it or don't, but that's where Kate is."

"No," the man said, shaking his head in denial. "Mr. Wesley had her phone tracked to The Memorizers underground location. She was there not even one day ago."

My heart sank and I stopped breathing for a second. *Crap.*

"Maybe she left her phone at The Memorizers, mister," said a small voice behind me. I knew she was there before I saw her. I turned around so fast, I swear I got whiplash; and it wasn't from the accident. Blood streaked down the side of her face, and for a moment, I could see her lying in the casket four years ago. Panic welled up inside me, and I blinked over and over to rid myself of the image. It was Leslie. She may be banged up, but she was alive.

Immediately I shoved her behind me, shielding her from the man's line of sight.

"Is your whole family stupid?!" the man asked, sarcasm dripping from his words.

I narrowed my eyes momentarily, holding back my need to say something in return.

"If you don't tell me what I want, then people will die."

Everything in that moment happened so slowly. The stranger turned abruptly to his right, swinging the gun around and aiming it at the woman who stopped to help us. He pulled the trigger. The blast of the gun assaulted everyone's ears, and the air was tainted with the acrid scent of gunpowder as the bullet hit the woman in the chest. Thrown back, she fell to the ground, eyes closed as the blood began to pool down her shirt onto the dirt road.

The sound rocked me backwards as I grabbed for Leslie, her body trembling beneath my hands.

The woman lay motionless; from where Leslie and I were standing I couldn't tell if she was dead or alive. Thomas had been just two steps away from her when the stranger fired his gun. *It could have been Thomas.* Those words kept repeating in my mind. Thomas kneeled down next to her. I watched with wide eyes as he checked to see if she was alive.

"She's still breathing," he said. "Please, sir, we could still save her!"

"Do you want to be next?!" threatened the man. He aimed his gun more pointedly at Thomas. "Get away from her!"

Thomas raised his hands, and stood back up. The woman's blood on his pants and fear in his eyes, he backed away. "Okay, okay, I was just trying to help her, man. You don't want her blood on your hands," Thomas choked out.

In the distance, my attention was pulled away for a moment at the sound of police sirens. *Did the woman call the police? Please God, let them come and save us from this nightmare.*

"Just get over there with the others," commanded the man to Thomas. He pointed in the direction of me and Leslie with his gun and began taking steps to close the gap between us.

Thomas walked over to where we were and nodded at me. A silent *"Are you okay?"* I felt so far from okay.

Behind me, I heard the sound of crunching gravel. *Who else got out of our car?* "Don't you get any closer to my daughters!" Dad yelled from behind me.

At the sound of Dad's request, the gunman's patience met its end and he swung the gun around and fired, missing the shot and causing Leslie and I to both instinctively duck. Before the stranger began firing again, the sirens were more noticeable now. Getting closer and louder with each passing second.

"Which one of you called the police?" he asked, derisively chuckling. "You know, Mr. Wesley controls the police. It's cute that you think that will matter."

"What's going on here?" asked a man from behind me. As I turned around, I noticed a truck parked a little farther ahead. He must have stopped when he saw the car flipped upside down and all of us standing outside along the road.

"We're just having a friendly chat," said the man with the gun sarcastically.

"With a gun?" asked the other man.

My eyes darted between both men and then back to Dad. *What was our plan? How could we get out of this mess?*

"How did this accident happen?" the second man asked, frantically. "Are any of you hurt?"

Poor guy. He looked friendly and helpful. Too bad Crazy Guy was probably going to shoot all of us.

I could tell the moment his eyes fell on the woman that was bleeding out on the road. "Oh my God. We have to help her!" the second man shouted. He ran over to the woman and knelt down beside her.

"Hey!" yelled the man with the gun. "She's fine. Leave her alone."

"I'm a doctor! Let me help her!" replied the second man, frantically. "She needs medical attention."

"Sure, you're a doctor, and I'm the Pope," laughed the first man. "Unless you would like to join her in the same spot, I suggest you MOVE!" He pointed the gun at the man claiming to be a doctor and frantically waved it toward us. Once the new stranger joined the rest of us, something in the dark caught my eye. It was Gill! *Thank God she is okay!* I was worried she wouldn't wake up.

Gill had a giant log in her hand and she was quietly creeping up behind the man trying to kill us all. Slightly crouched, she approached very slowly, silently, trying hard not to be found out.

Silently, I willed all of us to keep our mouths shut so that Gill had a chance to whack this crazy man over the head and give us an opportunity to escape.

"Here's how this is gonna go," said the gunman.

"Let me guess, you're going to monologue about why we should do what you say and then we're going to give you whatever you ask for?" Thomas retorted sarcastically.

Dad shot Thomas a warning glance, pleading with him to not make this worse.

"You think this is funny, kid?" asked the man.

"No, but I think you're in for a big surprise," replied Thomas. He was trying to keep the crazy man distracted and give Gill a chance to help us get free of all of this. Even still, I rolled my eyes at their exchange.

The man looked taken aback at Thomas's bravery a split second before Gill raised the log and hit him over the head. Hard. I heard him sink to the ground like a sack of potatoes.

"Take that!" shouted Gill.

Dad darted forward instantly, grabbing the gun that went awry when the man fell. I cautiously approached, but Dad held his hand out and stopped me. "Hold on," he said.

I waited until Dad checked the man's pulse.

"He's alive, but unconscious. I don't know how much time we have until he wakes up."

"Everyone okay?" asked Mom, as she climbed out of the car. We all nodded.

The man who had stopped to help us now moved urgently to the woman. I watched in horror as he knelt down and checked her pulse again. He searched in several different spots, as if something wasn't right.

He stood slowly.

"She's dead," he announced.

Gasping, I covered my mouth. Leslie stood at my side and turned her face into my shirt, as if hiding from the realization that the woman was alive one minute, and then dead the next. I put my arm around her and rubbed her back to comfort her. *How was anything going to be okay?*

"Are you really a doctor?" Dad questioned, looking at the man.

The man shook his head no. "I thought he might be more willing to let me help if he thought I was a medical professional. I'll call the police now if you want me to," he said.

"I thought I heard sirens a minute ago. They might already be on their way," I said.

"Let's hope that's true. This is all a mess. What did that guy want?" asked Gill, gesturing down to the unconscious psycho that ran us off the road.

Gill must have been unconscious this whole time. I'm glad she was okay now, but she could need medical attention.

"He was looking for Kate," I replied.

"Robert, we have to get out of here," Mom said, panic taking over. "We have a dead woman and an unconscious man on the ground, and you're holding a gun that doesn't belong to you. The SUV we 'borrowed' from someone who can be considered a terrorist is upside down. None of this looks good." She waved her hands wildly around the chaos surrounding us.

Dad sighed heavily. "I know, I know. Let me think."

The sirens resumed and turned off just as red and blue lights came into focus. Finally! It was a police car pulling over where we were all standing. I held my breath as he exited the vehicle.

"Everything okay here? Anyone hurt?" the police officer asked.

His eyes went wide as he saw the dead woman on the ground as well as the unconscious man.

"What is this?" he asked, his voice accusatory.

"Officer, we can explain," Dad said.

He immediately drew his gun and aimed it at Dad when he saw the gun at his side.

"Drop the weapon!" the officer yelled.

I watched as Dad put the gun down and then raised his hands in surrender.

"You have to understand. This man," Dad said, pointing to the unconscious guy, "ran us off the road, caused my family to crash our SUV, and then attempted to shoot at us. We had to do something!"

The officer took in everything at the scene with a skeptical look on his face. "And this woman? She was shot. How do I know it wasn't you?" he asked Dad.

Dad stood with his head held high and spoke calmly to the officer. "You don't. Arrest me if you must but leave my family out of this."

"Robert, no…" said Mom. I could hear the fear in her voice. As soon as Dad was arrested, they would realize who he was and I would most likely never see him again.

I felt a tear roll down my face. *How could this be happening?*

The officer spoke into his radio and called for backup, while keeping his gun aimed at Dad.

The man who stopped and tried to help us earlier interrupted the tense silence. "Look, officer. I'm Burton. This family didn't cause all of this. They are telling the truth. The psycho guy shot the woman and wouldn't let any of them try to help her. The only reason he hasn't killed all of us, myself included, is because this brave young lady," he continued, pointing to Gill, "hit him over the head with a log."

Gill gave the officer and Burton a fake smile. "Just trying to help," she said.

"And why should I believe you?" asked the officer, still not trusting any of us.

Burton's expression changed into something sinister. I felt a twisting in my gut. *Something was wrong.*

"Because if you don't, I'll make sure Mr. Wesley sees to it that you are killed."

Chapter 24

"Excuse me?" said the officer.

Judging by his reaction, I could tell it was news to him just like it surprised us.

"Did I stutter?" said Burton.

I couldn't believe that he pretended to be helpful and friendly. We were clearly surrounded on all sides by Memory Lane guards, spies, and people directly connected to Gideon Wesley.

Burton's actions confused me. First he told the officer that it wasn't our fault the woman was killed, which was true, but then he said he would turn the officer over to Mr. Wesley. *Was Burton really on our side? What was his end game?* My head was spinning in circles.

The man who ran us off the road groaned and stirred. "Ugh. My head," he said while reaching for the back of his head. He pulled back his hand to see blood running through his fingers. It seemed Gill got him really good. He sat up and blinked at all of us, with a dazed look on his face.

"Put your hands up!" yelled the officer. He pointed his gun at the man while the rest of us froze.

"I didn't do anything wrong! They knocked me out!"

"That's a lie!" Thomas and I shouted at the same time.

The officer looked at all of us as if trying to decide who was telling the truth. I could only hope that he believed my family.

"Everyone stop talking!" shouted the officer. "I want to know how this woman was shot!" he said, while pointing to the woman on the ground. Shivers ran up and down my spine as I remembered that she was dead and that we watched her die.

Dad made eye contact with the police officer. "This man," he said, while pointing to the crazy man sitting in the middle of all of us, "shot her. This is his gun. We took it away from him once he was knocked out. I was only trying to protect my family," Dad explained calmly.

"You can't prove that!" the crazy man growled.

"We certainly can arrest all of you and check for gunpowder residue," said the officer.

The logic of that made me feel better. My Dad never shot the gun. Maybe we could get out of this mess on actual evidence.

"Or," said Burton, "we could let Mr. Wesley sort this all out. I pressed a button on my phone to bring him here. And let me say, he doesn't come out for just anyone. I told him this was important."

What? Gideon Wesley was coming now?

"There's no such button," replied the officer.

"Believe whatever you want, but Mr. Wesley has a few of his most trusted individuals on speed dial at the touch of a button. I sent him an S.O.S. because we are in the presence of some celebrities," Burton said. He smiled cunningly and then pointed to me and Thomas.

"My chief of police assured me that we needed to divert the ambulances away from here when the call came in for this accident. 'Police only' was the directive given. You can't tell me that directive was because of Mr. Wesley. He has nothing to do with the police!" shouted the officer.

Burton smiled again. "I can assure you that he most certainly has a tremendous influence on the majority of the police departments in America."

I froze while Burton reached into his pocket for something.

Does he have a gun?

"What is that?" asked Thomas.

"Drop it!" shouted the officer.

I couldn't tell what Burton was holding. From where I was standing, it looked like a pen. He brought it up to his mouth slowly and aimed it in the direction of the officer.

What in the world?

I watched in horror as Burton blew into the pen-like object and a dart flew out, hitting the officer in the heart.

He collapsed with a small gasp immediately.

"That's more like it. So much talking, and he was too much trouble anyway. Mr. Wesley should be along in about half an hour," said Burton calmly.

Dad, Mom, Thomas, the crazy man, and Gill all stared at Burton with wide eyes.

"Did you just kill a police officer?" Dad choked out.

Instinctively, I pushed Leslie behind me, in case he had another dart in his pocket.

Burton nodded. "Just a little potassium chloride. We've been using it forever on hardened criminals on death row. It's a quick, painless way to die."

"We would have preferred you not kill him at all!" Dad shouted back.

"Well, I would have preferred a hot wife by my side, but we don't always get what we want, Mr. Healy," replied Burton wryly.

In less than 24 hours, we had heard so many gunshots, seen so many people hurt, and now we had two corpses on our hands. *Was any of this real?* I started to hyperventilate, thinking that there was no possible way we could get out of this. Leslie squeezed my hand and tried to calm me silently.

"By the way," said Burton, turning to face the crazy man in the middle, "you can stand up now, Jesus."

"I can't believe I had to get hit on the head in order to make this believable. Why couldn't it be you?" Jesus asked, rubbing his head and standing. He kicked the officer's body and grabbed his gun.

Burton and the crazy man—now apparently named Jesus—were partners? None of this made any sense.

"You played your part well, my friend. Mr. Wesley will reward you in time," Burton told Jesus. "Now, I need all of you to line up over here."

"Why should we listen to you?" asked Gill.

I locked eyes with Gill to tell her to shut up before we all got shot. I grabbed Leslie's hand and started to move over toward where Burton said we needed to line up. Thomas and my parents followed suit. Gill looked reluctant, but eventually lined up with all of us.

"Now, Mr. Wesley will be happy to see some of you. Especially you two," Burton said, pointing to me and Thomas.

We were trapped on the side of the road with nothing but thick brush behind us. Too thick to escape in. Did we put up a good fight? Was this all worth it, standing here at what felt like the literal end of the road? I couldn't answer that question any more than I could see a way out of this predicament. There was no way we were escaping this time. My heart sank as I realized that Leslie would probably go back into the program, and that my parents, Thomas, and I would be arrested and likely held at Memory Lane indefinitely. Tears rolled down my face as I accepted the fate of my family.

"How'd you do it, anyway?" asked Burton.

His question broke me out of my reverie and momentary wallowing.

Was he talking to me? I wondered.

"Yes, you," Burton said, gaining my attention. "How did you and Thomas break into Memory Lane?" He seemed to be in awe of what we did just a short time ago this summer.

I remained silent.

"Not a talker?" Jesus asked, invading my personal space. "We can make you talk," he said.

I shuddered as he got closer.

I felt Leslie squeeze my hand and that somehow gave me the confidence I needed to answer Burton and Jesus's stupid question.

"Are you upset that two teenagers got into your precious Memory Lane illegally? That we got past all of your security measures and still thwarted capture? That you still don't have a clue what memory I saw and won't ever get to find out?"

Jesus slapped me across the cheek, hard.

Mom screamed, and I felt Leslie grab my arm to steady me, as I was forced backward a few steps.

"Don't touch her!" I heard Dad yell at Jesus.

My chest was heaving as I grabbed my cheek to lessen the sting from his slap. I steadied my breath as I gathered the courage to respond.

"It's fine, Mom. He can't help it that he likes to hit little girls for fun. Makes him feel powerful. Whatever works, dude," I replied shrugging.

No one moved or made a sound. I felt everyone's eyes on me at that moment and it made me feel like I was an animal in a cage at the zoo being watched.

Burton spoke and broke the tension. "Jesus, watch yourself. We don't want them harmed just yet, not before Mr. Wesley arrives."

"He tried to kill us in a car crash!" Mom yelled. "This is ridiculous."

"Not to mention the emotional trauma we've all experienced tonight," added Gill. "Thanks for that, Burton and Jesus. Really, we should send you a gift basket. Hannah, don't forget to get their addresses for those family Christmas cards."

I tried to contain my chuckle, but it was too late.

"Mr. Wesley is perfectly happy taking you and her with him while you're unconscious," said Burton, pointing to me and Gill.

Mom shot me a warning look that told me to be quiet. I couldn't help myself sometimes with these people. They were just so high-and-mighty.

The distant sound of a helicopter above us stole my attention away from Burton and Jesus. I shielded my eyes with my hand from the dirt and dust as I glanced up to look at the helicopter approaching. The blades blew every bit of dust into the air. *Was that helicopter here for us? How many of us could fit in one?*

"Ah, the moment we've all been waiting for," said Burton.

The helicopter continued to fly above us for a solid minute or so. *Where was it going to land?* A search light came down from the helicopter while all of us were looking up at it. Burton and Jesus were waving their arms like crazy people, trying to let the pilot know where we were.

The helicopter started its descent on the other side of our wrecked car. It was the flattest spot other than the road, and I guess blocking traffic was ill-advised. As it landed, I watched the grass and dirt blow around, thinking about how the helicopter came in to disrupt this peaceful, grassy field much like Memory Lane had been disrupting my family's lives for over four years now. It was ironic how all the pieces kept coming together. Instead of resolution, it was just more pain.

All of us continued to watch the landing, when suddenly I saw Gill walk over, pat my shoulder, and then take off running in the opposite direction of the helicopter.

"Gill!" I shouted. "What are you doing?!"

She continued to run full speed away from us.

"Gill!" I shouted again. "Come back!"

Where was she going?

Jesus shot at Gill as she ran away and all of us instinctively ducked at the sound of the gun.

I assumed he was missing Gill each time he fired at her because she kept running full speed away from us down the road.

I prayed she just kept running. *Don't look back, Gill.* At least one of us was able to get away.

The helicopter landed and Jesus and Burton gave all of us a warning look that said, *"If you try what she did, you won't make it out of this alive."* The blades of the helicopter ceased their rotation momentarily and I watched in horror as Mr. Wesley climbed out. He straightened the lapels of his jacket and smoothed back his hair, sunglasses in place. You would have thought we were on set for a spy movie. His expensive dark suit looked perfectly tailored and he approached with an air of confidence and arrogance that came from his knowing that he needed help from no one.

I had not seen him since the funeral for Kate's Mom. The death he likely caused. Even with time, he still made me shiver from the creepy vibe he gave off. He approached Jesus and Burton and shook hands with them before taking off his sunglasses and looking over at me, Thomas, and my parents. Leslie was mostly hidden behind me. The night was lit only by the single streetlamp and the headlights of the dead woman's car. Despite the darkness, Mr. Wesley still felt the need to wear sunglasses. I always thought that people who wore sunglasses at night were trying too hard.

"Hannah. Thomas. Robert," Mr. Wesley said. "Good to see you again."

"The pleasure is ours," said Thomas.

Gideon Wesley smiled, but it didn't reach his eyes. The pretend smile gave away what he was hiding underneath his outward appearance. Clapping his hands together expectantly he asked, "Now, where is Kate?"

All of us stared at Mr. Wesley, pretending like we had no idea what he was talking about. I was thankful that my parents and Thomas were on board with the whole idea of keeping Kate away from her Dad.

Burton chose that moment to speak up. "About that. Sir, we didn't call you because we had Kate. We called you because we thought it was important to apprehend the fugitives."

Gideon blinked hard and fast a few times before turning to face Burton.

"You don't have Kate? Did you at least find out where she is?" he asked, visibly fuming that they had not completed what they had been assigned.

"No, sir."

"I see," said Mr. Wesley. He paused for a few seconds and narrowed his eyes. I pushed Leslie further behind me because Mr. Wesley looked on the edge of becoming enraged. I remembered this look from when Kate and I were kids. It didn't take much to get her in trouble. It could be any little thing and he would just absolutely lose it. One time, she left her food sitting in the Instapanel too long and he took it out and threw it at her. We were eleven years old. The memory of the rage on his face and the way he visibly shook at what he perceived to be a lack of respect from his daughter sent a shiver through me. I don't know how she survived his abuse and anger.

"So you are wasting my time," Gideon said, dismissively.

Jesus tried to explain this time. "We brought you fugitives that broke into Memory Lane. Not to mention, Kate's best friend. She will lead us to her in time. I guarantee it."

Gideon Wesley looked at Jesus and then at Burton. He smirked and then slapped Burton across the face and punched Jesus in the stomach. They both stumbled and grabbed the area that was in pain from Mr. Wesley's assault. "No one is safe from harm, you know. You should be more careful. Besides," Mr. Wesley said impatiently, "I don't have time for all of this. I need Kate. Now!"

Both Jesus and Burton continued to breathe heavily and stare at Mr. Wesley. The surprise and horror on their faces gave away their new fear. Perhaps they had dodged his anger all this time. Mr. Wesley was right, No one was safe. I guess they had nothing else to say. Either that, or they didn't want to get hit again.

Gideon made eye contact with me. "There are ways of making you talk so I get what I want."

"I'm not eleven years old anymore, Mr. Wesley. Neither is Kate. I'll do whatever it takes to make sure she doesn't ever have to see you again."

"I'm so glad you found some confidence, Hannah," he replied, cracking a smile that still didn't reach his eyes. "You may not be a child anymore, but there are certainly people in your life that are children who..."

I inhaled sharply and felt Leslie stiffen behind me.

"Is that a threat?" I asked.

Gideon Wesley chuckled, his eyes narrowing. "It's a promise."

No one blinked as we stared at each other.

"Now then," said Mr. Wesley, rubbing his hands together like a greedy child. "Are we doing this the hard way or the easy way?"

"Doing what?" asked Thomas.

"Getting in the helicopter."

"To go where?" Mom asked.

Mr. Wesley scoffed. "Memory Lane, of course. We have some catching up to do."

"We can't all fit," I said, pointing out the obvious.

"I'm certain there is room for the four of us," said Mr. Wesley.

The four of us? Who did that include? My heart was sure to explode out of my chest while I waited for Mr. Wesley to explain.

"No. We all stay together," said Dad.

Mr. Wesley walked over to where Dad was standing and put his hand on Dad's shoulder. "That's not really up to you, Robert."

"Like hell it isn't."

Mr. Wesley chuckled and pretended to shake with fear.

I rolled my eyes at Mr. Wesley poking fun at my father's protectiveness. My Dad wasn't perfect, but at least he wasn't abusive.

How could the whole world believe that Gideon had their best interest in mind? He could be the definition of charming and poised when in the public eye. Yet, in private, the true monster made his way out. I made a promise to myself to make it known to everyone who the real Mr. Wesley was. I refused to stand by and watch this any longer.

"Robert, you don't have to make this difficult," said Mr. Wesley. "Hannah, Thomas, and Leslie can join me calmly and we can be on our way."

No. No way was I letting Leslie come with Gideon. I'd rather die.

"You're crazy if you think I'm letting both of my daughters go any-where with you!" screamed Mom. She reached forward to slap him in the face but he dodged her attempts at violence. He grabbed her wrist and began to twist her arm. I watched in horror as she struggled against his grip.

"Linda. Don't hurt yourself," said Mr. Wesley.

"You're the one hurting her!" yelled Leslie from behind me.

Mr. Wesley dropped Mom's arm and turned back to face me and Leslie.

"My, my, aren't you feisty?" he asked Leslie.

She came out from behind me with her head held high. *Why did she have to be so brave?*

"If I agree to go back with you and join the program again, will you leave my family alone?"

My stomach dropped as my worst fears had just been realized.

Mr. Wesley smirked. "Now we're talking."

Chapter 25

The blood drained from my face and for a moment, the world began to spin. *She couldn't be serious?* "Are you insane? Leslie, you can't do that!"

Leslie crossed her arms in defiance. "I'm capable of making my own decisions, you know."

"You're still a child!"

Silence continued to ring in my ears as I became aware of everyone else staring at me and Leslie in that moment.

"While I appreciate this fine show of dramatic flair, we really need to be going," said Mr. Wesley, checking his watch. *Do you have somewhere else to be? Torturing some other family?*

"There is no way I am letting you go anywhere with Gideon Wesley!" shouted Mom.

"Over my dead body!" yelled Dad.

"But if I can help out—" Leslie started to say.

"Please, I won't lose you when I just got you back!" shouted Mom, tears running down her face. Her voice broke on the last word and Leslie reached out to hug her. I joined in. This was all just too much.

"Mr. Wesley, can't you just give us a few minutes to figure this all out?" Thomas begged, his voice filled with panic.

I shook my head. "We don't need to discuss anything. Come on, Thomas. Let's go. Leslie, you're staying with Mom and Dad."

"You can't make me stay!"

"Everybody just calm down for a minute," said Mr. Wesley. "I just want to study your brains. They fascinate me. I also want to find my daughter. I mean no harm."

I rolled my eyes. *Sure. I believe that to be true. And why did Mr. Wesley only want me, Thomas, and Leslie? What about Jesus and Burton? Was he just using them?*

"Are we just lying out loud now?" I asked, incredulously.

"None of us have to sit and talk," said Leslie. "I'm ready to go."

"No!"

"Hold up!" said Thomas. "Let's think about this logically."

All of us turned to look at Thomas as he seemed to gather himself before looking directly at Mr. Wesley.

"How does Leslie being in the program again help you find Kate?" he asked, calmly.

"The program does not reveal its secrets," he answered cryptically.

Mom scoffed and shook her head angrily. "Yeah, and I'm supposed to send my daughter with you."

Thomas interjected again. "I'm serious. What is the reason you need Leslie in the program? You say your end goal is to find Kate. How can Leslie help with that?"

"She's just an added bonus. I fully intend to take you and Hannah with me," replied Mr. Wesley.

At that moment, Leslie's eyes glazed over as her arms hung limply at her sides. Not again. I grabbed her hands and gently tugged on her, trying to get her attention, and bring her back to us, but she wasn't responding.

"Leslie? Come on. We really need you here right now. Can you hear me?" I asked.

Mom reached forward too and brushed the hair from Leslie's face "Honey, can you hear us?"

Looking up into Mom's face, I could see the panic rising.

Leslie continued to stare straight through me. It was the creepiest feeling. I could see her eyes but there was absolutely no recognition in them.

"What's wrong with her?" Mr. Wesley asked. He attempted to move closer to Leslie, but Mom and I blocked her with our bodies. We made sure that he didn't have access to her at the moment.

"Nothing. She's fine," I replied.

"She doesn't look fine." He moved closer again and tried to look around me at Leslie. "Her eyes look empty."

"It's just stress. Give her a minute." I looked back at Leslie and tried to get her attention again. "Les? Look at me. Come on." I shook her arm gently.

Mom looked at me nervously. We were both at a loss every time Leslie had one of these flashbacks or hallucinations. I was tired of this happening to her.

"Let me help," said Mr. Wesley.

"Don't touch her!" I shouted. Mom and I moved Leslie farther away from where Mr. Wesley was standing, continuing to block him with our bodies. My outburst caused Thomas to move closer and make sure that we were okay. Leslie started repeating words like she did some of the other times this happened. I could just barely make out her whispers.

"Leave me alone … leave me alone … leave me alone…"

"I have just the thing for this," Mr. Wesley announced. I turned around just as he reached into his pocket and pulled out a device that looked like an old laser pointer. My heart rate increased while I watched him point it at Leslie and press the blue button on the side.

"Stop! Wait!" I shouted.

It was too late. He pressed the button. *What kind of sicko does that to a kid who is obviously not even mentally present at the moment?*

My gaze shifted to Leslie, waiting to see what the button did.

I gasped as she grabbed her head and winced in pain. For a moment, fear rose up in me.

"What did you do to her!?!?" I yelled at Gideon. I felt the blood rush to my cheeks in anger.

"Hannah. Wait," Leslie spoke softly, squeezing my hands. "It stopped."

"What? You're back here with me?" I checked her face for recognition, and she nodded slowly. Mom made eye contact with Leslie next and then smiled, gently stroking her cheek. Relief flooded through me knowing that at least for now, Leslie was back.

"What did that thing do?" I asked Mr. Wesley, turning around and glaring at him.

"Isn't it obvious?" he asked, smirking.

Glaring at him, I could feel the puzzle pieces of Leslie's episodes all falling into place. We knew they had something to do with Memory Lane. Jenson had told us Leslie was on a list of children that had a chip implanted in their brains.

"It stopped Leslie from having a memory flashback. I control them, you see," he explained shaking the small controller to emphasis.

"What?!?! All this time you've been the one giving her these glimpses into her time in the program? When she doesn't know where she is or who she's with or who any of us are?"

"It was always going to end this way, Hannah."

I lunged forward to grab at Mr. Wesley's throat. "I'll kill you!" I shouted.

"Hannah, no!" screamed Mom and Thomas in unison. They both ran to stop me before I actually did kill him.

Thomas grabbed my arm and pulled me back into his chest. "Let me go!" I yelled at Thomas. "I'm not letting him get away with this!" I elbowed Thomas in the ribs as I continued to reach forward at Mr. Wesley. He backed away from me some, startled at how crazy I was acting.

Leslie came and stood in between me and Mr. Wesley. "Hannah! Stop! I'm okay!" She had her hands up in a surrender pose and was trying to get me to calm down.

"I promise I'm fine," Leslie repeated.

My chest was still heaving as I felt Thomas slowly relax his grip on my arms when I stopped reaching for Mr. Wesley.

"That wasn't very lady-like," said Mr. Wesley, brushing off his shirt as if he got dirt on it.

"Giving my sister hallucinations and flashbacks isn't very gentlemanly," I retorted.

"We're even then."

"We could never be," I replied. I held back the urge to spit right in his face.

"Anyway," Mr. Wesley deflected, completely ignoring my fury, "Now that you know the control I have over your sister, it is in all of your best interests to go with me to Memory Lane."

"Pardon me, sir, but what about our agreement?" asked Burton.

Mr. Wesley turned around to face him. The look he shot at Burton was one of disdain. Like Burton was the scum on the bottom of his shoe. So much for him being important and in Gideon's inner circle.

"Agreement?"

Burton looked down momentarily and then seemed to gather his confidence. "Yes, our agreement that I would be rewarded for services to Memory Lane."

"Ahh. That agreement."

Was Burton seriously asking for money right now?

"So, am I meeting you at Memory Lane later or what?" Burton asked, standing up a little straighter.

Mr. Wesley seemed to consider his answer carefully for a moment. "I'll tell you what. Why don't you and Jesus head on back to Memory Lane. Tell the receptionist that I asked for you both to wait for me in my second office. I'll be along later tonight."

"Perfect. Thanks," said Burton. "Come on Jesus. Let's go," he replied.

I watched as the two of them got into the car that Burton pulled over in, back when he was just a nice man trying to help us out. Crazy how things had changed in a short amount of time.

Mr. Wesley clapped his hands together, facing me, Leslie, Thomas, and my parents again. "Now. Where were we?" he asked.

All of us looked at each other, but no one said a word. I wasn't going to give him the satisfaction of speaking first.

"Oh right. I was taking your daughters and nephew to better understand the brain and how it stores memories."

"They aren't science experiments, Gideon!" shouted Mom.

Mr. Wesley looked offended for a second. "Of course not. They are more valuable than gold. Besides, I'm not a scientist. I hire people for that. The ideas are all mine though," he replied, pridefully.

I felt my cheeks get hot again. "You're a sick man!"

"I'm a father who wants to find his daughter. And I happen to have her best friend standing in front of me. I'm just capitalizing on that fortunate circumstance."

"I'll never tell you where she is."

"You won't have to. Your brain will do the talking for you," Mr. Wesley replied. "Now, it's imperative that we leave. You'll understand when we arrive."

How was I going to keep Kate's location a secret if Mr. Wesley put me in one of those machines?

"Can we have a minute to at least say goodbye?" asked Mom, hesitantly.

"If you must. Make it quick."

Mom and Dad rushed over to where we were standing and enveloped all of us in a hug. As soon as we were huddled together, hugging, it was like a wave of emotions came over me and I couldn't contain my tears. Something I had been holding back for days and days finally broke through. I sobbed harder than I had in a long time. Everything leading up to this moment just hit me like a ton of bricks, and I couldn't move past it. I cried for Leslie and her lost childhood because of the program. I cried for my parents who lost time with their youngest daughter. I cried for myself because I lost a best friend and a sister at the same time four years ago. Mom squeezed me hard and then we all took a step back from the hug.

I sniffled and then found myself wiping the tears off my face with my sleeve. Mom and Dad both smiled at me and Leslie. Their eyes were glistening with tears.

"We are so proud of both of you," Mom said.

"Take care of each other," added Dad.

Mom turned to look at Thomas. "I can't say how grateful I am knowing that my daughters will be with you." Mom choked back a sob. "Keep them safe, please." Mom struggled to hold back more tears.

Thomas smiled and nodded at Mom and I noticed his eyes were shining too. "Of course, Aunt Linda," he replied.

Leslie grabbed my hand and smiled up at me. I couldn't believe we were actually going back to Memory Lane with Mr. Wesley willingly. I hoped we would eventually find a way to escape, but all I could think at the moment was that at least I would be with Leslie to protect her this time. And that Kate was nowhere near Memory Lane so her father couldn't hurt her. She would never be safe with him again, especially after what happened regarding her Mom's death.

"Everybody ready to go?" asked Mr. Wesley, interrupting our goodbye.

He sounded a little too giddy for my taste.

"Why don't you take me in place of Hannah and Leslie?! You can study my brain again," said Dad, desperately.

His last-ditch effort to protect both of us made my eyes well up again. He stood in between us and Mr. Wesley as if his body could keep us safe from harm. If only it were that simple.

"That's cute. But no thanks, Robert. Leslie and Hannah's brains are worth ten times yours. They are young and pliable. Plus, Hannah and Thomas both need to be reprimanded for the break-in they orchestrated earlier this summer."

"Promise me that you won't kill them," said Mom. Tears rolled down her cheeks, and she made no attempt to wipe them away.

Mr. Wesley made eye contact with Mom. "I would never kill someone on purpose."

Mom lunged forward to attack Mr. Wesley.

At least I knew where I got my rage from.

"Linda!" yelled Dad. He grabbed Mom and pulled her away from Gideon. She was fighting him hard. I could tell Dad was struggling to hold her back.

Mr. Wesley calmly spoke to my parents. "If you can't control yourself, Linda, then I think some tranquilizers are in order. All of you are so worked up."

"Your solution is to just drug everyone into compliance?" I asked.

Mr. Wesley shrugged. "Whatever works."

"What is your plan for the bodies? The police officer and the woman died here. Our DNA is littered all over the crime scene," said Thomas.

I glanced over at my parents. Mom seemed to have calmed down a bit and Dad loosened his grip on her.

"You're just going to leave this poor woman and police officer to rot? What about their families?" asked Mom.

"I'll send some Memory Lane guards to clean up the mess in about an hour. Satisfied?"

"No! An officer was killed with a potassium chloride dart. In the heart. A woman was shot. Don't you think the police and FBI are going to have some questions?" Thomas demanded.

Mr. Wesley sighed heavily and acted like their dead bodies were such an inconvenience to him. *No wonder he had his wife killed.*

"Fine. I'll call the chief of police and the director of the FBI if necessary to let them know that all of this needs to be taken care of. What's a few more million dollars when you have so much?" he asked, chuckling to himself.

"And the families of both victims will be notified?" I pleaded. I couldn't imagine the families not knowing what happened to their loved ones.

Mr. Wesley waved my question off, as he was already on the phone with the chief of police, presumably. He was muttering and pacing while he talked.

Sorry the deaths of two people are such a burdensome task.

Leslie looked up at me. "Are you scared, Hannah?"

"Of course," I replied. After all that had happened, there was no need to lie to her and make her feel like she was the only one worried about what we were getting ourselves into.

She nodded. "I'm glad you're coming with me."

"Me too." I squeezed her hand. Just having her there was a comfort.

Mr. Wesley wrapped up his phone call and then turned back to us. "All taken care of. The police car and the woman's car are being towed back to the police station. Another tow truck is coming to get the car you guys crashed. The Memory Lane guards and the coroner are on their way to make sure the bodies get squared away. The police chief assured me the families would be notified. Now, we really must be going."

He started walking back to the helicopter and got about twenty steps away before he realized we weren't following him.

Was this really it? The last time I might see my parents?

I stifled a sob and hugged my parents one more time along with Leslie and Thomas.

"We'll come find you," Dad whispered. "No matter what."

I nodded and tried to shut out the dark thoughts that said there was no way Mr. Wesley was going to let my parents anywhere near Memory Lane while we were there. I had to hold onto hope that they would find a way to get us out.

"Keep each other safe," whispered Mom before squeezing me one last time.

"What are y'all gonna do?" I asked Dad.

He smiled. "Don't worry about us."

Thomas, Leslie, and I walked away from my parents and joined Mr. Wesley heading toward the helicopter. Mr. Wesley reached it first and climbed inside. Thomas got in next followed by me, and then Leslie. My eyes were shining with tears when I looked out and saw my parents waving at us. I refused to let the tears fall as I waved back at my parents.

Mr. Wesley gestured to the seat belts and I made sure we were all tightly belted and secured before reaching across Leslie and closing the door. Mr. Wesley pointed out the headphones that were hanging above each seat. They dampened some of the sound of the helicopter blades and made it where those on the helicopter could talk to each other. We all put them on as he started the helicopter. Even with the headphones, the sound was deafening as the blades continued to spin in the air.

"We should be there in about half an hour," Mr. Wesley said casually. He probably shouted it, but I could barely hear him over the sound of the helicopter blades. moments after the blades began to pick up speed, I felt us leave the ground. This was it. No turning back now. Leslie squeezed my hand at that exact moment and I squeezed her hand back. At least we were together.

She was practically sitting in my lap and my knees were touching Thomas's because there wasn't a whole lot of space in the helicopter. The houses and streets looked like tiny pinpricks of light from this perspective. It was breathtaking being this high up. If I focused on the view, I could almost forget that we were being held hostage by Mr. Wesley who had his wife killed, and was looking for Kate to do who knows what to her. The lights of the passing cars headed to their peaceful destinations were a welcome distraction from thinking about what they would do to Leslie's brain when we got back to Memory Lane. Were they going to pick it apart again? The way the stars dotted the sky, I had almost forgotten that Thomas and I were likely going to be arrested and probably have The Mnemonic used on us.

How had everything we'd been through led to here? We had evaded capture so many times and I got Leslie back only to be in a helicopter with Mr. Wesley himself headed back to Memory Lane. I had even started to fix things with Kate after all these years and now...

Leslie shifted against me and it brought me out of my thoughts.

"Hannah?" she shouted over the sound of the helicopter.

"What?" I yelled back.

Leslie looked at me with sadness in her eyes. "Are we gonna die?" she mouthed.

I couldn't respond. I didn't want to scare her, but I also didn't want to lie to her face. Leslie deserved more than that.

I pulled her even closer and replied, "Not if I can help it."

Chapter 26

Memory Lane came into view faster than I wanted it to and before we knew it, we were landing on the helicopter pad. As the helicopter landed, I felt Leslie squeeze my hand. She never did like landing or take-off on a plane. The helicopter experience was much different from any plane ride we had ever had and shook so much more when it landed. Squeezing her hand back, I looked up to see the whirring of the blades slowing down as we touched the ground. This was all too fast. Memory Lane was a few hundred feet away! I inhaled deeply, trying to ready myself for whatever Mr. Wesley had in store for me and Thomas. I shook my head before any thoughts of what his plans for Leslie might be just yet. I lied to myself, *"If I don't think about it, it isn't real."*

The blades of the helicopter stopped completely, and I removed the noise-canceling headphones from my ears. Leslie and Thomas followed suit.

"Everyone ready?" asked Mr. Wesley. Turning to look at us, he had sheer delight written on his face and if I didn't actually know better, you would think we were about to head off into the most fun adventure.

I shrugged. "Not really, but you haven't given us much of a choice," I replied.

Mr. Wesley frowned. "Don't be such a Debbie Downer."

I watched as Mr. Wesley got out of the helicopter and motioned for us to follow. Thomas got up to file out of the back, but I stopped him.

"Wait just a minute," I whispered.

He sat back down and looked at me expectantly. Leslie had a curious look on her face as they both waited for me to explain why I wanted to wait to get out of the helicopter.

"We need a way to communicate with each other if we're separated."

"I agree. Any ideas?" asked Thomas, keeping his voice low.

"We could start another fire," suggested Leslie with a smirk on her face.

I gently shoved her arm. "Funny," I said. "Because that went so well last time."

"How does a fire communicate anything anyway?" asked Thomas, egging Leslie on.

She took the bait. "I think it's pretty clear that it means get out of there fast."

"Guys, Mr. Wesley is looking at us funny. We need a real idea, now," I said.

"How about we just don't get separated?" Thomas nervously looked back over toward Mr. Wesley.

"Great idea, though I don't think Mr. Wesley is keen on keeping us together."

He was approaching the helicopter door again, presumably to see what was keeping us from exiting.

"Well, I don't really see that we have any options here."

"Plotting against me?" asked Mr. Wesley, poking his head in the helicopter, glaring at us suspiciously.

Leslie and Thomas both exchanged glances with me but none of us spoke.

"Do I need to remind you that I control Leslie's brain?" he added, with a sinister look in his eye. He pulled out the device that he showed me earlier when he stopped her flashback from happening.

Not wanting him to hurt Leslie, I resigned myself to getting out of the helicopter and following Mr. Wesley. *He really was such an evil man.*

The walk to the building felt so much shorter than any of our other walks into Memory Lane. Perhaps it was because this time we were being welcomed with open arms instead of breaking and entering. As we made our way into Memory Lane, Leslie reached for my hand and Thomas stood close by my side. A few women behind the desk who worked for Memory Lane and other patrons attempting to relive their memories stared as we entered the building. Mr. Wesley had that effect on people. I know because I had felt it. He was powerful, rich, in control of so much of our entire country and what made it worse, he knew it. Confidence, power, and control are hard things to fight against.

As we continued past the front and through the various hallways I noted the significant difference in how this particular Memory Lane was laid out compared to others. Mr. Wesley led us to a door marked with his name on it. He paused momentarily and punched in a code that then brought up a retinal scanner. He allowed it to get close to his face and scan his eye. A few seconds later, the scanner's light turned green and the door popped open. I wondered if Mr. Wesley had an office at every Memory Lane location.

Thomas, Leslie, and I followed him into his office and he gestured for us to sit. The room was enormous. It was easily as big as the first floor of my parents' house.

There were two gold chandeliers above his workspace, a huge desk made of dark wood, and at least three leather sofas and other comfortable looking chairs. *This was an office?* It could easily be someone's apartment.

All three of us were standing in awe at his space when Mr. Wesley cleared his throat and told us to sit down on one of the sofas directly in front of his desk.

As soon as we sat down, there was a beep and a voice spoke through an intercom near Mr. Wesley's desk.

"Jesus and Burton are waiting to speak with you, Mr. Wesley," the voice said.

"I have a Y-45 coming to them momentarily."

The voice on the other side of the intercom paused before speaking again. "I'll see to it that the Y-45 makes it to them."

What in the world is a Y-45?

"Now," said Mr. Wesley. "I've gathered you all here to ensure that—"

"You're an evil man!" screamed Leslie, rising from the sofa.

"Whoa! Calm down, Les."

"He's gonna have Jesus and Burton killed!" she yelled.

"What? How do you know that?" I asked incredulously.

Leslie crossed her arms and stared directly at Mr. Wesley. "Tell them. There's no need to lie now."

Mr. Wesley sighed, folded his hands and placed them on the desk, but didn't say a word.

"What is going on? Why are you accusing Mr. Wesley of killing Jesus and Burton?" asked Thomas.

"I have some distinct memories of my time in the program. I could hear the orders shouted in our area of Memory Lane sometimes by the guards. Anytime a Y-45 was issued, the people were always hauled off in body bags. Isn't that right, Mr. Wesley?"

"Those people committed crimes," he replied calmly.

"Killing them is a crime. So is killing your wife," I retorted.

Mr. Wesley stared into my eyes as if trying to read my mind. I stared right back. I refused to let him win this petty battle.

"That's none of your business."

"Murder is always illegal, Mr. Wesley. Or have you forgotten what it's like to have morals?" I asked.

Leslie gasped at my brazen comment. Mr. Wesley was obviously capable of murder and if I wasn't careful, I would be next.

Mr. Wesley chuckled. "I have morals, Hannah. More than you know."

"So you just ignore these so-called morals when you are stealing memories from people or killing them?"

"I do not steal memories. It's a business transaction. People agree to it."

I scoffed. "Yeah, like the majority of people can afford your fee."

"Don't blame me for capitalism. It's been around for hundreds of years."

"I blame you for taking people's precious memories!"

Mr. Wesley smiled. "I am merely providing a service to lessen the effects of ALD-87."

He sounded like the news or an ad that was rehearsed.

"Right. For a famine that you probably helped create," I replied.

Mr. Wesley stood up and reached forward across the desk to grab the collar of my shirt. The sudden movement took my breath away as I adjusted to the fact that Mr. Wesley was now in my face looking like he wanted to strangle me.

Thomas stood up in response to Mr. Wesley's aggression. He was breathing so hard his chest was heaving.

"I wouldn't hurt Hannah if I were you."

Mr. Wesley dropped the collar of my shirt and turned to Thomas.

"Yeah? What are you going to do about it?" he taunted.

I watched in horror as Thomas's fists clenched at his sides. He was gearing up for a fight I knew he would lose. Mr. Wesley had too many resources at his disposal. Too much money, power, and the right people on his side. There was no way that Thomas could hurt Mr. Wesley and continue to live.

"Thomas, don't," I said, gently grabbing the arm closest to me. "He's not worth it."

Thomas continued to stare down Mr. Wesley and breathe heavily, but his clenched fists relaxed slightly.

"Why did you bring us here?" Thomas asked.

Mr. Wesley dusted off his shirt and sat back down. He looked calm again while he gestured for us to sit.

"Do you believe that life is fair?" he asked.

Neither Thomas, Leslie nor I said anything for a solid thirty seconds. The three of us exchanged glances and then looked back at Mr. Wesley to see if we misunderstood the question.

"What?" I finally asked, confused.

"Do you believe life is fair?" he repeated. A woman entered the room through a side door holding a tray of tea and what I assumed were cookies. *Were we in England?* I tracked her movements as she brought the tray to Mr. Wesley and placed it on his desk. She offered him a pleasant smile before hurrying out of the room.

"What does that have to do with anything?"

Mr. Wesley grabbed a cup and poured himself some hot tea. He added sugar and then brought it up to his mouth to drink while staring at me.

"Answer the question," he said. Mr. Wesley took another sip of tea.

I took the bait and answered first. "I believe that bad things happen to everyone, if that's what you're asking."

Mr. Wesley smiled. "A pessimist, I see."

"I prefer the term realist. People don't just wake up lucky one day. Most people work hard for what they have. But sometimes things don't go as planned. Bad things touch everyone's life. Even famous people who seem to have it all figured out, are miserable behind closed doors. So yeah, life is fair in the sense that eventually we all have crappy things happen," I added.

"I too, believe that to be true. Life is equally terrible to everyone."

I glanced over at Leslie. "Not all of life is terrible."

She smiled at me. I couldn't bring myself to say that everything sucked when I got Leslie back. The current situation that we found ourselves in wasn't good, and I had no idea how we were going to get out of it, but I had to hold on to the small piece of goodness I had been given that was my little sister.

Thomas cleared his throat. "Well, that's a bunch of crap. Life is terrible sometimes, but it's often caused by horrible people. People like you," he said, staring at Mr. Wesley again.

Thomas's comment bounced right off Mr. Wesley as he sipped his cup of tea, and then placed it down and held up the tray containing the cookies.

"Want a cookie?" he asked all of us.

All of us shook our heads no. I couldn't be sure they weren't poisoned.

"Why do you hate me?" asked Mr. Wesley. He was looking right at Thomas.

"Gee, I don't know. You want a list?"

I had to hand it to Thomas. He was really laying it all on the line. I hated Mr. Wesley too, but I was trying to stay on his good side to protect Leslie as long as I could. I hoped that his being a father and wanting Kate back could be used to my advantage.

"Would a list help you get rid of your rage?"

"Rage!? You're the one that grabbed Hannah by the shirt!"

"After she insinuated that I started the famine in '87!" Mr. Wesley shouted. "I invented FastTrack packs so no one went hungry. How can you say that I caused the famine?!" For a moment, I could see a glimmer of humanity in Mr. Wesley.

Leslie's quiet voice broke through the shouting. "I have some reasons to hate you," she said.

I turned to look at her, trying to figure out what her plan was.

"I'm sure you do," replied Mr. Wesley.

I nudged Leslie to go on. I wasn't sure what she had to say, but I wanted to make sure that she knew I supported her no matter what. "You took me from my family when I was a child and attempted to control my memories and thoughts. You all but dissected my brain to figure out what made me different from other people. You told me that my parents were dead and that my sister never loved me. You. You did all of that to a nine-year-old child."

Leslie's arm was trembling against me. I couldn't even imagine what it must have taken to say all of that to Mr. Wesley, her captor. I wanted to kill him and it wasn't even me that was kidnapped and experimented on all those years.

Mr. Wesley sat across from us with his arms folded on the desk, silent.

"Was it worth it?" Leslie asked, in the smallest whisper.

I grasped her hand as she wiped a tear rolling down the side of her cheek.

"I have now mapped enough information about how memories are stored in the brain and my team has determined how to isolate the gene that retains memories. We are weeks away from being able to scan for it in infancy and remove it if necessary."

"Surgery on infants so you can potentially steal memories from them when they are adults?! You're sick!" I shouted.

Mr. Wesley shook his head. "You have it all wrong. I believe in technology. I believe in science. I believe in helping people."

Thomas rolled his eyes. "You sound like a campaign commercial. We aren't buying whatever you're selling."

"Enlighten me. How does performing brain surgery on babies help people?" I watched in silent rage as Mr. Wesley reached over and sipped more of his tea. Like we were just discussing his favorite TV show or where he wanted to get lunch.

"It allows Memory Lane to track their memories more fully when they are adults. You need to understand that eventually everyone will be required to come to Memory Lane for regular screenings. My team plans to use memories and scans of the brain as a way to identify people."

"Why are you telling us all of this?"

"To help you understand that I am not the bad guy. I am just someone who wants to advance the way we live even further."

"Pictures aren't good enough to identify people? We have to scan their brains and store their memories?" I asked.

"Were pictures of Leslie good enough when you assumed she was dead?" Mr. Wesley retorted.

I felt the blood rush to my face in anger. "That's not the same thing!"

Mr. Wesley took another sip of his tea. "I want everyone to have access to Memory Lane in the future. We are working to bring down the cost of reliving a memory so that more can participate and see how beneficial it is."

"How kind of you," said Thomas. "So instead of $50,000, it will be $30,000."

Mr. Wesley chuckled. "I knew you would assume that. But I am happy to arrange a simple neuroscan for people that cannot pay to reduce their costs to a few thousand dollars."

"Let me guess, it will cost even less for people with small children who want to scan them early?" I asked, with disdain.

"You're a smart girl, Hannah." He bit into a cookie after dipping it in his tea.

"When is all of this information hitting the public?" asked Thomas.

"Very soon."

Thomas and I exchanged a glance.

I shook my head in disbelief. "This is a far jump from watching memories on a screen. You're crazy to think the majority of people are ready to have their brains messed with even more than usual."

Mr. Wesley shrugged. "It's just a scan. Similar to a head CT."

"And what about when you find something you don't like? What if a person comes in and retains their memories like me? Do you perform surgery right then? Do you kill them?"

"Of course not. I present them with some options. I already told you, I'm not a monster."

"Options like what?" Leslie asked.

"Therapy or surgery."

"Therapy? What kind of therapy?" I asked.

"A newly developed therapy that is classified, I'm afraid."

"Now it's classified?" I asked, confused. "After all the information you just gave us? What's your endgame here, Mr. Wesley? I thought you wanted to see Kate again. You haven't mentioned her once."

"I do want to see my daughter again. I believe I figured out where she is."

My stomach dropped. *Did he really know? He certainly had the means to find her.*

"Why do you want to see her so badly anyway?" asked Thomas.

"What a ridiculous question. She's my daughter. I love her."

"You've got a funny way of showing it," I replied.

Mr. Wesley sipped more tea and ate another cookie in silence.

"I am trying to get Kate to see that what I am doing here is not a bad thing. That I am the same father she grew up with."

I stood up abruptly. "There is no way in hell Kate believes that anymore! Not after you had her Mom killed."

"It's in your best interest to stop accusing me of things, Hannah," Mr. Wesley replied calmly.

I crossed my arms in defiance and stared at him. I was at a true loss for words. I had nothing else to say to this man.

The side door to the office opened abruptly, and the three of us turned to see who had barged in. It was the same woman who brought in the tray of tea and cookies.

"Sorry to interrupt..."

"Sally, I already told you that I was in an important meeting and to buzz me on the intercom unless it was an emergency."

"I know, sir. But your daughter just arrived."

Chapter 27

"What?!" I shouted. My heart was hammering so hard I thought it might beat out of my chest. *How did Kate get here? Why was she here? Was she in immediate danger?*

Mr. Wesley stood up and started walking toward the side door of his office. He paused and turned around briefly to address Thomas, me, and Leslie. "Give me ten minutes." The door creaked closed, and a lock clicked into place on the other side.

As soon as he disappeared through the side door, I spoke. "How on earth did he find Kate?"

"Maybe Mr. Wesley is bluffing," Leslie suggested, shrugging.

"Or, we have been wrong this whole time and she is working for her Dad," said Thomas dryly.

I shook my head in disbelief. "Have you both lost your minds?"

Thomas ran his hand through his hair, deep in thought. "Come on, Hannah, how do we know that we can trust Kate one hundred percent?"

"All she's done is prove to us that she's on our side! She helped us break into Memory Lane, for goodness' sake!"

"Yeah, but blood is thicker than water," Thomas pointed out.

"What does that even mean?" I spat out.

"It means that Kate's loyalties might be to her father and we have to accept the fact that she played us," Thomas explained.

"There's no evidence of that," I said defiantly, unwilling to believe that Kate was just pretending to be done with her Dad and all of Memory Lane. It couldn't be possible! If it were true, then she was the world's best actress or I was a gullible idiot.

Leslie stood up and walked over to the side door of Mr. Wesley's office.

"What are you doing?" I asked.

Leslie started pulling on the handle of the door, but it was locked. "Got tired of listening to you and Thomas arguing so I decided to see if there was a way out of here."

For a moment, I smiled. "Good thinking."

"I'll check the front door," Thomas said. He jiggled the doorknob, but the door didn't open. Both doors were electronically locked.

"Well, so much for getting out of here," I scoffed, dropping back down on the sofa.

Thomas was persistent, though. He walked over to the desk and started lifting things and opening drawers. "Let's keep looking. Maybe there is a button we can press on Mr. Wesley's desk to get out. Surely he doesn't use a key on the inside of his office."

"Hold on a minute," I said, glancing around the room to look for cameras. "Is anyone else weirded out that Mr. Wesley left us alone in his office for ten minutes? Is he trying to see what we do? Why isn't there a guard in the room with us?"

Thomas stopped his hurried search of Mr. Wesley's desk. "You think this is a trap?"

"I wouldn't put it past him."

"So we just stand here like sitting ducks? We can't, I can't," begged Leslie. "I refuse to go back into the program or have anything to do with Mr. Wesley and his infant brain surgeries."

"That won't happen," I said to Leslie. "I won't let it."

"You can't guarantee that!" she cried. Her hands were shaking, and I could see that she was just barely holding it together.

The side door opened. Mr. Wesley and a Memory Lane guard stood at the entrance and stared at us. I can only assume they heard our argument.

"Well, isn't this nice. A family tiff, I see?" asked Mr. Wesley.

"It's nothing," I replied.

"Whatever it is or isn't will have to be tabled for now. We have some urgent business to take care of, Hannah. Please follow me through this door. I'll be back for Thomas in a moment."

"What!?! No way I'm leaving them and going anywhere with you!"

"I'm afraid you don't have a choice," replied Mr. Wesley calmly.

"There's always a choice."

"Right you are. But this choice will be heavily influenced by how much you value your sister's life."

My eyes went wide in horror as Mr. Wesley pulled out the pen-shaped dart containing what I could only assume was the same poison used to kill the police officer earlier in the evening.

"NO! DON'T!" I yelled, while lunging forward to block his access to Leslie. I acted on pure instinct. My own well-being was forgotten for the sake of Leslie's.

Mr. Wesley put the poisoned dart back in his pocket. "I thought that might convince you. Follow me," he said.

"Why can't Leslie come with me?" I asked, still trying to make sure that she made it out of this alive and that we stayed together.

"Because this conversation is solely between you and my daughter."

"Whatever Kate has to say to me she can say in front of Leslie," I replied.

Mr. Wesley shook his head. "I'm afraid that is not the case."

I remained silent, trying my best not to punch him in the face. *How dare he force me to separate from Leslie and Thomas.*

Leslie looked at me with tears in her eyes. "It's okay, Hannah. Go with him."

I hugged her and felt her sobbing against me. I didn't care that there were other people in the room at the moment. This whole situation was awful, cruel, and unfair.

After a short time, Leslie wiped her tears on my shirt. "Will I get to see you again?"

I squeezed her harder and shook my head, doing my best to assure her that I would make sure of it. Deep down, I hoped that I wasn't lying to her. "I am so proud of you."

Mr. Wesley cleared his throat to get my attention. "Wrap it up," he said curtly.

I shot him an angry glare and hugged Leslie again. Thomas caught my gaze, and I saw the sadness in his eyes. Sadness for all of us and everything we had lost. "Protect her as long as you can," I said to him.

"Of course," he replied.

I kissed the top of Leslie's head, wiped a stray tear from her cheek, and walked over to the side door to leave with Mr. Wesley. I couldn't look back at Leslie for fear of never actually leaving the room. I stepped through the doorway and stopped, waiting to hear the click of the door closing on what felt like all the family I had left. *Would I see them again? Were we all just game pieces in some weird experiment for Mr. Wesley?* As we walked down the hallway, my mind was spinning with questions about why Kate was here and how she even got here. *Why would she leave Jenson? Is she working with her Dad? Was everything since her return a lie?*

We walked for what felt like forever. Minutes passed and, despite trying to keep track of how many turns we made so that if I got free I could go back, I could not keep up. Instead we turned right, then left, and then right again. No matter what I tried, I lost count of the number of steps from his office. *So much for finding my way back.* Mr. Wesley opened a door to my right which led to a small foyer-type room. The Memory Lane guard ushered me inside and then Mr. Wesley scanned his retina again while also swiping a badge to unlock another door. *Was this extra protection that was added since our break-in at Memory*

Lane? This place was like a maze and I wasn't sure that I would remember the layout if I tried to leave this area on my own. The door beeped and both the guard and I followed him inside.

Kate was sitting on a red couch, facing the wall. The room was small, and not decorated other than a single painting. There were no electronics of any kind from what I could see. The overstuffed couch was the only place to sit in the entire room. Kate looked lost in thought, her face showing signs of the deep exhaustion that we all were suffering from. When the door closed behind me, the click of the lock startled Kate out of her thoughts.

"Hannah!" She ran over to give me a tight hug, but I left my arms hanging at my sides. My thoughts and feelings were muddled with confusion. I was so glad to see she was safe, but where was Jenson? Was he okay? I wasn't sure what her motives were just yet, and I didn't want to assume anything.

Kate looked confused at my non-reaction to her arrival and hug, but backed away anyway and took a seat on the couch again.

"Hannah, have a seat," said Mr. Wesley.

I stood there awkwardly, waiting for further instructions. Mr. Wesley obviously had a reason for making me come talk to Kate, but I wasn't about to give him what he wanted by making myself comfortable on the couch. I scanned the mostly empty room, hoping for some miraculous way to escape, to embed the details of the room in my head that might aid in my escape should I need to get out quickly. The Memory Lane guard stood like a sentry in front of the door. I was sure that wasn't a valid option for me getting out of the room. Mr. Wesley was also still in the room with me and Kate and I wasn't sure how long he planned to stay. The painting was the only thing that might be an option. I could only hope that there was some sort of secret passage behind it, but that seemed like a one-in-a-million chance.

"Sit," ordered Mr. Wesley.

"I think I'll stand," I muttered.

Mr. Wesley kept his face neutral, but I could tell that I was angering him. His right eye was twitching, and his casual demeanor had been replaced by one filled with anxiety. My resistance irked him to the core. "Hannah, I can make you sit, if you'd rather do it the hard way," he responded flatly.

Sighing, I took a seat on the red couch, crossing my arms over my chest and slouching into the cushions. My attempt at defiance wasn't getting me anywhere. *I just hope Leslie and Thomas are okay.* Kate adjusted herself on the couch, leaning forward, and wringing her hands. She seemed antsy and uncomfortable.

"What's going on? What is so important that you continue to hurt my family?" I asked. "I deserve to know the truth."

"Let's start with an update on current events, shall we?" Mr. Wesley suggested, gesturing to Kate as if this was a news broadcast and he was introducing a new guest. Kate closed her eyes to compose herself. She took a deep breath and turned to face me on the couch.

"Jenson is dead."

"What?!" I asked in disbelief. "You're lying." This couldn't be happening!

"It's true," Kate snapped back. You could see tears in her eyes, one slipping free and sliding down her cheek. "The doctors couldn't save him. I held his hand until he took his last breath."

I shook my head, willing it to be a lie. "No. He was talking in the ambulance; he squeezed my hand before I left. He was going to be okay." *"Trust no one,"* he had whispered in my ear before the paramedics took him to the ambulance. *How could this happen? Jenson was talking when we last left him with Kate.*

"The bullet wound in his stomach caused some internal bleeding which the doctors couldn't repair. He didn't even make it into surgery," Kate explained, tears streaming down her face.

I couldn't sit still any longer. Pushing myself off the couch, I started to pace, my thoughts coming in waves and my heart struggling to keep up with the information. "No. You called and said that he was shot in the spleen and that his surgery went fine. That all he needed was a pill to fight infections for the rest of his life."

"I didn't want to worry you with everything else that was going on," she said.

"So you lied?" I yelled, harshly. "Was there anything you DIDN'T lie about? You should have figured something else out!"

"Well, excuse me for not thinking straight. I was in shock. Jenson and I had meant something to one another; you just met him a few months ago."

There was an awkward silence while I stared at Kate. *Was she seriously implying that I shouldn't be upset at Jenson's death because I only met him a little while ago? He had saved my life several times, always having a plan to get out of the same kind of mess I was in right now.* All at once, the guilt began to eat away at me. I blinked as my own tears began to fall. It was my fault that Jenson was even dragged into any of this with Memory Lane and The Memorizers. If I hadn't needed someone to break into the computers at Memory Lane, he never would have been shot and died. I balled up my fists, knowing that if it wasn't for Jenson, I would never have gotten Leslie back. His blood was on all our hands. *If he knew this was how it would end, would he still be so willing to sacrifice to help us?*

"This is not the purpose of me bringing Hannah to you, Kate. Tell her why you needed to speak with her," said Mr. Wesley.

"I don't think she's ready," Kate pointed out.

"Well, she needs to be ready. We don't have time for this." Mr. Wesley insisted.

"Ready for what? Stop talking in circles and tell me what is actually going on," I demanded, hastily brushing the tears from my eyes as I tried to prepare myself for what new hell this could be.

Kate took another deep breath and motioned for me to sit back down on the couch. This time, I sat down. The fight in me was wearing thin. We had been running for so long, and here I was, the very place I had been running from.

Jenson was gone. How much more would Memory Lane take from me?

"Please understand, I never thought it would go this far and I never wanted you to find out," she began.

Find out what?

"I lied to you. Everything I said about running away, telling you I hate my Dad. It was all a lie. I've been working for him this whole time."

My heart stopped and so did time. I could feel the floor spinning beneath my feet and I saw spots in my vision. She couldn't... She wouldn't... I willed myself not to pass out. Thomas was right not to trust Kate. *How could I be so stupid?* I clutched the couch as if the entire world had shifted beneath me.

"How could you? Why did you lie?" I choked out, praying I could hold back the tears.

Kate's face maintained the same blank look that I had been staring at since Mr. Wesley showed up to tear us away from our parents. I shook my head, trying to process what was happening. Kate stood up from the couch and began pacing the small room.

She paused in front of me, "You don't understand. There's a bigger picture you have to consider here. Not everything is about any one of us."

"Bigger picture? I thought we were friends. You've been lying to me since finding me with The Memorizers. Was that all a set up too?"

"No!" Kate declared. For a moment, Kate looked hurt, then the mask was back on.

"How can I trust you?" I crossed my arms in anger, my body shaking from the betrayal. Every moment when I thought it couldn't possibly get worse, it did. I sat there, trying to listen to her excuses. I vowed that I would never trust Kate again, no matter what she said. She sat back down next to me on the couch and faced me, as if for a moment we were two friends rather than a liar and a hostage.

"Just listen for a minute. Things here at Memory Lane are in danger. Antoine has been plotting to take over Memory Lane. Dad needed me to be able to help him keep it safe."

"That makes no sense. Antoine hates Memory Lane; why would he want to take it?"

"I know it sounds crazy, but I promise that's the truth," revealed Kate.

"What can you do for your Dad? You just turned eighteen. It's not like you know anything about the business."

"In fact, I can do quite a bit. For starters, I can take control of the company," Kate said matter-of-factly.

"What?!"

"You heard that correctly, Hannah," said Mr. Wesley emphatically.

I turned to face Mr. Wesley. "This is too much information too fast. Look, this is confusing. Explain it with crayons and pictures like I'm a kindergartener."

"Don't talk about yourself like that," said Kate.

As if I needed her to "stand up for me" right now.

Mr. Wesley sighed as if I was bothering him with my questions. Did he seriously think I wasn't going to ask for clarification after everything he had done to my family? "Antoine is planning to kill me and then take over Memory Lane," he said.

"That's ridiculous," I scoffed. "Why would Antoine do that? He hates Memory Lane. Why else would he be building so much to tear it down?"

"Does he hate it?" Mr. Wesley asked. "Are you sure about that? Or perhaps he just wants the power for himself."

I blinked in disbelief. *How could I NOT have thought of that? With all the suspicious activity at The Memorizers complex?* My mind was racing trying to process all of this and I was quiet when I finally knew what to ask next.

"How do you know he wants to kill you?" I asked.

"I have my sources."

This man was incapable of being anything but cryptic.

"This still doesn't make any sense. Why does Kate have to run Memory Lane instead of you?" I asked. "Wouldn't Antoine just kill Kate and then take over?"

Mr. Wesley smiled. "I knew you were smart, Hannah."

"Smart or not, I still don't understand. You're going to sacrifice Kate?"

"Heavens no. We're going to take care of Antoine. We just need to buy some time."

"You mean kill him. So that's just what you do, isn't it? Kill people that are in your way. Is that what happened to your wife?" I asked angrily. *How could they just casually talk about killing someone like this?*

"He's trying to kill me!" Mr. Wesley retorted.

"I guess that makes it okay in your eyes. You and your family are sick." I turned to look at Kate in disgust. "You are just as bad as your Dad. I can't believe I ever trusted you." I got up from the couch and walked quickly over toward the exit. I couldn't stand to be near Kate or her Dad right now. The guard stopped me and before I could turn around I felt a hand touch my shoulder from behind. I whipped back around to face Mr. Wesley.

He spoke again, calmly this time. "Listen, you must understand that the technology and advancements that are taking place here at Memory Lane are for all people. It's not just my work. It's my life's mission."

"Your 'life mission' has been my entire family's misery."

"It is unfortunate that way," he replied. "There are things happening here that you just don't have a clear understanding of and we don't have a lot of time to truly bring you up to speed. We have a big announcement happening very soon."

"What announcement?" I asked. *Why was everything happening so fast? How was I supposed to come up with a plan to get away when the situation just got more and more complicated?*

329

"Kate is going live in about an hour. It will be all over the internet soon."

"Stop talking in circles," I shouted, "Is it really too hard just to tell the truth and say what is happening?"

Kate walked over to where I was standing near the door and smiled at me, and I was instantly filled with dread.

"You're going with me, Hannah. We're announcing that you are joining the company as my partner as soon as we reveal that my Dad is leaving due to his stage four lung cancer. He has weeks to live."

The room was spinning again, as if I was on some kind of carnival ride I didn't ask to be on. "Why do you think I would ever agree to do this? It's insane!" I shouted.

"Not even if Leslie and Thomas could be spared?" asked Kate, in a small voice.

Gasping, I stuck my finger in Kate's face angrily. "You don't bring her or Thomas up to me. Never again. Got it? Hasn't your family hurt us enough?"

She nodded yes, and for a moment I could see a flicker of fear in her eyes. After all we had been through, all we had run from together, you would think she would know better by now.

Shaking my head, I looked back at Mr. Wesley. "Wait, you have cancer?" I asked, shocked.

He shook his head, with a smile. "Of course not. To give us the time we need to plan, we need Antoine to think I am dying and soon so that Kate and your partnership and the subsequent takeover of Memory Lane isn't a stretch."

"This whole family has a PhD in lying!"

"So do all the politicians in this country. It's just how it is." Mr. Wesley shrugged.

"This whole scheme of yours will never work. My family will never believe that I agreed to run Memory Lane with Kate. They know I'm against everything you stand for. Besides, Thomas and I breaking in earlier this summer was all over the news. How are you gonna explain that?" I asked.

"My plan is to say that it was all part of a training exercise for my Memory Lane guards."

I laughed out loud. "And you think that will work?"

"The public will believe anything. Especially if this announcement is followed in the next few days by the reduction in prices to view memories at Memory Lane. They will be so ecstatic; they won't care about who is taking over."

"How can you expect me to do this?" I said to both Kate and Mr. Wesley.

"Kate and I are making the announcement with or without you present."

"Why do y'all need me anyway? Why can't Kate just take over on her own?"

Mr. Wesley's sinister smile said it all. "Because you're going to be our public guinea pig for Memory Lane's first brain scan. Nothing will help the people trust these changes more than seeing a true believer in what we are doing for everyone agree to get scanned."

Chapter 28

The terror of every moment just never seemed to end. How could they expect me to do this? How could they expect anyone?

My eyes went wide, horrified at the magnitude of what this meant. "There's… no way that… I'll agree to that," I stammered. I was losing it; there was only so much one person could take.

"Hannah, you are so predictable," Mr. Wesley stated tautly. He walked over to the wall that held the single painting in the room. Reaching into the pocket of his grey, perfectly pressed trousers, he pulled out a remote that looked similar to the one he used on Leslie. With a dramatic arm swish, he pressed the button as he pointed it at the painting. With a single beep, the painting slid down, revealing a huge security screen that looked like it was monitoring a room.

I should have known that the lone painting was placed in the room by design. Indignantly, I walked over toward it to get a better look. The room looked like some kind of cell, no doubt somewhere inside of Memory Lane. I could just make out two people blindfolded and tied up in chairs. The closer I got to the screen, the more my heart sank as I realized who I was looking at. It was Thomas and Leslie.

God, how could this be happening? Where are you in all this mess? I couldn't read the expressions on either of their faces because of the blindfold, which made me more anxious than I wanted to admit.

"Is this real?" I choked out. It was getting harder to keep it together.

"Yes," replied Mr. Wesley flatly. *Did the man have NO feelings?*

Kate put her hand on my shoulder in comfort. "I'm so sorry, Hannah."

"Don't touch me!" I jerked away from her grasp. "You did this!" I shouted at her.

I whipped my head around toward Mr. Wesley. "Untie them now!"

"I'm afraid that's not possible. This can easily be remedied by you agreeing to join Kate and me. Neither Leslie nor Thomas are being harmed right now. That is subject to change, depending on your next choices."

"How can you just hold innocent people hostage?!?"

"That's sort of how this works. I am using them as leverage to get what I want out of you."

The room was spinning again, and I felt as though I might actually throw up right then and there. I leaned toward the wall to gain my bearings. "You're sick, the both of you! I hope you rot in Hell for all the things you have done to my family and all the other families you have hurt to simply get your way!" I spat in his face and walked as far away from him as possible inside the room.

Mr. Wesley pulled a perfectly ironed handkerchief from his pocket and wiped his face, unfazed by my disrespect. He tucked the handkerchief back in his packet. "Hannah, we can do this the easy way or the hard way," he stated, no emotion on his face.

"You can lock me up with Thomas and Leslie because I'm not agreeing to be your puppet like your daughter."

"That's really how you want this to play out?"

I nodded my head and said, "Yes."

"Have it your way." With a quiet click, Mr. Wesley pressed the button on the remote, his face changing from indifference to menacingly smug.

I watched in horror as the room that Leslie and Thomas were in began to fill with water. They both turned their heads toward the sound of the rushing water, their eyes still covered by the blindfolds. I watched as they both jerked at the restraints that tied their hands behind their backs and tried to rock in their chairs. Hot tears streamed down my face. *Why? Why was everything always a matter of life and death? Would I ever be able to make a decision that didn't determine if others lived or died?* My mind raced to Jenson, alive in my mind one minute and dead the next. *How was I going to fix all of this?*

The water rose faster than I thought it could as the large pipes dumped water in droves into the tiny room. It was already up to their ankles.

"Can they hear us?" I asked desperately through tears.

"Why? What could you possibly need to say to them?" Mr. Wesley put his hands on his hips in mockery. "'Gee, I'm sorry I couldn't agree to do one simple task for Mr. Wesley, so you're going to drown now,'" he said sarcastically.

"I just wanted to say goodbye! You owe me that."

Mr. Wesley pushed a button on his remote. "Go ahead. You have one minute. And don't say anything that will tip them off about what you're doing for me."

I heard nothing indicating that the sound was on but I tried speaking anyway.

"Leslie? Thomas?"

Both of them turned their heads in the direction of my voice. *There must be an intercom in that room.*

"Hannah?" asked Leslie. "Help us! There's water filling up in this room and we're tied up!"

"I know, Les. I can see you now even if you can't see me."

"Are you gonna get us out then? My shoes are full of water and my shins are cold."

"I know. I'm so sorry, this isn't how I wanted this to go." I stifled a sob. I had to keep my composure so they wouldn't know what was happening.

"What are you talking about, Hannah?" asked Thomas.

"I don't have much time. I promise, it's going to be okay. Please know that I love both of you and I am grateful for the time you have been in my life. The water will stop soon and you both will be okay."

"What?! Why are you saying goodbye?" asked Leslie, panicking as the water continued to rise. The water was up to the seat of their chairs and I could feel my own panic rising.

"I can't explain that. You just have to trust me." I choked back the tears and the sob rising in my throat. It took everything in me to not reach across and strangle Mr. Wesley and Kate for what they had done, and kept doing to my family. I would make all of this right. I didn't know how right now, but I would figure it out.

"This doesn't make any sense. Where did Mr. Wesley take you? Did you find Kate?" asked Thomas.

"I can't answer that right now. I love you, Leslie. And thanks for everything, Thomas. I wouldn't have made it this far without you."

Then the sound cut off and I couldn't hear them and they couldn't hear me. I could see both of them yelling my name but it didn't matter. The sound was cut off but the water continued to rise.

"I'll do it. I will play your stupid game. Just turn the water off!" I yelled at Mr. Wesley.

"Good, I knew you would see it my way." Mr. Wesley clicked the button but the water continued to fill the room.

"I said I agreed. If anything happens to them I won't do a thing for you. Turn off the water!" I screamed.

"I'm pressing the appropriate button but it doesn't seem to be stopping the water." Mr. Wesley said, his voice filled with its own panic now. *They must really need me to make this work, or they would just kill us all.*

I watched in horror as the water continued to fill the room Thomas and Leslie were in. Mr. Wesley pressed the button on his remote but nothing seemed to be changing.

"Send someone in there to stop the water, please!" I yelled. "You have to do something."

"On it, sir," said the Memory Lane guard who was in the room with us. He turned to leave.

"Is this a test?" I asked Mr. Wesley, confusion filling my voice.

He looked confused at my question. "A test?"

"Is this real? Or is this some kind of simulation to make me think Thomas and Leslie are in danger so that I am willing to go along with your plan?"

"I assure you it's all real," he claimed, continuing to press the button on the remote.

"Even the broken remote that won't stop the water from rising?" I choked.

"Even that. Technology isn't perfect, Hannah," Mr. Wesley replied wryly.

The screen showed the water level stop rising. Leslie looked panicked and I could tell that Thomas was talking to her. I could only guess that he was trying to calm her down. *At least she isn't completely alone, like me.* I wished that I could be in the room with her, but took small comfort in the fact that Thomas was there.

"Happy?" asked Mr. Wesley. "They both seem fine. A little wet, but none too worse for the wear."

"You're just going to leave them in that room?"

"Until we have a deal that you are coming with Kate and me to make the announcement, yes. They are to remain in that room."

"Can I at least talk to them again and explain what is happening and why I am going to be working for Memory Lane with Kate?"

"No. That would be too risky. They can find out with everyone else."

My heart sank. *How was I going to explain all of this to Leslie and Thomas? There had to be a way to get a message to them.*

"Fine, I'll do it. But only if you let Thomas and Leslie out of those restraints and that terrible water torture room," I demanded.

Mr. Wesley nodded his head. "I'm not a monster." He clicked another button on the remote and the water began to drain from the room.

"I disagree." I crossed my arms. "I have your word that Thomas and Leslie will remain unharmed?"

Kate chimed in this time. "Yes, I'll make sure of it, Hannah." She put her hand on my shoulder, as if to comfort me.

I shrugged her hand off, rolling my eyes. "Oh, now I believe everything." It was still so hard to believe that Kate was two-faced this whole time. *I should have known deep down that nothing had changed four years ago. She abandoned me when Leslie disappeared, and she's been putting my family in danger this entire time.* I vowed to never forgive her.

Motion caught my eye on the screen as the remaining water drained from the room and I saw two Memory Lane guards come into view. They removed the blindfolds and then untied each of them. Then the guards carefully led both of them out of the room and off camera through the water. Thomas was fighting the guard and trying to walk on his own and I couldn't help but smile. I had to believe that they would be okay, that somehow everything would fall into place the way it should be.

The screen behind the painting went black and I watched as the painting slid back into place as if nothing ever happened.

"Alright, let's go get changed so we can make that announcement," Mr. Wesley said, while clapping his hands together.

"I don't have other clothes," I said, hoping the excuse would delay the inevitable.

"Don't worry, I think I have some that will fit you," replied Kate.

Great, now I have to wear my enemy's clothes.

I followed both Kate and her Dad out of the room and into the hallway where there appeared to be a lot of activity. Several people were walking at a brisk pace as if headed to the same place. I noticed they were dressed in their best clothes, as if anticipating something big happening. *Of course. The announcement. It will be televised.*

"The announcement is happening here?" I asked Kate as we continued to make our way through the hall.

"Of course," she replied.

Mr. Wesley stopped walking and turned around to face Kate.

"I'll meet you in half an hour," he said to her. I watched as he snapped his fingers and a Memory Lane guard appeared on command. It was freaky. The guard followed Kate and me to another location.

We took a few more right turns and then a left. Kate stopped in front of a door and swiped herself in. The guard stayed outside the door. As I followed her inside, I realized this must be her office and living space if she was here overnight. There was a large desk, a couch, and what looked like a Murphy bed folded up in the wall. Off to the side of the bed was another door. Kate walked over to it and gestured for me to have a seat on the couch.

As I sat down, I started thinking about everything leading up to this moment. I was about to embark on a journey of lies where my family would have no way of knowing that I didn't double-cross them. I could only hope that they knew me well enough to know that I was being forced into all of this. A part of me wished I could just kill Kate and Mr. Wesley both, and maybe this nightmare would end. But that would make me no better than they were. *How could they do this to me?*

Kate came out of what I assume was a closet holding a deep-plum colored business suit. "What do you think?" she asked, modeling it for me. Her tone had changed and it was as if everything that had transpired in the last six hours was just a dream. The suit had a pencil skirt and a blazer. Very professional. It would absolutely convince any crowd that I was serious about helping Kate run Memory Lane.

It was gorgeous and a small part of me was glad that she remembered I liked purple, but I still hated this whole situation. "It's fine."

"Great," she replied. "You wear this and I'll wear a black pant suit."

I stood up to get the purple suit from her and held it against me to see if it would fit. It looked pretty close to my size, but I still needed to try it on.

"So this announcement—am I giving a speech?" I inquired.

Kate nodded. "It's scripted. You just have to read it from the prompter."

"Do I get to see it beforehand?"

She shrugged. "Not sure. You'll have to ask my Dad."

Awesome. That probably meant the speech was full of more lies and other things that would make me look terrible to those who knew me. Not that the Wesleys cared at all.

"Where can I change?" I asked abruptly. I didn't want to be trapped with Kate any longer than I had to be.

"There's a bathroom right outside. Hannah, listen. I hope you know—"

"Stop. I don't want to hear it. Save your lies for the broadcast. I'll be right back."

I walked to the door of Kate's makeshift office with the purple suit in hand and was immediately met with the Memory Lane guard.

"Bathroom?" I asked, as politely as I could.

"Follow me," he replied.

Great. I can't even be trusted to go to the bathroom.

We walked just a few doors down until I spotted the bathroom on the left. The guard waited outside as I walked inside, closed the door, and then double-checked that it was locked. It was a bathroom with only one toilet and sink. I hung the suit up on the inside of the door, glanced in the mirror, and gasped at what I saw. I looked awful. The bags under my eyes could be sleeping bags for a homeless person. I really hoped the TV crew would have makeup powerful enough to make me look like a decent human being again. I needed a shower, but I didn't think I had enough time before the announcement.

As I stared in the mirror, my thoughts began to wander. *How was I going to contact Leslie, Thomas, and my parents to let them know that I was being forced into this whole thing?* I would die rather than betray them. Obviously, Kate and Mr. Wesley did not feel the same way. *Maybe I could give them a code word during the speech?* But how would they know what word? We didn't agree on one. Why did this have to be so complicated?

There was a knock on the bathroom door. "Are you almost done? We need to get you and Miss Wesley to hair and makeup," said the guard.

"Just a minute," I replied.

I quickly grabbed the purple skirt and blazer off the hanger. I put the blazer over my current shirt, hoping that it would close and look good enough. I slipped out of my pants and pulled on the skirt. It zipped on the side and seemed to fit okay. It was a little long, but fit well in the waist. It would have to do. I took another look in the mirror and gathered my pants off the floor.

Opening the door, I stepped out of the bathroom and followed the guard back to Kate's office. She was dressed in her black business suit, looking ready to go. *Was I really ready to do this? What other choice did I have?*

"That looks amazing on you, Hannah. Well, ready or not, let's go get prepped to be on TV," she announced.

Chapter 29

Have you ever walked through a moment in your life and felt like you must be dreaming? Walking through the bustling halls of Memory Lane, headed toward even more lies, felt surreal. In my head I knew it was real, but my heart hoped it was just a dream.

We left Kate's office and followed the Memory Lane guard back down the hall. I never realized how many doors there were in this building. The walk to the next room was short and yet it felt as though we passed a dozen doors. Were Leslie and Thomas behind one of those doors? Were they really safe? We stopped at a door that looked just like the other and yet it opened up into a large room full of people. It was bustling with activity. Cameramen, makeup artists, police, and more Memory Lane guards filled the room. My eyes scanned the faces and found Mr. Wesley. He had changed suits. This one larger than the last, still perfectly pressed and Lord knows it was expensive but it looked as though he had lost weight since I'd seen him only a half hour ago. Kate walked over to her Dad, and I followed.

"Almost ready, ladies?" he asked, his eyes closed as some kind of spray finished coating his face.

"We just need hair and makeup," replied Kate. An air of excitement lingered on her voice and it stung my heart. It reminded me of her betrayal and how trapped I was. We were supposed to be friends!

"You can have my chair. I think they're done with me now." As he stood up, I saw the makeup on his face. He had an unhealthy green undertone to his skin and the shading made his face look far thinner than it was. Only moments ago he looked healthy, as though he could run Memory Lane forever. Now, he had deep hollows in his cheeks and under his eyes that made it seem as though he might not last the broadcast. No doubt this was all to make him look pale and sickly to garner sympathy from the viewing audience.

Kate sat down in the chair first, and for the first time I got to see this new makeup technology in action. First, the digital screen came down to scan her face. It was looking to find her perfect skin tone shade. After scanning was complete, the scanning screen zoomed back up into the ceiling and two arms came down. One opened up like a sunning shield, positioned just below the chin, no doubt to protect her clothes from this process. The other arm was a sprayer and it started with the liquid foundation. It came out in a fine mist and lightly covered Kate's face.

Before the next stage of makeup, one of the makeup artists stepped in to examine and buff out the spray foundation. After the foundation was applied, the machine got closer to her eyes and applied eyeshadow, eyeliner, and mascara. It was almost sad. What were the makeup artists even there for, quality control? To buff out any mistakes? It was incredible that the machines did it all now.

"Here's your speech," Mr. Wesley said firmly, startling me and turning my attention away from Kate getting her makeup done.

I looked over to see him holding out a small digital tablet. I took it from his outstretched hand and I scanned it for a minute to see what it said. *What was I getting myself into?* Most everything I read was in line with what was discussed during their "presentation" of how things needed to be. The words that jumped out at me were "I am looking forward to this opportunity" and "Memory Lane is ready to welcome me to their company for the next step…"

Neither of those things were true, but based on this outline of the broadcast, it sounded like Kate was going to be speaking about the bulk of the new information and changes happening at Memory Lane. It was a relief that I didn't have much to say. Trying to sound convincing as a hostage was something I had never had to do. As I read through the speech on the tablet, I tried to see if there was a way I could change the wording to signal to my family that this was against my will. Surely, they would know I didn't want to take over Memory Lane with Kate.

Kate got out of the makeup chair and motioned for me to sit down. I handed the tablet back to Mr. Wesley.

"I'm going over there to get my hair styled. I'll be right back, Hannah," Kate said. A bubble of excitement seemed to be stirring just below the surface of her smile. It pained my heart to know that even with me standing here, a hostage forced into an agreement to fake taking over Memory Lane so Mr. Wesley could arrange to kill Antoine, that for Kate and Mr. Wesley, this was just a game to be played. I watched as both Kate and Mr. Wesley walked away from where we were currently standing by makeup.

I sat down in the chair and closed my eyes so the makeup scanner could read my face. After a few seconds, I felt a light mist of foundation being sprayed onto my face. Next was lip gloss, and I briefly opened my eyes so I could see the color chosen by the scanner. It was a nice compliment to my complexion. There was a digital readout that signaled to me eyeliner and mascara was next so I would be ready. A strange sensation came over me as a little miniature tool put precise amounts of eyeliner and mascara on my eyes. I didn't normally wear a full face of makeup so this felt like too much. As the machine finished with my eyes, I blinked rapidly and opened them to make sure it looked good on me. I waited a few more seconds for the blush to be applied to my cheeks and then glanced in the mirror one last time.

I appeared as professional as I could for TV. *Let's get this over with. Maybe they would let me see Leslie and Thomas once this part of the charade was over.*

Looking around the busy room, I tried to spot Kate and her Dad to see where they went, but I didn't see anyone I recognized. For a moment, I relished the fact that I was alone. Maybe I could come up with a plan. *Could I find a way out of this whole mess?* I walked around trying to get my bearings so that maybe I could figure out where Leslie and Thomas were being held and go to them. I tried to look innocent and lost, hoping that someone would ask me if I needed something. Most people in the room wouldn't even make eye contact with me. They were either too busy, self-involved, or just plain rude. There was no one I could trust here in this room and there were too many guards and police officers for me to actually try something. I felt defeated.

Just as I was about to give up, I felt a tap on my shoulder. Whirling around, I gasped in surprise.

"Gill!?!" I grabbed her arm and pulled her toward the wall, then hugged her tightly just to be sure it was really her. "What are you doing here?"

"Shhhhh," she whispered. "Follow me. Quickly."

Gill took my hand and made her way through the room with purpose, as if she had walked this room a thousand times. She knew each place to avoid and how to get around the guards and police officers. She stopped in a small corner of the room mostly obscured by cameras, lights, and reflectors.

"What's going on? Why are you here? How did you get here?" I asked in a hushed tone, trying not to draw attention to us.

"I'm here to make sure the announcement doesn't happen," she declared.

"What? How do you even know about it?"

"I put a tiny CLD on you when we were on the side of the road before I ran off. When I left The Memorizers, I grabbed a bunch of them from storage. I knew they would come in handy. I've heard everything Mr. Wesley and Kate told you."

I thought back to her strange departure and her patting my shoulder before running off. I smiled. "You're a genius."

She shrugged, but she couldn't hide the slight blush that hit her cheeks. "I try."

"By the way, Hannah. I'm sorry that Kate turned out to be a liar. Worse still, that she was always in on the things that were happening to your family. I wouldn't wish that on anyone." She looked at me with genuine sadness in her eyes.

"Thank you, Gill. I am grateful that you have stuck with us and you didn't turn out to be a criminal or a liar," I joked. Gill smiled and I knew she was the only one I could trust right now. "How are you going to stop the announcement?" I asked, keeping my voice low.

"It's best if you don't know. It'll ruin the look of surprise on your face. We don't want anyone to suspect you had something to do with it."

She had thought of everything. It all made me uneasy, but not as much as announcing to the world that I was helping Kate take over Memory Lane.

"How did you get in this room anyway?" I asked. "Or the building, for that matter," I whispered.

Gill pointed to her clothes. I was so caught up in seeing her again that I didn't realize she was wearing a uniform. She looked like one of the camera operators for TV.

"Did you steal clothes from someone?"

"No, that would have required knocking someone out and hoping the clothes fit. I may or may not have found the van with the extra clothes parked on the side and taken some things," Gill said, smirking.

"Has Mr. Wesley seen you?"

"Nope. I'm pretty sure he would have me removed, which is why I'm trying to keep a low profile."

I nodded in agreement and glanced around the room to see if Kate and Mr. Wesley were still occupied. I spotted them by the exit door that led to the stage outside. Kate was looking around anxiously.

"Well, I better go before Kate and Mr. Wesley kidnap and torture anyone else I care about," I balked sarcastically.

"See you later," replied Gill with a wink.

I made my way over to the exit door leading to the outside stage area and found Kate and Mr. Wesley with several Memory Lane guards in tow.

As I approached, Kate turned to me. "I thought you had changed your mind about the announcement since you disappeared. I was going to be sad that Leslie and Thomas would be tortured again," she said jokingly.

My face was devoid of emotion, and I crossed my arms indignantly. "I'm not a coward, Kate," I said tartly. "I love my family."

"And I don't?" she retorted.

"How's your Mom?"

For a moment, something flashed across Kate's face. I couldn't tell if it was pain or anger, but my comment hit the way I wanted it to. "If you love your family, you sure have a strange way of showing it."

The two of us stood in silence for a moment until I finally couldn't take it anymore.

"What broke you?" I asked with a note of sadness and loss in my voice that I couldn't restrain.

"What do you mean?"

"My old best friend would have never allowed my family to be tortured or held hostage. Let alone by her own father."

"You knew the old Kate. You can't seriously think I'm the same person as I was when I was thirteen. People grow up, Hannah. I thought it was common knowledge."

"People do grow up. But they don't change at their core."

Kate shrugged, acting like she was annoyed that we were even having this conversation.

Was Kate brainwashed? Were her memories of our friendship removed? Something more sinister? Could someone fake a whole friendship like that? These insane ideas popped into my head and I did my best to shove them down so I could focus on my current task at hand of attempting to convince everyone on TV that I was on board with the plan of helping run Memory Lane. I vowed to revisit them later to see if something else was really going on.

There were more people rushing over to where we were standing, and I stopped thinking abruptly. Camera people, newscasters, and Memory Lane guards were making their way to us as I poked my head out of the door. The crowd outside was growing. There were chairs set up facing a stage with a podium and a microphone. Giant lights aimed at the stage lit up a black backdrop and people stood around the chairs and flooded the lawn since the chairs were completely full of newscasters and what I assumed were other journalists. This announcement was going to be big.

The crew inside with us pushed their way through the exit door.

"I guess that's our cue," said Mr. Wesley. "Everyone ready?" he asked, looking at me and Kate. Before we could speak, a lady began the introductions at the podium with the microphone. She was standing center stage.

"Welcome everyone and of course our millions of viewers at home to this exciting news, live from Memory Lane."

There was a round of applause while the lady waited to continue.

"We are honored to have all of you join us as we witness history being made today. This has been a long time coming."

More applause from the crowd. I watched as several hands from the crowd went up into the air.

"There will be time for questions at the end. For now, I'm going to turn the microphone over to our founder, the brains behind Memory Lane, CEO, Mr. Wesley."

The crowd applauded even louder than before as the lady stepped aside so that Mr. Wesley could speak. He walked up to the podium and placed a digital tablet on it. I looked at Kate to see if she was going to go on stage and stand next to her Dad. She made no attempt to move from our position just yet, so I waited.

"Thank you all for being here today," began Mr. Wesley. "It brings me great joy to introduce everyone here and viewers across the country to my daughter, Kate Wesley."

He gestured to where Kate was standing, and she joined him on stage. She slowly walked to the podium and hugged her Dad.

The crowd applauded again, and reporters and journalists snapped so many pictures. The camera flashes were endless, and I wondered if I could go blind. Watching this farce play out before my eyes filled me with anger, bubbling up just below the surface. This whole thing was nothing but a publicity stunt. Not even two months ago, Kate told me she ran away from her Dad and hated everything that Memory Lane stood for. Now, she was hugging him and about to announce to the world that she was taking over the company. Something didn't add up. The more I thought about it, the more I was convinced that Kate had changed somehow. I wouldn't put it past Mr. Wesley to steal memories from his own daughter or brainwash her to get what he wanted.

"As many of you know," Mr. Wesley spoke again, "I am proud of everything that Memory Lane has accomplished since its establishment four years ago. We have brought the world a better way to see memories that have been forgotten due to the horrific famine of 2087. We graciously brought you nutrition in the form of FastTrack packs when times were tough. Memory Lane has been committed to serving this country from the very beginning of its existence. We are now proud to announce the next chapter of Memory Lane."

He paused, waiting for applause to cease from the crowd.

"Times change. Sometimes things happen in life that you don't expect. Last week I found out that I have stage four lung cancer. The prognosis is not good, even though I have access to the best physicians in the country. They have given me less than one month to live.

Effective immediately, my daughter, Kate Wesley, is going to take control of Memory Lane. She will be the new president and CEO."

There was a collective gasp from the crowd, and a deafening silence followed. Mr. Wesley gestured to Kate, and I watched as hundreds of hands went into the air, and numerous flashes went off again as reporters and TV newscasters took pictures to capture this incredible moment in Memory Lane history.

Mr. Wesley stepped aside, and Kate stepped up to the microphone. "Thank you, Daddy."

I watched from the sidelines as I waited for her to bring me to center stage as well. My eyes drifted to the crowd and scanned for Gill. She was nowhere that I could see. *Was she still here? What was she planning? How far was she going to let this announcement go before stopping it?*

Kate began speaking again, interrupting my thoughts. "Thank you everyone for being here on such short notice. I know you are all saddened by the news of my father's diagnosis. I am still struggling with it myself and I hold onto hope that maybe the doctors can find something to help him stay with us." She wiped a stray tear off her cheek, and I couldn't help but roll my eyes. I knew this was all a farce. Of course, the audience was eating this all up.

"Despite this big change, I wanted to make sure everyone here today and our viewers at home know that I am excited to embark on this journey with all of you. I am confident in my ability to lead Memory Lane into a brighter future than ever before." Kate glanced down at the tablet and then continued. "As you all know, we offer many services here at Memory Lane and we are proud to announce a reduction in the fees to relive memories by sixty-five percent." She paused for a significant amount of time to allow for applause. The crowd clapped loudly and a few people even screamed out in celebration.

"In addition to reduced fees for reliving memories, we are now proud to offer the latest technology in brain mapping. This technology is in its very early stages, but will help detect tumors, early forms of brain cancer, and numerous abnormalities regarding memory loss to help combat the effects of ALD-87. Signing your child up for the free brain scan at this time is of course optional but is highly recommended by doctors around the country for children of all ages starting as young as one month old. It is perfectly safe, but I know many of you will want to ask questions. More information will be coming out about this soon."

Kate took a deep breath and looked down at the tablet. "As an added bonus, if you sign your child up for a brain scan by August 1 of this year, you will get the opportunity to relive a memory at Memory Lane for free."

So now Kate and Mr. Wesley are going to bribe people to sign their children up for this brain scan thing? *This is insane.*

The audience stood up and clapped for the latest announcement about the brain mapping. These people are crazy. How are they automatically on board with everything Memory Lane comes out with? I couldn't fathom being that gullible.

After a few moments of applause, Kate spoke again. "Running Memory Lane is no small task, and there was careful consideration taken when deciding who I would like to join me on a journey like this. Let me introduce to you my friend who will be helping me run Memory Lane as we all embark on this next journey. Please give a warm welcome to Hannah Healy."

That was my cue. Taking a deep breath and squaring my shoulders, I thought about the water rushing into that room with Leslie and Thomas. *For them, I could do anything.* I slowly made my way over to the center of the stage and the podium where Kate and Mr. Wesley were standing. This was so awkward. My heart pounded in my chest as I faced the audience and tried to remember to breathe. A motion caught my eye from above. A black object was flying toward us.

What in the world?

Clapping continued all around me as I focused on the black object. It was buzzing loudly. *A bird? A drone?*

I grabbed the microphone and cleared my throat. My palms were sweating. I scrolled the tablet to where my speech was and took a deep breath.

"Thank you for joining us today. I am grateful and pleased to be a part of the operations at Memory Lane. The—"

In an instant there was a crash, so loud that I could no longer hear. The explosion surrounded the podium as the black object crashed into the stage where I was standing with Kate and Mr. Wesley.

Frantic screams erupted all around me as I dove out of the way of falling debris that had been caused by the explosion. My dive was too late and a metal bar from the stage fell on top of me, crushing my arm. I cried out in pain. Looking down, I saw the bone sticking out along with so much blood. My head was throbbing and my vision began to blur. I reached out with my good arm to touch my head, and my fingers were covered in blood. I felt my head swimming as the scene around me began to fade. Sounds were becoming muffled. My arm throbbed, and my head hurt so much that it was difficult to focus on anything. *Maybe, if I close my eyes for just a second. Just to push through the pain...*

****

I woke up to a woman shaking me awake, violently. I shrugged her hand off my shoulder and squinted into the light as I opened my eyes. I was becoming more and more aware of the throbbing in my arm. *What happened? Who was this?*

"Hannah, can you hear me?" asked the person, her voice was filled with fear and I could see that she cared. She was dressed in a uniform of some sort and looked to be around my age.

Did I know her? Where was I? "Who's Hannah?" I asked.

Acknowledgments

I have a few people to thank for supporting me again on my journey to becoming an author.

To the "group chat" students in my 5th period class of the 2021-2022 school year, thank you so much for opening up and trusting me to help you with not only academics, but with problems that you had outside of school. All of you are such hard-working, intelligent, and amazing kids. I am so thankful that you were in my class for the longest period of the day because you made my job that much better with your laughter and excellent, thought-provoking questions. Thank you for listening to me talk daily about reading books for pleasure instead of watching Netflix. Lastly, thank you for entertaining my lack of knowledge of popular terms among teenagers these days.

To my AP Chemistry students of the 2022-2023 school year, I was so blessed to be your teacher and I am beyond thankful for the amount of work you put into my class. There was something special about teaching most of you two years in a row. I was so moved when I saw several of you at my author event supporting me outside of just being your teacher. Many of you don't enjoy reading and you still purchased a signed copy of my book anyway. I appreciate that more than you will ever know. All of you are going to do amazing things and I look forward to staying in touch.

Thank you to my church family at Light of the World for being supportive and excited about the sequel to *Memory Lane*. Your encouragement and positive feedback were much needed and always welcomed. I persevered because of your faith and belief in me to get another book published.

A huge thank you to my beta reader who read each chapter carefully, provided feedback, and caught my mistakes. Your excitement and joy for this sequel is unparalleled and I cannot extend my gratitude enough. I appreciate you listening to me complain about how hard writing was some days and how other days I couldn't wait for you to read the crazy ending to the chapter. Your support along the way is what got me through the past year and a half of writing.

A tremendous thank you to Tiarra Tompkins for opening my eyes to the world of independent publishing and reminding me to rely on God in all things. I am so glad that your daughter ended up in my class last school year so I could meet you and have things fall into place with regard to editing and publishing.

To Brenda Rodriguez, there are not enough words to describe how thankful I am for your friendship and support. You bought the very first copy of *Memory Lane* and you were so excited to get to read it even though you don't like stories with multiple parts or the teen fiction genre. I have no doubt that you will be the first in line to buy *Memory Restored* and any book I write after that. I appreciate you recommending my book to your students and other people you meet so that my dream of being an author can become real. Thank you so much for always encouraging me to learn every day and for being a true friend.

Thank you to my sister, Andrea Scott, for the belief in me and encouraging words for getting this second novel published. Your BookTok ideas for my social media have been great and I cannot thank you enough for your help. You have shown incredible strength this past year and I am proud of you for overcoming so many obstacles. I hope you continue to find your joy.

I cannot thank my parents, Armando and Rebecca Diaz, enough for being such great role models and for supporting me on this wild journey to become an author. You never questioned that I had this dream and you fully believed me when I said I was going to do it. Thank you for reading my books and for being proud of my accomplishments.

Most importantly, I want to thank God for giving me the strength to continue writing daily. I am humbled by your grace, mercy, and love.

Author Bio

Amanda Diaz is an author, writer, and teacher. She lives in Fort Worth, Texas, where she teaches high school chemistry. Her passion for teaching inspired her to write, and her books have helped encourage her students to love reading as much as she does. *Memory Restored* is her second novel.

Printed in the USA
CPSIA information can be obtained
at www.ICGtesting.com
JSHW060933131123
51921JS00002B/2

9 781954 437937